LOVECRAFT UNBOUND

ALSO EDITED BY ELLEN DATLOW

Blood Is Not Enough
Alien Sex
A Whisper of Blood
Little Deaths
Off Limits
Twists of the Tale: Stories of Cat Horror
Lethal Kisses
Vanishing Acts
The Dark
Inferno
The Del Rey Book of Science Fiction and Fantasy
Poe: 19 New Tales Inspired by Edgar Allan Poe
The Best Horror of the Year, Volume One

WITH TERRI WINDLING

Sirens and Other Daemon Lovers
A Wolf at the Door and Other Retold Fairy Tales
The Green Man: Tales of the Mythic Forest
Swan Sister: Fairy Tales Retold
The Faery Reel: Tales from the Twilight Realm
Salon Fantastique
The Coyote Road: Trickster Tales
Troll's Eye View: A Book of Villainous Tales

THE ADULT FAIRY TALES SERIES

Snow White, Blood Red
Black Thorn, White Rose
Ruby Slippers, Golden Tears
Black Swan, White Raven
Silver Birch, Blood Moon
Black Heart, Ivory Bones
The Year's Best Fantasy and Horror:
First through Sixteenth Annual Collections

WITH KELLY LINK & GAVIN J. GRANT

The Year's Best Fantasy and Horror:
Seventeenth through Twenty-first Annual Collections

Edited by Ellen Datlow

LOVECRAFT UNBOUND

TWENTY STORIES

MILWAUKIE

Dark Horse Books, 10956 SE Main Street, Milwaukie, OR 97222 | darkhorse.com

Cover & book design by Tina Alessi
Special thanks to Daniel Chabon and Madeline Gobbo.

Library of Congress Cataloging-in-Publication Data

Lovecraft unbound : twenty stories / edited by Ellen Datlow. -- 1st Dark Horse Books ed. p. cm. ISBN 978-1-59582-146-1 (pbk.) 1. Horror tales, American. I. Datlow, Ellen. II. Lovecraft, H. P. (Howard Phillips), 1890-1937. PS648.H6L67 2009
813'.0873808--dc22

2009024683

ISBN 978-1-59582-146-1
First Dark Horse Books Edition: September 2009

Printed in the United States of America
1 3 5 7 9 10 8 6 4 2

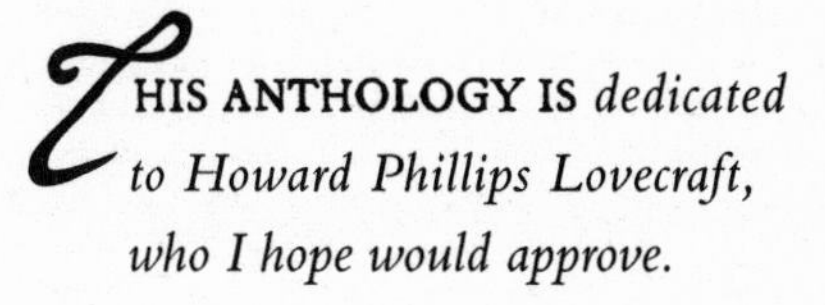

THIS ANTHOLOGY IS *dedicated to Howard Phillips Lovecraft, who I hope would approve.*

Contents

ELLEN DATLOW

Introduction

H. P. LOVECRAFT'S WORK, and fiction inspired by his entire mythos, continue to sell . . . and sell . . . and sell. In 1997, Ecco Press published *Tales of H. P. Lovecraft*, selected and edited by Joyce Carol Oates. Library of America recently collected Lovecraft's major novels and short stories in a volume introduced by Peter Straub. Even though so many reprint and original anthologies continue to be published, the taste for new Lovecraftian fiction seems to be growing rather than fading.

I read most of Lovecraft's fiction in my early teens, and even then, although I enjoyed it immensely, I noticed the difference between the wonder and embrace of the unknown in science fiction and the dread of the unknown in Lovecraft's work. Most of his fiction is characterized by this sense of dread. I've also read the multitudes of pastiches in anthologies of work "inspired" by Lovecraft, but most—for me, at least—are too obvious and bring little new to the table.

The title, *Lovecraft Unbound*, came to me in a flash, and from that came the idea. First, I took a few of the best *under*-reprinted subtley Lovecraftian stories I've read over the last several years. While I complain about the numerous Lovecraftian pastiches published, there is also a relatively small but solid body of Lovecraftian short fiction that is not pastiche—from those I chose four stories that have not been overexposed by appearing in a lot of other Lovecraftian anthologies (or elsewhere). Second, I commissioned the rest, eager to provide a showcase for writers whose Lovecraftian work I've enjoyed, such as Michael Shea, Marc Laidlaw, Michael Cisco, Elizabeth Bear, William Browning Spencer, Nick Mamatas, Sarah Monette, and Laird Barron. Third, some of the above suggested other writers with an interest in Lovecraft—a few of whom also submitted new stories that I bought for the anthology.

I asked for stories *inspired*—thematically and possibly—by plot points in Lovecraft's mythos. What I wanted was variety: in tone, setting, point of view, time. In fact, I'd prefer not to have any direct reference in the story to Lovecraft or his works. No use of the words "eldritch" or "ichor," and no mentions of Cthulhu or his minions. And especially, no tentacles.

As with most original theme anthologies, sometimes a story slips in with elements that go against the guidelines; so, yes, there are a few tentacles; and yes, there might even be some other overtly Lovecraftian trappings—and at least one story that uses them in a subversive celebration of H. P. Lovecraft's amazingly resilent universe.

DALE BAILEY & NATHAN BALLINGRUD

The Crevasse

WHAT HE LOVED was the silence, the pristine clarity of the ice shelf: the purposeful breathing of the dogs straining against their traces, the hiss of the runners, the opalescent arc of the sky. Garner peered through shifting veils of snow at the endless sweep of glacial terrain before him, the wind gnawing at him, forcing him to reach up periodically and scrape at the thin crust of ice that clung to the edges of his facemask, the dry rasp of the fabric against his face reminding him that he was alive.

There were fourteen of them. Four men; one of them, Faber, strapped to the back of Garner's sledge, mostly unconscious, but occasionally surfacing out of the morphine depths to moan. Ten dogs, big Greenland huskies, gray and white. Two sledges. And the silence, scouring him of memory and desire, hollowing him out inside. It was what he'd come to Antarctica for.

And then, abruptly, the silence split open like a wound:

A thunderous crack, loud as lightning cleaving stone, shivered the ice, and the dogs of the lead sledge, maybe twenty-five yards ahead of Garner, erupted into panicky cries. Garner saw it happen: the lead sledge sloughed over—hurling Connelly into the snow—and plunged nose first through the ice, as though an enormous hand had reached up through the earth to snatch it under. Startled, Garner watched an instant longer. The wrecked sledge, jutting out of the earth like a broken stone, hurtled at him, closer, closer. Then time stuttered, leaping forward. Garner flung one of the brakes out behind him. The hook skittered over the ice. Garner felt the jolt in his spine when it caught. Rope sang out behind him, arresting his momentum. But it wouldn't be enough.

Garner flung out a second brake, then another. The hooks snagged, jerking the sledge around and up on a single runner. For a moment Garner thought that it was going to roll, dragging the dogs along behind it. Then the airborne runner slammed back to earth and the sledge skidded to a stop in a glittering spray of ice.

The dogs boiled back into its shadow, howling and snapping. Ignoring them, Garner clambered free. He glanced back at Faber, still miraculously strapped to the travois, his face ashen, and then he pelted toward the wrecked sledge, dodging a minefield of spilled cargo: food and tents; cooking gear; his medical bag, disgorging a bright freight of tools and the few precious ampoules of morphine McReady had been willing to spare, like a fan of scattered diamonds.

The wrecked sledge hung precariously, canted on a lip of ice above a black crevasse. As Garner stood there, it slipped an inch, and then another, dragged down by the weight of the dogs. He could hear them whining, claws scrabbling as they strained against harnesses drawn taut by the weight of Atka, the lead dog, dangling out of sight beyond the edge of the abyss.

Garner visualized him—thrashing against his tack in a black well as the jagged circle of grayish light above shrank away, inch by lurching inch—and he felt the pull of night inside himself, the age-old gravity of the dark. Then a hand closed around his ankle.

Bishop, clinging to the ice, a hand-slip away from tumbling into the crevasse himself: face blanched, eyes red rimmed inside his goggles.

"Shit," Garner said. "Here—"

He reached down, locked his hand around Bishop's wrist, and hauled him up, boots slipping. Momentum carried him over backwards, floundering in the snow as Bishop curled fetal beside him.

"You okay?"

"My ankle," he said through gritted teeth.

"Here, let me see."

"Not now. Connelly. What happened to Connelly?"

"He fell off—"

With a metallic screech, the sledge broke loose. It slid a foot, a foot and a half, and then it hung up. The dogs screamed. Garner had never heard a dog make a noise like that—he didn't know dogs *could* make a noise like that—and for a moment their blind, inarticulate terror swam through him. He thought again of Atka, dangling there, turning, feet clawing at the darkness, and he felt something stir inside him once again—

"Steady, man," Bishop said.

Garner drew in a long breath, icy air lacerating his lungs.

"You gotta be steady now, Doc," Bishop said. "You gotta go cut him loose."

"No—"

"We're gonna lose the sledge. And the rest of the team. That happens, we're all gonna die out here, okay? I'm busted up right now, I need you to do this thing—"

"What about Connell—"

"Not now, Doc. Listen to me. We don't have time. Okay?"

Bishop held his gaze. Garner tried to look away, could not. The other man's eyes fixed him.

"Okay," he said.

Garner stood and stumbled away. Went to his knees to dig through the wreckage. Flung aside a sack of rice, frozen in clumps; wrenched open a crate of flares—useless—shoved it aside; and dragged another one toward him. This time he was lucky: he dug out a coil of rope, a hammer, a handful of pitons. The sledge lurched on its lip of ice, the rear end swinging, setting off another round of whimpering.

"Hurry," Bishop said.

Garner drove the pitons deep into the permafrost and threaded the rope through their eyes, his hands stiff inside his gloves. Lashing the other end around his waist, he edged back onto the broken ice shelf. It shifted underneath him, creaking. The sledge shuddered, but held. Below him, beyond the moiling clump of dogs, he could see the leather trace leads, stretched taut across the jagged rim of the abyss.

He dropped back, letting rope out as he descended. The world fell away above him. Down and down, and then he was on his knees at the very edge of the shelf, the hot, rank stink of the dogs enveloping him. He used his teeth to loosen one glove. Working quickly against the icy assault of the elements, he fumbled his knife out of its sheath and pressed the blade to the first of the traces. He sawed at it until the leather separated with a snap.

Atka's weight shifted in the darkness below him, and the dog howled mournfully. Garner set to work on the second trace, felt it let go, everything—the sledge, the terrified dogs—slipping toward darkness. For a moment he thought the whole thing would go. But it held. He went to work on the third trace, gone loose now by some trick of tension. It too separated beneath his blade, and he once again felt Atka's weight shift in the well of darkness beneath him.

Garner peered into the blackness. He could see the dim blur of the dog, could feel its dumb terror welling up around him, and as he brought the blade to the final trace, a painstakingly erected dike gave way in his mind. Memory flooded through him: the feel of mangled flesh beneath his fingers, the distant *whump* of artillery, Elizabeth's drawn and somber face.

His fingers faltered. Tears blinded him. The sledge shifted above him as Atka thrashed in his harness. Still he hesitated.

The rope creaked under the strain of additional weight. Ice rained down around him. Garner looked up to see Connelly working his way hand over hand down the rope.

"Do it," Connelly grunted, his eyes like chips of flint. "Cut him loose."

Garner's fingers loosened around the hilt of the blade. He felt the tug of the dark at his feet, Atka whining.

"Give me the goddamn knife," Connelly said, wrenching it away, and together they clung there on the single narrow thread of gray rope, two men and one knife and the enormous gulf of the sky overhead as Connelly sawed savagely at the last of the traces. It held for a moment, and then, abruptly, it gave, loose ends curling back and away from the blade.

Atka fell howling into darkness.

They made camp.

The traces of the lead sledge had to be untangled and repaired, the dogs tended to, the weight redistributed to account for Atka's loss. While Connelly busied himself with these chores, Garner stabilized Faber—the blood had frozen to a black crust inside the makeshift splint Garner had applied yesterday, after the accident—and wrapped Bishop's ankle. These were automatic actions. Serving in France, he'd learned the trick of letting his body work while his mind traveled to other places; it had been crucial to keeping his sanity during the war, when the people brought to him for treatment had been butchered by German submachine guns or burned and blistered by mustard gas. He had worked to save those men, though it had been hopeless work. Mankind had acquired an appetite for dying; doctors had become shepherds to the process. Surrounded by screams and spilled blood, he'd anchored himself to memories of his wife, Elizabeth: the warmth of her kitchen back home in Boston, and the warmth of her body, too.

But all that was gone.

Now, when he let his mind wander, it went to dark places, and he found himself concentrating instead on the minutiae of these rote tasks like a first-year medical student. He cut a length of bandage and applied a compression wrap to Bishop's exposed ankle, covering both ankle and foot in careful figure eights. He kept his mind in the moment, listening to the harsh labor of their lungs in the frigid air, to Connelly's chained fury as he worked at the traces, and to the muffled sounds of the dogs as they burrowed into the snow to rest.

And he listened, too, to Atka's distant cries, leaking from the crevasse like blood.

"Can't believe that dog's still alive," Bishop said, testing his ankle against his weight. He grimaced and sat down on a crate. "He's a tough old bastard."

Garner imagined Elizabeth's face, drawn tight with pain and determination, while he fought a war on the far side of the ocean. Had she been afraid too, suspended over her own dark hollow? Had she cried out for him?

"Help me with this tent," Garner said.

They'd broken off from the main body of the expedition to bring Faber back to one of the supply depots on the Ross Ice Shelf, where Garner could care for him. They would wait there for the remainder of the expedition, which suited Garner just fine, but troubled both Bishop and Connelly, who had higher aspirations for their time here.

Nightfall was still a month away, but if they were going to camp here while they made repairs, they would need the tents to harvest warmth. Connelly approached as they drove pegs into the permafrost, his eyes impassive as they swept over Faber, still tied down to the travois, locked inside a morphine dream. He regarded Bishop's ankle and asked him how it was.

"It'll do," Bishop said. "It'll have to. How are the dogs?"

"We need to start figuring what we can do without," Connelly said. "We're gonna have to leave some stuff behind."

"We're only down one dog," Bishop said. "It shouldn't be too hard to compensate."

"We're down two. One of the swing dogs snapped her foreleg." He opened one of the bags lashed to the rear sledge, and removed an Army-issue revolver. "So go ahead and figure what we don't need. I gotta tend to her." He tossed a contemptuous glance at Garner. "Don't worry, I won't ask *you* to do it."

Garner watched as Connelly approached the injured dog, lying away from the others in the snow. She licked obsessively at her broken leg. As Connelly approached she looked up at him and her tail wagged weakly. Connelly aimed the pistol and fired a bullet through her head. The shot made a flat, inconsequential sound, swallowed up by the vastness of the open plain.

Garner turned away, emotion surging through him with a surprising, disorienting energy. Bishop met his gaze and offered a rueful smile.

"Bad day," he said.

Still, Atka whimpered.

Garner lay wakeful, staring at the canvas, taut and smooth as the interior of an egg above him. Faber moaned, calling out after some fever phantom. Garner almost envied the man. Not the injury—a nasty compound fracture of the femur, the product of a bad step on the ice when he'd stepped outside the circle of tents to piss—but the sweet oblivion of the morphine doze.

In France, in the war, he'd known plenty of doctors who'd used the stuff to chase away the night haunts. He'd also seen the fevered agony of withdrawal. He had no wish to experience that, but he felt the opiate lure all the same. He'd felt it then, when he'd had thoughts of Elizabeth to sustain him. And he felt it now—stronger still—when he didn't.

Elizabeth had fallen victim to the greatest cosmic prank of all time, the flu that had swept across the world in the spring and summer of 1918, as if the bloody abattoir in the trenches hadn't been evidence enough of humanity's divine disfavor. That's what Elizabeth had called it in the last letter he'd ever had from her: God's judgment on a world gone mad. Garner had given up on God by then: he'd packed away the Bible Elizabeth had pressed upon him after a week in the field hospital, knowing that its paltry lies could bring him no comfort in the face of such horror, and it hadn't. Not then, and not later, when he'd come home to face Elizabeth's mute and barren grave. Garner had taken McReady's offer to accompany the expedition soon after, and though he'd stowed the Bible in his gear before he left, he hadn't opened it since and he wouldn't open it here either, lying sleepless beside a man who might yet die because he'd had to take a piss—yet another grand cosmic joke—in a place so hellish and forsaken that even Elizabeth's God could find no purchase here.

There could be no God in such a place.

Just the relentless shriek of the wind tearing at the flimsy canvas, and the death-howl agony of the dog. Just emptiness, and the unyielding porcelain dome of the polar sky.

Garner sat up, breathing heavily.

Faber muttered under his breath. Garner leaned over the injured man, the stench of fever hot in his nostrils. He smoothed Faber's hair back from his forehead and studied the leg, swollen tight as a sausage inside the sealskin legging. Garner didn't like to think what he might see if he slit open that sausage to reveal the leg underneath: the viscous pit of the wound itself, crimson lines of sepsis twining around Faber's thigh like a malevolent vine as they climbed inexorably toward his heart.

Atka howled, a long rising cry that broke into pitiful yelps, died away, and renewed itself, like the shriek of sirens on the French front.

"Jesus," Garner whispered.

He fished a flask out of his pack and allowed himself a single swallow of whiskey. Then he sat in the dark, listening to the mournful lament of the dog, his mind filling with hospital images: the red splash of tissue in a steel tray; the enflamed wound of an amputation, the hand folding itself into an outraged fist as the arm fell away. He thought of Elizabeth, too, Elizabeth most all, buried months before Garner had gotten back from Europe. And he thought of Connelly, that aggrieved look as he turned away to deal with the injured swing dog.

Don't worry, I won't ask you to do it.

Crouching in the low tent, Garner dressed. He shoved a flashlight into his jacket, shouldered aside the tent flap, and leaned into the wind tearing across the waste. The crevasse lay before him, rope still trailing through the pitons to dangle into the pit below.

Garner felt the pull of darkness. And Atka, screaming.

"Okay," he muttered. "All right, I'm coming."

Once again he lashed the rope around his waist. This time he didn't hesitate as he backed out onto the ledge of creaking ice. Hand over hand he went, backward and down, boots scuffing until he stepped into space and hung suspended in a well of shadow.

Panic seized him, the black certainty that nothing lay beneath him. The crevasse yawned under his feet, like a wedge of vacuum driven into the heart of the planet. Then, below him—ten feet? twenty?—Atka mewled, piteous as a freshly whelped pup, eyes squeezed shut against the light. Garner thought of the dog, curled in agony upon some shelf of subterranean ice, and began to lower himself into the pit, darkness rising to envelop him.

One heartbeat, then another and another and another, his breath diaphanous in the gloom, his boots scrabbling for solid ground. Scrabbling and finding it. Garner clung to the rope, testing the surface with his weight.

It held.

Garner took the flashlight from his jacket, and switched it on. Atka peered up at him, brown eyes iridescent with pain. The dog's legs twisted underneath it, and its tail wagged feebly. Blood glistened at its muzzle. As he moved closer, Garner saw that a dagger of bone had pierced its torso, unveiling the slick yellow gleam of subcutaneous fat, and deeper still, half visible through tufts of coarse fur, the bloody pulse of viscera. And it had shat itself—Garner could smell it—a thin gruel congealing on the dank stone.

"Okay," he said. "Okay, Atka."

Kneeling, Garner caressed the dog. It growled and subsided, surrendering to his ministrations.

"Good boy, Atka," he whispered. "Settle down, boy."

Garner slid his knife free of its sheath, bent forward, and brought the blade to the dog's throat. Atka whimpered—"Shhh,"

Garner whispered—as he bore down with the edge, steeling himself against the thing he was about to do—

Something moved in the darkness beneath him: a leathery rasp, the echoing clatter of stone on stone, of loose pebbles tumbling into darkness. Atka whimpered again, legs twitching as he tried to shove himself back against the wall. Garner, startled, shoved the blade forward. Atka's neck unseamed itself in a welter of black arterial blood. The dog stiffened, shuddered once, and died—Garner watched its eyes dim in the space of a single heartbeat—and once again something shifted in the darkness at Garner's back. Garner scuttled backward, slamming his shoulders into the wall by Atka's corpse. He froze there, probing the darkness.

Then, when nothing came—had he imagined it? He must have imagined it—Garner aimed the flashlight light into the gloom. His breath caught in his throat. He shoved himself erect in amazement, the rope pooling at his feet.

Vast.

The place was vast: walls of naked stone climbing in cathedral arcs to the undersurface of the polar plain, and a floor worn smooth as glass over long ages, stretching out before him until it dropped away into an abyss of darkness. Struck dumb with terror—or was it wonder?—Garner stumbled forward, the rope unspooling behind him until he drew up at the precipice, pointed the light into the shadows before him, and saw what it was that he had discovered.

A stairwell, cut seamlessly into the stone itself, and no human stairwell either: each riser fell away three feet or more, the stair itself winding endlessly into fathomless depths of earth, down and down and down until it curved away beyond the reach of his frail human light, and further still, toward some awful destination he scarcely dared imagine. Garner felt the lure and hunger of the place singing in his bones. Something deep inside him, some mute inarticulate longing, cried out in response, and before he knew it, he found himself scrambling down the first riser, and then another, the flashlight carving slices out of the darkness to reveal a bas relief of inhuman creatures lunging at him in glimpses: taloned feet and clawed hands and sinuous Medusa coils that seemed to writhe about one another in the fitful and imperfect glare. And through it all the terrible summons of the place, drawing him down into the dark.

"Elizabeth—" he gasped, stumbling down another riser and another, until the rope, forgotten, jerked taut about his waist. He looked up at the pale circle of Connelly's face far above him.

"What the hell are you doing down there, Doc," Connelly shouted, his voice thick with rage, and then, almost against his will, Garner found himself ascending once again into the light.

No sooner had he gained his footing than Connelly grabbed him by the collar and swung him to the ground. Garner scrabbled for purchase in the snow but Connelly kicked him back down again, his blonde, bearded face contorted in rage.

"You stupid son of a bitch! Do you care if we all die out here?"

"Get off me!"

"For a dog? For a goddamned *dog*?" Connelly tried to kick him again, but Garner grabbed his foot and rolled, bringing the other man down on top of him. The two of them grappled in the snow, their heavy coats and gloves making any real damage all but impossible.

The flaps to one of the tents opened and Bishop limped out, his face a caricature of alarm. He was buttoning his coat even as he approached. "Stop! *Stop it right now!*"

Garner clambered to his feet, staggering backward a few steps. Connelly rose to one knee, leaning over and panting. He pointed at Garner. "I found him in the crevasse! He went down alone!"

Garner leaned against one of the packed sledges. He could feel Bishop watching him as he tugged free a glove to poke at a tender spot on his face, but he didn't look up.

"Is this true?"

"Of course it's true!" Connelly said, but Bishop waved him into silence.

Garner looked up at him, breath heaving in his lungs. "You've got to see it," he said. "My God, Bishop."

Bishop turned his gaze to the crevasse, where he saw the pitons and the rope spilling into the darkness. "Oh, Doc," he said quietly.

"It's not a crevasse, Bishop. It's a stairwell."

Connelly strode toward Garner, jabbing his finger at him. "What? You lost your goddamned mind."

"Look for yourself!"

Bishop interposed himself between the two men. "*Enough!*" He turned to face Connelly. "Back off."

"But—"

"I said back off!"

Connelly peeled his lips back, then turned and stalked back toward the crevasse. He knelt by its edge and started hauling up the rope.

Bishop turned to Garner. "Explain yourself."

All at once, Garner's passion drained from him. He felt a wash of exhaustion. His muscles ached. How could he explain this to him? How could he explain this so that they'd understand? "Atka," he said simply, imploringly. "I could hear him."

A look of deep regret fell over Bishop's face. "Doc . . . Atka was a just a dog. We have to get Faber to the depot."

"I could still hear him."

"You have to pull yourself together. There are real lives at stake here, do you get that? Me and Connelly, we aren't doctors. Faber needs *you*."

"But—"

"Do you get that?"

"I . . . yeah. Yeah, I know."

"When you go down into places like that, especially by yourself, you're putting us all at risk. What are we gonna do without Doc, huh?"

This was not an argument Garner would win. Not this way. So he grabbed Bishop by the arm and led him toward the crevasse. "Look," he said.

Bishop wrenched his arm free, his face darkening. Connelly straightened, watching this exchange. "Don't put your hands on me, Doc," Bishop said.

Garner released him. "Bishop," he said. "Please."

Bishop paused a moment, then walked toward the opening. "All right."

Connelly exploded. "Oh for Christ's sake!"

"We're not going inside it," Bishop said, looking at them both. "I'm going to look, okay, Doc? That's all you get."

Garner nodded. "Okay," he said. "Okay."

The two of them approached the edge of the crevasse. Closer, Garner felt it like a hook in his liver, tugging him down. It took an act of will to stop at the edge, to remain still and unshaken and look at these other two men as if his whole life did not hinge upon this moment.

"It's a stairwell," he said. His voice did not shake. His body did not move. "It's carved into the rock. It's got . . . designs of some kind."

Bishop peered down into the darkness for a long moment. "I don't see anything," he said at last.

"I'm telling you, it's *there*!" Garner stopped and gathered himself. He tried another tack. "This, this could be the scientific discovery of the century. You want to stick it to McReady? Let him plant his little flag. This is evidence of, of . . ." He trailed off. He didn't know what it was evidence of.

"We'll mark the location," Bishop said. "We'll come back. If what you say is true it's not going anywhere."

Garner switched on his flashlight. "Look," he said, and he threw it down.

The flashlight arced end over end, its white beam slicing through the darkness with a scalpel's clean efficiency, illuminating flashes of hewn rock and what might have been carvings or just natural irregularities. It clattered to a landing beside the corpse of the dog, casting in bright relief its open jaw and lolling tongue, and the black pool of blood beneath it.

Bishop looked for a moment, and shook his head. "God damn it, Doc," he said. "You're really straining my patience. Come on."

Bishop was about to turn away when Atka's body jerked once —Garner saw it—and then again, almost imperceptibly. Reaching out, Garner seized Bishop's sleeve.

"What now, for Christ's—" the other man started to say, his voice harsh with annoyance. Then the body was yanked into the surrounding darkness so quickly it seemed as though it had vanished into thin air. Only its blood, a smeared trail into shadow, testified to its ever having been there at all. That, and the jostled flashlight, which rolled in a lazy half circle, its unobstructed light spearing first into empty darkness and then into smooth cold stone before settling at last on what might have been a carven, clawed foot. The beam flickered and went out.

"What the fuck . . ." Bishop said.

A scream erupted from the tent behind them.

Faber.

Garner broke into a clumsy run, high-stepping through the piled snow. The other men shouted behind him, but their words were lost in the wind and in his own hard breathing. His body was moving according to its training, but his mind was pinned like a writhing insect in the hole behind him, in the stark, burning image of what he had just seen. He was transported by fear and adrenaline, and by something else, by some other emotion he had not felt in many years or perhaps ever in his life, some heart-filling glorious exaltation that threatened to snuff him out like a dying cinder.

Faber was sitting upright in the tent—it stank of sweat and urine and kerosene, eye-watering and sharp—his thick hair a dark corona around his head, his skin as pale as a cavefish. He was still trying to scream, but his voice had broken, and his utmost effort could now produce only a long, cracked wheeze, which seemed forced through his throat like steel wool. His leg stuck out of the blanket, still grossly swollen.

The warmth from the Nansen cooker was almost oppressive.

Garner dropped to his knees beside him and tried to ease him back down into his sleeping bag, but Faber resisted. He fixed his eyes on Garner, his painful wheeze trailing into silence. Hooking his fingers in Garner's collar, he pulled him close, so close that Garner could smell the sour taint of his breath.

"Faber, relax, relax!"

"It—" Faber's voice locked. He swallowed and tried again. "It laid an egg in me."

Bishop and Connelly crowded through the tent flap, and Garner felt suddenly hemmed in, overwhelmed by the heat and the stink and the steam rising in wisps from their clothes as they pushed closer, staring down at Faber.

"What's going on?" Bishop asked. "Is he all right?"

Faber eyed them wildly. Ignoring them, Garner placed his hands on Faber's cheeks and turned his head toward him. "Look at me, Faber. Look at me. What do you mean?"

Faber found a way to smile. "In my dream. It put my head inside its body, and it laid an egg in me."

Connelly said, "He's delirious. See what happens when you leave him alone?"

Garner fished an ampule of morphine out of his bag. Faber saw what he was doing and his body bucked.

"No!" he screamed, summoning his voice again. "No!" His leg thrashed out, knocking over the Nansen cooker. Cursing, Connelly dove at the overturned stove, but it was already too late. Kerosene splashed over the blankets and supplies, engulfing the tent in flames. The men moved in a sudden tangle of panic. Bishop stumbled back out of the tent and Connelly shoved Garner aside—Garner rolled over on his back and came to rest there—as he lunged for Faber's legs, dragging him backward. Screaming, Faber clutched at the ground to resist, but Connelly was too strong. A moment later, Faber was gone, dragging a smoldering rucksack with him.

Still inside the tent, Garner lay back, watching as the fire spread hungrily along the roof, dropping tongues of flame onto the ground, onto his own body. Garner closed his eyes as the heat gathered him up like a furnace-hearted lover.

What he felt, though, was not the fire's heat, but the cool breath of underground earth, the silence of the deep tomb buried beneath the ice shelf. The stairs descended before him, and at the bottom he heard a noise again: A woman's voice, calling for him. Wondering where he was.

Elizabeth, he called, his voice echoing off the stone. Are you there?

If only he'd gotten to see her, he thought. If only he'd gotten to bury her. To fill those beautiful eyes with dirt. To cover her in darkness.

Elizabeth, can you hear me?

Then Connelly's big arms enveloped him, and he felt the heat again, searing bands of pain around his legs and chest. It was like being wrapped in a star. "I ought to let you burn, you stupid son of a bitch," Connelly hissed, but he didn't. He lugged Garner outside—Garner opened his eyes in time to see the canvas part in front of him, like fiery curtains—and dumped him in the snow instead. The pain went away, briefly, and Garner mourned its passing. He rolled over and lifted his head. Connelly stood over him, his face twisted in disgust. Behind him the tent flickered and burned like a dropped torch.

Faber's quavering voice hung over it all, rising and falling like the wind.

Connelly tossed an ampule and a syringe onto the ground by Garner. "Faber's leg's opened up again," he said. "Go and do your job."

Garner climbed slowly to his feet, feeling the skin on his chest and legs tighten. He'd been burned; he'd have to wait until he'd tended to Faber to find out how badly.

"And then help us pack up," Bishop called as he led the dogs to their harnesses, his voice harsh and strained. "We're getting the hell out of here."

By the time they reached the depot, Faber was dead. Connelly spat into the snow and turned away to unhitch the dogs, while Garner and Bishop went inside and started a fire. Bishop started water boiling for coffee. Garner unpacked their bedclothes and dressed the cots, moving gingerly. Once the place was warm enough, he undressed and surveyed the burn damage. It would leave scars.

The next morning, they wrapped Faber's body and packed it in an ice locker.

After that they settled in to wait.

The ship would not return for a month yet, and though McReady's expedition was due back before then, the vagaries of Antarctic experience made that a tenuous proposition at best. In any case, they were stuck with each other for some time yet, and not even the generous stocks of the depot—a relative wealth of food and medical supplies, playing cards and books—could fully distract them from their grievances.

In the days that followed, Connelly managed to bank his anger at Garner, but it would not take much to set it off again; so Garner tried to keep a low profile. As with the trenches in France, corpses were easy to explain in Antarctica.

A couple of weeks into that empty expanse of time, while Connelly dozed on his cot and Bishop read through an old natural history magazine, Garner decided to risk broaching the subject of what had happened in the crevasse.

"You saw it," he said, quietly, so as not to wake Connelly.

Bishop took a moment to acknowledge that he'd heard him. Finally he tilted the magazine away, and sighed. "Saw what," he said.

"You know what."

Bishop shook his head. "No," he said. "I don't. I don't know what you're talking about."

"Something was there."

Bishop said nothing. He lifted the magazine again, but his eyes were still.

"Something was down there," Garner said.

"No there wasn't."

"It pulled Atka. I know you saw it."

Bishop refused to look at him. "This is an empty place," he said, after a long silence. "There's nothing here." He blinked, and turned a page in the magazine. "Nothing."

Garner leaned back onto his cot, looking at the ceiling.

Although the long Antarctic day had not yet finished, it was shading into dusk, the sun hovering over the horizon like a great boiling eye. It cast long shadows, and the lamp Bishop had lit to read by set them dancing. Garner watched them caper across the ceiling. Some time later, Bishop snuffed out the lamp and dragged the curtains over the windows, consigning them all to darkness. With it, Garner felt something like peace stir inside him. He let it move through him in waves, he felt it ebb and flow with each slow pulse of his heart.

A gust of wind scattered fine crystals of snow against the window, and he found himself wondering what the night would be like in this cold country. He imagined the sky dissolving to reveal the hard vault of stars, the galaxy turning above him like a cog in a vast, unknowable engine. And behind it all, the emptiness into which men hurled their prayers. It occurred to him that he could leave now, walk out into the long twilight and keep going until the earth opened beneath him and he found himself descending strange stairs, while the world around him broke silently into snow, and into night.

Garner closed his eyes.

DALE BAILEY has published three novels, *The Fallen*, *House of Bones*, and *Sleeping Policemen* (with Jack Slay, Jr.). A fourth novel, *The Clearing* (also with Jack), is forthcoming. His short fiction—which has won the International Horror Guild Award and has been twice nominated for the Nebula Award—has been collected in *The Resurrection Man's Legacy and Other Stories.*

BAILEY SAYS: *I first encountered Lovecraft when I stumbled across a battered paperback reprint of* The Horror in the Museum *in a used bookstore. I fell for it right away, as any self-respecting twelve-year-old would. But what has sustained my interest well into adulthood is the horror of Lovecraft's central observation: that the universe is inconceivably more vast, strange, and terrifying than mere human beings can possibly imagine. That seems to me fundamentally true, if not particularly reassuring, and I think that much of my own fiction—while not often explicitly "Lovecraftian"—circles around that same issue. I still have that paperback, by the way. The cover is a work of genius. And the title story still gives me nightmares.*

NATHAN BALLINGRUD lives with his daughter just outside of Asheville, NC. His stories have appeared in *Inferno: New Tales of Terror and the Supernatural, The Del Rey Book of Science Fiction and Fantasy, SCIFICTION,* and the forthcoming *Naked City: New Tales of Urban Fantasy.* He recently won the Shirley Jackson Award for his short story "The Monsters of Heaven."

BALLINGRUD SAYS: *I respond most directly to the nihilism in Lovecraft's fiction, to its antagonistic relationship with the reader. While so much horror fiction comes from a standpoint of moral conservatism, Lovecraft's fiction is decidedly anarchic in nature. The stories are a direct assault on the comforts of society and religion. If the horror genre has a noble purpose—and I believe that it does—this is where it lies.*

Also, he had some of the best story titles ever. "The Dunwich Horror," "The Dreams in the Witch-House," "The Horror at Red Hook," "The Colour Out of Space"—those are just awesome.

RICHARD BOWES

The Office of Doom

THE VIEW FROM the University Science Reference Desk is all about dark and light. It looks out over a balcony into an illuminated twelve-story atrium. The front of the library building has ranks of tall windows. Outside are the dark trees of New York's Washington Square and beyond them, the lights of the brownstones and skyscrapers on the far side of the park.

My thoughts ran to the past on a night when I sat behind that desk waiting with curiosity and a bit of dread for an old acquaintance to reappear. I was in the last months before my retirement from this University where I'd been employed for most of my adult life. Until the day before, I'd enjoyed the freedom that came from no one knowing what to do with me.

Once I announced I was leaving after thirty-five years, I was kind of beyond the law. I could sit at the Information Desk—I'd been a library reference assistant for most of those years—making notes for stories I was writing, and neither the librarians nor the public could quite bring themselves to bother me.

Then my boss asked me to see if there was anything of archival interest in the Office of Doom before it got renovated. She was very polite about it and I couldn't really refuse. Also, I did feel some desire to tie up all my affairs, including some troublesome ones, before I left.

She didn't call it the Office of Doom, of course. She referred to it as Room 975, which is the number on the door. I was among the last ones who remembered the nickname.

The office is in a far corner of our floor, and for many years it had been used for nothing but the storage of boxes of old university records. Those had been moved out, but the dust remained. There were roach motels in the corners, a glue trap under the desk, and strange stains on the rug. An old wooden hat rack was missing two of its hooks. The only thing on it was a gnarly woolen scarf in a rusty orange shade. The lock on one of the desk's side drawers had been broken open at some time in the past.

Even for a building designed by a former admirer of Hitler and financed by the man who put Richard Nixon in the White House, the room had always been especially creepy. I'd brought a rolling plastic trash bin with me and used it to keep the door propped open, so as not to get shut in. Then I dusted off the swivel chair and sat at the desk.

Room 975 got its nickname among the lower echelon library staff because when the place first opened in the early 1970's, this windowless ten-foot by six-foot hole was where they stuck people who had fallen from grace and were on their way out.

Pulling up the creaking chair, I went through the desk drawers, not expecting to find anything much after all these years but wanting to make sure. It was mundane stuff at first: jotted notes, a photo of an office party from a couple of decades back with some people who almost looked familiar, pamphlets, and outdated fire evacuation instructions. Everything went into the trash.

Then, way in the back of a bottom drawer, I found a small plastic nail manicure kit with the words *50th Annual Convention of the Financial Officers of New York State* in gold lettering.

The first occupant of the Office of Doom was a pale weasel of a man named Siddons. He had been the chief financial officer to the president of the University, William "Dollar Bill" Bradshaw, who built this very library and brought the school nearly to bankruptcy doing it. When Bradshaw was abruptly axed by the board of trustees, Siddons found himself in this office. He spent his days whispering into the phone and doing his nails (which I must admit were quite immaculate and trim). Then one day he was gone to a place where apparently his reputation had not yet traveled.

I tossed the manicure kit into the bin.

That set me looking for signs of the Office of Doom's next occupant, Dr. Harold Kassin. Known to us all as "Kassin the Assassin" he had been the hatchet man for a very aggressive Dean of Libraries. The Dean and Dr. Kassin wanted to fire everybody. But one morning the Dean was called into the office of the University President who succeeded Bradshaw, and was summarily dismissed for forging documents. He was escorted off the premises by security guards as we all cheered. Kassin was in this office the very next day.

He had a face like an ax. At one time or another he'd confronted just about everyone in the library and told them he was watching them and they'd better straighten up. We practically ran group tours for all the people who wanted to look in and see his disgrace. He too was gone without any forewarning one fine day. Word was that he'd taken a job as head of a small library in New Jersey. I pitied the staff.

The desk yielded no traces of Kassin, which didn't really surprise me. He was careful in the way of professional killers. I stood up and riffled through the file cabinet. Old folders full of invoices got tossed with scarcely a second glance. If anyone had been seriously interested in evaluating this stuff, they wouldn't have given this assignment to me.

Then I found a stack of menus for long gone pizza parlors, announcements of music acts at the Bottom Line and CBGB's, flyers from comic-book stores on Bleecker Street and horror film festivals at the Waverly theater.

After they ran out of disgraced administrators, the office got returned to library use. For a few years it was where our student assistants got stashed.

Among the artifacts were a few scribbled notes, and I recognized the handwriting. Chris McLaren was a film major who worked for us in the early '80s, a skinny kid who wore black clothes and spiked hair and had an intense interest in Aleister Crowley, Roman Polanski, the Illuminati, and role-playing games. Even when you were face to face with him he seemed to be staring at you slightly askance from around some corner only he could see.

Chris and I got along okay. We shared a certain detachment and interest in the strange. I'd told him about the nickname we'd given the room and he loved it.

As I riffled through the next layer of folders I realized the material I was tossing in the trash had been left behind by Frances Hooker, a librarian and the last occupant of this office. With that name, her life in junior high school must have been a living hell. I felt not an iota of sympathy for her.

Miss Hooker was youngish but wore dresses that fell below the knee and blouses that came up to her chin. She never smiled and only discussed business.

The student employees lost their office when she arrived. For that and for reasons of temperament, she and Chris hated each other from the start. I hadn't been entirely sad about this. She and I didn't get along either, and Chris kept her distracted. I don't feel proud about not having tried to protect him.

Then, as if remembering those two had evoked it, I spotted an old Interlibrary Loan shipping envelope addressed to Chris. Scrawled in black marker was *Necronom/Miskaton.*

Careful not to disturb it in any way, I quickly shut the drawer and got outside. Then I locked the office and told everyone I was going to lunch.

What I actually did was to visit the Strega, the witch who worked among us.

Her office was on the east side of Washington Square Park. Back before the University became an academic high-roller, this was a gritty urban campus with a bunch of old commercial buildings converted to classrooms. I went in the side entrance of one of these, took a turn just inside the door, walked down a short corridor, descended spiral metal stairs, and found myself in Central Supply.

Years ago the place had hummed. Anyone who wanted anything had to get a requisition order and bring it here. Normally there was a line and three or four clerks behind a tall counter handling requests, making sure everything was filled out correctly and properly signed and dated and then piling office supplies on the counter. If there was a problem, Ambrose was the man you saw first, a black guy built like a walking bunker who was always a little too busy to listen.

Central Supply was almost deserted now. Piles of dusty, broken furniture—tables, desks, and chairs sat where lines once formed. Ambrose was still at the counter, but no one else was. He sat, older, bigger but somehow frail, absorbed in whatever was on his computer screen. I had to say "Hello" twice before he looked up.

"Is Mrs. Rossi here?" Once upon a time, only unusual requests from the highest University echelon or esoteric problems that defied clear definition got referred to Teresa Rossi.

Now Ambrose nodded without looking up and called out, "Teresa, someone for you."

"I know," was the answer, like, somehow, she expected me. "Send him in."

With no more formality than that, I lifted a hinged section of the counter and walked back to her office.

The University locksmith many years ago was a tiny man with a large head and a beautiful face—like the ones on shepherds in Renaissance nativity paintings. He had come from Palermo and lived in Greenwich Village. Once he said that back when he first arrived here, Teresa Rossi's mother had been the neighborhood Strega. He mentioned that her mother was a witch with great respect and added as an afterthought that her father had a hardware shop on Mercer Street.

All else had changed but Teresa Rossi, at first glance, was just the same: dark hair with little highlights, nice but anonymous at-work dress, and jewelry that caught the eye—was that a minute owl's face staring out from that earring?—but when you looked closely seemed perfectly mundane.

"You're still here," she said expressing no surprise. Part of her shtick was that she was never surprised.

"For a little while longer," I said. "You too."

She shrugged. "Each department orders everything online from Staples now. What we do is receive broken furniture and call for carting companies to come and haul it away."

"But you're still in business?" She nodded and waited for me to speak. "There was a kid working for us years ago who pulled a stupid prank with Interlibrary Loan."

"Chris McLaren," Teresa Rossi said, like it happened earlier in the week and not twenty-five years before. "That went way beyond being a prank. I thought all that had been taken care of." She showed a flash of irritation. At moments she could be chilling.

"Something connected to that turned up today." I told her what I'd found.

"You didn't touch it."

"No."

"It will have to be dealt with when there's nobody around."

"I work late tomorrow night."

"That will be good." And the session was over.

Many years before, I had brought Chris with me to help carry stuff back to our department. We were waiting in line when Teresa emerged from her office with the University Counsel and escorted him out as he babbled his gratitude. "Don't know how you found those letters. The secretary swore she'd discarded them years ago." The Strega nodded as if this was nothing.

Chris was fascinated by Teresa Rossi. Something made her notice him, too. I stepped up to place my order and she motioned him over and spoke to him. Later I asked what she'd had to say.

"She wanted to know who I was. Said not to trust you too far, but I think she was kidding."

I told him what the locksmith told me and about the stories of how she had certain control over lost objects and future events.

"People like her and you are like the limbic system of this place," he said. "You know how in our brains, behind all the recent flashy developments that gave us stuff like emotions and aesthetics and cosmic awareness, there's this lizard brain. It's what makes the heart beat and what stays alert to odd noises and sudden movements in the dark while we sleep. Don't wonder where the dinosaurs went, there's a bit of one inside each of us."

"So Mrs. Rossi and I are ancient lizards?"

"Yeah man. You're the Old Ones and it's cool."

Thinking back, I can remember Chris talking about H. P. Lovecraft and the evil book the *Necronomicon* and Miskatonic University, the accursed New England institution of higher learning that shows up in Lovecraft stories.

We joked about accursed universities not being that far fetched. I remember him talking about doing an Interlibrary Loan request for the *Necronomicon*. I even showed him how to search the huge print tomes of library holdings, as one did in those pre-internet years, and as part of the gag I approved the ILL request for him.

He told me, months, maybe a year later, that the book had arrived. I said, "It's probably some kind of cheap reprint."

"It's close enough," he said peeking around the invisible corner, and I assumed he was joking.

By the time Chris got the book, Frances Hooker had been hired. She apparently never slept, never went home, and had no interest in life except library science. Even other librarians didn't like her, but they agreed that she was excellent at her work and shut themselves in their offices when she was round.

I had to deal with her and found she hated me because I didn't have a library degree. I believe she hated everyone who was not a librarian. She thought that librarians should be addressed as "Curator" in the same way as medical people are called "Doctor." No one went along with this.

Mad librarians were no novelty. The first one I worked for at the University was Alice Marlow. She had dyed blonde hair and, though somewhat pudgy, wore leather mini-skirts and mesh stockings. It was 1970, and stuff like that did get worn, but not by any other librarians that I can recall.

The main library hadn't yet been built, and departments and collections were stuck in odd places around campus. We had been installed in a small office on the floor above the Gates of Eden Beer Hall, a student hangout on Waverly Place. There was a men's hat manufacturer on the floor above us in those dusty, far gone days. Alice was erratic, sweet and zaftig one minute, insanely suspicious the next. I was no prize either, always slipping down to the Gates of Eden to get drunk or over to Washington Square to cop drugs. She threatened to fire me for being habitually late to work.

She'd usually forget about that but I made it a point to come in early the next day. She never showed up and wasn't there the day after that either. I began to wonder what had happened. That afternoon two people from administration came and took all her personal effects. It seemed she'd gone berserk in the West Fourth Street subway station two days before, screaming that people were putting LSD in her coffee, and her family had her committed.

Hooker was unpleasant to me, but she was hell on Chris, who was used to easy-going supervision. I assumed that was what made him increasingly twitchy. I tried telling him not to let her get to him. He stopped speaking to anyone and then stopped coming to work. I made inquiries and got nowhere.

His roommates said he'd gotten very moody and had taken off suddenly. "He talked about needing to go somewhere up in New England, man," one of them said.

Later I was told to go through his locker. There was the *Necronomicon* with leather binding and gold lettering that looked not at all cheap or new. I won't say that it exuded evil, but I'd read enough Lovecraft not to touch it. While I stood wondering what to do, Frances Hooker walked by. I thought it was Fate.

"This looks like a rare book," I said, "It's from Interlibrary Loan and I don't know how to handle something like this." I didn't even have to say that was because I wasn't a librarian. She glared at me, gathered up the volume, and stalked off to the Office of Doom.

Ms. Hooker's behavior over the next year or so grew stranger than Marlow's ever had been. The cleaning people heard her shrieking in her office late at night. On one occasion she stood up at a faculty meeting and spoke in tongues. The rare books librarian said that once when she spoke to him, a tongue long and forked like a snake's lolled out of her mouth. But he drank, and nobody but me believed him. Then she disappeared, leaving a disjointed note about mountains and madness and needing to travel.

Even at the time I felt a certain amount of guilt about having knowingly let Frances Hooker have the *Necronomicon*. When I was ordered to clear out her office, the book was in the top drawer of her desk. I went to Central Supply and told Teresa Rossi what had happened. She was not pleased. "Chris brought the *Necronomicon* to this place. He's young but not a child and will pay a price." The witch looked me in the eye, "You're a disappointment." She shrugged. "Stay at work late and someone will be there."

That someone appeared just before closing time. It was early fall and not that cold, but he wore an overcoat, a wide brimmed hat, and dark glasses, and carried a leather satchel. Chris had barely been gone twelve months, but from what I could see he looked twenty years older, gaunt and stone faced.

Without a word, he went into the Office of Doom and came out with something in his satchel. "Chris, I'm sorry..." I said.

"It's OK." The voice was faint and from far away. Then he was gone.

I was the one who suggested that the now vacant Office of Doom be used as a storage space. Everyone thought it was a good idea.

Twenty-five years later, in the digital age, students and faculty no longer come into the libraries. And yet the surroundings are pleasant enough, and the computer facilities are excellent. So just before eleven o'clock on the night I sat waiting once again, the place was full of foreign doctors from around the world studying to pass their U.S. equivalency exams.

Busy, conspiratorial, they would jump up and dash downstairs to smoke foul smelling cigarettes outdoors. And as always, they watched me from the corners of their eyes convinced that I worked for the secret police and was going to turn them in.

Their names, Visascia, Yadaminia, sounded like obscure nineteenth-century diseases. The one thing they all wanted was to pass their exams and go work in American emergency rooms.

They barely looked up when Chris McLaren appeared. In fact nothing about him would have attracted their attention. Things apparently had gotten easier for him. Except for a certain wariness, he looked like a guy you'd see in any suburban mall, balding, a bit overweight, a little pressed for time. He carried a satchel.

"You're still here." The voice was a breath, a whisper. He showed no surprise.

I let him into the Office of Doom, showed him where I'd found the envelope, and left. They announced closing time over the loud speakers as he came back to the desk.

He peered at me from around his corner. "Some kind of errata sheet," he said. "Must have missed it the last time. I've gotten better over the years."

"Chris, what happened to you?"

"Awful stuff at first. Mrs. Rossi, though, told me who to talk to, how to throw myself on their mercy. She said they always need someone to clean up little mistakes."

"What happened with Frances Hooker bothers me . . ." I trailed off.

Chris gave what might have been the ghost of a smile. Then he turned and was gone.

Everyone thought my retirement party was quite a success: a large crowd, a couple of my young relatives in attendance, plenty of sentimental and funny gifts.

Teresa Rossi showed up unexpectedly. People asked her when she was going to call it quits and she said, "Soon, maybe." At one point when we were alone, she told me, "An old friend wants you to know the case is closed and nobody holds any grudge against you." When I started to thank her she added, "It's not strictly justice. But ones like us don't always want that."

RICHARD BOWES has written five novels, the most recent of which is the Nebula Award–nominated *From the Files of the Time Rangers.* His most recent short fiction collection is *Streetcar Dreams And Other Midnight Fancies* from PS Publications. He has won the World Fantasy, Lambda, International Horror Guild, and Million Writers Awards.

Recent and forthcoming stories appear in *The Magazine of Fantasy and Science Fiction*, *Electric Velocipede*, *Clarkesworld*, and *Fantasy* magazines and in the *Del Rey Book of Science Fiction and Fantasy*, *Year's Best Gay Stories 2008*, *Best Science Fiction and Fantasy*, *The Beastly Bride*, *Haunted Legends*, *Fantasy Best of the Year 2009*, *Year's Best Fantasy* and *Naked City* anthologies. Several of these stories are chapters in his novel in progress, *Dust Devil on a Quiet Street.*

His home page is www.rickbowes.com.

BOWES SAYS: *Thinking about it, I had no idea why I chose to write a story for* Lovecraft Unbound. *I first read him fifty years ago when I was a kid working in the Boston Public Library in Copley Square with plenty of time on my hands. It was a collection of his best-known short stories, and it stuck with me, but not in a major way. Years later when I worked at NYU's Bobst Library in Washington Square, we did joke about ordering the* Necronomicon *via interlibrary loan. But that's really not enough.*

Then, just now, I went into my bedroom to find something else, and Lovecraft looked down on me. He's dull metallic grey. His head is elongated, his eyes blank discs. It's a bust of the author I received years ago for winning an award, and it's always seemed scary.

For a while I dressed him up in a D'Artagnan hat, complete with plume, and a pair of sunglasses with pink heart-shaped rims. But a young visitor wanted those for her Barbie. Now he has a bronze-blond fright wig. And "fright" is the defining word.

There, I believe, is the answer: a decade's cohabitation and Lovecraft has seeped into my consciousness. As further evidence that this is possible, the editor of Lovecraft Unbound has maybe a dozen similar busts staring down on visitors in her apartment.

ANNA TAMBOUR

Sincerely, Petrified

ON THE APPROACH, it's the world's most unassuming national park. Not here, the jutting majesty of organ cacti, buttes, cathedral rocks. Though the Painted Desert is technically part of it, you wouldn't know that here, in this flat, dry ex-floodplain. Only a few scattered stumps and a red brick building greet the drive-in tourist to the Petrified Forest. Within easy walking distance, everything's flat as a Roman ruin pre-restoration. The usual walk-around outdoors, though littered with surprises, lasts less than half an hour; and would, for most visitors, be a visit soon sunk below memories of the shopping at Silver City, fried breads at that little place in Taos, the lonely cliffdrop down to the rushing Colorado at Mexican Hat, and those Western-movie backdrops around Moab.

What catches pretty much everyone, however, is the museum/gift shop. It's like that thing in the tequila bottle—the worm that bores into the flesh of cactus, deep enough to kill it.

Architecturally, the low-slung building is pure highway office, Department of Motor Vehicles. The gift shop has Navajo silver jewelry inset with paint-bright stones, string ties, belt buckles, bookends, and bric-a-brac. The petrified wood in them is certified "from sites outside the park, but of the same quality." For kids, there's Magic Crystals, plastic dinosaurs and rubber rattlesnakes, a

Junior Scientist Guide to Rocks, unconvincing chunks of "fool's gold," and a Genuine Tooled Leather Wallet Kit. No food here, and the only drink is water from the restroom sink. Most visits would end now, but it's the rec-room size museum, oddly enough, that makes visitors stop, stare through the glass, actually read, and more amazingly, remember.

Yosemite, so photogenic that it loses nothing in black and white, was given park status in 1906 with a sweep of the great-white-hunter president's pen. But since the late 1800s, when Wild Bill Hickok made the West interesting, experts argued about making *this* place known. Park status would draw attention to it, a damnably fool idea. Others argued that this elitist attitude was what made the East what it was—somewhere to escape from. "Our corner should have its national park," said a faction known by the watch chains stretched across their heavy tums. But all sorts of people agreed, many who would not agree with each other on anything else. "All Americans should have the same right to enjoy what only a few enjoy now," railed the Summer 1909 *Allaeompic Light*, a short-lived journal owned by two men and a woman: two naturists and a naturalist.

Yet unlike Yosemite, Pike's Peak, or Mt. Rushmore, the attractions of *this* place are portable.

Want a polished slice of *Araucarioxylon arizonicum*? Once, in the highlands, a stand of great pre-redwoods shaded tyrannosaurs, only to fall and be washed down into this floodplain where proto-crocodiles and salamanders the size of great white sharks slid amongst the cycads—before the volcanoes. After, ash fell over the logs, buried and washed through them; and then the logs and broken forest detritus slowly dried. And so, like candying fruit, where the sugar permeates and preserves, the mineral-thick bath dried over 225 million years, and quartz and other minerals replaced the cellulose. Depending upon the mineral, the wood looked almost as it had in life, down to the cell structure—or altogether different. The long-grained purplish red pieces broken from the heartwood, streaked with fat-white quartz—like corned beef.

But that is by the way. What matters is that before it was a park, every year more of the petrified wood just disappeared—casually souvenired, deliberately collected.

In 1907, the first committee formed to solve the problem. And then came: War. Depression. War. Deaths and birth. The story of the committees. No agreement reached within any of these short-lived collections of geographically scattered folks who had only one common interest. Finally, in 1960, when urgently finding a solution had become a necessity, given the fact that the place was becoming more known every summer vacation, the newest committee recommended a solution. Simple. Logical. American. It could not have been proposed in the days when the West was wild. No, this recommendation was a product of the post-war, Peace Corps, think-not-what-you-can-do-for-yourself time: Law.

So, in 1962 Congress legislated the Petrified Forest National Park into being, and also laid down the law about taking anything from it, other than memories and purchases from the shop.

The opening day of the park was the same day that its museum/ shop opened.

Walter R. Wilder and Hugh Krey had been on that committee and attended that penultimate meeting at the University of Arizona. The air conditioner's noise was so loud that other members yelled louder than normal, and the meat-packing-room cold made Wilder wish he'd brought a jacket. Krey's monosyllabic scorn for law thrilled and rather frightened Wilder, who doodled something shaggy on his yellow pad, and noted: *K-Wolf eyes.*

Neither man proposed another plan. When the meeting ended with some backslapping, these men slipped out, avoiding human contact—each going his separate way. On the train home, Wilder's imagination served up scenes of what would happen to the petrified forest, the . . . the final devastation. And while he couldn't visualize a lighthearted Krey, Wilder had felt Krey's frustration, and suspected that he too, was depressed enough for Valium.

Professor Wilder taught psychiatry at the University of Chicago. Dr. Krey, a geologist with a huge reputation for his work on cryptobiotic soils, was a lecturer at U of C's School of Geophysical Sciences.

In a campus famed for eccentric dressers, Wilder, an over-ripe-pear-shaped man, wore string ties: leather plaited thinner than a whipsnake, caught with a decorative silver choke. He had a collection of them and seemed to wear them according to some presentiment of what mood the day would bring. Some chokes were Navajo myth-themed: the turquoise-winged thunderbird, yellow-and-white-striped squash blossom, thundercloud—as common thematically in their homeland as caps with flaps are, in Chicago—yet the stones in these pieces were choice. Most of his chokes were simply-mounted stones, each a head-turner in its own way. One of them cried out for rye, sauerkraut, and mustard. He didn't look any sillier in his string ties than Theo Grossner (Dean of the School), who wore sandals and socks throughout Chicago's winter. Both men, however, left their pet peccadilloes in Chicago. At a conference at, say, Harvard, only their words were notable.

The living room of Wilder's apartment could have been a museum, so well had he bought and displayed his collection. The sparkling halite crystals from the Wieliczka Mine—to other tastes, mere salt to be crushed. Mouthwatering wulfenite from the Red Cloud Mine in Arizona, as red as a blood orange. Great rock-candy mimetite protruding from what looked like a slagheap of burnt sugar, coming all the way from Johanngerogendtadt in Saxony, where Siegfried and Kriemhild's love had ended in bitterness and blood. Atacamite from Wallaroo, chrysoberyl from Takovaja, rutile from Pfitsch, and brookite from Froßnitz. The pieces showed a wide and particular taste. The Alexandrite from the emerald mines along the Takovaja Urals had cost more than its worth, but what a history. Then there were the grotesqueries. The iron-flower from the Erzberg in Styria. The writhing horse of lead. Nothing here was shaped by human hand.

His second bedroom held his books. He was divorced, with one surprising issue from the marriage—a daughter in her twenties whom he loved uncomplicatedly and who taught, of all things, home economics.

Dr. Hugh Krey was a long jerky strip of a man, in clothes he ordered when the ones he had wore out, from the Sears, Roebuck catalogue or picked up at someplace local (since he'd arrived in Chicago, Kresge's Dollar Store was the place—cheapest and closest). His eyes were the color of a snow-laden sky, with pinprick pupils. They disconcerted people, attracted women who loved dangerous men. Not that he was predatory. He just used women same as they used him.

Even though there was the odd coincidental interest that both men had in the petrified forest, Wilder had always avoided Krey, who hadn't seemed to notice Wilder. The psychiatrist didn't blame the man. Wilder had always shied away or been tongue-tied in front of the famed geologist—the shyness of an amateur in an expert's presence. Now at last, he had something to offer—a thought hatched from his own expertise.

A month after the Arizona meeting, on a stinking-hot September day the first week of the new semester, Professor Wilder rang the geology lecturer at work, made a wry observation about the committee's balls, and invited the geologist to his apartment "for a beer after work." The address he gave was 3C, to which Krey said, " 'Kay."

Wilder had lived in the same Hyde Park apartment in Chicago's South Side for thirty years, Krey for two—a once-gracious brownstone a block from Lake Michigan. The phone call from Wilder was the first time they'd spoken. Krey wondered what beer Wilder would drink. Decided Pabst Blue Ribbon, in a glass. Which was another reason Krey always preferred drinking beer alone, but he approved Wilder's lack of chattiness, his silence when others in that committee spoke so authoritatively about the psychological effect of harsh penalties on the guilty. *He must have been laughing up his ass.* Yeah, Krey knew what Wilder was and would have been willing to listen to him, up to a point. *What came first, crazy people or shrinks?* So Krey didn't mind the invitation. It intrigued him.

Wilder opened the door holding a Budweiser that he handed Krey. Then he stepped aside. "I'll get mine," he said, flicking some switches on the wall and escaping down the dark hall to the kitchen, not that Krey noticed. The stuff in the cases had caught all of his attention.

Light poured over, pierced, probed, and petted the rocks and minerals. Krey walked slowly around the room, not noticing the widening wet around his armpits. The night was sweltering, and though there were no visible lamps in the room, all the wattage in those subtly hidden light sources could have fried an egg. When Wilder entered, bottle in hand, Krey was bent over, gazing, not at the picnic-table-size slice of *Araucarioxylon arizonicum* mounted on the wall, but at something in the case just to the left.

Wilder's hand squeaked against the neck of his bottle. "I'm just an amateur."

"Hn," said Krey.

"Ready for another?" said Wilder. He reached out.

"Whoa." Krey drank, one eye on Wilder, as if the bottle were a glass of milk and Wilder was his mother watching.

Wilder was in agony, awaiting the judgment of this expert. His right big toe flexed so hard he heard the knuckle crack. His guts felt stirred with a wooden spoon.

"Thanks," said Krey.

Wilder took the bottle and scurried to the kitchen. The contents of his own bottle, he poured into a jar and put in the fridge. He picked a fresh cold one from the pack in the fridge and returned with it, hovering around Krey, not knowing if the man wanted it or not.

"That," Krey pointed, and laughed, sort of. "It brings back memories."

Wilder's laugh exploded. No "What a fine collection" or "Nice stuff." No appreciative comments at all.

"Your collection must be so much better," he blurted before he could stop himself.

He mopped his face with his handkerchief. Did that disguise the redness that he felt rise up his neck? His eyes must have been closed, because when he opened them again, Krey's back was to him. The man was mumbling to himself, bent over a clump of epidote from, Wilder had been told, Knappenwand in Untersulzbachtal.

His toe shredded the sock.

Krey finally turned to him. "I wouldn't say that. Different, is all. Got another beer?"

He handed it to Krey and scurried back to the kitchen.

Krey thought of his own collection, every piece of which he had personally found. A source of pride, but a limit. Display? He'd never thought that way. He'd always hoarded them. Home? His bed stuck in an arroyo that wound between buttes of books, papers, and boxes that had once held shoes, booze, artillery shells. He was almost jealous. He'd heard that some professor at the university had fallen heir to a bottled orange juice fortune, but that he continued living as he had—teaching. Krey hadn't paid attention to the name then, but remembered now: Wilder. Krey remembered how disgusted he'd been—and resentful. How he'd thought of the discoveries he'd make, contrasted with that dumbass—a fortune wasted on a drone with so little imagination, he'd continue teaching. Now, he looked again at that hunk of soberyl, and had to do something before he felt sorry for himself. Wilder was no dumbass.

He wandered to the kitchen door, where he watched Wilder pour a bag of beer nuts into a bowl. A red shell floated to the table.

Wilder sponged it off before taking two beers out of the fridge, putting them and the bowl on a tray. He opened a cupboard and was looking into it when Krey entered, pulled out one of the two kitchen chairs, and sat, digging a handful of nuts from the bowl.

"Have a drink," said Krey.

Wilder let the bottles accumulate on the table. But by his third, his toes were still as herrings in a can, not because of the beer (straight vodka was his drink) but because of Krey. The geologist was telling of the time when the sphalerite in his pants gave him crotch rash at a Bulgarian border post, while the guards tore his rickety British van apart because they spotted a dirty magazine he'd planted on the back seat.

"But why cause them to suspect you? What about the van?"

"They're Bulgarians! I threw them a bone. As long as they didn't chew the wheels, I was happy. And I *was, very* happy. There's nothing like a bracing border search." Krey's eyes sparkled like Wilder thought a mad dog's would, terribly exciting, but odd. *Krey a chatterbox? or is he lying? and why? Does he think I don't know value? Is he laughing at me? No. He really* does *admire my collection. Is he a little jealous? I* hope *so . . .*

Krey's long legs had tipped his chair back, its front legs reared up. Wilder would have been furious if anyone else had done this to his furniture, and almost didn't notice now.

"But we still have that problem," Krey said, sitting up abruptly.

Wilder looked into Krey's eyes. He hadn't bruised the floor to be offensive.

"Decidedly." In all the excitement, Wilder had almost forgotten what he'd planned to say to Krey.

"Of course this is *your* expertise." Krey's expression was receptive, respectful, expectant.

"I wouldn't say that," Wilder smiled, thrilled beyond words. This was the first time he'd brought an expert to see his collection, and to be treated like a peer—

Krey's forearm jerked forward, sweeping salt and peanut crumbs onto Wilder's spotless floor. "Isn't behavior your specialty?"

"Certainly. Of course." Wilder felt his neck burning, wished he wasn't wearing one of those new white nylon open-neck shirts. "Absolutely."

Krey pulled a pipe, tobacco pouch, and wooden box of matches out of the left breast pocket of his shirt, and paid them undivided attention. Wilder escaped to the bedroom where he dug a cigar from his night table, collected the cutter and box of matches, and steadied his breath before he returned to the kitchen, where he replaced the empty peanut bowl with a heavy ashtray, and sat at the table preparing his cigar. Then he wasted a good smoke, pulling on it with as much introverted eye-avoidance as Krey, who in his absence had produced a notepad and pencil.

Krey smoked as if his pipe and thoughts were his only companions.

Eventually Wilder stubbed out his cigar stub, left the kitchen with no comment, got his own writing materials and returned with them. Ostentatiously, he took the hood from his pen.

Krey's smoke floated between them.

Wilder's big toe cracked. *I'll be damned if I break first.*

Krey prepared another pipe, and *still*, Wilder didn't say a word, but now that he *thought* about what he'd liked about Krey in the first place, his anger slipped. The man was honest. He didn't shit around. "You were saying?" he invited.

Krey knocked the pipe in the ashtray, and stuck it headfirst, in his pocket. "What'll a law do?"

"You mean, prohibiting collection?"

"Yeah. Fines, jail, criminal record, what have you."

"What's prohibition ever do," Wilder said. "The stuff'll skyrocket in price and be trucked out before you can say black market."

"Normal Joes couldn't afford it. Not unless they bootlegged, or sold white slaves."

Krey's eyes narrowed, spreading the crows-feet. "Or were heirs to stinking fortunes." It was humor. He wasn't being offensive. Just signaling.

"Rotten stinking fortunes," corrected Wilder.

Wilder left for another cigar. He needed a break to get his thoughts together, as now he really didn't want to sound stupid. Now that he was sure Krey was the man he most wanted to expose them to, and to act in concert with.

Alone, Krey smiled with his teeth showing, something he never did in the presence of others.

Krey spoke first, not even giving Wilder a chance to sit. "What does law create, doctor?"

A growl of happiness escaped the older man. "Desire," he said in the voice that had laid waste dozens of female students some years ago.

"And?" Krey asked.

"And what?" Wilder was confused, not used to questions he hadn't planted. *Prohibition creates desire. Desire above all . . . but law, penalties, the hunt . . . the thrill of—*

"This isn't Psych 101," Krey snapped. "You can't treat me as a peer, I know, but—"

Wilder held up his pen, for silence. "The greatest motivator in the human psyche," he said, "is fear."

"Why, give the man a coconut."

"Fear" was what Krey was aiming for, in his attempt to get Wilder to think of a solution. Krey had examined his own psyche well enough, he reckoned, to know that fear gave him purpose. It distinguished desiring women. The ones married to colleagues wafted the most danger, and amongst them were the most desire-worthy, for a while. Every specimen he'd ever smuggled to his craggy but cozy little lairs bore a worth proportionate to the fear attached to its acquisition. Like neighborhoods jostling, contentment and resentment lived neck and neck in his thoughts, as they did in the nation. Money could buy anything, but for a man like him, even on a dean's salary—*if I'd been law abiding, what would I have?* That petrified forest irked him immensely. Only obscurity had saved it from being carted away to the moneyed, as wholesale as a feedlot of steers to the Armour sausage mill, to be consumed with as much intelligence as America does its hot dogs. *That slab on the wall here . . . polished! How big is mine?* Krey clicked his tongue, comparing, remembering. His largest piece of the Petrified Forest was a 386.5 lb splitfaced-broken length of *Schilderia* (rarer than the *Araucarioxylon arizonicum*) pried out of the ground by himself and a wetback who was pathetically grateful to do it for ten bucks and a ride into Flagstaff. Three hours from home (Denver, then) at dusk on an evil incline, the last drop of oil from his rundown Ford leaked, and the pistons melted solid.

He had the hood open and was leaning over the dead engine when two singing saviors pulled beside him on the one-lane road, in a bad excuse for a truck. No more than ten words were exchanged. They took over his Ford pickup and the situation. First, they shoved the pickup into a little hide of firs just up the road a bit, the kind of place you'd expect to find, if you're alone at night, half a dead woman. They smelled worse than two drunk skunks, but next, they tossed out the cord of wood they had in the back of their truck as if the split logs were toothpicks, and they lined the truckbed with burlap sacks one of them fetched from somewhere inside the truck. Then, grinning like maniacs, they pushed him out of the way and hefted the unwieldy rock from Krey's pickup to their truck. They tossed in his pick and shovel, and tied it all down till the tires could bounce along a logging track and the load would stay quiet as a body. Git in, said the one with the most teeth. The passenger door was opened for Krey by Eustace. Clive (he was called) rode shotgun, literally. Eustace drove with one hand on the wheel. He was generous, pulling out (with his teeth) a cork stopping a bottle that said Nehi, and wiping the bottle on his shirt before handing it to their guest. His own bottle was Heinz Ketchup.

He didn't ask questions, but served up stories wrapped around homilies like "Johnny Walker's for the ladies" and "The gubermint persues happiness, to arrest it." In their youth in Kentucky, they'd made a hassled living as "distillers." Krey shook his head. The stuff was cloudy as the water in Cubatão, and twice as deadly. They hadn't been going to Denver, but since that was where he was going, that was where they went because, as Eustace said, it was a thing he'd do for them if they were up shit creek.

When they reached his embarrassingly suburban house (a university rental property), they carried in his things, keeping the burlap wrapping on everything including the pickaxe till they got indoors, where they didn't dump stuff, but asked him where he'd like each item placed. Clive folded the wrapping neatly and took it to the truck, returning with a full Dr. Pepper. Happy home, he said. So long, said Eustace, and they left. Krey knew they wouldn't take money, but he'd laid the keys to the Ford on Eustace's seat. He had just closed his door when there was a knock, and Eustace appeared, dangling the keys.

He loved that rock, but not for itself. He loved the way it challenged him to think he knew something when he analyzed its samples. Within its seemingly static cells, as dead as Pluto, it encapsulated life, death, transformation. It was what religion *should* be, mushed myth to the pap of rubes. There was nothing flashy, obvious, easy about this rock—or anything in his collection. His slivers weren't biopsies, teeming with marvelous virulence. His petrified woods, like a crystal rose, globules of obsidian, every rain-pouring grain of simple salt, was *life*. Life in a timeframe that dwarfed science itself—science—the only truth worth seeking. Sure, he'd washed that hunk of stone once, but he never lost sight of what it was. It lived near his bed, covered in a patina of greasy, cat-fur-laden dust. When Denver had imploded and he'd had to move to Chicago, real moving men from Mayflower had packed his belongings with mostly silent distaste—"You got any furniture?"—until they got to *it*, leaning against the corner nearest where his bed had been. "Bud," the bigger one said to Krey, "That's a hernia. You want that mountain? You move it outn." He sat heavily on the floor. $20 each moved him and his colleague to move the mountain. Even then, once the Mayflower van's back doors were locked, the poet came back and put his hand out, bold as a bellhop. "Suspicious load," he laughed. Krey meekly forked over another two fives because he didn't trust them not open the van and *look* for something to take. And the Mayflower sailed away. *Chump*! Krey threw the university's house keys into the hydrangeas. *What's to stop them?* Not that he had anything they'd know to take. *Nothing like Tiffany's here with the glass cases, everything spotless and sparkling Precious Find. I've got nothing that Money values.*

Krey thought of his cat, Punk, who only enjoyed food that wasn't his. Krey helped Punk pursue happiness. The steak on a mousetrap was the most pleasure so far. The steak on the rat-trap, Punk left. He must have considered that a trap too dangerous to play against. Instead, he watched it and ate the rat who judged incorrectly.

"Am I interrupting an internal dialogue?" Wilder smiled. "Want some eggs?" He emptied the ashtray down the dumbwaiter.

Wilder cooked pedantically, using more utensils than Krey would take for a dig. The plate he slung in front of his guest had six colors on it, and that was just the food. Until that moment, Krey never knew that parsley existed outside of restaurants. He ate it first, so as not to be rude.

They finished the meal with black stewed coffee. Proper prospector's mud. It made up for the eggs.

Wilder wiped his mouth on a linen napkin, collected the plates, and stacked them by the sink. "Fear is what I was thinking of," he said as he placed a fresh ashtray on the table, and a pack of Marlboros and book of matches that said *Macello Ristorante.*

"Go on," said Krey.

"We gotta cut the balls off desire. Replace them with a special kind of fear. Know what I mean?"

"Of course."

"What?"

"Fear . . ."

Wilder held the Marlboros out to Krey, who shoved them away. "Tell me, doc."

"Dread," grinned Wilder. "That's the worst kind of fear. Dread of what will happen."

Krey blew a smoke ring. He'd lit up without knowing what he was doing, but now he needed time. Wilder's words were what he'd thought himself, but thinking as he did of people, he hadn't trusted himself. Sure, people are stupid, but just how stupid are they, and how do you make them fear something (he hadn't figured that brilliant *dread*)—how do you make people fear something to the point of it being *too* dangerous to ignore, taunt, steal its threat from under it and laugh all the way to the bank or wherever—if making *theft* a criminal offense only makes it more attractive, a mere mousetrap to a Punk? Krey was confused, but possibly Wilder had figured something out.

Krey snorted. "It's only property. Congress is hardly going to strap someone in the chair for stealing rocks, even diamonds at Tiffany's."

"Congress! What are they compared to gods?"

"Gods?"

"You haven't read my monographs of course, but did you happen to see the *Saturday Evening Post* of March 6, 1958. 'Deities of the Desert?' No? A little interest of mine, you see."

"You collect myths, too? So Indians prayed to the rain god." Krey rubbed his eyes. They felt sandy. "Capture it on Kodak."

"Want some raisin toast?"

"No goddamn raisin toast. Get to the point."

"We need a myth."

"And you'll make one?"

"I thought something along that line."

"You're a regular rattler in the grass," Krey laughed. "Make toast. I'll open the window."

"I wouldn't do that."

But Krey already had. The room filled with a sickening warm fust. The washing line that stretched between Wilder's window and the apartment on the other side of the open square (garbage cans and cats' playground below) was filled with diapers.

"I wish that woman would get a washing machine," Wilder sighed, but really, he couldn't care less.

He ran his hand over the strands of hair on his dome, delighted that he'd assessed the world renowned scientist correctly. For a while there, Krey had scared him in all the wrong ways—the man's lack of social skills, his sense of grievance, something else that left a chip on his shoulder. But looking at Krey's back now, Wilder was not only proud of his own ability to assess someone he'd only observed briefly, but felt true warmth inside. Camaraderie.

Krey's unusually small teeth gleamed—unconscious, open-mouthed admiration. Wilder was definitely not what a nice rich psychiatrist with a tenured professorship should be. *And for some reason, he trusts me.*

Krey ate his toast like a dog—fast, without chewing. He was getting it out of the way. Wilder poured two mugs of coffee.

"That dread," said Krey. "Are you talking cause and effect?"

"I never thought of it that way, but yes. Think of it as the expectation of a reaction from a previous action. Be bad and you won't get anything from Santa, or the Easter Bunny won't lay you an egg. And other myths, all implanted in the human psyche for a purpose."

"Control!"

"Egg . . . zakly. You wouldn't be a Trotskyite?"

"I'm eggnostic."

"Touché."

"So you're going to fake some story of the god who looks after the petrified forest."

Wilder waggled a finger in Krey's face. "Better than that. Fake? What *is* reality? I'll implant the scholarly records. Remember, I have a reputation."

At night in various deeply uncomfortable places, Krey had read lurid-covered rubbish to escape the weather, wildlife, and other people. He never *remembered* any of that trash as such, but . . . "I know that story of mine about the crotchrash was bullshit," he said. "I'm sorry, but it's not like I made it up. It's a goddamn cliché."

"I know," said Wilder, remembering that the man was telling the truth when he had said "your expertise." *He respects me, I think. Maybe even my collection, just a little.*

"I'm just telling you this because you've lit my fuse, but you're the expert here. You were talking dread?"

"An emotion you might regard unworthy of rational beings." Wilder wasn't being ironic.

"I've read papers in front of colleagues, too, you know." Krey poured himself cold coffee. He was actually nervous.

"I promise I won't laugh," said Wilder.

"It's eight o'clock. Don't you think we should call in sick?"

"The ring of the telephone," said Krey. "The knock on the door. A man lives in a neat little house. He opens the door in the morning and reaches out. What should he expect? A rolled-up *Tribune* and a bottle of milk. Implant dread, and you could pay him a million dollars, he won't open that door. Ask him what he expects, and a million to one, he can't tell you. Not a rattlesnake coiled in the Sports section. No strychnine in the milk. He just *expects*. Nameless dread."

"Or as I once wrote: paranoia is the key."

"Exactly! But I don't know how to do it," Krey ended.

Wilder had put much thought into his faux myth. He hadn't reached the stage of myth invention, but telling Krey of the idea, *false myth*—had led to Krey's gestalt—and Krey had in turn, inspired him, especially Krey's idea of "nameless dread."

"Did I tell you," said Wilder, "that I'm retiring this year? That I applied for and was accepted as Director of the Petrified Forest National Park Museum?"

Krey's mouth fell open.

"Don't congratulate me."

"What'll you put in it?" Krey shouted. "Petrified wood and signs? You romantic fool. You'd get more respect running a Dairy Queen."

"I did it for love," Wilder said. "And you're right. I rather dreaded that it would be hard to curate compellingly . . . until you."

— 2 —

"Superstitious, I wasn't," reads a penciled crumpled scrap of butcher paper. "However, more bad luck has happened to me than any one person could rationally have experienced. Take this back." It is signed, "A cynic no more, Scranton, Pennsylvania."

A typed letter on expensive blue Cross stationery reads:

> *To Whom It May Concern:*
> *Please warn everybody Not to Take the Petrified Wood from the Park. My husband just died. My daughter is sick. Before he took what was nothing really, just a little pebble, we were such a happy family. I warned him but he took it anyway. He had it made into this pendant that he gave me for our anniversary. He didn't tell me that this was the pebble till he was going in for the operation. I'm a good Christian woman, so take this and bury it or something, please please please. It's more evil than the snake in the Garden of Paradise.*
>
> *Yours sincerely,*
> *Mrs. John S.*
> *Los Angeles.*

A ruled page filled to the edges with words:

> *Before. Yes, before, I sailed my little boat on a placid sea of ignorance. Was I blissful? Oh my, yes. Before the truth floated like jetsam towards me, fouling my rudder . . .*

A telegram:

STOP THIS CURSE STOP TELL THEM IM SORRY STOP HERES THE STONE

A letter in German. Several in semi-American, one of which mentioned mummies and the Hope Diamond. One letter with an envelope marked Beverly Hills in which a woman states that her mother-in-law "stole" a tiny piece of petrified wood on her honeymoon in 1911, but didn't find out about the curse till 1954. "Is this (see enclosed) why my husband dropped dead at 49? Is this why my granddaughter has seizures and my grandson got a bee in his ear? Is this why I never win the lottery?"

These were only some of the great pile of letters and pieces of petrified stone in the central display case when the museum opened—all Krey and Wilder productions.

A few months later, Krey's game was up in Chicago—something about a Mrs. Everly. He took early leave and was accepted for the next year at West Virginia Tech.

Dear Hugh,
You might enjoy the cutting.

Fondly,
Walt

P.S. How are you faring so far from civilization?

The Tucson Star, Wednesday, June 6, 1963:

The Curse of the Petrified Wood
by Phillip Joy
. . . Dr. Walter Wilder, the head of the museum and a noted authority on myth, had this to say: "Myths have their purpose and should, even in our scientific times, be respected, as the underlying strata of our

> value systems. Some myths, like this one about the curse of taking petrified wood from the park, are so old that they predate historical knowledge, but that doesn't make them any less worthy—we know to avoid snakes without being taught at school. We instinctively avoid fire . . ."

Krey read it in his windowless office at the Tech. His door had been closed at the time, but that didn't stop his unseemly laughter traveling down the hall and penetrating the ears of at least one envious colleague.

Hugh was faring fine. He was, for the first time in his adult life, in love. And the woman wasn't even married. They walked arm in arm, under the black limbs of hickories and talked as Hugh had never talked with anyone before. Especially a woman. "I'm opening like a flower," he told her.

September 8, 1964

Dear Hugh,
You won't believe it! Letters and rocks are coming in from everywhere! Someone shipped us a whole log! These tales are unbelievable. I am going to write a book. When the Silent Psyche Speaks the Truth. *You're a loss to the psych profession.*

Walter,
A little something for your collection. Your personal *collection!*
Fondly,
Hugh

"Hugh?"

"Walter?"

"I had to ring you. I've looked everywhere. What is it?"

Krey's laugh startled Walter, it was such a rippling stream.

"Moissanite, Walt. Dropped from the heavens to West Virginia."

"It's beautiful. How can I thank you?"

"No thanks needed, Walter. That's nothing compared to the beauty here beside me."

Walter heard some scuffling, and a giggle.

"Am I disturbing you?"

"Yes."

"Oh, I'll—"

"No you won't," laughed Krey. "You already have disturbed me. How ya doin', you old conman?"

"Hugh?"

"Hugh who?"

"I'm serious. My collection. You truly think it has a worth?"

"Are you kidding? I'd give my eyeteeth for it."

Walter Wilder's eyes closed. He'd wanted to hear that line for so long that he almost didn't believe it. "You really mean that?"

"Who *wouldn't*, Walter?"

"I've been thinking a lot about it. Do you know where I live out here?"

Krey hadn't asked. Wilder's letters had the park as return address.

"In a trailer," Wilder said. "The collection is in storage in Chicago. I would like to give it to you . . . Hugh?"

Wilder heard whispers on the line, then what he thought might be a door closing. He waited.

"That's almost the nicest thought anyone's ever had for me. But you can't be serious."

"You seem to appreciate it. Are you just flattering me?" Wilder's voice almost wheedled for a *no*. He couldn't know that for a moment, Krey had trembled with desire.

"The Wilder collection would make the finest museum proud. Give it to the Field, or . . . God! The University of Chicago. The Wilder Collection, in its own wing, in of the School of Geophysical Sciences."

"You really think so?"

"It *is* a fucking museum."

"You really think so?"

"Are you breast-feeding deprived or something? Yes, yes, great ballsa yes!"

"Your old school?"

"How many times do I have to—uh, except for one piece. That polished slab of petrified wood on the wall."

Walter Wilder was finding it difficult to concentrate, but he tried, through the fog of his confused happiness. "Why?"

"It's not science."

"Doesn't it show what it's like crosscut?"

"Yes," Krey admitted, "but it's beautiful. Decorative."

"I thought so, too."

"It doesn't belong in a museum, Walter."

"It must belong somewhere."

"A mafia coffeetable," slipped out of Krey's mouth. "No," he said. "I didn't mean that."

"Yes you did." But Wilder wasn't upset. "What do you advise?"

"Well . . . Arizona! The state capital. They'll hang it there."

"I'll ring the governor. And thank you, Hugh. But are you sure you don't want—"

"Part of me does, Walt. The unscientist part. I *am* part human, as you might have guessed." Krey waited for Wilder's laugh, then continued. "I only keep what I collect myself. I'm kinda proud of it. And I only collect to study it, as a scientist."

"I admire you," Wilder said, and hung up.

February 5, 1965

Hugh,

Here's a handful from our mailbag from just this week. *You would be amazed at the tonnage we're getting back with it. Last month a 250 lb piece came by UPS. I couldn't do with it what I do with all the others, a ritual I really love. Every evening after the park has closed, I walk out under the stars and toss the send-backs out, like a farmer sowing oats. Rather like God tossing stars into the heavens.*

"Dr. Wilder, please."

"Please hold."

"Wilder here."

"Fuck, Walt."

"Eh?"

"I just got your letter."

"Hugh?"

"Who else. Gimme your home number. I'll ring you tonight."

"Walter?"

"Yes, Hugh."

"You wouldn't take a body and open up the skull, and stick the hypothalamus where the fuckassimus would be, would you?"

"Whatever are you saying."

"Or reverse the liver and spleen. And have anatomy students study the cadaver?"

"Why would anyone do something that crazy? That's nothing short of despoilment."

"So why the fuck are you despoiling the land?"

"Are your underpants too tight, Hugh?"

"Look, I know what you *thought* you were doing. Your intentions are noble, but this is the problem with amateurs when they think they're doing good. What you've engaged in is . . . as bad as pop psych."

"But what?"

"The wood that comes back. Don't put it back, Walt. Just don't. You don't know where it came from, and spreading it around only despoils the body of the land. No one can study it when you do that, because you're throwing spleens around as if they belong in armpits."

Walter Wilder broke out into a cold sweat. He pinched his leg viciously, he was so angry. "God, I'm sorry. I can't pick them up.

I can't undo what I've . . . what an idiot. I'll never forgive—"

"Shut up, Walter. You understand. We all make mistakes. Just don't do it again."

"Believe me, I'd have my arms cut off first. But what'll I do with the returns?"

"Anything but that. Why don't you give 'em to all those Navajo jewelers you know? They don't care where the stuff comes from."

"They don't, do they?"

"It's not in their interest to know."

"Thank you, Hugh."

"Thank *you*, Walter. I'm sorry I was a bit harsh."

"I was a slow student," Wilder chuckled. "But am I wrong in something I do know a bit about?"

"Do you know a bit about anything?"

"The human heart. Have you given yours away?"

" . . . Yes. Her name's Ann. We're getting married in June. She's making invitations. It'll be her family. I don't have any."

"Yes, Hugh. You do."

Walter Wilder wasn't surprised that there was a delay in response, and an unmanly wet sound. "I forgot to tell you," he said. "Congratulate me. I'm going to be a grandfather."

On a bleak day in April, just before the first crocuses broke through the sodden gray of autumn leaves, Ann, that was her name, Krey's love, got Stage 1 of Dying Stupidly. A scratch from a squirrel she was feeding got infected. Some days later, they gave her penicillin. Then they put her in the hospital where she got streptococcal pneumonia. From scratch to burial took a month.

'69:

Merry Christmas, Hugh.
You don't have to write,
but I'd love to hear from you.

In 1971, Walter Wilder retired from his directorship of the museum, nothing that made any news stories, but a few months earlier, his granddaughter, the one he gave a rattle made of petrified stones that he'd personally picked for her from the returns, was diagnosed with encephalitis. On taking the directorship of the museum back in '62, Wilder had had his collection of string tie chokes remade into necklaces and bracelets and given them to his daughter.

> Her Majesty put on rubber boots and a Burberry mackintosh; the president changed into cowboy boots, denim jacket, and western string tie.
>
> —*"The Queen Makes a Royal Splash" by Kurt Anderson,* Time, *March 14, 1983*

> Sales of string ties (the "bolo," the official state neckwear of Arizona since 1973) have gone up 12,000 percent since President Reagan took office.
>
> —Menswear Marketwatch, *March 20, 1985*

Two pages typed on an old manual:

To Whom This Should Concern:

Damn you.

Nothing I did deserved this. Three deaths in my family in the past year: my parrot Rudy, our loving dog Kevin and a kitten my youngest daughter brought home when she found it crying in the snow the day after Christmas. I would be sleepless from fear if my husband's sleeplessness didn't keep me awake. These days our home, instead of a WELCOME mat, seems to have a sign on the lawn: MORGUE. No one visits. We missed the last neighborhood party. I used to be the organizer. Do you know what it takes to organize potato salad for 150 people? My husband's manager hates him. My oldest boy's intelligence is measurably diminishing. My oldest daughter is secretly meeting a boy who has just one thing on his mind, not that she cares. When I think that only two years ago when we visited your park, she was going to be a scientist, I want to scream, but that accomplishes nothing. I tried to communicate with you, in your visitors' book, my disgust for your display of naked superstition completely inappropriate in a museum supposedly dedicated to the exploration and elucidation of natural phenomenae. I yearned then to state my true name, to speak to your staff face to face, but didn't because my daughter was so impressed with the site that she expressed an interest in working at the park when she matured. I was loath to prejudice her chances. The blessing was, she never saw that hogwash under glass—all that please forgive me. I took this *absolute* s★★t. *Yes, s★★t. You need to be shocked out of your complacency. Not all of us are stupid. She wanted all of her time during our visit to be spent outside, something I was thankful for, and to which I attributed her intelligent upbringing. This sensible attitude of hers only made me more furious at that insult to science that you display in what has to be pride of place.*

So just before we left, while my family were in the restrooms, I strolled outside till I found the biggest piece of petrified wood that I could fit in my handbag. I took it.

I used to keep it hidden indoors but recently buried it in a wasteland where no children play and real estate conditions are so depressed, it is safe from development unless our species spreads its infestation thoroughly across the land. WARNING: I can dig it up and send it to a lab at any time.

Why am I giving you notice? Because you should tell first. I shouldn't foot the bill to discover your sordid secret. Why did you think rational people would stay quiet forever? I won't.

You've ruined countless lives, yet you didn't have *to. You could have posted signs. Something polite and decent like* Please don't step on the grass—pick the flowers—run in the hallway. *People are used to signs. You didn't have to slow poison us.*

You are, after all, not vengeful gods, but creepy little bureaucrats. Mark my words. It's only a matter of time before Truth Will Out. In the meantime: Find out how to clean up your site and DO IT, or do you have just as much of a clue about that as about uranium, or what they put in Colonel Sanders' chicken spice?

Very truly,
A. Ware
Somewhere,USA

"What the—"

"Hello . . . hello . . . Is this Hugh Krey?"

"Depends."

"This is Walt, Hugh. Walter Wilder."

"Walter, do you know what time it is here? How the fuck did you find me?"

"You didn't make it easy. It took a week. Listen, Hugh. Did you see Reagan on TV?"

"When?"

"Last week."

"Are you kidding? This is Nigeria. And why would I want to watch the Ray Gun?"

"Don't make fun of him."

"You aren't serious."

"If you saw his rendezvous with destiny speech you couldn't say that. The man understands the human psyche."

Hugh reached out his toe and flicked the fan to high, now that he was fully awake. "You can't want to talk politics."

"Did you see that picture showing the president in his string tie, with the Queen?"

"Gosh," Krey said. "I didn't get my last issue of *Menswear Daily*. Walter, are you seeing anyone for this?"

"This is serious. It was in all the papers."

"When?"

"Back in '83."

"Eleven years ago? I was prospecting in hell."

"The string tie was a hunk of petrified wood."

"You remember the date?"

"People here framed the pictures. You really didn't see?"

"*The Hades Chronicle* doesn't even have funnies."

"The point *is*, and *please pay attention.* Now President Reagan has Alzheimer's. He announced it last week."

"So that's his excuse."

"You don't get it?"

"What's to get? He can't remember the Iran Contras. Yeah, I do get that."

"I'm not talking politics, thickhead. That's petrified wood from the Petrified Forest. I'm sure of it."

"Where?"

Wilder's sigh was louder than the crackles in the line. "His tie, Hugh. His string tie choke."

"Dr. Wilder. Good night, or morning or whatever the fuck. I need my rest. Get medicated."

It's a rest home only people with money can afford. There's a pretence of dignity. One old man is sitting beside the bed of another. It's a "private room."

"I couldn't open my door," says the one in the bed. "Too afraid."

"It's no shame to be here. They do the maidwork," Krey says.

"Don't," says Wilder. "I asked you here because I want to warn you." He rises up on his sticklike arms. "Get rid of your pieces."

"Or I won't get the girls," smiles Krey. His lips champ over teeth that make a dull grinding sound, like a melamine cup on a melamine saucer that doesn't fit.

"Get *rid* of them. There might be something left in your life."

Krey laughs. "You sound like a believer."

"There *is* a curse. I just didn't believe it before."

Krey's eyes cloud. "You made it—*We* made it up, Walter. Remember?"

"I remember all sorts of things, like my Wendy and her beautiful daughter. Like that love of your life. And your career."

"Bad luck."

"Too much bad luck."

"We're scientists, Wilder! Don't you remember what you said: Paranoia is the key?"

"I also remember what I said: Myths have their purpose."

"That was between us. A joke, remember? A white lie for the good of the site. We're scientists, you and I. We *implanted*, Doctor. Please remember. Walter. Come back to me."

Krey reaches out. His arthritic hand looks like an exotic fruit that hasn't sold—something purplish and overripe. Wilder's is bones in rice paper. It is cold.

Eventually the nurse comes in. She rolls up a wheelchair with a colorful crocheted throw disguising an overthick seat.

"Mr. Wilder. It's time for your lunch. Should I tell the dining room that there will be another guest?"

Wilder turns his head to Krey. "Want lunch? We're having oysters Rockefeller, roast grouse, and some kind of gateau."

The nurse's eyes signal professional sympathy to Krey, who for some reason doesn't notice her. Then she's all business with Wilder.

"No sir. It's tomato soup and fruit cup, and a birthday cake for Mrs. Wood."

"I was jesting," says Wilder, his eyes locked on Krey's. "He's leaving."

And he does leave, quickly and wordlessly, but not fast enough before the nurse throws back the covers and exposes Wilder.

Krey drives away, slowly and very carefully. He doesn't dare stop, so he has to swallow the bile that's refluxing with volcanic violence. "We did it. We planted those expectations. We sinned against science." Krey weeps as he mistakes the fast lane for the slow one.

Don't trifle with the curse of the Petrified Forest. Steal a piece of ancient wood . . . and some version of hell on earth will surely come your way. That's what park rangers suggest to visitors, and the hundreds of letters they've received prove it.

—Leo Banks, "Petrified with Fear! The curse of an ancient forest dogs park troopers," Tucson Weekly, *December 15, 1997*

Unfortunately, in spite of severe penalties, written and verbal warnings and the opportunity to legally obtain petrified wood, thoughtless visitors continue to steal over one ton each month.

—Petrified Forest National Park Information Page, http://www.petrified.forest.national-park.com/info.htm

---

ANNA TAMBOUR lives in an area of Australia where the rocks on high, forested ridges include fossilized seashells two days' walk from today's seashore. Some recent and upcoming publications that include her stories are the anthologies *The Del Rey Book of Science Fiction and Fantasy*, *Paper Cities*, *Interfictions*, and *Sky Whales and Other Wonders*; and the magazines *Subterranean*, *Andromeda Spaceways Inflight Magazine*, and *Asimov's Science Fiction*. For more about her stories and books, see www.annatambour.net

TAMBOUR SAYS: *Lovecraft could have been the inspiration for the command, "put up or shut up." Yet this murky aspect of his stories is perversely also the strength of those other great successes: religion and neuroses. Both hold minds in dark, fear-driven thrall despite science's sparks of enlightenment and reason flaring up in various places for many centuries. Scientists have recently mapped fear in the human brain (and they're prospecting for superstition) yet maybe knowledge isn't power, for science is weak against that certain something that Lovecraft, religion, and the normal irrational human mind all do so dreadfully well.*

BRIAN EVENSON

The Din of Celestial Birds

WHEN HE RETURNED, stumbling down the mountain and out of the jungle, he did not remember anything beyond having entered the stone hovel and seen, in the far corner of the dirt floor, a cage, partly covered in a feathered cloak. Even from the door, it did not seem that the hovel had been entered or the cage touched in months. He approached and brushed the feathers with his hand, brought his palm away covered with dust, and was surprised to hear a dull rattling from within or perhaps behind the cage. He remembered tugging off the heavy cover, feathers coming loose in his hands, and then remembered nothing until he was stumbling down the mountain, his body cut and bruised, his clothing torn and rotting away, his hair littered with pieces of frond and feathers.

It had been four mouths. The villagers were surprised to see him. When he first disappeared they had assumed he had fled to join the rebels, which rumor had it were massing on the southern half of the island. Nonetheless, two days after his disappearance and at his wife's request they had agreed to search in the area he had last been seen, and accordingly a team of men had climbed the mountain, traversing the narrow switchbacks until they came, as he himself had come, to the old stone hovel constructed into the side of the cliff. They had looked into the hovel with a torch, but found it empty, the dirt floor undisturbed and thick with dust.

"And the cage?" he asked, when they later told him the story.

"Cage?" asked the leader of the search party. "There was no cage."

"In the corner?" he asked. "Covered in a cape of feathers?"

The man shook his head. "Nothing had been in there for years."

Yet he was certain he had entered it.

There were, he learned from the Indians living in the shanty on the edge of the village, certain rumors about the hovel. Some said it had belonged to a *cjlanuk* driven out of the valley by the other Indians before the Europeans had come, that it had been built by legged serpents and from it he had practiced a dark intercourse which had rapidly consumed him. Others claimed it was the dwelling of an early German monk whose party had been slaughtered. He had built the house and slowly gone mad in it, stripping away the flesh from his legs with his own knife until he died. All among the Indians agreed, however, that the place should not be approached, that he had made a tremendous mistake in going there.

In the interest of science, he was taken to the capital to speak to a neurologist, who measured his head and examined it for evidence of concussion or injury, who shined a light into his eyes, who asked him a series of questions to which there seemed no correct answers and nodded as he answered. He was hypnotized but still recalled nothing, "as if," the neurologist said, raising an eyebrow and considering the case study he would write, "a portion of your brain has been removed or rewired," though the doctor also said not to worry, that his mind in time would find its way back to what it had lost.

At first, he had trouble sleeping and would remain awake for hours as his wife slept beside him. Often he would leave his bed to throw open the shutters, watching the bats throwing themselves about before the town's only streetlight. The night calmed him somewhat and he liked to sit crouched on the sill and feel the slight air against his skin. When he did manage to sleep, his arms and legs often thrashed about and he made uncanny half-strangled noises until his wife shook him awake. The neurologist advised that instead of waking him she sit beside the bed during the spells and chart any shift in motion or sound and loaned them a clock to record the time. Thus, he often found when he awoke, tacked to the wall behind the bed, notes made from the night before:

> *3:50. Movement restricted to a shivering of the legs and a twitch on the right side of the torso. A periodic, high-pitched rapid barking.*

None of the notes led him anywhere. He remained as ignorant of what happened to him as he had been before.

The national police came and interrogated him about his whereabouts over the past four months, accusing him of having associated with the rebels, of trying to unsteady the already instable political situation. Even after being beaten severely and being prompted with leading questions that already assumed his guilt, he could recall nothing about what had happened after he lifted the cover from the cage. His refusal to cooperate angered the police, and they might have killed him had it not been for the intervention of the mayor and his presentation of a letter on gilt-edged paper from the neurologist.

His body had a peculiar feeling to it all the time, as if it was not entirely his own. He was awkward on his feet and had difficulty sometimes recalling and then carrying out the simplest of dynamics, the movement of his spoon from bowl to mouth, for instance, or the arc of a scythe through the grain. He could not bear being around others and only just tolerated his wife and her attempts to comfort him and to prod him into remembrance. He grew reclusive, withdrawn. He became concerned about his physical condition. What he had at first thought to be cuts and scratches from his journey down the mountain quickly took on a different character for him, for there were some wounds that after crusting over remained red and puckered and tender and did not subside, and others that never scarred or crusted over at all but remained bloodless and open, minuscule inverse cones dotting his stomach and thigh. Indeed, these seemed to be increasing in number. They seemed to him important to understanding his illness, but for whatever reason he had the instinct to keep them hidden from the neurologist and from his wife as well.

A month later, late at night, rebels passed through the town, on retreat from an abortive attack on the capital. They dragged the mayor out of bed and beat his head in with their rifle butts, bullets being too valuable to waste. They left him dead in the square, head unfurled like a flattened balloon, and moved quickly on. By morning the town was occupied by national police, patrolling the town in search of rebels. He and most of the other men of the town were dragged to the central square, were interrogated and were as well beaten by a colonel missing an eye and a hand.

With the help of a neighbor, his wife carried him home. She cleaned his visible wounds then removed his clothing to bathe him, was horrified to find his thighs and belly pitted and covered with holes, some of them big enough to prod her little finger into.

"What are these?" she asked. "How did the soldiers do this to you?"

He shook his head. She left the house and returned with the local doctor, who examined the pits and could not make sense of them, and was incensed for having been taken away from those beaten more severely. She went back out and returned several hours later with the Indian shanty's *cjlanuk*. He approached, looked gravely into the pits. He rubbed a handful of red powder over the man's belly and thighs until the man cried out.

"*Xalagmua*," the *cjlanuk* said. "He is dead already. There is nothing to be done for him." He said nothing more beyond advising the wife to bury her husband alive or at the very least to have him imprisoned.

"Is the disease infectious?" she asked.

He shook his head. "You are in great danger," he insisted.

"What sort of danger?"

"*Xalagmua*," the *cjlanuk* said again, and left.

His wife was mostly of European blood and thus had no temptation to follow the *cjlanuk*'s unexplained advice. After her husband had recovered from the beating she saw no reason to mistrust him, for he seemed as normal as he had seemed since his return from the mountain, even if the pits and holes on his lower body did not fade and in fact seemed to spread farther along the surface of his skin.

His struggles and movements during the night seemed to have decreased as well. In their place, however, as he admitted neither to his wife nor to the neurologist, came dim dreams that seemed to have some connection to the absent four months. Of these, he could recall only scattered images, the most frequently recurring of which was that of a cage made of bones, lacquered and held together with strips of tanned skin, the doors of the cage consisting of two interlocked skeletal hands. Behind or inside was what appeared to him a flash of light, in constant and frenetic motion. He often heard as well, in his different dreams and their different situations, a great chorus of cries, birdlike but oddly distorted and ethereal, creating what he thought of upon awakening as being the din of celestial birds.

He felt famished even after he had eaten, a constant nagging emptiness tugging at the base of his spine. He ate more but did so privately so as not to upset his wife. He did not seem to gain any weight. He felt trapped, paced back and forth through the house, spent hours wandering through the jungle outside, at home found it more and more difficult to keep up an appearance of novelty.

When the neurologist told him that the four missing months might never come back, he knew they were already on their way. He dreamt of clouds of transparent and sharp-beaked birds, their din immense as they swept over him. He woke up with the feeling that his thighs and chest were bloody, the sense of something feeding on him. He stood and brushed at his body, but the feeling did not vanish until he had fled the house through the window and stood below the town's streetlight. Looking down, he saw he had not bled at all, but that the pits in his body had deepened and had spread to all parts of his skin except his hands and his face.

He returned to bed but woke later to the sound of birds, naked, in the middle of the jungle, at the base of the mountain, his hands and body smeared with blood. He washed himself in a stream, managed to stumble his way back to his house and into bed before his wife awoke. The next morning, he claimed illness, remaining in bed until late in the day, terrified of himself, wondering what would happen next.

He dreamt his body was a cage, that lining his chest and cradled in his hips were caches of eggs, slowly hatching into tightly folded birds, the strange pitting of his skin coming from their attempts to pull open a hole. He awoke shivering and was afraid to go back to sleep.

He kept awakening bloody, far from home. Reports began to drift in of national police and rebels found dead around the town, their eyes gone and their skulls cracked, gaping holes in their bodies. The Indians claimed it was the return of *Xjalagmua*—some sort of ancient creature or spirit, his wife said, though she herself believed the stories of the deaths to be fabricated by the national police as a means of trying to keep the rebels out of the jungles and to locales where they could be more easily captured.

He was willing to agree, to justify the blood on his body as having welled up mysteriously from the normally dry holes and pits, as a spontaneous upswelling of some kind. He continued to believe that until he woke one night at the base of a mountain dragging a carcass through the darkness. He left it and ran before he knew if it were human or animal.

The slaughters in the jungle increased. Oddly, the dead were always of European blood. Even before sleep came, he felt himself drawn to the window and out into the jungle. He tried to believe it was a dream, tried to claim he was not responsible for whatever his body did without him.

He awoke to find himself prowling the edge of the indian shanty, but oddly unable to force himself to walk past the outer circle of shacks. He recognized, at a little distance, standing before a fire, the *cjlanuk*, dashing his arms back and forth, pointing at him. He realized he was holding something in one hand, looked down to see a pale-skinned child, his fingertips pushed through the skull and holding the child's head like a ball.

He shook the thing off his fingers, let it fall in a stiff heap. The *cjlanuk* beckoned him forward and he found himself able to come among the shacks and move toward the man. When he tried to turn to one side, however, he found he could not. He tried to go back, but his feet carried him forward until he found himself standing before the fire, regarding the *cjlanuk* on the opposite side.

"*Xalagmua*, you have come," he said.

"What is happening to me? What is wrong with my body?" the man asked.

"I do not speak to you," said the other. "You are dead."

"Please," said the man. "I did not mean to kill the child. I am not responsible."

The *cjlanuk* shook his head. "Come forward," he said.

He tried to pass around the fire, found he could not, found himself inclined instead to walk into the flame. The *cjlanuk* lifted his hands, drew patterns in the smoke, making a narrow path that seemed to tug him forward. He tried to resist, but his feet shifted, stepped forward onto the coals.

He felt the pain and then bursting from his body thousands of insubstantial birds. They whirled about him, turning into flame and smoke. He smelt his flesh burn, felt himself fall.

The local doctor cleaned his burns and rubbed them with ointment. He bound his legs up in cloth, telling his wife to change the dressing twice daily. When the doctor was gone, she asked him how he had come to be in the Indian shanty at night and he could not explain it, only that he had awakened and had been there. There had been, she said, a child found dead near there, the crown of its head pierced roundabout as if it had been taken into the mouth of a wolf or grasped by a giant claw. The child was fair-skinned, she said, drained of blood, and the police thought it must be the doing of Indians or rebels. He just nodded, tried to sleep.

He woke up halfway out the window, pus running down his legs, his wife shaking him, drawing him in. With her encouragement, he allowed himself to be led back into the room. He lay down on the bed, allowed her to change his dressing.

She left briefly, returned with a rope. She tied one end to the leg of the bed, tied the other end around his waist.

"To keep you safe," she said. She brewed a rich tea for him, a narcotic of some kind that the doctor had given to her, and came to bed, looping the rope around her ankle. He drank and fell asleep.

The sun was rushing in upon him. His legs hurt, his head as well. He tried to roll his way out of bed, found himself restrained by the rope. He turned back around in bed to find his wife dead beside him, her eyes missing, great gouges out of her flesh.

He lay there regarding her for some time, trying to feel something, but feeling nothing. He was, he remembered the *cjlanuk* saying, already dead. He could bring himself to not feel himself responsible.

He sat up in bed long enough to untie the rope, roll her out of the bed, hide her underneath. He lay in bed most of the day, feeling the pain in his legs. Near evening he got out of bed and made his painful way into the kitchen, remaining long enough to light a fire, heat the pot of tea that she had made earlier. He was there, preparing to drink the tea, when the local doctor arrived and scolded him for being out of bed then inquired why his wife had let him do such a thing.

"She isn't here," he said. "She's gone out."

"Out?" the doctor asked. "Someone should be with you."

The man shrugged, allowed the doctor to help him back to bed, begging him once there to give him something for the pain.

The doctor looked astonished, "But I gave her something for you," he said.

"I want something that will not put me asleep," he said. "I need to be awake when she comes home."

Grumbling, the doctor opened his bag, removed a vial of fluid and a hypodermic syringe, the needle of which he heated in the fire to sterilize it. He gave the man an injection, the man feeling a numbness rapidly spread through his body.

"You would like me to remain until your wife returns?" the doctor asked. "I'll have to charge for my time, of course."

The man waved him away.

When the doctor was gone, the man worked his way out of bed. He stood, tested his legs. The pain was still present, but the injection made him no longer care that it was there, made it feel as if he were observing it rather than feeling it for himself. He made his way into the kitchen and took the last of the matches, then went to the door and out into the darkness.

He limped past the street lamp. He passed through the east side of the town, moving into the jungle and toward the mountain. The walk was difficult, and he often felt faint and had to rest, and once fell and had a struggle getting up. He reached the base of the mountain and realized he had gone too far south, had to walk a kilometer north until, by moonlight, he discovered the trail leading up.

He set about climbing, negotiating the narrow trail in the dark by touch. The dressing on his legs had become sodden with blood and other fluids and was making a damp sound as he walked. His breath, too, came only narrowly, and by the time he had climbed three hundred meters, he had difficulty breathing at all. He turned and looked down, back at the town, the single light and then a few lights still in houses, then turned and kept climbing.

By the time he reached the stone hovel, the medicine was wearing off. He felt he was going to lose consciousness. He tried to avoid looking at his legs or thinking about them. He knew he could not make it back down again.

He put his head to the opening of the hovel. He struck a match, held it in.

In the far corner was a cage, partly covered by a feathered cloak. He made his way toward it slowly, stopping before it. Reaching out his hand, he took the cloak by the corner, pulled it quickly away.

The cage was empty. He stumbled forward, collapsed onto the dirt floor. He lay there as his body dissolved into uncanny birds and fluttered away, the birds crying out, the wings knocking against what was left of him until nothing at all was left of him and he found himself turning and wheeling and dissolving into all portions of the night.

BRIAN EVENSON is the author of ten books of fiction, most recently the story collection *Fugue State* and the novel *Last Days*. His novel *The Open Curtain* was a finalist for an Edgar Award and an International Horror Guild Award and was among *Time Out New York*'s top books of 2006. Other books include *The Wavering Knife* (winner of the IHG Award for best story collection) and the tie-in novel *Aliens: No Exit*. He has received an O. Henry Prize as well as an NEA fellowship. He lives and works in Providence, Rhode Island, where he directs Brown University's Creative Writing Program.

EVENSON SAYS: *As somebody living in Lovecraft's hometown, I find myself thinking about his writing or walking past places from his stories and houses he lived in almost every day. "The Din of Celestial Birds" was written when I was reading a lot of magic realism and simultaneously rediscovering Lovecraft's work, reading a few of his best stories over and over again. It tries to capture both his mood and some of what I admire about the way Lovecraft's protagonists stumble into situations they don't begin to understand until it's too late. I couldn't have written it without him.*

AMANDA DOWNUM

The Tenderness of Jackals

THE TRAIN CHASES the setting sun, but can't catch it. Not even the high-speed line can catch the sun, and the InterCity Express slides into the Hannover Hauptbahnhof as purple dusk gives way to charcoal. In the hum and whine of its wheels, Gabriel hears the wolves.

Soon, they whisper.

He drags on his cigarette, watching the sinuous white-and-red curve of the train vanish behind the station. Eyes flash in the darkness, nearly lost in the neon and glitter of the promenade shops. Smoke curls from his nose, twists a sharp-jawed head toward him before it unravels on the breeze. *Hungry*, it growls.

He waits a moment longer; reluctant, if not defiant. Savoring the smoke and the night, air that doesn't reek of the tunnels—musk and meat and thickening tension, the ghouls snapping as often as they spoke and the changelings cowering out of their way. Everyone knowing the wolves were waiting and no one wanting to answer the call. Until finally, Gabriel, newcomer, interloper that he is, couldn't stand it anymore and went above to face them.

Thinking about it is enough to ruin the taste of his cigarette. He crushes the butt underfoot and goes inside, accompanied by ghostly wolves. It's easier to acquiesce. Everyone does, they tell him.

Too bright inside, new glass and metal guts dressed in old stone skin—glowing screens and signs, light gleaming on the tiles, restaurants and expensive shops. He watches the train disgorge its Berlin passengers. Footsteps and hushed voices echo through the vaulted room, eerily muted, ghosts of sounds. Commuters and students, tourists, a pair of grey-coated Bundeswehr officers. Nothing that looks like prey.

The tightness in his chests eases. Maybe not this train. Maybe it won't be tonight. Maybe he won't be the one to feed the wolves after all.

Then he sees the boy.

He might almost be a uni student, or at least pass for one. Fashionably threadbare jeans and t-shirt, a sweatshirt tied around his waist in spite of the heat, a backpack stiff with paint and patches hanging off one thin shoulder. Dark hair falls over his eyes, but can't hide the sleepless shadows under them. He glances around, shoulders hunched, hands tight on the straps of his bag. Too far away for Gabriel to smell his nervous sweat, but he imagines the scent of it clearly.

So do the wolves.

One of the soldiers moves past the boy with the barest brush of sleeves; the boy shudders. Gabriel shivers too—for an instant the light is wrong, twisting and dimming. The station darkens, shrinks. The soldier glances down, his face scarred and shadowed, his uniform stained and decades out of date.

Then it's gone and the soldier walks on, neat and pressed once more. The boy's face drains grey. It's always easier for the walls to slip here, in the between-places. Too bad he can't understand the warning.

Their gazes meet, hold for an instant before the boy looks away. Gabriel steps back, wraps himself in a shadow and watches the boy glance at the ticket counter before turning toward the exit. The wolves breathe hot and hungry on his neck.

The strays, the runaways, the lonely and the lost—these have always been their prey.

The killings started in 1918, when the war had left Germany worn and starving, left more children with nowhere to go. At least twenty-four young men and boys lured away from the train station with promises of jobs or food or a place to sleep, or even just a cigarette and a soft word. Gabriel knows the taste of that desperation; it's how he first found the ghouls, after all.

At least twenty-four people murdered here in six years, probably more. Such a small number, really, not even a dent in the population. Not like the genocide Gabriel's grandparents escaped in 1915, or the holocaust that swept Europe with the next war, or even the civil war that Gabriel survived. Insignificant, as atrocities go. But it was enough to birth the wolves.

Gabriel wonders how many more people have been killed in Hannover since they came. Killed by people like him.

He follows the boy outside, away from the wicked lights. The last bruise of dusk has faded and the night closes around him warm and heavy, full of the rush of fountains and the hum and purr of traffic, footsteps and voices. The wolves follow, full of hunger and approbation. So much easier to give them what they want—what he wants too, they insist. He knows the hunger, doesn't he? The desire for the chase, to feel skin part and blood flow, the taste of hot meat. Gravemeat can never truly sate.

His nails carve crescents of pain in his palms. *You're nothing,* he tells them. *Nothing but ghosts and shadows, echoes. Specters to be laid to rest.*

Their toothy laughter echoes in his head. Maybe, but they're not wrong.

The prey—the boy, he corrects himself savagely—pauses beneath the statue of Ernst August, sinking heel to haunch and leaning against the plinth. His movements are jerky with fatigue, and as soon as he thinks no one's watching, his expression flattens, eyes hollow as pits. As if looking alive is too much effort any more. He tugs a pack of cigarettes out of his pocket, shakes out nothing but a few flakes of tobacco. He crumples the box with a soft curse.

Gabriel's cue. The wolves urge him on, intangible noses nudging his back. They've seen this play acted out a hundred times. They know the lines.

He steps out of the gloom of the betweens, and his shadow falls over the boy's face. He holds out his own pack. "Willst du eine Kippe?"

The boy startles, tenses. His wary thoughts are easy to read—he should say no, should leave, get back to the light, to the laughable safety of other people. Sensible prey-thoughts.

Instead he pulls a smile on like an ill-fitting mask, and nods. Humans are rarely sensible enough. "Danke."

Gabriel raises an eyebrow at his accent. His lighter cracks and orange flame dances over the boy's face. Childhood softness still clings to him, despite his lanky limbs and thin cheeks. His skin has a smoothness that won't survive a razor. The flame catches flecks of gold in his hazel eyes as he leans in and drags deep. A pretty boy—the wolves approve. Gabriel lights a cigarette of his own and flips the lighter shut, letting the dark lap over them again.

"American?" Smoke leaks out of his mouth around the word—innocent coils, this time.

The boy nods. Salt-sweat and unwashed hair, the cloying chemical tang of cheap soap, and under it all the metallic richness of flesh and blood. He pushes himself up, still leaning against the concrete pedestal and trying to look nonchalant.

"What are you doing in Hannover?" He tries to quash his curiosity—whatever the boy's story is, he doesn't need to know it.

"Just passing through." His voice is dull—not shy or sullen, but uncaring. Going through the motions.

Gabriel watches the lights of the promenade. People ebb and swirl heedlessly around them, blind to the sharp-toothed shadows. Sweat prickles his back and hair sticks and itches on his neck. The wolves are quiet. They don't care about the particulars of the hunt, only the red and messy end.

"What's your name?" he asks. He doesn't need to know that, either, but anything's better than *boy*, or *prey*.

"Alec. You?"

He pauses, thinks of a lie. But what's the point? "I'm Gabriel."

Alec studies his cigarette. "You're not German either."

Gabriel smiles. "No. Armenian, by way of Beirut."

"What are you doing in Hannover?"

"Talking to you." He grimaces as soon as the words leave his mouth.

Alec snorts, the most expression he's shown yet. "That's a lousy line."

"It is. Sorry. But really, I don't know anymore."

Liar, mock the wolves, their eyes glinting in the shadows.

The boy smiles slowly, a better fit than the last one. "That sounds like a line too." Engaging now, like this is familiar. Gabriel nearly shakes his head; a stranger trying to pick up teenagers shouldn't be reassuring.

He might be a monster, but he's not that kind. Tires squeal on the street and he hears the wolves' laughter. *Whatever gets you through the night.*

"How old are you?" he asks. It's expected.

"Eighteen." Not even trying to sound convincing.

Gabriel drags on his cigarette. "Does that ever fool anyone?"

Alec shrugs. "No, but it makes them feel better. Whatever gets them through the night, I guess. If I said sixteen, would you walk away?"

"No," he says after a moment.

The boy lifts his eyebrows, but his stomach growls before he can reply. He grimaces, his cynical façade crumbling till he's just a kid again.

"Come on," Gabriel says, crushing the cigarette under his heel. "There's a kebab stand down the street. I'll buy."

Alec hesitates, another flash of wariness. Instincts trying to save his life. But they're too far into the game now, or he just doesn't care. He nods, and follows Gabriel away from the train station.

The wolves stalk silently behind them.

Selim is working the imbiss tonight. He nods at Gabriel as they approach, glances at Alec and asks a silent question with one eyebrow. The boy's stomach rumbles again at the smell of meat and grease, garlic and onion and cumin.

Gabriel shakes his head—*not one of us*. Selim frowns as he realizes what's happening; he's seen the wolves himself. He hands Alec his döner—made with safe meat, not what the ghouls eat—and takes Gabriel's money, his face creasing into an unhappy glower.

"What's his problem?" Alec asks softly as they leave.

Gabriel fights a frown of his own. "He doesn't approve." Selim was a changeling like him, taken as a child instead of born to the tunnels. Maybe it's easier for the ones who never had a human life; he's never asked.

The boy snorts, but the food distracts him. Gabriel watches with amusement as the sandwich disappears with the speed only the starving and adolescent can manage. When it's gone, Alec crumples the wrapper and licks tzatziki off his fingers.

"Thanks." Honest gratitude, no coyness, and Gabriel can't meet his eyes. But everywhere else he looks he sees the wolves. He swallows hungry spit, thinks of turning around. But gravemeat won't sate this hunger.

They walk through the dark streets, away from the crowds. The noise of traffic fades as they follow the Altstadt's narrow cobbled streets. Shops are closing, people heading for home. Alec shifts his bag from shoulder to shoulder occasionally but doesn't complain. By the time they reach the river, though, he's growing restless. So are the wolves.

"Do you have a room somewhere?" he asks. "Somewhere we could go?"

"No. Should I?"

Alec frowns and shrugs. "I guess not." There are always alleys for this kind of thing, after all, whether it's prostitution or murder. Not affected nonchalance, Gabriel decides—the boy really doesn't care. He wishes he could wonder what could crush someone so young that way, but he knows all too well.

They cross the river and turn at the Leine Palace, its long pale façade facing the water and the greenway on the other side. The building is dark and quiet, streetlamps shedding pools of yellow over grass and trees and empty benches. Traffic flows on the other side of the park, but Gabriel isn't worried about being interrupted. People know when to look away.

He stops at the little bridge leading to the palace's glass doors. The metal railing is still warm; the river ripples black and gold below. Stairs descend to the water, but he can't see how to reach them from here. The bittersweetness of water and wet rock fills his nostrils. It's a cleaner river than some—fish still live in it; the whisper of death is only his imagination.

Alec stands beside him, propping his elbows on the stone. "Looks like a nice place to dump a body," he says with a crooked smile.

Gabriel's lips pull back. "Twenty-four of them, actually." He chuckles as Alec starts. "Not me."

"No, I mean—" The boy laughs, a breathless nervous rush. "I was only joking."

"I wasn't. Hannover had a serial killer once. Fritz Haarmann—do you know the story?"

"No." Hair flops over his eyes as he shakes his head. "I never went in for true-crime stuff."

"He killed a lot of people. When he was done with the bodies, he dumped them in the river."

Alec makes a face, stares down at the water in disgust and fascination. "What you mean," he asks a second later, "when he was done with them?"

"He sold the meat on the black market. That was the rumor, anyway."

"God. Why do people read about stuff like that?"

"They think monsters are interesting." His mouth twists wryly as he remembers his own horror and fascination when he realized the shadows prowling the bombed ruins of his neighborhood at night weren't soldiers or thieves, weren't anything human. Easy to admire their teeth and claws and strength when he was weak and helpless. Easy to want to join them when he was alone and starving. But he's still alone, still starving.

Alec snorts. "You don't need to kill twenty-four people to be a monster."

"No." Gabriel picks at a rust spot, trying to ignore the rasping breath of wolves. "It's much easier than that."

Something in his voice makes Alec look up and swallow, Adam's apple bobbing in the slender softness of his throat. The prey part of his brain sees what the thinking part tries not to—Gabriel's night-shining eyes, the length of his teeth and thickness of his nails. And finally, a real reaction—fear threads through his scent, acrid beneath garlic and cumin. His pupils dilate, black swallowing hazel. No doubt his hands are tingling as his heart pumps faster, as the atavistic survival instinct screams at him to *run run run*.

He'll run, and Gabriel will give chase, ghost-wolves beside him, and the night will wash red and none of them will be hungry anymore. For a while.

Alec's bag slips off his shoulder, thumps against the cobbles. His narrow chest hitches with breath, the sound loud and ragged in Gabriel's ears. He can hear the boy's heart now, and his vision tunnels. Hunger clenches his stomach, makes his teeth ache.

But the boy doesn't run. His hand tightens white-knuckled around his backpack strap—an awkward sort of weapon, and he doesn't swing it.

"What are you?"

Gabriel lets out a breath he hadn't realized he'd drawn, and the red fades from his vision. The wolves whine and growl.

"I'm a monster. A *ghul*—an eater of the dead. And I'm a killer too." Alec stares at his face; Gabriel can feel himself changing. Nothing drastic, but the bridge is enough of a between-place to allow it. His teeth sharpen, crowding in his still-human jaw. Nails curve into claws and his vision brightens.

"And that's why you picked me up? To kill me. To eat me?" He nods slowly.

"Well." The boy shakes his hair back, trying for that cynical affectation again. "At least you're not just another asshole john."

"This isn't a joke."

"No." Alec reaches out to touch Gabriel's face, traces a fingertip down his temple and the length of his jaw. Stubble rasps against his nail and Gabriel feels it in the roots of his teeth. "I can see that."

Wonder in his voice, or something like it, and while his fear hasn't faded, neither has it worsened. Gabriel catches his hand, feels the boy's pulse fast and strong against his fingers. Like looking into the past, into a mirror. The wolves whine, confused and annoyed.

Footsteps echo on the sidewalk. A woman walks along the river, a pocket-sized dog straining against its leash ahead of her. The Pomeranian growls as it passes the bridge, yips and dances. The woman looks up, hurries her pace when she sees Alec and Gabriel, tugging the dog away. The streetlight shows her moue of distaste.

"*Schlampe*," Alec says, loud enough to carry. The woman stiffens, but keeps walking, disappearing into the shadows of the park. Gabriel's lip curls, but the wolves ignore the interlopers. Easier prey, perhaps, but not to their taste.

Gabriel realizes he's still holding the boy's hand. He lets go, scrubs his palm on his pants. "Go. Follow her. Get on a train and get out of the city. You'll be safe."

"Safe?" Alec laughs, hard and sharp. "You're kidding, right?"

"Better than dead."

"I'm not sure about that." He lifts his chin. Adolescent defiance, but something deeper and uglier beneath it. "You think I don't know what happens to kids like me? You think I don't know about monsters?" He jerks his sleeve up, baring the edge of one thin shoulder, round blistered burn scars and a purple-green bruise. His fear is gone now, buried in rising anger.

Gabriel takes a step backward and the railing gouges his back. "It's easy to think you want to die when you're young. Trust me, you don't."

"Really?" His face flattens again, and it's all Gabriel can do to meet his eyes.

"I don't want to hurt you." It comes out a growl and they both flinch. "They do."

He points past the bridge, to the wolves lurking at the edge of the lamplight. Alec frowns at the shadows. "What—" He stops, mouth sagging open. Eyes gleam back at them, red and gold and copper-green. "What are they?"

"They're ghosts, but not the ghosts of men. Enough death and pain in one place start to wear patterns. They're the ghosts of acts, of madness and hunger and murder."

"And they want . . . more?"

"What I told you before, about human meat sold on the black market? It was more than a rumor. But Haarmann and Grans weren't selling it to the people of Hannover. They were selling it to ghouls. To my people.

"We're monsters, but not killers. We try, at least. They knew where that meat was coming from, but they chose not to ask, to look the other way. And so more people, more children, kept dying. And the wolves wormed their way into their hearts." He shakes his head. "All our hearts. Maybe they've been there all along."

Alec looks at him, shadows hiding his face. "And you?"

"I killed someone, a long way from here. He called himself a soldier, but he wasn't much older than you, young and foolish. I didn't plan on it, didn't mean to, but I killed him and ate him. It's the law—no fresh meat. Once you break it, once you taste fresh blood, you want more. I ran, came here to hide, but the wolves were waiting for me."

"And now they have you," Alec whispers, "and me."

Gabriel nods. Hunger cramps his stomach, but he's so tired. The wolves wait, mockery silenced.

"Go ahead." Alec moves closer, meets his eyes. "I mean it. I'm going to die anyway, right? I'd rather you killed me than somebody else." Gabriel tries to turn away, but the boy grabs his shoulder. "Please! I can't keep doing this. I'm so fucking *tired*."

"Then find another way. You don't want this."

"Fuck you." He jerks away with a snarl. "Don't you fucking tell me what I want." He reaches into his pocket and pulls out a butterfly knife.

Gabriel tenses. The wolves tense. He feels them quivering, mouths watering.

The knife flips open, light running yellow along the blade. Gabriel waits for the attack, but instead Alec brings the edge down against the inside of his forearm. Blood wells, floods the night with red and copper. Gabriel swallows.

"What are you—"

"This is what you want, isn't it? What they want?" He gestures toward the wolves, flinging drops of blood onto the sidewalk. The shadows seethe, their hunger a burning weight in Gabriel's head, his own hunger a weight in his stomach.

He clenches his fists, claws digging into his palms. "Don't."

"What, do I need to run?" Alec's lip curls. "There's always a game, isn't there. Fine, I can run if that's what it takes." He raises his bleeding arm towards Gabriel. "Catch me."

And he bolts for the park. The wolves bay, so loudly Gabriel thinks his ears will burst. The night washes red and roaring and his vision locks on the boy's slender back. Muscles bunch and tighten and before he can stop himself he's giving chase. Wind in his face, his pulse nearly drowning the rasp of denim, the crunch of grass under Alec's boots.

The boy makes it halfway across the greenway before Gabriel catches him with a tackle that knocks the air from both their lungs. They fall in a tangle of elbows and knees, the roots of a tree hard beneath them.

He wants this, the wolves chorus. *Give him what he wants. You'll be kinder than the others. Go for the throat.*

Alec curses, struggles. The knife traces a line of heat across Gabriel's arm before he knocks it away. The boy's hand knots in his hair as his teeth graze skin, and he can't tell if it's an attack or an encouragement. Soft flesh parts, sweat and blood slicking his lips, salt and seaweed. He growls at the taste of it and the wolves howl their victory, drowning Alec's sobs.

His jaw aches as he stops, trembling with the need to bite. One hand gouges the dirt, the other tugging the boy's head back. Alec's chest heaves against his, breath wet and ragged. Tears leak down his cheeks, drip down his neck to smear the blood.

"No," Gabriel breathes, though the effort dizzies him. "I'm not this kind of monster." He pushes himself off, disentangling his legs. He shakes his head, inhales the scent of crushed grass and earth along with salt and blood and fear.

Alec sobs, curling on the ground, one hand touching his bleeding throat. "It figures," he chokes. "Of all the monsters I meet, you're not monster enough."

"I'm a ghoul, not a killer. A jackal, not a wolf." He crouches beside the boy, hands between his knees. Adrenaline tingles in his cheeks and fingers, pushing back the hunger, clearing his head. "We haunt graveyards, eat corpses. We skulk in the shadows and the seams of the world, in the between-places. We steal children and raise them in the dark."

Alec sits up with a wince, smearing dirt on his face as he wipes at the tears and snot. At the last, he glances up, eyes red-rimmed and glistening.

"That's what I am," Gabriel says, not sure if he's telling the boy or himself. "I won't kill you. But—" He swallows against the thought. But it's all he can offer. "I can steal you. You may not thank me when you see what it means," he warns, as the boy's eyes widen. "You'll never escape it, once you know. Hunger and shadows and dead things. That's what I can give you." Not here, not the Hannover warrens with their miasma of guilt and yearning, but there's a whole world to see. He started over once—maybe he can do it again. Maybe Alec can too.

The hope on Alec's face is terrible, hope and fear and longing. A second's doubt, and then he pulls his mask of unconcern on again. "Why didn't you say so?" He stands awkwardly, favoring his wounded arm.

Gabriel finds the fallen knife, closes it and hands it back. The wolves watch from the darkness, whining and slinking.

There will be more. They always come, the killers and their prey. You won't stop us. You can't atone so easily.

"But I won't be your killer," he whispers to the dark. "And he won't be your prey." It's not enough, but it's something.

It's a life.

AMANDA DOWNUM lives near Austin, Texas, in a house with a spooky attic. She keeps a fluctuating menagerie of cats, dogs, and novels, and one long-suffering husband. Her short fiction is published in several places, including *Strange Horizons*, *Realms of Fantasy*, and *Weird Tales*. Her first novel, *The Drowning City*, will be released by Orbit Books in the fall of 2009. For more information on Amanda or her writing, visit www.amandadownum.com.

AMANDA DOWNUM SAYS: *I fell in love with Lovecraft just after college, but prefer the eldritch, alien, and unknowable without the racism and misogyny so common in his work. I also love fish, perhaps unhealthily.*

JOEL LANE

Sight Unseen

IN OCTOBER 2008, I had a call from my mother to let me know my father had died. I offered to go and see her, but she said it wasn't necessary. We live about thirty miles apart. Apparently I was down as his next of kin. Which surprised me, as I hadn't been sure he was still alive. Neither of us had seen him since 1982.

"There are some things of his you're entitled to," my mother said. "Not much. He was living in a hostel. His body was found in Salford."

"What happened to him?" I asked.

"They don't seem to know. Maybe a stroke or a heart attack. Someone found him near the river, just lying there. That's care in the community, I suppose." Her voice sounded brittle.

"Are you sure you're okay?"

"It's just a shock, David." She paused. "If you'd told me a week ago he was still alive, I'd have said I didn't give a fuck. He left us both. But now I can't help wondering what happened to him. The police said he was living there alone, no partner, nothing. Maybe they came for him after all."

"Who?" She didn't answer. "Oh, you mean … But if so, they didn't take him, did they?"

"Maybe they didn't like what they found. Oh don't worry, David. I'm not going mad. I'm just upset. And I'm sad for you. All these years."

"Don't worry. I'm all right." The part of me that cared was lost in time. It might as well have been abducted by aliens.

"The police want to talk to you." She gave me a number with an 0161 prefix: Manchester. "There'll be an inquest. Oh, something I forgot—he was registered blind. Don't know why he went out somewhere on his own."

"People's habits don't change."

She laughed quietly. "I'll speak to you soon, David. Take care."

"And you." I put the phone down and stared at the number I'd written on a scrap of paper. In the window, the September daylight was fading. The gray wall of next door's garage was marked with some regular scratches that didn't quite make an image. I reached for the keypad, then realized my fingers were trembling too much to dial.

I don't remember my father very clearly. He left home when I was seven. After that, my mother destroyed every picture of him that had been in the house. I remember him as a thin man with dark hair, angular cheekbones, and uneven teeth. But that may all be inaccurate.

What I'm sure of is that when the sun went down, he would never put the light on unless he wanted to read. I remember him and my mother arguing about it. *It's not safe*, she'd say. *David could walk into something and hurt himself.* He would say that artificial light cost money.

Another thing I recall is his collection of fossils. They were in the front room, on the shelves of the bookcase. Some were entire shells turned to stone; others were polished surfaces that held skeletons, whorls, segmented forms. He let me hold them, said it was like being able to touch the past. Behind the fossils, the shelves were full of his books about UFOs and pyramids and magic. He

said I could read them when I was old enough. But by then
gone and taken the books with him, and I wouldn't have wanted to read them anyway.

It's hard for me to separate what I saw then from what my mother told me later. My father started coming and going at odd hours, sometimes just sitting in the front room when the rest of us got up in the morning. Sometimes he wouldn't speak to me or my mother all day. Then they'd start arguing during the night. *My body's not my own*, he said. *This life is a disguise. They'll come for me again. I don't belong here.* It didn't make any sense to me—or to my mother, who shouted that he needed to get help, he was going mad, he was a danger to me.

In retrospect, of course, he was going through a breakdown. And my mother did succeed in getting him onto medication, though he said she was just trying to stop him seeing. I'm not sure exactly what he believed, but the core of it was that he had been abducted by aliens when he was a teenager. They wanted to use him as an observer, he said. He told me several times that if I was approached by anyone who wasn't human, too pale or thin to be a person, I should tell him at once.

Shortly before he left, he started going into trance-like states. He'd stop whatever he was doing, then move his head slowly like a camera. "They want to see," he explained when my mother tried to make him snap out of it. A few times she broke down, wept with frustration and grief at what was happening to him. He cried too, wrapping his face in his hands, shaking. There was a terrible darkness in his eyes. I started to believe he really wasn't human.

One night I heard my mother screaming and jerked awake in the dark, trying to hear and not hear at the same time. *What do they want to see? This? What do you want me to show them? You're mad. Get out of here. Get out! GET OUT!* I heard him walk slowly down the stairs. My mother carried on crying. I curled up in the bed, my hands over my ears, a noose of tension gripping my throat.

The next day, my father packed a suitcase and left. He came back for the rest of his possessions during the week, while I was at school. The house felt invaded by emptiness. My mother said it was better for him not to be there at all than to be there in body but somewhere else in his mind. I didn't show her the note he'd left on my bed. *Dear David*, it said, *I'm sorry to leave you, but this isn't what I am. I need to find my real self. One day you'll see and understand. Love always, Dad.* I stole a few matches from the kitchen, then took the note to the local wasteground and burned it.

My father didn't try to keep in touch after the divorce went through. We knew he'd moved to Wales. When people asked, my mother said he was on another planet. I was vaguely aware of missing him, but the thought was bound up with resentment and fear. *Fuck it*, I thought eventually. *If he doesn't want to know me, I don't want to know him.* There was no surrogate father, either, though after I left home there were men in my life. But never for too long. I always walked away before they had the chance to abandon me.

The train from Birmingham to Manchester passed through the badlands of the north Midlands, stopping at Derby and Stoke-on-Trent as if to make a point. The view was crowded with damaged factories, rusting sheets of corrugated iron, gray brick walls tattooed with bright swirls of spray paint. A station waiting room with tatters of broken glass like loose skin in its windows. How could people live in ruins?

I was vaguely aware of the sounds in the train carriage. A child imitating mechanical noises, a young woman on the phone to her lover, a dog barking out of sight. But I felt like a camera focused on the images beyond the window. Had my father's blindness been caused by some hereditary disease? Did I have that to look forward to? Beyond that, more difficult questions were lurking. What would it have been like if he'd stayed with us? Would I understand him? Questions that couldn't be asked, let alone answered.

At Manchester Piccadilly I was met by Steve Cohn, a plain-clothes police officer I'd spoken to on the phone. Where non-suspects are concerned, the police are a lot less formal than they used to be. We picked up coffees at the station, and he drove me to a nearby park overlooked by flaking tower blocks. "I'm sorry about your dad," he said.

The coffee tasted like tarnished metal. "It was a long time ago," I said. "There's nothing to go back to. He changed."

"I need a statement from you. Nothing too detailed. And then I'll be happy to answer any questions you have. If I know the answers."

The statement established that I'd had no contact with my father for twenty-five years, and that I had no claim on his estate (such as it was) beyond the standard legal rights. I also volunteered the information that I'd suspected he was mentally ill, but hadn't tried to contact him for family reasons. My words didn't taste much better than the coffee, but the policeman didn't offer any comment.

When he'd recorded my statement, I asked, "Could I see his room?"

"I'm afraid it's been cleared out. But his possessions are at the coroner's offices in Salford. I can arrange for you to see them and take anything you'd like to keep, as long as you have ID on you." I did. "One hostel room is very much like another," Cohn said. "To be honest, all it will tell you is that he lived in a very limited space."

"That's not how I think of him. At least he died in the open air. Could I see where . . ."

"Of course." Cohn gave me a photocopied page from a map, with an X marked in red next to the river Irwell. "There's a slope they call the Landslide, where a street collapsed in 1927. Your dad was lying at the bottom of the slope, looking up into the sky. He wasn't entirely blind, you know. He could see a bright light."

"What was wrong with his eyes?"

"Some kind of tumor. He'd had a few operations for it, so the tissue around his eyes was badly scarred. He'd been on and off radiotherapy for years. That could have brought on the seizure that killed him. The people who found your dad, some local teenagers, said he was reaching up in the air."

I didn't ask if I could see him. Often I wish I had. I'd been struggling with that all day, finally decided to ask, but when it came down to it I was afraid. That the old man's face wouldn't inspire any recognition in me. That his damaged eyes would see through me. I bit my lip.

Cohn drove me to Salford. It reminded me of north Birmingham: new roads, garages and fast-food restaurants juxtaposed with much older, all but derelict housing. He stopped outside the coroner's office. "I'll come in with you." He spoke to the receptionist, who checked my Council Tax booklet and called someone on the phone. "I'll leave you to get on with it," Cohn said. "Feel free to contact me if you have any questions. Take care."

A tall, bald man appeared, blinked at me as if I were a neon sign, then led me down a corridor and through several fire doors to an office at the back of the building. He unlocked the door and said, "Alan Kinver's things are in this room on the left. Take your time, and put aside anything you'd like to keep. You'll need to fill in some forms, but that won't take long. I'll come back in an hour to see how you're getting on."

The office was lined with metal shelves bearing gray plastic crates, like a warehouse. Nine crates had stickers marked with my father's name and date of death. I moved them all to the floor, then sat on a chair to examine their contents. The first two were shirts, trousers and shoes—faded, torn and dusty, nothing a charity shop would have accepted. The third was cooking pans and crockery that hadn't been cleaned in a long time. The fourth was an assortment: two white plastic sticks, a traditional walking-stick, a compass, a pair of binoculars, a small telescope, a radio and a wristwatch with a cracked face, the hands stuck at three o'clock.

At the bottom of the fourth crate was a flat cardboard box that opened at the top. It was full of small chunks or flakes of stone, each bearing a fossil. There were coiled ammonites, segmented trilobites, white *dastilbe* or fossil fish, a leaf, a bird's skull, some kind of crayfish. He'd probably bought most of them in craft shops or museums, though a few rougher ones might have come from beaches. I closed the box and put it by my chair to take home.

The next two crates were full of books. All of the kind I remembered from the house in Smethwick: encounters with aliens, UFOs, the occult, theosophy, the Kabbalah, pyramids, ley lines. Most were dog-eared paperbacks from the sixties and seventies, but a few were older and more scarce hardbacks from specialist publishers. I took half a dozen of the latter to give me some insight into my father's world. By this time, my eyes were blurred with tears.

The seventh crate contained old sheets and blankets. They didn't rise up and make faces at me, but they were badly stained and had a faintly acrid, metallic smell I had to assume was my father's. The eighth crate contained several dozen cassettes—electronic, jazz and modern classical music—and a portable cassette player, plus a hundred or so yellowing issues of *Prediction*, *Fortean Times*, and similar magazines. Again there were some rarer titles, but I left them alone.

The bald man dropped by to check how I was. I told him I was okay and would go back to reception when I'd finished. The ninth crate was filled with paperwork. Notebooks of various shapes and sizes, loose-leaf binders and folders, letters in opened envelopes, press cuttings about disappearances and mysterious sightings. I opened a small memo book and read:

I am a witness, a living satellite. My eyes are alien. What my eyes record goes to their world, but the white people don't tell me what it means to them. My mind is human, but my eyes are not. The doctors deny that because they know. If they were merely ignorant, the facts would destroy them. Their role is to see nothing. Mine is to see everything. What a privilege, and what a terrible price.

My father's handwriting was small and blocky, like the text on an old home computer. It was hard to read—not because it was untidy, but because the letters had been simplified to vestiges intended for his eyes only. A diary for 2005 was densely inscribed with notes and symbols that seemed to combine physics, astrology and ritual magic. Certain dates were highlighted in red and given old-fashioned names: *Roodmass, May Eve, Hallowmass.* Time after time, with the imperishable faith of a Jehovah's Witness, he'd written: *They will come for me.*

One hard-bound notebook seemed more recent: the larger, more chaotic handwriting suggested a time when my father's sight was failing. On a typical page, the words were slanting up and down, and any attempt at structure had been abandoned. The notes were half prayer and half solitary rant:

a cold flame in the night – a promise never kept – the phases of a different moon – the coiled staircase inside – the language of fossils – these eyes aren't mine – a secret path through the rock – a woman with stars in her breasts – the smell of rotting stone – the eternal witness – trapped between worlds – never able to belong

Somewhere near the bottom of the last crate, I found a few small manila envelopes that contained photographs. One I remembered as having been on the wall above one of my father's bookcases: a blind white salamander that lived in underground rivers. Its eyelids were sealed, and it had pale, feathery feelers on either side of its head. Suddenly I heard my father saying: *This is an olm.*

Another envelope contained two small photos in black and white. The first was of a small child I didn't recognize, walking on a wall; his face was in sunlight, laughing. Could that be a stepbrother I'd never met? Then I looked at the second photo and recognized my mother as a young woman. The child was me. I stared at the image, trying to see another face through it.

The cobbled street ended in a jagged ledge. The slope from there down to the Irwell was too steep to walk down steadily. Loose bricks and cobblestones lay between tree roots and jutted from mounds of earth. The surface was overgrown with moss and grasses, but showed little evidence of post-disaster human activity. It was like the war damage that survived in parts of Manchester and East London: if you couldn't repair it, you got used to it.

I worked my way cautiously down the slope, holding onto pieces of rubble to keep my balance. How had my father managed it? And more to the point, why? It had to be one of the places and times he'd marked out for *contact.* Because it was exposed and largely abandoned, or for some deeper reason to do with the psychic residue of the landslide? I couldn't fathom his thinking any more now than in the past. Words from his insane diary rattling through my head, I climbed over the shapeless ruins to the wooden bridge in the crevice of the valley. That was where they'd found him.

It was beginning to get dark, at least this far below street level. There were no streetlights down here, and it would be dangerous to stay much longer. But I couldn't help pausing on the bridge, crouching, letting my gaze climb slowly from the trees on the far bank to the slate-gray university buildings, and on into the dull evening sky. Threads of light were tangled among masses of torn cloud. I felt a buried excitement—part fear and part anticipation—grip me as I waited there. But only nightfall happened. I tried to say goodbye to my father, but the words wouldn't come. All I could think of was his still body lying here on the bridge, his damaged eyes gazing into the sky as if back up a flight of stairs he'd fallen down.

Several hours later, I was drinking in a basement bar near Whitworth Street. I'd booked a cheap hotel room in case the police and coroner business took longer than expected, but that was all in hand. The books, papers, and other bits and pieces I'd salvaged from my father's possessions were back at the hotel. Now I just needed something to escape into. Alcohol, music, and decent-looking men would serve that purpose. They generally did.

The bar was done out in a mock-warehouse style: cheaply white-washed stone walls decorated with Tom of Finland prints, empty oil drums for seats. The music was a subdued pulse of techno. The air was cool, and the beer was cold. Middle-aged guys in leather vests and trousers mingled with younger, more brightly-dressed lads from the dance floor who'd come down here to chill out. I got talking to one of the latter, a dark-haired youth with bruised eyes and a flat Salford accent. We went upstairs and danced together for a while. Nothing more. That was as much contact as I needed.

A few nights later, I had a dream that woke me up breathless and shivering. I was sitting at my desk, reading, while night fell outside. Then I got up to close the curtains. In the window, I could see a classic harvest moon: yellow and almost full, its scars clearly visible. It was moving steadily downward and to the left. In another minute, it had dropped out of the sky. The scientific part of my mind informed me that, according to Newton's laws of motion, such a dramatic change in the moon's orbit around the earth would displace the earth from its own orbit around the sun. I gazed into a suddenly empty night sky, realizing that all human life was going to end within a few hours.

On the last evening in October, I caught a bus out to the Sandwell Valley: a region of woodland with patches of open ground and a few wartime bomb shelters. It was a couple of miles from the house I'd lived in as a child, and I knew it had been one of my father's favorite places. These days I had friends who went there to cruise, but open-air sex had never been my thing. In fact, I couldn't really have explained why I was going there.

On the way, I saw a bunch of teenagers mooching from house to house in plastic ghost masks. Early fireworks cracked open the sky above the terraced houses. I was thinking of my father's last, barely readable diary: *you can't go through—you're caught between worlds—trapped in time like a fossil in stone.* Over the past few weeks, I'd been alternating between grief, bitterness, and indifference towards him. Gradually I'd become aware that these feelings were held in different layers of my own past. I wondered if he'd struggled with that too.

By the light of a half moon and some constellations I didn't recognize, I made my way down into the forest. Dead leaves and branches obliterated the footpath. The smell of decay mingled with fresh smoke. I could hear the trickling of a river, but didn't see it. The sense of buried excitement returned to me, making me so tense it was an effort to breathe. I remembered my adolescent dreams of gypsies, hunters, outlaws. The eyes watching from the darkness. The moon clouded over until I had to reach in front of me to fend off overhanging branches. Then the foliage thinned out, and I felt a cold wind blowing through an open space ahead.

Without the trees, I could see the blurred orange glow of the city's light pollution. And something flickering and shifting on the edge of vision—like a distant fire, but not bright enough, unless it was wrapped in smoke. The ground under my feet was harder than before. As my eyes adjusted to the near dark, I saw that I was approaching a hilltop on which some kind of stone circle had been left to fall apart. Was this an observation point from wartime? The ruins looked much older than that. Then I glimpsed a thin figure waiting among the stones.

He stepped forward to meet me. I couldn't breathe. What could I say to him? *How have you been, apart from dying*? As he came closer, I saw he was moving his head slowly from side to side. Was that a message? Then the moonlight grew brighter, and I saw his face. The next thing I remember is running, tripping over roots, stumbling through branches, tearing my hands, not caring how much

I hurt myself if the pain could help me believe that I hadn't seen white feelers reaching out of his eyes.

Eventually I realized I was back in the streets, somewhere on the edge of north Birmingham. The houses looked unreal, like a film set hastily constructed and damaged to give the impression of age. A black cab drove past and I waved it down. The driver was concerned, wanted to take me to the City Hospital, but I asked him to take me home. He gave me some tissues to clean the blood from my hands before I sat down. "Been in a fight?" he asked. I shook my head.

When I got back to my flat, it was just after midnight. I locked and bolted the door, checked the window locks, then went into the bedroom and pulled down the blind. But I didn't undress, or turn out the light. I got my electric torch from the bathroom in case the light bulb failed. Then I sat on the bed, reading film magazines and waiting for the dawn. At some point, a memory came back to me that had been lost for years: how for a long time after my father left, I used to sleep with the bedside lamp on for fear of what I might learn to see in the dark.

JOEL LANE'S publications include two collections of supernatural horror stories, *The Earth Wire* and *The Lost District and Other Stories*; two novels, *From Blue To Black* and *The Blue Mask*; a novella, *The Witnesses are Gone*; and two collections of poems, *The Edge of the Screen* and *Trouble in the Heartland.*

Lane is the editor of the anthology of subterranean horror stories *Beneath the Ground* and co-editor (with Steve Bishop) of the crime fiction anthology *Birmingham Noir.* He has written several articles on great weird fiction authors for the critical journal *Wormwood.* His short story "My Stone Desire" won a British Fantasy Award in 2007.

Forthcoming books include a third novel, *Midnight Blue*, and a collection of supernatural crime stories.

LANE SAYS: *Lovecraft's work was an obsession of my teens. His dramatic sense of alienation and hopelessness spoke powerfully to my small and useless adolescent self. Coming back to his work in my thirties, and again in my forties, I've found that what affects me most in his stories is the sense of personal loss wrapped up in the "cosmic" metaphors. So many of his stories deal with broken families, corrupt or absent fathers, a loss of trust. My favorite Lovecraft story, "The Shadow Out of Time," is about a man becoming alienated from his family and his world. "Sight Unseen" is my own take on that theme.*

HOLLY PHILLIPS

Cold Water Survival

NOVEMBER 11:
Cutter is dead and I don't know what to feel. Andy is crying and Miguel is making solemn noises about the tragedy, but I think they're acting. Not their grief—that's real—but their response to it. I think they're just playing to what's expected out there in the world. I can't, and I don't think Del can either. I've seen the shining in his eyes, and it isn't tears. There's a kind of excitement in the air, the thrill of big events, important times: death. It's a first for all of us. For Cutter, too.

[The viewer of the digital video camera is like a small window onto the past, shining blue in the dull red shade of my tent.]

There's a sliver of indigo sky, and the white glare of snow, and the far horizon of ocean like a dark wall closing us in. There are the climbers, incongruous as candy wrappers in their red and yellow cold-weather gear. But they're like old-time explorers, too, breath frosting their new beards and snow shades hiding their eyes. [Only because I know them do I recognize Cutter on the left in yellow, Del on the right in red.] Their voices reach the small mic through gusts of wind so strong it sways the videographer [me], making the scene tilt as if the vast iceberg rose and fell like a ship to the ocean swells. It doesn't. Bigger than Denmark, Atlantis takes the heavy

Antarctic waves without a tremor. But this is summer, and we haven't had any major storms yet.

I can hear them panting through my earbuds, Cutter and Del digging down to firm ice where they can anchor their ropes. Rock can be treacherous; ice, more so; surface ice that's had exposure to sun and wind, most of all. They hack away with their axes, taking their time. Bored, the videographer turns away to film a slow circle: the dark line of the crevasse, the trampled snow, the colorful camp of snow tents, disassembled pre-fab huts, crated supplies, and floatation-bagged gear. I remember with distaste the dirty frontier mess of McMurdo Station, an embarrassment on the stark black-white-blue face of the continent, but I can sympathize, too. The blankness of this huge chunk of broken ice sheet is daunting. It's nice to have something human around to rest your eyes on.

Full circle: the climbers are setting their screws. They aren't roped together; ice is too untrustworthy. The videographer approaches the near side of the crevasse as they come up to the far lip, ready to descend. Their crampons kick ice shards into the sunlight; the focus narrows: spike-clad boots, ice spray, the white wall of ice descending into blue shadow. The climbers make the transition from the horizontal surface to the vertical, as graceless as penguins getting to the edge of the water, and then start the smooth bounding motion of the rappel. The lip of the crevasse cuts off the view. [A blip of blackness.] A better angle, almost straight down: the videographer has lain down to aim the camera over the edge. The climbers bound down, the fun of the descent yet to be paid for by the long vertical climb of the return. The playback is nothing but flickering light, but in it is encoded the smell of ancient ice, the sting of sunlight on the back of my neck. I must have sensed those things, but I didn't notice them at the time. I didn't notice, either, that I only watched the descent through the tiny window of the camera in my hand.

They're only twenty meters down when Cutter's screws give way. *Shit*, he says, *Del*—And he takes a hack with his axes, but the ice is bad, and the force of his blows tips him back, away from the wall—his crampons caught for another instant, so it's like he's standing on an icy floor where Del is bounding four-limbed like an ape, swinging left on his rope, dropping one ax to make a grab—and the camera catches the moment when the coiling rope slaps the failed screw into Cutter's helmet, but by then he's falling. Del looses the brakes on his rope and falls beside him, above him, reaching, but there's still friction on his rope, and anyway, no one can fall faster than gravity. *Cutter,* says the videographer, and the camera view spins wide as she finally looks down with her own eyes. The camera doesn't see it, and I don't now except in memory. The conclusion happens off-screen, and we, the camera and I, are left staring at the crevasse wall across the way.

And so it's only now, in my red tent that's still bright in the polar absence of night, that I see it—them—the shapes in the ice.

November 12:

We spent the morning sawing out a temporary grave, and then we laid Cutter, shrouded in his sleeping bag, into the snow. It was a horrible job. Cutter, my friend, the first dead person I'd laid hands on. It should have been solemn, I know, and I have somewhere inside me a loving grief, but Christ, manhandling that stiff broken corpse into the rescue sled, limbs at all the wrong angles and that face with the staring eyes and gaping shatter-toothed mouth. Oh Cutter, I thought, stop, don't do this to me. Stop being dead? Don't inflict your death on me? On any of us, I guess, himself included. I hated to do it, but the others aren't climbers, so it was Del and me, all too painfully conscious of how bad the ice could be. We made a painstaking axes-and-screws descent, crampons kicking in until they'll bear your weight, not trusting the rope as you dig the axes in. In spite of everything, it was a good climb, no problems at all, but there was Cutter waiting at the bottom for us. His frozen blood was red as paint on the ice-boulders that choked the throat of the crevasse.

It was so blue. Ice like fossilized snow made as hard and clear as glass by the vast weight and the uncountable years. An eon of ice pressed from the heart of the continent out into the enormous ice sheet that is breaking up now, possibly for the first time since humans have been around, and sending its huge fragments north to melt into the oceans of the world. Fragments of which Atlantis is only one, though the only inhabited one. Like a real country now, we have not only a population, but a graveyard, a history, too.

And an argument. Andy made her case for withdrawal—playing the role, I thought, that began with her tears—but none of us, not even her, had thought to call in the fatality the day it happened. "Why not?" I asked, and nobody had an answer for me. "Why didn't you?" said Miguel, but I hadn't meant to accuse. I had wanted someone to give me an answer for my actions, my non-action. Not reporting the death will mean trouble, and we're already renegades, tolerated by the Antarctic policy-makers only because no one has ever staked a claim on an iceberg before. We set up McMurdo's weather station and satellite tracking gear and promised them our observations, but we aren't scientists, we're just adventurers, coming along for the ride. And now Cutter's dead, out here in international waters, and though I guess the Australians will want some answers at some point—I know his parents will—Oz is a long way away. I almost said, *Earth is a long way away.* Earth is, dirt is, far from this land of ice and sea and sky.

[Camera plugged into laptop, laptop sucking juice from the solar panels staring blankly at the perpetual northern sun.]

I watch the fall, doing penance for my curiosity. My own recorded breath is loud in my earbuds. The camera's view flings itself in a blurry arc and then automatically focuses on the far wall. Newer ice that's really compacted snow is opaquely white, glistening as the fierce sun melts the molecular surface. Deeper, it begins to clarify, taking on a blue tone as the ice catches and bends the light. Deeper yet, it's so dark a blue you could be forgiven for thinking it's opaque again, but it's even clearer now, all the air pressed out by millennia of snow falling one weightless flake at a time. Some light must filter through the upper ice because the shapes [I pause] are not merely surface shapes, but recede deep into the iceberg's heart.

Glaciers (of which Atlantis was one) form in layers, one season's snow falling on the last, so they are horizontally stratified. But glaciers also move, flowing down from the inland heights of the continent, and that movement over uneven ground breaks vertical fault lines like this crevasse all through the vast body of ice. So any glacial ice face is going to bear a complex stratigraphy, a sculpting of horizontal and vertical lines. This is part of ice's beauty, this sculptural richness of form, color, light, that can catch your heart and make you ache with wonder. And because it is the kind of harmony artists strive for, it's easy to see the hand of an artist in what lies before you.

But no. I've seen the wind-carved hoodoos in the American southwest, and I've seen the vast stone heads of Rapa Nui, and I know the difference between the imagination that draws a figure out of natural shapes and the potent recognition of the artifact. These shapes [I zoom twenty percent, forty percent] in the ice have all the mystery and meaning of Mayan glyphs, at once angular and organic, three-dimensional, fitting together as much like parts in a machine as words on a page. What are they? I've been on glaciers from the Rockies to the Andes and I've never seen anything like this. My hands itch for my rope and my axes. I want to see what's really there.

November 13:

I wondered if Del would object to another climb—he came up from retrieving Cutter stunned and pale—but the big argument came from Miguel, who talked about safety and responsibility to the group. I said, "Have you looked at the pictures?" and he said, "All I see is ice." But Miguel's a sailor, one of the around-the-world-in-a-tiny-boat-alone kind, and ice is what he keeps his daily catch in. Andy said he had a point about safety, if things go really wrong we're going to need one another, but she kept giving my laptop uneasy looks, knowing she'd seen something inexplicable.

I said, "Isn't this why we're here? To explore?"

"What if it's important?" Andy said, changing tack. "What if it really is something? The scientists should be studying it, not us."

"Ice formations," Miguel said. "How important is that? It's all going to melt in the end."

"Are we always going to argue like this?" This from Del. "If we're going to quit, then let's get on the satellite phone and get the helo back here to pick us up."

"I'm just saying," Miguel said, but Del cut him off.

"No. We knew why we were doing this when we started. I hate that Cutter's dead, but I wouldn't have come to begin with if we'd laid different ground rules, and if we're going to change now, I don't want to be here. I've got other things to do."

I backed him up. This was supposed to be our big lawless adventure, colonizing a chunk of unreal estate that's going to melt away to nothing in a couple of years—not for nationalism or wealth—maybe for fame a little—but mostly because we wanted to be outside the rules, on the far side of every border in the world. Which is, I said, where death lies, too.

Taking it too far, as usual. Andy gave me another of those who-are-you looks, but I fixed her with a look of my own. "Get beyond it," I said. "Get beyond it, or why the hell are we here?"

And then I remembered why these people are my closest friends, my chosen family, because they did finally give up the good-citizen roles and tapped into that excitement that was charging the air. Most people would think us heartless, inhuman, but a real climber would understand: we loved Cutter more, not less, by moving on. Going beyond, as he has already done.

So Del and I roped up again and went down.

[The images come in scraps and fragments as the videographer starts and stops the camera.]

The angle of light changes with the spinning of the iceberg in the circumpolar current. For this brief hour, it slices into the depths of the crevasse, almost perfectly aligned with the break in the ice. So is the wind, the constant hard westerly that blows across the mic, a deep hollow blustering. Ice chips shine in the sunlight as they flee the climber's crampons kicking into the crevasse wall. The tethered rope trails down into the broken depths. Everywhere is ice.

[Blip]

The crevasse wall in close-up. Too close. [The videographer leans out from a three-point anchor: one ax, two titanium-bladed feet.] Light gleams from the surface, ice coated in a molecule-thick skin of melt water, shining. All surface, no depth. *Shit*, the videographer [me] says. *Look*, the other climber [Del] says. The camera eye turns toward him, beard and shades and helmet. He points out of the frame. A dizzying turn, the bright gulf of the crevasse, the far wall. More shapes, and Christ, they're big. The crevasse is only three meters wide at this point, and measuring them against a climber's length, they're huge, on the order of cars and buses, great whites and orca whales.

[Blip]

A lower angle. [Pause, zoom in, zoom out.] These shapes swirl through the ice like bubbles in an ice cube, subtle in the depths. Ice formations, Miguel said. Ice of a different consistency, a different density? Ice is ice, water molecules shaped into a lattice of extraordinary strength and beauty. The lattice under pressure doesn't change. Deep ice is only different because air has been forced out, leaving the lattice pristine. So what is this? The camera's focus draws back. They're still there, vast shapes in the ice. The wind blusters against the mic.

[Blip]

The floor of the crevasse—not that a berg crevasse has a floor. There's no mountain down there, only water three degrees above freezing. But the crack narrows and is choked with chunks of ice and packed drifts of snow, making a kind of bottom, though a miserable one to negotiate on foot. The camera swings wildly as the videographer flails to keep her balance. Blue ice walls, white ice rubble, a flash of red—Cutter's frozen blood on an ice tusk not too far away.

[Blip]

A still shot at last. A smooth shard of ice as big as a man, snow-caked except where Del is sweeping it clear with his ax handle. *It could be*, he says panting, *or part of one*. My own voice, sounding strange, as it always does on the wrong side of my eardrums: *So it broke out when the crevasse formed?* Del polishes the ice with his mitts. The camera closes in on his hands, the clear ice underneath his palms. It *is* ice. The videographer's hand reaches into the frame to touch the surface. Ice, impossibly coiled like an angular ammonite shell.

November 15:

Del and I hauled the ice-shape up in the rescue sled as if it was another body, but by the time we had it at the surface, the constant westerly, always strong, was getting stronger, and Miguel was urgent about battening down the camp. We'd been lazy, seduced by the rare summer sun, and now, with clouds piling up into the blue sky, we had to cut snow blocks and pile them into wind breaks—and never mind the bloody huts that should have been set up first thing. Saw blocks of Styrofoam-like snow, pry them out of the quarry, stack them around the tents and gear, all the time with the wind heaving you toward the east, burning your face through your balaclava, slicing through every gap in your clothes. The snow that cloaks the upper surface of the berg blows like a hallucinatory haze, a Dracula mist that races, hissing in fury, toward the east. It scours your weather gear, would scour your flesh off your bones if you were mad enough to strip down.

The bright tents bob and shiver. McMurdo's satellite relay station on its strut-and-wire tower whines and howls and thrums—Christ, that's going to drive me mad. Clouds swallow the sun, the distant water goes a dreadful shade of gray. And this isn't a spell of bad weather, this is the norm. Cherish those first sunny days, we tell each other, huddled in the big tent with our mugs of instant cocoa. Summer or not, this gray howling beast of a wind is here to stay. Andy uplinks on her laptop, downloads the shipping advisories, such as they are for this empty bit of sea. There are deep-sea fishing boats out here, a couple of research vessels, the odd navy ship, but the Southern Ocean is huge and traffic is sparse. We joke about sending a Mayday—engine failure! we're adrift!—but in fact we're a navigation hazard, and the sobering truth is that if it came down to rescue, we could only be picked up by helicopter: there's no disembarking from the tall rough ice-cliffs that form our berg-ship's hull. And land-based helos have a very short flight range indeed.

Like most sobering truths, this one failed to sober us. Castaways on our drifting island, we turned the music up loud, played a few hands of poker, told outrageous stories, and went early to bed, worn out with the hard work, the cold, the wind. And for absolutely no reason, I thought, with Del puffing his silent snores in my ear, We're too few, we're going to hate each other by the end. And then I thought of Cutter lying cold and lonesome in the snow.

November 16:

Another work day, getting the huts up in the teeth of the wind. Miguel, sailor to his bones, is a fanatic for organization. I'm not, except for my climbing gear, but I know he's right. We need to be able to find things in an emergency. More than that, we need to keep sane and civilized, we need our private spaces and our occupations. We also need to keep on top of the observations we promised McMurdo, if we want to keep their good will—more important than ever with Cutter dead—which was my excuse for dragging Andy away from camp while the men argued about how to stash the crates. Visibility wasn't bad, and we laid our first line of flags from the camp to the berg's nearest edge. Waist-high orange beacons, they snapped and chattered in our wake.

Berg cliffs are insanely dangerous because bergs don't mildly dwindle like ice cubes in a G&T. They break up as they melt, softened chunks dropping away from the chilled core, mini-bergs calving off the wallowing parent. All the same, the temptation to look off the edge was too powerful, so we sidled up to it and peered down to where the blue-white cliff descended into the water and became a brighter, sleeker blue. The water was clearer than you might suppose, and since we were on the lee edge, there wasn't much surf. We looked down a long way. Andy grabbed my arm. "Look!" she said, but I was already pulling out the camera.

[Tight focus only seems to capture the water's surface. As the angle widens, the swimming shadows come into view.]

Deep water is black, so the shapes aren't silhouettes, they're dim figures lit from above, their images refracted through swirling water. Algae grows on ice, krill eat the algae, fish eat the krill, sharks and whales and seals and squids and penguins and god knows what eat the fish. God knows what. The mic picks up me and Andy arguing over what we're seeing. They move so fluidly they must be seals, I propose, seals being the acrobats of the sea. *Could be dolphins*, Andy counters, but when the camera lifts to the farther surface [when I, for once, take my eyes off the view screen and look unmediated] we see no mammal snouts lifting for air. *Sharks*, I say, but sharks don't coil and turn and dive, smooth and fluid as silk scarves on the breeze, do they? *Giant squid*, Andy says, and the camera's focus tightens, trying to discern tentacles and staring eyes. Gray water, blue-white ice. Refocus. The dim shapes are gone.

November 17:

The huts are up and we sent a ridiculously expensive e-mail to our sponsors, thanking them for the luxuries they provided: chairs, tables, insulated floors—warm feet—bliss. Andy uploaded our carefully edited log to our website while she was online, saying that Cutter had been hurt in a climbing mishap and was resting. We'd agreed on this lie—having failed to report his death immediately, there seemed no meaningful difference between telling his folks days or months late—but once it was posted I realized, too late, what we were in for. Not just hiding his death, but faking his life, his doings, his messages to his family. "We can't do this," I said, and Andy met my eyes, agreeing.

"Too late," Del said.

"No," Andy said. "We'll say he died tomorrow."

"We can't leave now," said Miguel. "We just got set up."

"We can't do this," I said again. "Him dying is one thing. Faking him being still alive is unforgivable. Andy's right. We have to say he died tomorrow."

"They'll pull us off," said Del.

"Who will?" I said, because we're not really under anyone's jurisdiction. "Listen, if his folks want to pay for a helo to come out from McMurdo—"

"We're too far," Andy said, "it'd have to be a navy rescue."

"They can get his body now or wait until we're in shouting distance of New Zealand," I said. "If we upload the video—"

"We can't make a show of it!" Miguel said.

"Why not?" Del said. "It's what people want to see."

"We can send it to the Aussies," I said, "to show how he died. It was a climbing accident, no crime, no blame. If they want the body, they can have it."

Del was convinced that someone—who? the UN?—was going to arrest us and drag us off for questioning, but I just couldn't see it. Someone's navy hauling a bunch of Commonwealth loonies off an iceberg at gunpoint because a climber died doing something rash? No. The Australians wouldn't love us, god knows Cutter's parents wouldn't, but nobody was going to that kind of effort, expense, and risk for us.

"So why the fuck didn't you say so two days ago?" Del said to me.

"Well," I said, "my friend had just died and I wasn't thinking straight. How about you?"

[The camera's light is on, enhancing the underwater glow of the blue four-man tent.]

The coiled ice-shape gleams as if it were on the verge of melting, but the videographer's breath steams in the cold. The videographer [me] is fully dressed in cold-weather gear, a parka sleeve moving in and out of view. The camera circles the ice shape in a slow, uneven pan [me inching around on my knees] and you can see that the shape isn't a snail-shell coil, it's more like a 3D Celtic knot, where only one line is woven through so many volutions that the eye is deceived into thinking the one is many. The camera rises [me getting to my feet] and takes the overview. There, not quite at center, like a yoke in an egg: the heart of the knot. What? The camera's focus narrows. In the gleaming glass-blue depths of the ice, an eye opens. An eye as big as my fist, translucent and alien as a squid's. The camera's view jolts back [me falling against the tent wall] and only the edge of the frame catches the fluid uncoiling of the ice shape, a motion so smooth and effortless it's as though we're underwater. The camera's frame falls away, dissolves, and then there's only me in the blue-lighted tent, me with this fluid alien thing swirling around me like an octopus in a too-small aquarium, opening its limbs for a swift, cold embrace—

[And I wake, sweating with terror, to see Del twitching in his dreams.]

November 18:

Cutter died again today. We sent the video file (lacking its final seconds) to our Australian sponsors, asking them to break the news to Cutter's family. Andy wrote a beautiful letter from all of us, mostly a eulogy, I guess, talking about Cutter and what it was like to be here now that he was dead. She did a brilliant job of making it clear that we were staying without making us sound too heartless or shallow. So this is us made honest again, and somehow I miss Cutter more now, as though until we told the outside world his death hadn't quite been real. I keep thinking, I wish he was here—but then I remember that he is, outside in the cold. Maybe I'll go keep him company for a while.

[The laptop screen is brighter than the plastic windows of the hut, the image perfectly clear.]

The camera jogs to the videographer's footsteps, the mic picks up the Styrofoam squeak-crunch of snowshoes. There's the team on the move, two bearded men and a lanky woman taller than either, in red and blue and green parkas, gaudy against the drifting snow. The camera stops for a circle pan: gray sky, white surface broken into cracks and tilting slabs. Blown snow swirls and hisses; a line of orange flags snaps and shudders in the wind. The videographer [me] sways to the gusts, or the ice-island flexes as it spins across its watery dance floor. Full circle: the three explorers up ahead now, the one in green reaching into the snow-haze to plant more flags.

[Blip]

Broken ice terrain, the sound of panting breath. Atlantis as a glacier once traveled some of the roughest volcanic plains on the planet, and these fault-lines show how rough it was, the ice all but shattered here. You have to wonder how long it's going to hold together. *Hey!* The explorer in blue gives a sweeping wave.

You guys! You have to see this! Shaky movement over tilted slabs of ice, a lurch—

[Blip]

A crevasse, not so deep as the one near camp, with the shape of a squared-off comma. In the angle, ice pillars stand almost free of the walls. Blue-white ice rough with breakage. Slabs caught in the crevasse's throat.

[Miguel, watching at my shoulder, says, "That's not what we saw. You know that's not what we saw!"]

November 20:

Miguel keeps playing the video of today's trek. Over and over, his voice shouts *You have to see this!* through the laptop's speakers. Over and over. Del's so fed up with it he's gone off to our hut and I'm tempted to join him, but it's hard to tear myself away. Andy isn't watching anymore, but she's still in the main hut, listening to our voices—hushed, strained, hesitant with awe—talk about the structures (buildings? vehicles? Diving platforms, Andy's voice speculates) that the camera stubbornly refused to record. At first I thought Miguel was trying to find what we saw in the camera images of raw ice, but now I wonder if what he's really trying to do is erase his memory and replace it with the camera's. I finally turned away and booted my own computer, opening the earlier files of the first ice-shapes I found. Still there? Yes. But now I wonder: *could* they be natural formations?

Could we be so shaken up by Cutter's death that we're building a shared fantasy of the bizarre?

I don't believe that. We've all been tested, over and over, on mountains and deserts, in ocean deeps and tiny boats out in the vast Pacific. Miguel's told his stories about the mind-companions he dreamed up in his long, lonely journey, about how important they became to him even though he always knew they were imaginary. I've been in whiteouts where the hiss of blowing snow conjures voices, deludes the eyes into seeing improbable things.

Once, in the Andes, Cutter and I were huddled back-to-back, wrapped in survival blankets, waiting for the wind to die and the visibility to increase beyond two feet, and I saw a bus drive by, a big, diesel, city bus. I had to tell Cutter what I was laughing about. He thought I was nuts.

So we've all been there, and though we all know what kinds of crazy notions people get when they're pushed to extremes—I've heard oxygen-starved climbers propose some truly lunatic ideas when they're tired—we aren't anything close to that state. Fed, rested, as warm as could be expected . . . No.

But if we all saw what we think we saw, then why didn't the camera see it too?

[Bubbles rise past the camera's lens. The mic catches the gurgle of the respirator, the groaning of the iceberg, the science-fiction sound effects of Weddell seals.]

The camera moves beneath a cathedral ceiling of ice. Great blue vaults and glassy pillars hang above the cold black deeps, sanctuary for the alien life forms of this bitter sea. Fringed jellies and jellies like winged cucumbers, huge red shrimp and tiny white ones, skates and spiders and boney fish with plated jaws. Algae paints the ice with living glyphs in murky green and brown, like lichen graffiti scrawled on a ruin's walls. Air, the alien element, puddles on the ceiling, trapped. The water seems clear, filled with the haunting light that filters through the ice, but out in the farther reaches of the cathedral, the light turns opaquely blue, the color of a winter dusk, and below, there is no light at all. Bubbles spiral upward, beads of mercury that pool in the hollows of the cathedral ceiling, forming a fluid air-body that glides along the water-smoothed ice. It moves with all the determination of a living thing, seeking the highest point. [The camera follows; bubbles rise; the air-creature grows.] The ceiling vault soars upwards, smeared with algae [Zoom in; does it shape pictures, words?] and full of strange swimming life [Are there shadows coiling at the farthest edges of the frame?], and it narrows as it rises to a rough chimney. Water has smoothed this icy passage, sculpted it into a flute, a flower stem . . . a birth canal. The air-body takes on speed, rising unencumbered into brighter and brighter light. The upward passage branches into tunnels and more air-bodies appear, as shapeless and fluid as the first. Walls of clear ice are like windows into another frozen sea where other creatures hang suspended, clearer than jellyfish and more strange. And then the camera [lens streaked and running with droplets] rises from the water [How?], ascending a rough crevice in the ice. The air-bodies, skinned in water—or have they been water all along?—are still rising too, sliding with fluid grace through the ice-choked cracks in the widening passage. [The videographer sliding through, too: how?] The host seeks out the highest places and at last comes up into the open air—ice still rising in towering walls, but with nothing but the sky above. Gray sky, blue-white ice, a splash of red. What is this? Fluid, many-limbed, curious, the water-beings flow weightlessly toward the splash of scarlet [blood]. They taste [blood], absorb [blood], until each glassy creature is tinted with the merest thread of red.

[And I close the file, my hands shaking as if with deadly cold, because these images are impossible. I'm awake, and my camera shows battery drain, and none of us, not even Andy, came prepared to dive in this deadly sea.]

November 22:

Miguel watched the impossible video and then walked out of the tent without a word. Andy sat staring at the blank screen, arms wrapped tight around her chest. And after a long silence, Del said calmly, "Nice effects." I knew what he meant—that I was hoaxing them, or someone was hoaxing me—but I can't buy it. Even if any of us had the will we don't have the expertise. We're explorers, not CG fucking animators. And who made us see what we saw in that inland crevasse? Who's going to make the evidence of that disappear on the one hand, and then fake a school of aliens on the other?

"Aliens," Andy said, her face blank and her eyes still fixed on the screen. "Aliens? No. They belong here. They're the ones that belong."

"Hey," I said, not liking the deadness in her tone. "Andy."

"Screw this," Del said, and he left too.

Miguel's not in camp. It took us far too long to realize it, but we spent most of the day apart, Andy in her hut, Del in ours, me in the big one brooding over my video files. We left the tents up for extra retreat/storage/work spaces and Miguel could have been in one of them—Andy assumed he was, since he wasn't in the hut they share—but when Del finally pulled us together for a meal, we couldn't find him. And the wind is rising, howling through the satellite relay station's struts and wires—wires that are growing white with ice. The wind has brought us a freezing fog that reeks of brine. If it were Del out there, I could trust him to hunker down and wait for the visibility to clear, but does Miguel the sailor have that kind of knowledge? We all did the basic survival course at McMurdo, but the instructors knew as well as Del and I that there's a world of difference between knowing the rules and living them. The instinct in bad weather is to seek shelter, and god knows it's hard to trust to a reflective blanket thin enough to carry in your pocket. But it's worse not to be able to trust your comrade to do the smart thing. We're all angry at Miguel, even Andy. He's put us all at risk. Because of course we have to go and find him.

November 24:

We're back. McMurdo's relay station is an ice sculpture, and our sat phone, even with its own antenna, isn't working. I don't know what we're going to do.

We went after Miguel, the three of us roped up and carrying packs. Our best guess was that he'd gone back to the crevasse where we saw, or didn't see, the buildings, structures, vehicles—whatever they were in the ice. So we followed the line of orange flags inland.

Standing by one, you could see the next, and barely discern the next after that, which put the visibility roughly at six meters. But with the icy fog blasting your face and your breath fogging up your goggles, the world contracts very quickly to within the reach of your arms. Walking point is hard, but it's better than shuffling along at the end of the rope, fighting the temptation to put too much trust in a tiring leader. I was glad when Del let me up front after the first hour. Andy, who has the least experience with this kind of weather, stayed between us, roped to either end.

A long hike in bad weather. The sun, already buried behind ugly clouds, grazed the horizon, and the day contracted to a blue-white dusk. We huddled in a circle, knee-to-knee, with our packs as a feeble windbreak. I fell into a fugue state. The blued-out haze went deep and cold and still, like water chilled almost to the point of freezing. The wind was so constant it no longer registered; the hiss of it against our parkas became the hiss of water pressure on my ears. And the whiteout began to build its illusions. Walls rose in the haze, weirdly angled, impossibly over-hung. Strange voices mouthed heavy, bell-like, underwater sounds. Something massive seemed to pass behind me without footsteps, its movement only stirring the water-air like a submarine cutting a wake. No different than the bus I saw on that Andean mountain, except that Andy jerked against me while Del muttered a curse.

And then the ground moved.

Ground: the packed snow and ice we sat upon. It gave a small buoyant heave, making us all gasp, and then shuddered. A tremor, no worse than the one I'd sat through when I was visiting Andy in Wellington, but at that instant, all illusion that Atlantis was an island died. This was an iceberg, already melting and flawed to its core, and there was nothing below it but the ocean. Another small heave. Stillness. And then a sound to drive you insane, a deep immense creaking moan that might have come from some behemoth's throat. I grabbed for Del. Andy grabbed for me.

The ice went mad.

We were shaken like rats in a terrier's mouth. The toe spikes on someone's snowshoes, maybe my own, gouged me in the calf. I didn't even notice it at the time. We lurched about, helpless as passengers in a falling plane, and all the time that ungodly noise, hugely bellowing, tugged at flesh and bone. I knew for a certainty that Atlantis was breaking up and that we were all already dead, just breathing by reflex for a few seconds more. I flashed on Cutter falling, knowing he was dead long before he hit the ground. I was glad we'd told his folks; glad Andy had sent that beautiful letter, eulogy for us all. And then the ice went still.

I lay a moment, hardly noticing the tangle we were in, my whole being focused on that silence. Quiet, quiet, like the final moment in free fall, the last timeless instant before the bottom. But it stretched on, and on, and finally we all picked ourselves up, still unable to believe we were alive. "Jesus," Del said, and I had to laugh.

We went on, me in the middle this time because of my limp, with Andy bringing up the rear. Tossed around as we had been, none of us was sure of our directions, and because of the berg's motion, GPS and compass were both useless. Blown snow and fog-ice erased our footprints as well as Miguel's. In the end, all we could do was follow the line of flags in the direction of our best guess and resolve that if it led us back to camp, we would turn and head straight back out again. I was feeling Miguel's absence very much by then, so much so that a fourth figure haunted the edges of my vision, teasing me with false presence. But maybe that was Cutter, not Miguel.

Flags lay scattered among huge tilted slabs of packed snow. We replanted the slender poles as best we could, and by this time I was starting to hope we *had* been turned around and were heading back to camp. If the berg-quake had scattered the whole line of flags, they were likely to be buried by the time we turned around, and if they were, we were screwed. But we couldn't do anything but what we were already doing. We clambered through the broken ice field, hampered by the rope between us and already tired from the wind. Del got impatient and Andy snapped that she was doing the best she could. "You're fine," I said. "Del, ease off." He went silent. We re-roped, and I took point, limp and all.

Spires of ice rose like jagged minarets above the broken terrain. Great pillars, crystalline arches, thin translucent walls. Scrambling with my eyes always on the next flag, I took the ice structures for figments of the whiteout at first, but then we were in among them and the wind died into fitful gusts. The line of flags ended, irredeemably scattered, unless this was its proper end and the former crevasse was utterly transformed. It was beautiful. Even exhausted and afraid I could see that, and while Andy shouted for Miguel and Del hunkered over our packs digging out the camp stove and food, I pulled out my camera.

[Digital clarity is blurred by swirling fog. Yet the images are unmistakable, real.]

Crystalline structures defy any sense of scale. This could be a close-up of the ice-spray caught at the edge of a frozen stream, strands and whorls of ice delicate as sugar tracery, until the videographer turns and gets a human figure into the frame. The man in red bends prosaically over a steaming pot, apparently oblivious to the white fantasia rising up all around him. The mic picks up the sound of a woman's voice hoarsely shouting, and the camera turns to her, a tall green figure holding an orange flag, garish among all the white and blue and glass. *Andy*, says the videographer. *Hush a minute, listen for an answer.* The human sounds die, there's nothing but the many voices of the wind singing through the spires. A long slow pan then: pillars, walls, streets—it's impossible not to think of them that way. A city in the ice. An inhuman city in the ice.

Movement.

The camera jerks, holds still. There's a long, slow zoom, as though it's the videographer rather than the lens that glides down the tilt-floored icy avenue. [The static fog drifting, obscuring the distant view.] Maybe that's all the movement is, sea-fog and wind swirled about by the sharp, strange lines of the ice-structures. [The wind singing in the mic, glass-toned, dissonant.] But no. No. It's *clarity* that swirls like a current of air—like a many-limbed being with a watery skin—gliding gravity-less between the walls, in and out of view. [Pause. Go back. Yes. A shape of air. Zoom. A translucent eye. Zoom. A vast staring eye.]

The camera lurches. The image dives to the snow-shoe-printed ground. The videographer's clothing rustles against the mic, almost drowning her hoarse whisper. *We have to get out of here. Guys! We need to—*

We roped Miguel between Del and me, with Andy again bringing up the rear. It was an endless hike, the footing lousy, the visibility bad, all of us hungry and aching for a rest. Del tried to insist that we eat the instant stew he'd heated before we left, but I was seeing transparent squids down every street, and when Miguel stumbled out of the ice, crooning wordlessly to the wind even as he clutched at Andy's hands, Del let himself be outvoted. "This is how climbers die," he said to me, but I said to him, "If you're on an avalanche slope you move as fast and as quietly as you can, no matter how hungry or tired you are." Death is here: I wanted to say it, and didn't, and while I hesitated the silence filled with the glass-harmonica singing of the wind—with Miguel's high crooning, which was the same, the very same. So I didn't need to say it. We followed the broken line of scattered flags back to camp.

And now I sit here typing while the others sleep (Miguel knocked out by pills), and I look up and see what I should have seen the instant we staggered in the door. All of our gear, so meticulously sorted by Miguel, is disarranged. Not badly—we surely would have noticed if shelves were cleared and boxes emptied on the floor—but neat stacks and rows have become clusters and piles, chairs pushed into the table are pulled askew, my still camera and its cables are out of its bag my hands are shaking as I type this there's a draft the door is closed the windows weatherproofed I'm pretending I don't notice but there's a draft moving behind me through the room

November 25:

I took my ax to the tent where we still kept the ice-shape Del and I brought up from the bottom of the crevasse. I was past exhaustion, spooked, halfway crazy. It was just a lump of ice. I took my ax to it, expecting it to bleed seawater, rise up in violent motion, fill the tent with its swirling arms. I swung again and again, flailing behind me once when paranoia filled the tent with invisible things. Ice chipped, shattered. Shards stung my wind-burned face. The noise woke Del in our hut nearby. He came and stopped me. There was no shape left, just a scarred hunk of ice. Del took the ax out of my hand and led me away, gave me a pill to let me sleep like Cutter. I mean, like Miguel. I'm still doped. Tired. I can feel them out there in the wind.

The relay tower is singing outside.

November 27:

The ice is always shaking now. New spires lean above our snow wall, mocking our defenses. Miguel cries and shouts words we can't understand, words so hard to say they make him drool and choke on his tongue. The wind sings back whenever he calls. The sat phone has given nothing but static until today, when it, too, sang, making Del throw the handset to the floor. The radio only howls static. The fog reeks of dead fish, algae, the sea. Everything is rimed in salt ice. Andy hovers over Miguel, trying to make him take another pill: Del threatened him with violence if he doesn't shut up. I grabbed Del, dragged him to a chair, hugged him until he gave in and pulled me to his lap. We're here now, all four of us together. None of us can bear to be alone.

November 28:

A new crevasse opened in the camp today, swallowing two tents and making a shambles of the snow wall. Is this an attack? Our eviction notice, Andy says, humor her badge of courage. But I wonder if they even notice us, if they even care. Atlantis is theirs now, and I suppose it always has been, through all those long cold ages at the heart of the southern pole. Now the earth is warming, the ancient ice is freed to move north, to melt—and then what? What of this ice city growing all around us like a crystal lab-grown from a seed? If the clues they've given us (deliberately? I do wonder) are true, then they are beings of water as much as of ice. It won't happen quickly, but eventually, as the berg travels north out of the Southern Ocean and into the Atlantic or Pacific, it will all melt. Releasing . . . what? . . . into the warming seas of our world. Our world *is* an ocean world, our over-burdened continents merely islands in the vast waters of misnamed Earth. What will become of us when they have reclaimed *their* world?

Del and Andy, in between increasingly desperate attempts to bring our sailor Miguel back from whatever alien mindscape he's lost in, are concocting a scheme to get our inflatable lifeboat, included in our gear almost as a joke, down the ice cliffs to the water. Away from here, they reason, we should be able to make the sat phone work, light the radio beacon, call in a rescue. I have a fantasy—or did I dream it last night?—that the singing that surrounds us, stranger than the songs of seals or whales, has reached into orbit, filling satellite antenna-dishes the way it fills my ears, drowning human communication. I imagine that the first careless assault on human civilization has already begun, and that the powers—the human powers—of Earth are looking outward in terror, imagining an attack from the stars, never dreaming that it is already here, has always been here, now waking from its ice-bound slumber. It is we who have warmed the planet; we, perhaps, who have brought this upon ourselves. But brought what, I wonder? And when Andy appeals to me to help her and Del with their escape plan, I find I have nothing much to say. But I suppose I will have to say it before long: why should we leave—*should* we leave—just when things are getting interesting?

Get beyond it, I'll have to tell them, as I did when Cutter died. We have to look beyond.

In the meantime, though, I'll make a couple of backups, downloading this log and my video files onto flash drives that will fit into a waterproof container. My message in a bottle. Just in case.

HOLLY PHILLIPS is a professional fantasist, which is to say, a full-time writer and occasional editor. She has been nominated for various awards and won the 2006 Sunburst Award for her story collection *In the Palace of Repose.* Her latest book is *The Engine's Child.* Holly lives in a small city on a large island off Canada's western coast.

PHILLIPS SAYS: *Lovecraft appeals to me for several reasons: that connection he draws between insanity and the perception of the inhuman universe (and which comes first?); the thoroughly satisfying notion of ancient, alien civilizations buried under this thin skin of humankind; his baroque weirdness. It amuses me to think we might actually be related (Howard Phillips Lovecraft was named for his maternal grandfather, Whipple Phillips), though the likelihood is vanishingly small. Still, that sort of hidden connection to the past, and to tainted bloodlines, seems very Lovecraftian, don't you think? And here I am, drawn against my will into an obsession with the strange, dark underbelly of fiction, dabbling in fantastical forces beyond my understanding . . .*

WILLIAM BROWNING SPENCER

Come Lurk with Me and Be My Love

WHEN WALLY BENNETT was a kid, his parents taught him to say this prayer:

Now I lay me down to sleep. I pray the Lord my soul to keep. If I should die before I wake, I pray the Lord my soul to take.

He had stopped saying the prayer at nine or ten, and he had always found it disturbing, for two reasons. One: Dying in his sleep was not a pleasant thought, not something Wally wished to entertain; the idea that the Lord was poised above his sleeping form like some immense holy vulture waiting to grab his soul—and do exactly *what* with it?—was unsettling, to say the least. And two: There was always the implicit suggestion that, should he *forget* to say this prayer, something awful would occur. One of Satan's minions might drag him into the abyss.

Wally hadn't thought about God much in years. Now here he was, reading a book entitled *Of Pandas and People* and thinking about . . . well, actually, Flower. Her name was Flower, oddly imprecise for one so much *herself*, as though her parents had wrestled with names like Daisy, Violet, and Rose, lost their way amid so many choices, and settled for this generic solution.

Wally was in love with Flower, love like a rat in his vitals, love that gnawed at his sleep, love that made his time away from her feel like bad television, like exile.

He had met Flower at a craft fair in Warrenton. Like all males, Wally hated craft fairs, but he had accompanied his married friends, Ben and Sarah, because they had insisted—well, Sarah had—that he needed to get out more. Wally and Sarah both worked for a small, desperate ad agency (Blitz Media) in Arlington, Virginia, and, more often than not, Wally worked on Saturdays, preparing for some Monday presentation while the rest of the office, people with lives, celebrated the weekend.

"You've got to get out of this office," Sarah had said. "You're like one of the undead, like a blind cave salamander."

So Wally had said sure he'd go, why not?

At first, the fair seemed to answer that question. Unruly children screamed and chased each other through the crowd. Coils of smoke unfurled from the slow-cooking carcasses of pigs and chickens and rose into the cloud-heavy sky. The beer in cardboard cups was tepid but, alas, not undrinkable, and Wally drank way too much, and a bluegrass band wailed, miserably authentic, thin, clenched voices harried by a banjo and a mandolin. The day, unseasonably chilly for late April, threatened rain, and Wally wished he'd worn something warmer than a t-shirt.

He stared at the crafts and the people who had crafted them and was appalled at how the creative impulse could so easily lose its way. The beer got him, and, for a moment, a rush of idiot compassion urged him to hug a pinch-faced man in brown overalls who sat on a stool surrounded by primitive paintings of Jesus engaged in various farm chores (milking a cow, driving a tractor, killing a hog), but the desire to comfort the untalented, the misguided, left Wally before he could act.

He had lost sight of his friends amid the milling throng, but Ben had anticipated that possibility and suggested that they meet back at the SUV at 4:00 should they become separated.

Wally looked at his watch. It was only 2:15, and he felt exhausted, which manifested in a flare of self-pity: *I am thirty-two years old, and the best I can do on a Saturday is accompany my married friends to a craft fair.* The thought inspired an instant twitch of self-loathing, because it was such a lame lament. You put something like that in your suicide note, and the cops would have a good laugh. "My wife burned dinner," someone would say. "I think I'll hang myself." Another wit would say, "Hell, nothing but reruns on. I'm gonna get the shotgun out of the attic and blow my damned head off."

Wally found himself resenting these imagined cops. What did they know about his life? A shy person, Wally had grown up in a family of extroverts, shouters, backslappers, people who could tell a dirty joke, heartily curse the referee at a football game, watch sitcoms and laugh like crows. He was the youngest, with three brothers and two sisters. He could never shake the feeling that he had arrived at the party too late. Everyone assumed he knew what the celebration was about, but he didn't have a clue.

"So, do you want to buy that?"

Wally looked up and saw the most exotic, most beautiful creature he had ever seen. Her eyes were a breathtaking blue, her lips full and dark purple, almost black, and she stood, bare feet planted on a small stool, swaying slightly as though to music, perhaps practicing some feminine martial art. Clouds had obscured the sun, but a single shaft of light escaped to bathe this child-woman in gold, as though God were throwing a spotlight on His glorious creation.

She had a Goth look to her, spiky black hair, a black t-shirt, and black cargo pants, but Wally knew—the way you know a thing when love pierces you like a sword—that she heeded no one's fashion, was, indeed, incapable of being, of looking, like anyone other than who she was. And Wally knew, having beheld her, that an after-image would burn in his mind for the rest of his life.

Now, three weeks later, sitting on the sofa in his apartment with *Of Pandas and People* on his lap, Wally thought again about that first meeting. Had he been immediately smitten, or was this a lover's revisionist history? It was, he thought, every bit as real as a car crash he had been in when he was twenty-four and a car filled with teenagers had run a stop sign and broadsided him. His car had seemed to spin slowly, leisurely, and images of the surrounding buildings, the clouds, and the stark winter trees had been shuffled like cards and slapped down one at a time in the middle of his mind, too surreal to comprehend and yet leaving him with the reality of a twice-broken arm. In just this way had his heart been altered, irrevocably, by Flower. Why else would he be reading *Of Pandas and People*? He read:

> Of Pandas and People *is not intended to be a balanced treatment by itself. We have given a favorable case for intelligent design and raised reasonable doubt about natural descent.*

This was the book that the people in Flower's commune were using to homeschool their children, and Flower had urged it on him with a mixture of diffidence and desperation. Clearly, his opinion of the book was important to her, so important (Wally suspected) that his negative opinion could scuttle their fledgling romance. All right: Wally knew that this intelligent design thing used to be called "creationism," which maintained that mankind did not evolve through the random action of physical forces. Intelligent design (aka God—and a Christian one at that) had to get Life going. And once Life got going, something as complicated as a giraffe was never going to evolve without divine meddling.

How would one know when something was created by the application of intelligence? How could one *recognize* intelligence? According to the authors of *Pandas*, seeing and knowing this intelligence was largely common sense. "Most of us do it without even thinking," they wrote. Consider those ripples in the sand that you observed when walking on the beach. Anyone could see that this pattern was a natural phenomenon created by the rhythmic action of the ocean's waves. But suppose you walked down that same beach and came upon the words JOHN LOVES MARY written in the sand. You'd know the waves hadn't created that pattern. Those words were created by intelligence! Probably, the authors added, by an intelligence named John or Mary. To illustrate this principle, the authors included a photo of sand in which the words JOHN LOVES MARY were written. *Proof!* (Wally was inclined to think that the *photographer* was the intelligence behind this pattern and that neither John nor Mary had anything to do with the words; he realized, however, that this thought was completely irrelevant.)

Wally read on, but his question wasn't "Can I honestly say I believe this crap?" No, his question was a simpler one: "Can I lie to Flower to win her love?" And the answer to that was a resounding, "Yes!" Love that can't trump intellectual integrity isn't worth the name.

On that day when they met, her first words were: "So, do you want to buy that?"

He could not say whether she repeated this sentence or whether the words simply hung in the air until he was able to process them. He saw that he was holding in his hands a small smooth object, a carving of some sort.

He studied it. It was a primitive wood carving of a man, standing, his legs disappearing into the blocky base of the carving. Cradled in his arms was a child—no, a tiny woman; her breasts were fully developed—and this woman was also holding something in her arms, a dog-like creature whose mouth opened to display ragged teeth. Man, woman, and dog-thing all faced forward, eyeless, mouths open. *Howling*, Wally thought.

"What is it?" Wally said, or heard himself saying. Was that a rude question? He couldn't think.

"You don't have to buy it," the girl said, jumping down from the stool. She was smiling, dimples in her cheeks.

"How much is it?"

"Twenty dollars, I guess." She looked at him, as though trying to puzzle out the effect such a sum would have.

"Okay," Wally said, and he fished in his pocket, pulled out some crumpled bills, and found a twenty among them. He handed this to the girl, who beamed, a smile worth all the twenties he had. She laughed, a musical trill that made Wally dizzy.

She took the carving from him and placed it in a small brown paper bag. She creased and folded the bag's top carefully, as though there was a formula for this folding, and, as she bent over, engrossed, the thick spikes of her hair leaned forward, suggesting the fronds of some jungle plant. Wally watched his hand move toward her hair, a hand in thrall. She looked up, and he dropped his hand and looked away, saw the card table covered with carvings, and examined another one. This one was a sort of frog creature with its mouth open. Within its mouth, he could see another frog peering out.

"You want that one, too?" she asked.

"Did you carve all these?"

"Yes," she said.

"That must have taken a long time." *Jeez.* Was this his best shot at conversation?

"I got a lot of time, that's for sure. Dah always says, 'More you wait, the sooner you're late!'" She giggled. "You can have that one, too, if you want it." And she looked down when she said that, at once demure, shy.

"How much?" Wally didn't know how much money he'd brought with him. Whatever, it was hers.

She shook her head, not looking up. "Free, is all," she said.

"That wouldn't be right. I really like it!"

She looked up, rocked him with her smile again, and said, "That's the price then. Liking. I give it to you for the liking of it. And because . . ." She was coy now; her head canted to the side and away, eyes looking back.

"Because?"

"I like you, too."

Then it was after four o'clock, and Ben was standing by his side, miffed. "We said we'd meet at the car at four," he said. "I've been looking all over for you. Sarah's got a headache. We need to get going."

Wally had lost track of time, sitting there with the girl.

"This is Flower," he told Ben. "She lives on a commune, and she carves these amazing figures."

"Nice meeting you," said Ben, but he was in a hurry, almost rude, a quick dismissive glance at her art, and Wally reluctantly stood up and followed him back to the SUV.

The next morning, Wally was in the parking lot before the craft fair opened. He'd come alone this time, and he spent the morning sitting with Flower, talking to her, passing the time, watching the people go by, ambivalent when people stopped and purchased one of her carvings. He liked seeing the smile a sale induced, but he didn't want anyone to own something Flower had touched and laboriously carved and sanded and graced with the sweet weight of her concentration.

At noon, Flower stood up and announced that she was closed for lunch. She walked around the table and out into the aisle, where a new batch of craft fair attendees jostled each other, picked through jewelry and junk, and purchased hot dogs and giant pretzels from a vendor wearing, for reasons of his own, a Spider-Man costume. Wally and Flower purchased fried chicken and fries and soft drinks from another food vendor and climbed to the top of a hill where they could look down on the fair. Flower pointed to the blue mountains to the west. "I live there," she said.

"Can I visit you sometime?" Wally asked.

"Oh, sure. I'd like that. I'll have to draw you a map, though. It's not easy to find, kind of a lurk, you know?"

"Lurk?"

"You know, like a hideaway. We don't want people to come mucking around in our business, so we lie low."

Flower reached forward and squeezed his arm. "If you really want to know about us, there's a book you should read. I mean, it's important. I can't even tell you how important." She let go of his arm and hugged herself, as though constraining something wild and sensuous within—or perhaps she was just responding to the chill, for the day had grown overcast, blustery, and was full of the stubborn remnants of winter.

Three extremely long weeks had passed since he had last seen Flower. He had watched her climb into her van, a wobbly, ancient vehicle, dirty-white with patches of gray primer, and he had waved goodbye—*idiot that he was!*—and, dazed by the kiss she had bestowed on his cheek, he had failed to follow her. Yes, he had the map she had drawn for him, and he had her promise that she would call him—she had carefully tucked away the business card he gave her (a card he'd made when he planned to escape the drudgery of Blitz Media by going freelance)—but he should have followed her. Because he knew just how forgettable he was.

Back in the days when he went to bars, when he made some effort to pick up women, he saw in their eyes this phenomenon of effacement. He would evaporate, even as he spoke. At first these women he approached would seem slightly annoyed, aware that their attention was being demanded by someone unremarkable, but then they'd look dazed, bemused, and turn to the girlfriend who'd accompanied them or shout to the bartender for a refill. Wally would know that, as far as they were concerned, he was gone, not even snubbed, which would have left some mental residue, some knowledge that he had *been* there.

Perhaps, driving down the highway, Flower had glanced in the rearview mirror, seen him waving, and wondered who he was. *Oh yes: a customer.*

He had asked her for a phone number, and she had told him there was no phone because "Dah don't hold with them. Not the lines nor the cells." She said she would drive to where there was a phone and call as soon as she could. And she had warned Wally that she'd have to "acclimate" her father (the formidable "Dah") to the notion of a visitor from the outside.

Naturally, Wally had grown impatient and tried to find her with her map. The map led him west on Lee Highway and north on 688, traveling through rainy, smudged-watercolor fields, black cattle, and barns as red as blood. He stopped at gas stations and antique shops and asked about the Hewlitt Farm or Skunk Cabbage Creek, but no one had heard of Flower's landmarks. Both weekends he'd hunted her, quitting at dark and driving home to study the map, which he had memorized and could see with his eyes closed—and which now looked so spare and unforthcoming that he wondered why, when she gave it to him, he hadn't laughed bitterly, shook his head, and said, "If you don't want me to visit, just say so."

Once he thought he was close. He'd driven past what looked like an abandoned gas station, but he'd seen the screen door swing open, emitting a cat before banging shut, so he'd turned around and gone back. He'd gotten out of his car and gone up to the screen door and peered in. He couldn't see into the gloom, but someone shouted "Hey!" and he turned around and saw an old man who must have come around the side of the building. He wore brown gloves and gripped a hoe in his right hand. His chin was pocked with white stubble, and the gray of his eyes was the color of rain water in a tin cup.

"You don't want to peep into a man's house like that. You give an honest knock is what you do."

"I was just—"

"We ain't got any gas. Does this look like a flourishing establishment?"

"I just wanted to ask directions. I'm looking for some people." Wally walked back to his car. He opened the door and prepared to get in. It didn't look like he was going to get anything but aggravation from this old buzzard.

"What kind of people?"

"I believe they live in a commune."

"Like hippies?"

"Well no, I think this is a Christian-based commune, actually."

"Something like those Mormoners, with their sacred underwear and their child brides?"

"No." Wally climbed in the car and turned the ignition on.

Just then the screen door opened, and a woman came out. She was wearing a green bathrobe over a blue nightgown, and pink slippers. She was as ancient as the man, but fleshier. Her eyes seemed very large behind her gold-framed glasses.

"What does he want?" she shouted to the old man.

"Wants to know where some people are, but he's mighty vague about them, mostly knows who they aren't."

That's when Wally saw Flower's carvings on the seat next to him. He couldn't say why he'd brought them with him. "For luck," he would have said if anyone had asked. Now he realized that there was an absolutely rational reason for bringing them along. They were evidence of Flower's existence.

Wally reached out and picked up the man-woman-dog carving and swung back out of the car, leaving the engine running.

"Maybe you've seen someone selling these carvings?" he said, holding up the carving. "At a fair or—"

"Damn you!" the man shouted, and he ran at Wally, swinging the hoe, and Wally ducked, which wouldn't have saved him, but the hoe's blade overshot, banging against the car's roof, and Wally slipped on the cracked asphalt, and thought he heard the old man grunt with frustration. He heard shouts, the old woman hollering, he couldn't make out what. The rusty blade winged by again, quick as a bat, inches from his left eye, and he heard a sharp bang, something cracking, and then he was standing, lurching forward, and the hoe's shaft slammed down on his left shoulder, knocked him to his knees, and he hollered, "Ow!" which seemed, even in the moment, a pathetic expression for the considerable pain.

"Okay, okay! That's enough, Paw! What the hell you doing, anyway?"

Squinting, hands in front of his face to fend off the next blow, Wally looked up to see the old man struggling with a thin, hard-muscled man in a flannel shirt and jeans. The family resemblance was obvious, the same muscle in the jaw, the same taut frame, same eyes.

"I ain't gonna let you go till you calm!" the younger man said, clutching the older man's arms from behind. The older man said nothing, glaring, the hoe on the ground by his feet.

Wally sat on the asphalt, his legs stretched out in front of him, his back against his car door, and rubbed his shoulder. He became aware that someone was casting a shadow over him, and he looked up and saw the old woman. She leaned over and offered him a can of beer.

"Thanks," Wally said. He popped the top of the can and took a long swallow.

"It ain't your fault," the woman said. "You just poked a sore."

After the old man and his son had gone back in the house, she explained about the sore. There had been a grandson, their daughter Laurel's boy. The boy, Dean, wasn't right in the head, and he was too much for Laurel, so she'd run off. The old woman and her husband had had the raising of the boy. "And no trouble at all. He was the sweetest little fellow, addled, but angel sweet."

One day they found him dead in a creek bed, his neck broken, and likely it was an accident, but Horace, her husband, had had a run in with some gypsies who'd stopped at the station—that was back when the place was a going concern—and these raggedy folk had been selling carvings that must have looked like the one Wally had (although she couldn't say for certain they were the same; she hadn't seen them).

She hadn't been home when Horace had the encounter, but he told her about it. Apparently, a big old whiskered fellow, the leader, had seen Dean and it set the old patriarch off. He said that Dean was nature gone awry, was an abomination to the great plan (something like that) and had no business living.

"You ever heard such a thing?" she asked. And it was no more than a week later that Dean was dead, and Horace went crazy, sure it was those gypsies, and he kept after the sheriff, who, to his credit, did what he could, but those travelers were gone, and no one else had set eyes on them.

"Not a bit of that is your fault," she told Wally, "but here you come, ignorant as a newborn, and stick your hand right in the hornet's nest."

Wally had thanked her for the beer, found Flower's carving where it had rolled up against the back tire, and climbed back into his car. His shoulder throbbed like a bad tooth, and he just wanted to get out of there. He was worried that Horace might give his son the slip and return with a shotgun. He was clearly a volatile man.

As he backed up, the woman shouted after him, "You seem like a nice man. You remind me a little of our Dean, though. He was always one to rush in without thinking. You might not want to find those people, is all I'm saying."

Wally was convinced that he wasn't going to find Flower. So why, then, did he continue to read *Of Pandas and People*? He supposed he read it because Flower said it was important. The book was a connection to her—and a stupid waste of a Sunday, no doubt. He was drinking beer on top of the pain killers his doctor had prescribed for his shoulder, and that was, no doubt, interfering with his concentration, but, really, what was so damned important about reconciling Genesis with evolution anyway? He read on, and in a chapter entitled "Genetics and Macroevolution," he read that the intelligent design blueprints were actually *protected* by natural selection. An evolutionist improbably named Bumpus had made a study of English sparrows and discovered that those sparrows killed by a severe winter were "more extreme in their physical characteristics." The normal sparrows survived. What the book called "stabilizing selection" kept the optimal (intelligence-designed, God-wrought) sparrows alive and eliminated the mutants.

Wally put the book down and walked to the window of his apartment. The view consisted of other apartment buildings and a parking lot. Heavy rain swept over the parked cars, pummeling them, generating a silvery nimbus that enclosed them. As he watched, a figure emerged from between two parked cars, surrounded in the same shimmer of atomized raindrops. This lithe, elegant apparition strode purposefully across the lot, oblivious to the downpour. *Flower!* Wally knew her instantly, by her grace, the way she moved as though partnered with some elemental force. She looked up and stared directly at him. He thought she might have heard the hitch in his breath and felt the rush of joy that flooded his heart. Wally turned, ran to the door of his apartment, flung it open, raced down the hall, down two flights of stairs, and ran out and into the rain, ran to her, and she smiled, hands at her sides, waiting, and he threw his arms around her and felt the lovely curve of her spine, the sweet animal truth of its history. What could be more wonderful, more mysterious than two creatures, shaped by huge forces, by fire, wind, and rain, by boundless, implacable time, finding each other in the terrible random turnings of the world?

The rain was a roaring in their ears and she had to shout: "I ran away!"

Inside Wally's apartment, she could not stop shivering, from the chill of the rain, from fatigue, and from, Wally understood, her own recklessness, the wild thing inside her that had torn her world asunder. Wally had read of children raised in strange cults, immersed in inflexible systems of belief, defined by rituals; children warned, more often than not, of the horror and death that awaited them if they turned away from the one true path. How hard it must be to forsake one's kin and country.

While she was showering, Wally undressed, toweled dry, and put on clean clothes. Then he fumbled through his closets for something that Flower could wear. Everything was too big, of course, but she could roll the cuffs of the pants . . . they'd have to buy stuff . . . he could wash and dry what she'd worn . . . had she hitchhiked? How could anyone be so brave?

Wally emptied the pockets of her sodden pants. There were some coins, a few bills, an ink pen, the business card he'd given her—which, incredibly, must have led her here—and a curious medallion about the size of a quarter. The medallion was warm to the touch and etched with a holographic image of something that looked a little like a trilobite, that ancient arthropod that suggested a many-segmented cockroach and turned up in fossils that were two or three hundred million years old. When Wally turned the medallion over, he saw the same hologram on the other side, although the effect was more one of the image *rolling* over to the other side than of a second image being revealed. He closed his fist on the medallion, and the sensation was quite pleasant, like holding a warm stone that sent waves of warmth pulsing up his arm, filling him with cozy omniscience.

He was sitting on the couch when Flower came out of the bathroom. She was wearing the clothes he had found for her, and she looked like a child playing dress-up. *Good God! What if she isn't even eighteen!* Without makeup, without the spiky hair and the deep purple lipstick, she seemed newborn, no more than fourteen.

"How old are you?" he asked.

Flower frowned. "Dah says likely 411 years, but the birthing logs were lost in a fire in 1810, and he says he might not have the count-back right."

Wally nodded. No problem, then. He was feeling pretty good, the thrum filling up his body with a soft, cottony certainty.

Flower said. "Did you take my little pocket piece?"

Wally nodded. "Yep." He uncurled the fingers of his fist to show her, but the medallion was gone. *Poof!* Like a magic trick. He giggled. "Gone," he said. He felt a little drunk. He remembered Flower's bravery, and he wanted to comfort and reassure her. "I read the panda people book you lent me. I don't have any problem with your being a Christian. I mean, if you think God created the world in six days, if you think dinosaurs shared the earth with men, that's okay with me."

"But I don't," Flower said, eyes wide. She seemed shocked, possibly offended. She frowned, then a knowing light came into her eyes, and she nodded as though in agreement with some internal voice. "You mean because of the book, how it's Christian and all. I just wanted you to read the book because then I wouldn't have to explain so much. I mean, it tells how we made the world and all, but the god of that book, he's not real. He's just a story. Dah says there are more story gods than you can hit with a stick."

Wally nodded, although he didn't think he was understanding her perfectly.

Flower's next words didn't seem to make complete sense either: "You're being sorted right now. I think it is a good sign that you found the kinstone before I gave it to you. Dah teases me, calls me superstitious, but I believe in omens. You finding it yourself, that's a good omen."

"Okay," Wally said. He was tired, maybe a little queasy, and he needed to rest before he examined all this new, confusing info. He closed his eyes.

He was jostled awake. He was lying on a thin air mattress in . . . it took a minute to get his bearings . . . a van. He had no memory of walking to the van. He saw the back of Flower's head and shoulders, and he pushed himself into a sitting position.

Flower must have seen the movement in the rearview mirror. She turned around, her smile more radiant than ever.

"Dah wasn't going to let you visit. So I ran off to fetch you. He won't fuss so much now, because you been sorted and you are definitely kin. You aren't some stranger he can smite with his wrath."

"Good," Wally said, but he was nervous all the same.

"If you are feeling better, why don't you come on up front and sit with me," Flower said.

Wally nodded. "Okay." He stood up, felt momentarily dizzy, and braced himself with a hand on the van's wall. They were still bouncing over rough road, but Wally wobbled and lurched his way to the passenger seat, clambered over it, and slid down. Rain splattered the windshield, but it was nothing like the earlier deluge.

"Where—" he began, but Flower yanked the wheel to the left and pointed them straight toward a cluster of massive granite boulders protruding from a sheer wall of red clay in which some gnarled, stunted pine trees had found grim purchase. Wally screamed.

Darkness enveloped them, stole the light, stole the thoughts in his head, stole the sound of his scream. He had no idea who or what he was. And then they were back, or at least they were somewhere.

"Here we are," Flower said. She turned the engine off, turned in her seat, threw her arms around Wally and squeezed him. "This is a pretty good lurk, huh?"

Wally climbed out of the van and turned slowly in a circle. There were thousands of tiny lights overhead, and, at first, he thought they were stars, but he realized that they blinked on and off, creating patterns that shifted and repeated.

"Come on," Flower said, taking his hand. She led him down a flight of metal stairs. Yellow lamps on the tunnel's walls illuminated other doors. Wally heard what sounded like the rush of water, the creak and clang of ancient machinery. "Where are we?" Wally asked, his words echoing around him like startled birds.

"We're inside a mountain," Flower said.

Wally didn't think there were any caves in these mountains. The caves were all farther west where underground streams carved elaborate limestone caverns.

Flower might have read his thoughts, for she said, "Dah says these caves were created by the Ur Gods and here is where they birthed the world. This is where they created the Gatherers, who were the first sons of mankind."

It seemed to Wally that he marched down countless steps and navigated a vast labyrinth before Flower opened a door that revealed the living room of what could have been a somewhat rundown Victorian home. It was a chilly room, poorly-lit by several dim gas-fueled globes. Logs were burning in the fireplace, and shadows licked the faded wallpaper, an intricate ivy print. Flower called out, "Dah, I want you to meet someone."

Several overstuffed armchairs faced the fire, and from one of them a figure emerged, expanding as it turned toward Wally and Flower.

"What have you done, daughter?" The voice was deep and bullhorn loud, and the man stepped into the light. He looked like Walt Whitman, Wally thought, if that great poet had weighed an additional three hundred pounds, had a thick slab of a brow that kept his eyes in constant shadow and a voluminous beard, mottled with gray-green moss or lichen.

"I've found a man to love," Flower said. "For the line and for love."

Her father seemed to have some difficulty breathing. Each expansion of his lungs—a visible effort—was accompanied by a rusty wheeze. He wore a ragged, ancient suit that appeared to be fashioned out of burlap or hair. "I told you, daughter, we cannot deal with the daylighters. We lurk in the shadows for a reason."

Flower walked up to her father and stood on her toes and said, "He's kin, Dah."

"Kin?"

Flower nodded her head.

"He's been sorted? You've had a stone look him over?" he asked.

"I have."

"Well." The monstrous man approached Wally and leaned forward. "Are you looking to marry my daughter or merely mount her?"

"Ah—" Wally began.

The old man's face loomed close. Where the flesh surfaced amid whiskers, it was infinitely creased, and Wally could see the man's eyes, as blue and quick as Flower's. "I'll know a lie," the man cautioned.

"Marry," Wally said.

"Good answer," the old man said, and he extended his hand. Wally shook it. Flower came up and hugged him.

Flower turned to her father, bowed, and left the room.

The old man gestured to another armchair, indicating that Wally be seated.

"My name is Garth, and you may call me that," he said, sinking into his own armchair. "I am glad you are one of the true, glad you are kin. My daughter has been disappointed before."

"Disappointed?"

Garth nodded. "She has loved unwisely, found outsiders who proved impure." He paused, slapped his massive hands down on his knees, and leaned forward. "You read the book?"

Wally didn't have to ask what book. "Most of it," he said.

"Well, the book is true, and then again, it's all cockeyed. Does it say why all this fuss was made? Does it say why some vast intelligence would fashion us?"

"I don't know," Wally said.

"Of course you don't. I do. I will tell you. The Ur Gods live in the vast reaches of time and span universes but their eyes are finite. They cannot monitor every future. And so they came upon this planet and thought, 'In time it will have its uses,' and they planted a seed. They drew man to their specifications and made him breathe. And what are we designed for?"

This time Wally was pretty sure the question was rhetorical, so he waited.

"We are designed to gather information. Yes! We assimilate the universe. We study, we experiment, we compile. And when the Ur Gods return, they will find us and our knowledge will be theirs."

"Well," Wally said. "That's something." This was fairly confusing stuff. "How exactly will they acquire this knowledge that we have gained over thousands of years?"

Garth smiled, as though a bright student had asked a particularly astute question. "They will devour us."

"Devour? What—"

Garth nodded. "Eat. Chew up and swallow. Devour. You make a sandwich and you devour it. Fry some eggs, bake a cake. What for? To eat!" Garth put his hands together. "What a fine thing. To be swallowed by a God!"

Wally was stumped. He couldn't think of a thing to say. Wait, there was something else he wanted to ask: "I understand that I am one of your line, an intelligently designed ancestor, not some strayed mutant, right?"

"Yes."

"How exactly do you know this?"

"My daughter gave you a kinstone. This is a technology from the stars, bequeathed to us by the Ur Gods. It glides beneath your flesh. It looks within you. And if it finds you wanting, it kills you."

"I could have been killed?" Wally said. Flower had been playing with his life? *Jeez.*

Garth shrugged. "You are alive. The Gods have blessed you. Among those my daughter has taken a fancy to, you are the first one who has survived. Be grateful." He sighed. "I only wish her mother had lived to see Flower's joy. But Rachel was burned for a witch. That is the nature of our calling: Mostly we weed, but sometimes we are weeded."

Garth showed Wally to his room. They climbed a narrow staircase and came out, again, into the vast light-speckled cavern. Far below, Wally saw several shadowy figures moving, illuminated by the light from a ghostly projection, a flickering holographic statue, a fifty-foot homage to some ancient alien voyager, perhaps, that resembled nothing so much as a giant trilobite.

They re-entered a world of shabby Victorian furnishings, and Garth ushered Wally into a dingy bedroom.

"We will talk tomorrow about your wedding," Garth said, and he extended his hand again. "I am pleased to welcome you back to your family."

Wally sat on the bed. He was too tired to make a careful assessment of his surroundings. He untied his shoes. He was tugging his shoes off when something fell onto the rug. It glittered there, like a malevolent insect, silver wings twitching. Wally recognized it. He guessed it had been lying in the cuff of his pants where it had fallen. This was the medallion, the *kinstone*, that was supposed to have slid beneath his flesh and vouched for his pedigree. Only it hadn't. It had fallen out of his hand because he had been drunk and wrecked on oxycodone.

Just great. He could pick it up. He could close his fingers over it and let it do its job. He suspected he was genetically fraudulent, an off-shoot, and so it would kill him. So what? If he just went ahead and married Flower, she'd find out soon enough, wouldn't she? *If you were a human being, could you marry into a clan of vampires without them noticing you weren't one of them?*

Wally took his shoe and pushed the holographic medallion under the bed and out of sight. *I am so screwed!* he thought. And then, because he was already on his knees, he put his elbows on the bedspread, folded his hands together, and began: "Now I lay me down to sleep—"

WILLIAM BROWNING SPENCER is the author of four novels and two collections of short stories. Spencer's satirical horror novel *Résumé With Monsters* describes a corporate America in which Lovecraftian monsters haunt the workplace. The novel won the International Horror Critics Award for Best Novel. Various creatures from Lovecraft also inhabit his novel *Irrational Fears* in which alcoholics are discovered to be the progeny of an ancient underground tribe who worship Tsathoggua.

His short stories have been included in *The Year's Best Science Fiction* and *The Year's Best Fantasy and Horror* and have been finalists for the Bram Stoker, World Fantasy, and Shirley Jackson awards. He currently lives in Austin, Texas, and is completing his novel *My Sister Natalie: Snake Goddess of the Amazon*, which will be published by Subterranean Press.

SPENCER SAYS: *I first encountered Lovecraft in the classic anthology* Great Tales of Terror and the Supernatural *(still in print sixty-five years after its original publication—and still brilliant). I think what drew me to him was the authority in his voice. He was the master of a kind of cumulative dread that arose in spite of the narrator's rational tone. The teller of these tales tries, by all the tricks of civilized speaking, to hold a steady course, but the monstrous indifference of space and time and history always wrests control from him. Of course, I didn't identify this lunatic spiraling into the abyss as the source of Lovecraft's power back in my teens when I first read him. I just thought he was brilliantly creepy.*

CAITLÍN R. KIERNAN

Houses Under the Sea

WHEN I CLOSE my eyes, I see Jacova Angevine.

I close my eyes, and there she is, standing alone at the end of the breakwater, standing with the foghorn as the choppy sea shatters itself to foam against a jumble of gray boulders. The October wind is making something wild of her hair, and her back's turned to me. The boats are coming in.

I close my eyes, and she's standing in the surf at Moss Landing, gazing out into the bay, staring towards the place where the continental shelf narrows down to a sliver and drops away to the black abyss of Monterey Canyon. There are gulls, and her hair is tied back in a ponytail.

I close my eyes, and we're walking together down Cannery Row, heading south towards the aquarium. She's wearing a gingham dress and a battered pair of Doc Martens that she must have had for fifteen years. I say something inconsequential, but she doesn't hear me, too busy scowling at the tourists, at the sterile, cheery absurdities of the Bubba Gump Shrimp Company and Mackerel Jack's Trading Post.

"That used to be a whorehouse," she says, nodding in the direction of Mackerel Jack's. "The Lone Star Café, but Steinbeck called it the Bear Flag. Everything burned. Nothing here's the way it used to be."

She says that like she remembers, and I close my eyes.

And she's on television again, out on the old pier at Moss Point, the day they launched the ROV *Tiburon II.*

And she's at the Pierce Street warehouse in Monterey; men and women in white robes are listening to every word she says. They hang on every syllable, her every breath, their many eyes like the bulging eyes of deep-sea fish encountering sunlight for the first time. Dazed, terrified, enraptured, lost.

All of them lost.

I close my eyes, and she's leading them into the bay.

Those creatures jumped the barricades

And have headed for the sea

All these divided moments, disconnected, or connected so many different ways, that I'll never be able to pull them apart and find a coherent narrative. That's my folly, my conceit, that I can make a mere *story* of what has happened. Even if I could, it's nothing anyone would ever want to read, nothing I could sell. CNN and *Newsweek* and *The New York Times*, *Rolling Stone* and *Harper's*, everyone already knows what they think about Jacova Angevine. Everybody already knows as much as they want to know. Or as little. In those minds, she's already earned her spot in the death-cult hall of fame, sandwiched firmly in between Jim Jones and Heaven's Gate.

I close my eyes, and "Fire from the sky, fire on the water," she says and smiles; I know that this time she's talking about the fire of September 14, 1924, the day lightning struck one of the 55,000-gallon storage tanks belonging to the Associated Oil Company and a burning river flowed into the sea. Billowing black clouds hide the sun, and the fire has the voice of a hurricane as it bears down on the canneries, a voice of demons, and she stops to tie her shoes.

I sit here in this dark motel room, staring at the screen of my laptop, the clean liquid-crystal light, typing irrelevant words to build meandering sentences, waiting, waiting, waiting, and I don't know what it is that I'm waiting for. Or I'm only afraid to admit that I know exactly what I'm waiting for. She has become my ghost, my private haunting, and haunted things are forever waiting.

"In the mansions of Poseidon, she will prepare halls from coral and glass and the bones of whales," she says, and the crowd in the warehouse breathes in and out as a single, astonished organism, their assembled bodies lesser than the momentary whole they have made. "Down there, you will know nothing but peace, in her mansions, in the endless night of her coils."

"*Tiburon* is Spanish for shark," she says, and I tell her I didn't know that, that I had two years of Spanish in high school, but that was a thousand years ago, and all I remember is *sí* and *por favor.*

What is that noise now? What is the wind doing?

I close my eyes again.

The sea has many voices.

Many gods and many voices.

"November 5, 1936," she says, and *this* is the first night we had sex, the long night we spent together in a seedy Moss Point hotel, the sort of place the fishermen take their hookers, the same place she was still staying when she died. "The Del Mar Canning Company burned to the ground. No one ever tried to blame lightning for that one."

There's moonlight through the drapes, and I imagine for a moment that her skin has become iridescent, mother-of-pearl, the shimmering motley of an oil slick. I reach out and touch her naked thigh, and she lights a cigarette. The smoke hangs thick in the air, like fog or forgetfulness.

My fingertips against her flesh, and she stands and walks to the window.

"Do you see something out there?" I ask, and she shakes her head very slowly.

I close my eyes.

In the moonlight, I can make out the puckered, circular scars on both her shoulder blades and running halfway down her spine.

Two dozen or more of them, but I never bothered to count exactly. Some are no larger than a dime, but several are at least two inches across.

"When I'm gone," she says, "when I'm done here, they'll ask you questions about me. What will you tell them?"

"That depends what they ask," I reply and laugh, still thinking it was all one of her strange jokes, the talk of leaving, and I lie down and stare at the shadows on the ceiling.

"They'll ask you everything," she whispers. "Sooner or later, I expect they'll ask you everything."

Which they did.

I close my eyes, and I see her, Jacova Angevine, the lunatic prophet from Silinas, pearls that were her eyes, cockles and mussels, alive, alive-o, and she's kneeling in the sand. The sun is rising behind her, and I hear people coming through the dunes.

"I'll tell them you were a good fuck," I say, and she takes another drag off her cigarette and continues staring at the night outside the motel windows.

"Yes," she says. "I expect you will."

— 2 —

The first time that I saw Jacova Angevine—I mean, the first time I saw her in *person*—I'd just come back from Pakistan and had flown up to Monterey to try and clear my head. A photographer friend had an apartment there, and he was on assignment in Tokyo, so I figured I could lay low for a couple of weeks, a whole month maybe, stay drunk and decompress. My clothes, my luggage, my skin, everything about me still smelled like Islamabad. I'd spent more than six months overseas, ferreting about for real and imagined connections between Muslim extremists, European middlemen, and Pakistan's leaky nuclear arms program, trying to gauge the damage done by the enterprising Abdul Qadeer Khan, rogue father of the Pakistani bomb, trying to determine exactly what he'd sold and to whom. Everyone already knew—or at least thought they knew—about North Korea, Libya, and Iran, and American officials suspected that al Queda and other terrorist groups belonged somewhere on his list of customers, as well, despite assurances to the contrary from Major-General Shaukat Sultan. I'd come back with a head full of apocalypse and Urdu, anti-India propaganda and Mushaikh poetry, and I was determined to empty my mind of everything except scotch and the smell of the sea.

It was a bright Wednesday afternoon, a warm day for November in Monterey County, and I decided to come up for air. I showered for the first time in a week and had a late lunch at the Sardine Factory on Wave Street—Dungeness crab remoulade, fresh oysters with horseradish, and grilled sanddabs in a lemon sauce that was a little heavy on the thyme—then decided to visit the aquarium and walk it all off. When I was a kid in Brooklyn, I spent a lot of my time at the aquarium on Coney Island, and, three decades later, there were few things a man could do sober that relaxed me as quickly and completely. I put the check on my MasterCard and followed Wave Street south and east to Prescott, then turned back down Cannery Row, the glittering bay on my right, the pale blue autumn sky stretched out overhead like oil on canvas.

I close my eyes, and that afternoon isn't something that happened three years ago, something I'm making sound like a goddamn travelogue. I close my eyes, and it's happening now, for the first time, and there she is, sitting alone on a long bench in front of the kelp forest exhibit, her thin face turned up to the high, swaying canopy behind the glass, the dapple of fish and seaweed shadows drifting back and forth across her features. I recognize her, and that surprises me, because I've only seen her face on television and in magazine photos and on the dust jacket of the book she wrote before she lost the job at Berkeley. She turns her head and smiles at me, the familiar way you smile at a friend, the way you smile at someone you've known all your life.

"You're in luck," she says. "It's almost time for them to feed the fish." And Jacova Angevine pats the bench next to her, indicating that I should sit down.

"I read your book," I say, taking a seat because I'm still too surprised to do anything else.

"Did you? Did you really?" and now she looks like she doesn't believe me, like I'm only saying that I've read her book to be polite, and from her expression I can tell that she thinks it's a little odd, that anyone would ever bother to try and flatter her.

"Yes," I tell her, trying too hard to sound sincere. "I did really. In fact, I read some of it twice."

"And why would you do a thing like that?"

"Truthfully?"

"Yes, truthfully."

Her eyes are the same color as the water trapped behind the thick panes of aquarium glass, the color of the November sunlight filtered through saltwater and kelp blades. There are fine lines at the corners of her mouth and beneath her eyes that make her look several years older than she is.

"Last summer, I was flying from New York to London, and there was a three-hour layover in Shannon. Your book was all I'd brought to read."

"That's terrible," she says, still smiling, and turns to face the big tank again. "Do you want your money back?"

"It was a gift," I reply, which isn't true, and I have no idea why I'm lying to her. "An ex-girlfriend gave it to me for my birthday."

"Is that why you left her?"

"No, I left her because she thought I drank too much, and I thought she drank too little."

"Are you an alcoholic?" Jacova Angevine asks, as casually as if she were asking me whether I liked milk in my coffee or if I took it black.

"Well, some people say I'm headed in that direction," I tell her. "But I did enjoy the book, honest. It's hard to believe they fired you for writing it. I mean, that people get fired for writing books." But I know that's a lie, too; I'm not half that naive, and it's not at all difficult to understand how or why *Waking Leviathan* ended Jacova Angevine's career as an academic. A reviewer for *Nature* called it "the most confused and preposterous example of bad history wedding bad science since the Velikovsky affair."

"They didn't fire me for writing it," she says. "They politely asked me to resign because I'd seen fit to publish it."

"Why didn't you fight them?"

Her smile fades a little, and the lines around her mouth seem to grow the slightest bit more pronounced. "I don't come here to talk about the book, or my unfortunate employment history," she says.

I apologize, and she tells me not to worry about it.

A diver enters the tank, matte-black neoprene trailing a rush of silver bubbles, and most of the fish rise expectantly to meet him or her, a riot of kelp bass and sleek leopard sharks, sheephead and rockfish and species I don't recognize. She doesn't say anything else, too busy watching the feeding, and I sit there beside her, at the bottom of a pretend ocean.

I open my eyes. There are only the words on the screen in front of me.

I didn't see her again for the better part of a year. During that time, as my work sent me back to Pakistan, and then to Germany and Israel, I reread her book. I also read some of the articles and reviews, and a brief online interview that she'd given Whitley Strieber's *Unknown Country* website. Then I tracked down an article on Inuit archaeology that she'd written for *Fate* and wondered at what point Jacova Angevine had decided that there was no going back, nothing left to lose and so no reason not to allow herself to become part of the murky, strident world of fringe believers and UFO buffs, conspiracy theorists, and paranormal "investigators" that seemed so eager to embrace her as one of its own.

And I wondered, too, if perhaps she might have been one of them from the start.

— 3 —

I woke up this morning from a long dream of storms and drowning and lay in bed, very still, sizing up my hangover and staring at the sagging, water-stained ceiling of my motel room. And I finally admitted to myself that this isn't going to be what the paper has hired me to write. I don't think I'm even trying to write it for them anymore. They want the dirt, of course, and I've never been shy about digging holes. I've spent the last twenty years as a shovel-for-hire. I don't think it matters that I may have loved her, or that a lot of this dirt is mine. I can't pretend that I'm acting out of nobility of soul or loyalty or even some selfish, belated concern for my own dingy reputation. I would write exactly what they want me to write if I could. If I knew how. I need the money. I haven't worked for the last five months, and my savings are almost gone.

But if I'm not writing it for them, if I've abandoned all hope of a paycheck at the other end of this thing, why the hell then am I still sitting here typing? Am I making a confession? Bless me, Father, I can't forget? Do I believe it's something I can puke up like a sour belly full of whiskey, that writing it all down will make the nightmares stop or make it any easier for me to get through the days? I sincerely hope I'm not as big a fool as that. Whatever else I may be, I like to think that I'm not an idiot.

I don't know why I'm writing this, whatever this turns out to be. Maybe it's only a very long-winded suicide note.

Last night I watched the tape again.

I have all three versions with me—the cut that's still being hawked over the Internet, the one that ends right after the ROV was hit, before the lights came back on; the cut that MBARI released to the press and the scientific community in response to the version circulating online; and I have the "raw" footage, the copy I bought from a robotics technician who claimed to have been aboard the *R/V Western Flyer* the day that the incident occurred. I paid him two thousand dollars for it, and the kid swore to both

its completeness and authenticity. I knew that I wasn't the first person to whom he'd sold the tape. I'd heard about it from a contact in the chemistry department at UC Irvine. I was never sure exactly how she'd caught wind of it, but I gathered that the tech was turning a handsome little profit peddling his contraband to anyone willing to pony up the cash.

We met at a Motel 6 in El Cajon, and I played it all the way through before I handed him the money. He sat with his back to the television while I watched the tape, rewound, and started it over again.

"What the hell are you doing?" he asked, literally wringing his hands and gazing anxiously at the heavy drapes. I'd pulled them shut after hooking up the rented VCR that I'd brought with me, but a bright sliver of afternoon sunlight slipped in between them and divided his face down the middle. "Jesus, man. You think it's not gonna be the exact same thing every time? You think if you keep playing it over and over it's gonna come out any different?"

I've watched the tape more times than I can count, a couple hundred, at least, and I still think that's a good goddamned question.

"So why didn't MBARI release this?" I asked the kid, and he laughed and shook his head.

"Why the fuck do you think?" he replied.

He took my money, reminded me again that we'd never met, and that he'd deny everything if I attempted to finger him as my source. Then he got back into his ancient, wheezy VW Microbus and drove off, leaving me sitting there with an hour and a half of unedited colour video recorded somewhere along the bottom of the Monterey Canyon. Everything the ROV *Tiburon II*'s starboard camera had seen (the port pan-and-tilt unit was malfunctioning that day), twenty miles out and three kilometers down, and from the start I understood it was the closest I was ever likely to come to an answer, and that it was also only a different and far more terrible sort of question.

Last night I got drunk, more so than usual, a *lot* more so than usual, and watched it for the first time in almost a month. But I turned the sound on the television down all the way and left the lights burning.

Even drunk, I'm still a coward.

The ocean floor starkly illuminated by the ROV's six 480-watt HMI lights, revealing a velvet carpet of gray-brown sediment washed out from Elkhorn Slough and all the other sloughs and rivers emptying into the bay. And even at this depth, there are signs of life: brittlestars and crabs cling to the shit-colored rocks, sponges and sea cucumbers, the sinuous, smooth bodies of big-eyed rattails. Here and there, dark outcroppings jut from the ooze like bone from the decaying flesh of a leper.

My asshole editor would laugh out loud at that last simile, would probably take one look at it and laugh and then say something like, "If I'd wanted fucking purple I'd have bought a goddamn pot of violets." But my asshole editor hasn't seen the tape I bought from the tech.

My asshole editor never met Jacova Angevine, never listened to her talk, never fucked her, never saw the scars on her back or the fear in her eyes.

The ROV comes to a rocky place where the seafloor drops away suddenly, and it hesitates, responding to commands from the control room of the *R/V Western Flyer.* A moment or two later, the steady fall of marine snow becomes so heavy that it's difficult to see much of anything through the light reflecting off the whitish particles of sinking detritus. And sitting there on the floor between the foot of the bed and the television, I almost reached out and touched the screen.

Almost.

"It's a little bit of everything," I heard Jacova say, though she never actually said anything of the sort to me. "Silt, phytoplankton and zooplankton, soot, mucus, diatoms, fecal pellets, dust, grains of sand and clay, radioactive fallout, pollen, sewage. Some of it's even interplanetary dust particles. Some of it fell from the stars."

And *Tiburon II* lurches and glides forward a few feet, then slips cautiously over the precipice, beginning the slow descent into this new and unexpected abyss.

"We'd been over that stretch more than a dozen times, at least," Natalie Billington, chief ROV pilot for *Tiburon II*, told a CNN correspondent after the internet version of the tape first made the news. "But that drop-off wasn't on any of the charts. We'd always missed it somehow. I know that isn't a very satisfying answer, but it's a big place down there. The canyon is over two hundred miles long. You miss things."

For a while — exactly 15.34 seconds — there's only the darkness and marine snow and a few curious or startled fish. According to MBARI, the ROV's vertical speed during this part of the dive is about thirty-five meters per minute, so by the time it finds the bottom again, depth has increased by some five hundred and twenty-five feet. The seafloor comes into view again, and there's not so much loose sediment here, just a jumble of broken boulders, and it's startling how clean they are, almost completely free of the usual encrustations and muck. There are no sponges or sea cucumbers to be seen, no starfish, and even the omnipresent marine snow has tapered off to only a few stray, drifting flecks. And then the wide, flat rock that is usually referred to as "the Delta stone" comes into view. And this isn't like the face on Mars or Von Daniken seeing ancient astronauts on Mayan artifacts. The lowercase δ carved into the slab is unmistakable. The edges are so sharp, so clean that it might have been done yesterday.

The *Tiburon II* hovers above the Delta stone, spilling light into this lightless place, and I know what's coming next, so I sit very still and count off the seconds in my head. When I've counted to thirty-eight, the view from the ROV's camera pans violently to the right, signaling the portside impact, and an instant later there's only static, white noise, the twelve-second gap in the tape during which the camera was still running, but no longer recording.

I counted to eleven before I switched off the television, and then sat listening to the wind, and the waves breaking against the beach, waiting for my heart to stop racing and the sweat on my face and palms to dry. When I was sure that I wasn't going to be sick, I pressed EJECT and the VCR spat out the tape. I returned it to its navy-blue plastic case and sat smoking and drinking, helpless to think of anything but Jacova.

— 4 —

Jacova Angevine was born and grew up in her father's big Victorian house in Salinas, only a couple of blocks from the birthplace of John Steinbeck. Her mother died when she was eight. Jacova had no siblings, and her closest kin, paternal and maternal, were all back east in New Jersey and Pennsylvania and Maryland. In 1960, her parents relocated to California, just a few months after they were married, and her father took a job teaching high-school English in Castroville. After six months, he quit that job and took another, with only slightly better pay, in the town of Soledad. Though he'd earned a doctorate in comparative literature from Columbia, Theo Angevine seemed to have no particular academic ambitions. He'd written several novels while in college, though none of them had managed to find a publisher. In 1969, his wife five months pregnant with their daughter, he resigned from his position at Soledad High and moved north to Salinas, where he bought the old house on Howard Street with a bank loan and the advance from his first book sale, a mystery novel titled *The Man Who Laughed at Funerals* (Random House; New York).

To date, none of the three books that have been published about Jacova, the Open Door of Night sect, and the mass drownings off Moss Landing State Beach, have made more than a passing mention of Theo Angevine's novels. Elenore Ellis-Lincoln, in *Closing the Door: Anatomy of Hysteria* (Simon and Schuster; New York), for example, devotes only a single paragraph to them, though she gives Jacova's childhood an entire chapter. "Mr. Angevine's works received little critical attention, one way or the other, and his income from them was meager," Ellis-Lincoln writes. "Of the seventeen novels he published between 1969 and 1985, only two—*The Man Who Laughed for Funerals* [sic] and *Seven at Sunset*—are still in print. It is notable that the overall tone of the novels becomes significantly darker following his wife's death, but the books themselves never seem to have been more to the author than a sort of hobby. Upon his death, his daughter became the executor of his literary estate, such as it was."

Likewise, in *Lemming Cult* (The Overlook Press; New York), William L. West writes, "Her father's steady output of mystery and suspense potboilers must surely have been a curiosity of Jacova's childhood, but were never once mentioned in her own writings, including the five private journals found in a cardboard box in her bedroom closet. The novels themselves were entirely unremarkable, so far as I've been able to ascertain. Almost all are out of print and very difficult to find today. Even the catalog of the Silinas Public Library includes only a single copy each of *The Man Who Laughed at Funerals*, *Pretoria*, and *Seven at Sunset*."

During the two years I knew her, Jacova only mentioned her father's writing once that I can recall, and then only in passing, but she had copies of all his novels, a fact that I've never seen mentioned anywhere in print. I suppose it doesn't seem very significant, if you haven't bothered to read Theo Angevine's books. Since Jacova's death, I've read every one of them. It took me less than a month to track down copies of all seventeen, thanks largely to online booksellers, and even less time to read them. While William West was certainly justified in calling the novels "entirely unremarkable," even a casual examination reveals some distinctly remarkable parallels between the fiction of the father and the reality of the daughter.

I've spent the whole afternoon, the better part of the past five hours, on the preceding four paragraphs, trying to fool myself into believing that I can actually write *about* her as a journalist would write about her. That I can bring any degree of detachment or objectivity to bear. Of course, I'm wasting my time. After seeing the tape again, after almost allowing myself to watch *all* of it again, I think I'm desperate to put distance between myself and the memory of her. I should call New York and tell them that I can't do this, that they should find someone else, but after the mess I made of the Musharraf story, the agency would probably never offer me another assignment. For the moment, that still matters. It might not in another day or two, but it does for now.

Her father wrote books, books that were never very popular, and though they're neither particularly accomplished nor enjoyable, they might hold clues to Jacova's motivation and to her fate. And they might not. It's as simple and contradictory as that. Like everything surrounding the "Lemming Cult"—as the Open Door of Night has come to be known, as it has been labeled by people who find it easier to deal with tragedy and horror if there is an attendant note of the absurd—like everything else about *her,* what seems meaningful one moment will seem irrelevant the next. Or maybe that's only the way it appears to me. Maybe I'm asking too much of the clues.

Excerpt from *Pretoria*, pp. 164-165; Ballantine Books, 1979:

> Edward Horton smiled and tapped the ash from his cigar into the large glass ashtray on the table. "I don't like the sea," he said and nodded at the window. "Frankly, I can't even stand the sound of it. Gives me nightmares."
>
> I listened to the breakers, not taking my eyes off the fat man and the thick gray curlicues of smoke arranging and rearranging themselves around his face. I'd always found the sound of waves to have a

welcomed tranquilizing effect upon my nerves and wondered which one of Horton's innumerable secrets was responsible for his loathing of the sea. I knew he'd done a stint in the Navy during Korea, but I was also pretty sure he'd never seen combat.

"How'd you sleep last night?" I asked, and he shook his head.

"For shit," he replied and sucked on his cigar.

"Then maybe you should think about getting a room farther inland."

Horton coughed and jabbed a pudgy finger at the window of the bungalow. "Don't think I wouldn't, if the choice were mine to make. But she wants me here. She wants me sitting right here, waiting on her, night and day. She knows I hate the ocean."

"What the hell," I said, reaching for my hat, tired of his company and the stink of his smoldering Macanudo. "You know where to reach me, if you change your mind. Don't let the bad dreams get you down. They ain't nothing but that, bad dreams."

"That's not enough?" he asked, and I could tell from his expression that Horton wished I'd stay a little longer, but I knew he'd never admit it. "Last night, goddamn people marching into the sea, marching over the sand in rows like the goddamn infantry. Must of been a million of them. What you think a dream like that means, anyway?"

"Horton, a dream like that don't mean jack shit," I replied. "Except maybe you need to lay off the spicy food before bedtime."

"You're always gonna be an asshole," he said, and I was forced to agree. He puffed his cigar, and I left the bungalow and stepped out into the salty Santa Barbara night.

Excerpt from *What the Cat Dragged In*, p. 231; Ballantine Books, 1980:

> Vicky had never told anyone about the dreams, just like she'd never told anyone about Mr. Barker or the yellow Corvette. The dreams were her secret, whether she wanted them or not. Sometimes they seemed almost wicked, shameful, sinful, like something she'd done that was against God, or at least against the law. She'd almost told Mr. Barker once, a year or so before she left Los Angeles. She'd gone so far as to broach the subject of mermaids, and then he'd snorted and laughed, so she'd thought better of it.
>
> "You got some strange notions in that head of yours," he'd said. "Someday, you're gonna have to grow out of crap like that, if you want people round here to start taking you seriously."
>
> So she kept it all to herself. Whatever the dreams meant or didn't mean, it wasn't anything she would ever be able to explain or confess. Sometimes, nights when she couldn't sleep, she lay in bed staring at the ceiling, thinking about the ruined castles beneath the waves and beautiful, drowned girls with seaweed tangled in their hair.

Excerpt from *The Last Loan Shark of Bodega Bay*, pp. 57-59; Bantam Books, 1982:

> "This was way the hell back in the fifties," Foster said and lit another cigarette. His hands were shaking and he kept looking over his shoulder. "Fifty-eight, right, or maybe early fifty-nine. I know Eisenhower was still president, though I ain't precisely sure of the year. But I was still stuck in Honolulu, right, still hauling

lousy tourists around the islands in the Saint Chris so they could fish and snap pictures of goddamn Kilauea and what have you. The boat was on its last leg, but she'd still get you where you were goin', if you knew how to slap her around."

"What's this got to do with Winkie Anderson and the girl?" I asked, making no effort to hide my impatience.

"Jesus, Frank, I'm getting to it. You want to hear this thing or not? I swear, you come around here asking the big questions, expecting the what's-what, you can at least keep your trap shut and listen."

"I don't have all night, that's all."

"Yeah, well, who the hell does, why don't you tell me that? Anyway, like I was saying, back about fifty-nine, and we was out somewhere off the north shore of Molokai. Old Coop was fishing the thousand fathom line, and Jerry—you remember Jerry O'Neil, right?"

"No," I said, eyeing the clock above the bar.

"Well, whatever. Jerry O'Neil was mouthing off about a twelve-hundred pounder, this big-ass marlin some Mexican businessman from Tijuana had up and hooked just a few weeks before. Fish even made the damn papers, right. Anyway, Jerry said the Mexican was bad news and we should keep a sharp eye out for him. Said he was a regular Jonah."

"But you just said he caught a twelve-hundred pound marlin."

"Yeah, sure. He could haul in the fish, this chunt son of a bitch, but he was into some sort of Spanish voodoo shit and had these gold coins he'd toss over the side of the boat every five or ten minutes. Like goddamn clockwork, he'd check his watch and toss

> out a coin. Gold doubloons or some shit, I don't know what they were. It was driving Coop crazy, 'cause it wasn't enough the Mexican had to do this thing with the coins, he was mumbling some sort of shit non-stop. Coop kept telling him to shut the hell up, people was trying to fish, but this guy, he just keeps mumbling and tossing coins and pulling in the fish. I finally got a look at one of those doubloons, and it had something stamped on one side looked like a damn octopus, and on the other side was this star like a pentagram. You know, those things witches and warlocks use."
>
> "Foster, this is crazy bullshit. I have to be in San Francisco at seven-thirty in the morning." I waved to the bartender and put two crumpled fives and a one on the bar in front of me.
>
> "You ever head of the Momma Hydra, Frank? That's who this chunt said he was praying to."
>
> "Call me when you run out of bullshit," I said. "And I don't have to tell you, Detective Burke won't be half as understanding as I am."
>
> "Jesus, Frank. Hold up a goddamn second. It's just the way I tell stories, right. You know that. I start at the beginning. I don't leave stuff out."

These are only a few examples of what anyone will find, if he or she should take the time to look. There are many more, I assure you. The pages of my copies of Theo Angevine's novels are scarred throughout with yellow highlighter.

And everything leaves more questions than answers.

You make of it what you will. Or you don't. I suppose that a Freudian might have a proper field day with this stuff. Whatever I knew about Freud I forgot before I was even out of college. It would be comforting, I suppose, if I could dismiss Jacova's fate as the end result of some overwhelming Oedipal hysteria, the ocean cast here as that Great Ur-Mother savior-being who finally opens up to offer release and forgiveness in death and dissolution.

— 5 —

I begin to walk down some particular, perhaps promising avenue and then, inevitably, I turn and run, tail tucked firmly between my legs. My memories. The MBARI video. Jacova and her father's whodunits. I scratch the surface and then pull my hand back to be sure that I haven't lost a fucking finger. I mix metaphors the way I've been mixing tequila and scotch.

If, as William Burroughs wrote, "Language is a virus from outer space," then what the holy hell were you supposed to be, Jacova?

An epidemic of the collective unconscious. The black plague of belief. A vaccine for cultural amnesia, she might have said. And so we're right back to Velikovsky, who wrote, "Human beings, rising from some catastrophe, bereft of memory of what had happened, regarded themselves as created from the dust of the earth. All knowledge about the ancestors, who they were and in what interstellar space they lived, was wiped away from the memory of the few survivors."

I'm drunk, and I'm not making any sense at all. Or merely much too little sense to matter. Anyway, you'll want to pay attention to this part. It's sort of like the ghost story within the ghost story within the ghost story, the hard nugget at the unreachable heart of my heart's infinitely regressing babooshka, matryoshka, matrioska, matreshka, babushka. It might even be the final straw that breaks the camel of my mind.

Remember, I am wasted, and so that last inexcusable paragraph may be forgiven. Or it may not.

"When I become death, death is the seed from which I grow." Burroughs said that, too. Jacova, you will be an orchard. You will be a swaying kelp forest. There's a log in the hole in the bottom of the sea with your name on it.

Yesterday afternoon, puking sick of looking at these four dingy fucking walls, I drove down to Monterey, to the warehouse on Pierce Street. The last time I was there, the cops still hadn't taken down all the yellow CRIME SCENE–DO NOT CROSS tape. Now there's only a great big FOR SALE sign and an even bigger NO TRESPASSING sign. I wrote the name and number of the realty company on the back of a book of matches. I want to ask them what they'll be telling prospective buyers about the building's history. Word is the whole block is due to be rezoned next year, and soon those empty buildings will be converted to lofts and condos. Gentrification abhors a void.

I parked in an empty lot down the street from the warehouse, hoping that no one happening by would notice me, hoping, in particular, that any passing police would not notice me. I walked quickly, without running, because running is suspicious and inevitably draws the attention of those who *watch* for suspicious things. I was not so drunk as I might have been, not even so drunk as I *should* have been, and I tried to keep my mind occupied by noting the less significant details of the street, the sky, the weather. The litter caught in the weeds and gravel — cigarette butts, plastic soft-drink bottles (I recall Pepsi, Coke, and Mountain Dew), paper bags and cups from fast-food restaurants (McDonalds, Del Taco, KFC), broken glass, unrecognizable bits of metal, a rusted Oregon license plate. The sky was painfully blue, the blue of nausea, with only very high cirrus clouds to spoil that suffocating pastel heaven. There were no other cars parked along the street, and no living things that I noticed. There were a couple of garbage dumpsters, a stop sign, and a great pile of cardboard boxes that had been soaked by rain enough times it was difficult to tell exactly where one ended and another began. There was a hubcap.

When I finally reached the warehouse—the warehouse become a temple to half-remembered gods become a crime scene, now on its way to becoming something else—I ducked down the narrow alley that separates it from the abandoned Monterey Peninsula Shipping and Storage Building (established 1924). There'd been a door around that way with an unreliable lock. If I was lucky, I thought, no one would have noticed, or if they had noticed, wouldn't have bothered fixing it. My heart was racing and I was dizzy (I tried hard to blame that on the sickening color of the sky) and there was a metallic taste in the back of my mouth, like a freshly filled tooth.

It was colder in the alley than it had been out on Pierce, the sun having already dropped low enough in the west that the alley must have been in shadow for some time. Perhaps it is always in shadow and never truly warm there. I found the side door exactly as I'd hoped to find it, and three or four minutes of jiggling about with the wobbly brass knob was enough to coax it open. Inside, the warehouse was dark and even colder than the alley, and the air stank of mould and dust, bad memories and vacancy. I stood in the doorway a moment or two, thinking of hungry rats and drunken bums, delirious crack addicts wielding lead pipes, the webs of poisonous spiders. Then I took a deep breath and stepped across the threshold, out of the shadows and into a more decided blackness, a more definitive chill, and all those mundane threats dissolved. Everything slipped from my mind except Jacova Angevine, and her followers (if that's what you'd call them) dressed all in white, and the thing I'd seen on the altar the one time I'd come here when this had been a temple of the Open Door of Night.

I asked her about that thing once, a few weeks before the end, the last night that we spent together. I asked where it had come from, who had made it, and she lay very still for a while, listening to the surf or only trying to decide which answer would satisfy me. In the moonlight through the hotel window, I thought she might have been smiling, but I wasn't sure.

"It's very old," she said, eventually. By then I'd almost drifted off to sleep and had to shake myself awake again. "No one alive remembers who *made* it," Jacova continued. "But I don't think that matters, only that it was made."

"It's fucking hideous," I mumbled sleepily. "You know that, don't you?"

"Yeah, but so is the Crucifixion. So are bleeding statues of the Virgin Mary and images of Kali. So are the animal-headed gods of the Egyptians."

"Yeah, well, I don't bow down to any of them, either," I replied, or something to that effect.

"The divine is always abominable," she whispered and rolled over, turning her back to me.

Just a moment ago I was in the warehouse on Pierce Street, wasn't I? And now I'm in bed with the Prophet from Salinas. But I will not despair, for there is no need here to stay focused, to adhere to some restrictive illusion of the linear narrative. It's coming. It's been coming all along. As Job Foster said in Chapter Four of *The Last Loan Shark of Bodega Bay*, "It's just the way I tell stories, right. You know that. I start at the beginning. I don't leave stuff out."

That's horseshit, of course. I suspect luckless Job Foster knew it was horseshit, and I suspect that I know it's horseshit, too. It is not the task of the writer to "tell all," or even to decide what to leave in, but to decide what to leave *out*. Whatever remains, that meager sum of this profane division, that's the bastard chimera we call a "story." I am not building, but cutting away. And all stories, whether advertised as truth or admitted falsehoods, are fictions, cleft from any objective facts by the aforementioned action of cutting away. A pound of flesh. A pile of sawdust. Discarded chips of Carrara marble. And what's left over.

A damned man in an empty warehouse.

I left the door standing open, because I hadn't the nerve to shut myself up in that place. And I'd already taken a few steps inside, my shoes crunching loudly on shards of glass from a broken window, grinding glass to dust, when I remembered the Maglite hidden inside my jacket. But the glare of the flashlight did nothing much to make the darkness any less stifling, nothing much at all but remind me of the blinding white beam of *Tiburon II*'s big HMI rig, shining out across the silt at the bottom of the canyon. *Now*, I thought, *at least I can see anything, if there's anything to see*, and immediately some other, less familiar thought-voice demanded to know why the hell I'd want to. The door had opened into a narrow corridor, mint-green concrete walls and a low concrete ceiling, and I followed it a short distance to its end—no more than thirty feet, thirty feet at the most—past empty rooms that might once have been offices, to an unlocked steel door marked in faded orange letters, EMPLOYEES ONLY.

"It's an empty warehouse," I whispered, breathing the words aloud. "That's all, an empty warehouse." I knew it wasn't the truth, not anymore, not by a long sight, but I thought that maybe a lie could be more comforting than the comfortless illumination of the Maglite in my hand. Joseph Campbell wrote, "Draw a circle around a stone and the stone will become an incarnation of mystery." Something like that. Or it was someone else said it and I'm misremembering. The point is, I knew that Jacova had drawn a circle around that place, just as she'd drawn a circle about herself, just as her father had somehow drawn a circle about her—

Just as she'd drawn a circle around me.

The door wasn't locked, and beyond it lay the vast, deserted belly of the building, a flat plain of cement marked off with steel support beams. There was a little sunlight coming in through the many small windows along the east and west walls, though not as much as I'd expected, and it seemed weakened, diluted by the musty air. I played the Maglite back and forth across the floor at my feet and saw that someone had painted over all the elaborate, colorful designs put there by the Open Door of Night. A thick gray latex wash to cover the intricate interweave of lines, the lines that she believed would form a bridge, a *conduit*—that was the word that she'd used. Everyone's seen photographs of that floor, although I've yet to see any that do it justice. A *yantra*. A labyrinth. A writhing, tangled mass of sea creatures straining for a distant black sun. Hindi and Mayan and Chinook symbols. The precise contour lines of a topographic map of Monterey Canyon. Each of these things and *all* of these things, simultaneously. I've heard that there's an anthropologist at Berkeley who's writing a book about that floor. Perhaps she will publish photographs that manage to communicate its awful magnificence. Perhaps it would be better if she doesn't.

Perhaps someone should put a bullet through her head.

People said the same thing about Jacova Angevine. But assassination is almost always unthinkable to moral, thinking men until *after* a holocaust has come and gone.

I left that door open, as well, and walked slowly towards the center of the empty warehouse, towards the place where the altar had been, the spot where that divine abomination of Jacova's had rested on folds of velvet the color of a massacre. I held the Maglite gripped so tightly that the fingers of my right hand had begun to go numb.

Behind me, there was a scuffling, gritty sort of noise that might have been footsteps, and I spun about, tangling my feet and almost falling on my ass, almost dropping the flashlight. The child was standing maybe ten or fifteen feet away from me, and I could see that the door leading back to the alley had been closed. She couldn't have been more than nine or ten years old, dressed in ragged jeans and a T-shirt smeared with mud, or what looked like mud in the half light of the warehouse. Her short hair might have been blonde, or light brown, it was hard to tell. Most of her face was lost in the shadows.

"You're too late," she said.

"Jesus *Christ*, kid, you almost scared the holy shit out of me."

"You're too late," she said again.

"Too late for what? Did you follow me in here?"

"The gates are shut now. They won't open again, for you or anyone else."

I looked past her at the door I'd left open, and she looked back that way, too.

"Did you close that door?" I asked her. "Did it ever occur to you that I might have left it open for a reason?"

"I waited as long I dared," she replied, as though that answered my question, and turned to face me again.

I took one step towards her, then, or maybe two, and stopped. And at that moment, I experienced the sensation or sensations that mystery and horror writers, from Poe on down to Theo Angevine, have labored to convey—the almost painful prickling as the hairs on the back of my neck and along my arms and legs stood erect, the cold knot in the pit of my stomach, the goose across my grave, a loosening in my bowels and bladder, the tightening of my scrotum. My blood ran cold. Drag out all the fucking clichés and there's still nothing that comes within a mile of what I felt standing there, looking down at that girl, her looking up at me, the feeble light from the windows glinting off her eyes.

Looking into her face, I felt *dread* as I'd never felt it before. Not in war zones with air-raid sirens blaring, not during interviews conducted with the muzzle of a pistol pressed to my temple or the small of my back. Not waiting for the results of a biopsy after the discovery of a peculiar mole. Not even the day she led them into the sea, and I sat watching it all on fucking CNN from a bar in Brooklyn.

And suddenly I knew that the girl hadn't followed me in from the alley, or closed the door, that she'd been here all along. I also knew that a hundred coats of paint wouldn't be enough to undo Jacova's labyrinth.

"You shouldn't be here," the girl said, her minotaur's voice lost and faraway and regretful.

"Then where *should* I be?" I asked, and my breath fogged in air gone as frigid as the dead of winter, or the bottom of the sea.

"All the answers were here," she replied. "Everything that you're asking yourself, the things that keep you awake, that are driving you insane. All the questions you're putting into that computer of yours. I offered all of it to you."

And now there was a sound like water breaking against stone, and something heavy and soft and wet, dragging itself across the concrete floor, and I thought of the thing from the altar, Jacova's Mother Hydra, that corrupt and bloated Madonna of the abyss, its tentacles and anemone tendrils and black, bulging squid eyes, the tubeworm proboscis snaking from one of the holes where its face should have been.

Mighty, undying daughter of Typhaôn and serpentine Ecidna—Υδρα Λερναια, *Urda Lernaia, gluttonous whore of all the lightless worlds, bitch bride and concubine of Father Dagon, Father Kraken*—

I smelled rot and mud, saltwater and dying fish.

"You have to go now," the child said urgently, and she held out a hand as though she meant to show me the way. Even in the gloom, I could see the barnacles and sea lice nestled in the raw flesh of her palm. "You are a splinter in my soul, always. And she would drag you down to finish my own darkness."

And then the girl was gone. She did not vanish, she was simply not *there* anymore. And those other sounds and odors had gone with her. There was nothing left behind but the silence and stink of any abandoned building, and the wind brushing against the windows and around the corners of the warehouse, and the traffic along roads in the world waiting somewhere beyond those walls.

— 6 —

I know *exactly* how all this shit sounds. Don't think that I don't. It's just that I've finally ceased to care.

— 7 —

Yesterday, two days after my trip to the warehouse, I watched the MBARI tape again. This time, when it reached the twelve-second gap, when I'd counted down to eleven, I continued on to twelve, and I didn't switch the television off, and I didn't look away. Surely, I've come too far to allow myself that luxury. I've seen so goddamn much—I've seen so much that there's no reasonable excuse for looking away, because there can't be anything left that's more terrible than what has come before.

And, besides, it was nothing that I hadn't seen already.

Orpheus's mistake wasn't that he turned and looked back towards Eurydice and Hell, but that he ever thought he could *escape*. Same with Lot's wife. Averting our eyes does not change the fact that we are marked.

After the static, the picture comes back and at first it's just those boulders, same as before, those boulders that ought to be covered with silt and living things—the remains of living things, at least—but aren't. Those strange, clean boulders. And the lines and angles carved deeply into them that cannot be the result of any natural geological or biological process, the lines and angles that can be nothing but what Jacova said they were. I think of fragments of the Parthenon, or some other shattered Greek or Roman temple, the chiseled ornament of an entablature or pediment. I'm seeing something that was *done*, something that was consciously fashioned, not something that simply happened. The *Tiburon II* moves forward very slowly, because the blow before the gap has taken out a couple of the port thrusters. It creeps forward tentatively, floating a few feet above the seafloor, and now the ROV's lights have begun to dim and flicker.

After the gap, I know that there's only 52.2 seconds of video remaining before the starboard camera shuts down for good. Less than a minute, and I sit there on the floor of my hotel room, counting—one-one thousand, two-two thousand—and I don't take my eyes off the screen.

The MBARI robotics tech is dead, the nervous man who sold me—and whoever else was buying—his black-market dub of the videotape. The story made the Channel 46 evening news last night and was second page in the *Monterey Herald* this morning. The coroner's office is calling it a suicide. I don't know what else they would call it. He was found hanging from the lowest limb of a sycamore tree, not far from the Moss Landing docks, both his wrists slashed nearly to the bone. He was wearing a necklace of *Loligo* squid strung on baling wire. A family member has told the press that he had a history of depression.

Twenty-three seconds to go.

Almost two miles down, *Tiburon II* is listing badly to starboard, and then the ROV bumps against one of the boulders and the lights stop flickering and seem to grow a little brighter. The vehicle appears to pause, as though considering its next move. The day he sold me the tape, the MBARI tech said that a part of the toolsled had wedged itself into the rubble. He told me it took the crew of the *R/V Western Flyer* more than two hours to maneuver the sub free. Two hours of total darkness at the bottom of the canyon, after the lights and the cameras died.

Eighteen seconds.

Sixteen.

This time it'll be different, I think, like a child trying to wish away a beating. *This time, I'll see the trick of it, the secret interplay of light and shadow, the hows and whys of a simple optical illusion—*

Twelve.

Ten.

And the first time, I thought that I was only seeing something carved into the stone or part of a broken sculpture. The gentle curve of a hip, the tapering line of a leg, the twin swellings of small breasts. A nipple the color of granite.

Eight.

But there's her face—and there's no denying that it's *her* face—Jacova Angevine, her face at the bottom of the sea, turned up towards the surface, towards the sky and Heaven beyond the weight of all that black, black water.

Four.

I bite my lip so hard that I taste blood. It doesn't taste so different from the ocean.

Two.

She opens her eyes, and they are *not* her eyes, but the eyes of some marine creature adapted to that perpetual night. The soulless eyes of an anglerfish or gulper eel, eyes like matching pools of ink, and something darts from her parted lips—

And then there's only static, and I sit staring into the salt-and-pepper roar.

All the answers were here. Everything that you're asking yourself . . . I offered all of it to you.

Later—an hour or only five minutes—I pressed EJECT and the cassette slid obediently from the VCR. I read the label, aloud, in case I'd read it wrong every single time before, in case the timestamp on the video might have been mistaken. But it was the same as always, the day before Jacova waited on the beach at Moss Landing for the supplicants of the Open Door of Night. The day before she led them into the sea. The day before she drowned.

I close my eyes.

And she's here again, as though she never left.

She whispers something dirty in my ear, and her breath smells like sage and toothpaste.

The protestors are demanding that the Monterey Bay Aquarium Research Institute (MBARI) end its ongoing exploration of the submarine canyon immediately. The twenty-five mile long canyon, they claim, is a sacred site that is being desecrated by scientists. Jacova Angevine, former Berkeley professor and leader of the controversial Open Door of Night cult, compares the launching of the new submersible Tiburon II *to the ransacking of the Egyptian pyramids by grave robbers.* (*San Francisco Chronicle*)

I tell her that I have to go to New York, that I have to take this assignment, and she replies that maybe it's for the best. I don't ask her what she means; I can't imagine that it's important.

And she kisses me.

Later, when we're done, and I'm too exhausted to sleep, I lie awake, listening to the sea and the small, anxious sounds she makes in her dreams.

The bodies of fifty-three men and women, all of whom may have been part of a religious group known as the Open Door of Night, have been recovered following Wednesday's drownings near Moss Landing, CA. Deputies have described the deaths as a mass suicide. The victims were all reported to be between 22 and 36 years old. Authorities fear that at least two dozen more may have died in the bizarre episode and recovery efforts continue along the coast of Monterey County. (CNN.com)

I close my eyes, and I'm in the old warehouse on Pierce Street again; Jacova's voice thunders from the PA speakers mounted high on the walls around the cavernous room. I'm standing in the shadows all the way at the back, apart from the true believers, apart from the other reporters and photographers and camera men who have been invited here. Jacova leans into the microphone, angry and ecstatic and beautiful—*terrible*, I think—and that hideous carving is squatting there on its altar beside her. There are candles and smoldering incense and bouquets of dried seaweed, conch shells and dead fish, carefully arranged about the base of the statue.

"We can't remember where it began," she says, "where *we* began," and they all seem to lean into her words like small boats pushing against a violent wind. "We can't remember, of course we can't remember, and they don't want us to even *try*. They're afraid, and in their fear they cling desperately to the darkness of their ignorance. They would have us do the same, and then we would never recall the garden nor the gate, would never look upon the faces of the great fathers and mothers who have returned to the deep."

None of it seems the least bit real, not the ridiculous things that she's saying, or all the people dressed in white, or the television crews. This scene is not even as substantial as a nightmare. It's very hot in the warehouse, and I feel dizzy and sick and wonder if I can reach an exit before I vomit.

I close my eyes, and I'm sitting in a bar in Brooklyn, watching them wade into the sea, and I'm thinking, *Some son of a bitch is standing right there taping this and no one's trying to stop them, no one's lifting a goddamn finger.*

I blink, and I'm sitting in an office in Manhattan, and the people who write my checks are asking me questions I can't answer.

"Good god, you were fucking the woman, for Christ's sake, and you're sitting there telling me you had no *idea* whatsoever that she was planning this?"

"Come on. You had to have known *something*."

"They all worshipped some sort of prehistoric fish god, that's what I heard. No one's going to buy that you didn't see this coming—"

"People have a right to know. You still believe that, don't you?"

Answers are scarce in the mass suicide of a California cult, but investigators are finding clues to the deaths by logging onto the Internet and Web sites run by the cult's members. What they're finding is a dark and confusing side of the Internet, a place where bizarre ideas and beliefs are exchanged and gain currency. Police said they have gathered a considerable amount of information on the background of the group, known as the Open Door of Night, but that it may be many weeks before the true nature of the group is finally understood. (CNN.com)

And my clumsy hands move uncertainly across her bare shoulders, my fingertips brushing the chaos of scar tissue there, and she smiles for me.

On my knees in an alley, my head spinning, and the night air stinks of puke and saltwater.

"Okay, so I first heard about this from a woman I interviewed who knew the family," the man in the Radiohead T-shirt says. We're sitting on the patio of a bar in Pacific Grove, and the sun is hot and glimmers white off the bay. His name isn't important, and neither is the name of the bar. He's a student from LA, writing a book about the Open Door of Night, and he got my e-mail address from someone in New York. He has bad teeth and smiles too much.

"This happened back in '76, the year before Jacova's mother died. Her father, he'd take them down to the beach at Moss Landing two or three times every summer. He got a lot of his writing done out there. Anyway, apparently the kid was a great swimmer, like a duck to water, but her mother never let her to go very far out at that beach because there are these bad rip currents. Lots of people drown out there, surfers and shit."

He pauses and takes a couple of swallows of beer, then wipes the sweat from his forehead.

"One day, her mother's not watching, and Jacova swims too far out and gets pulled down. By the time the lifeguards get her back to shore, she's stopped breathing. The kid's turning blue, but they keep up the mouth-to-mouth and CPR and she finally comes around. They get Jacova to the hospital up in Watsonville and the doctors say she's fine, but they keep her for a few days anyhow, just for observation."

"She drowned," I say, staring at my own beer. I haven't taken a single sip. Beads of condensation cling to the bottle and sparkle like diamonds.

"Technically, yeah. She wasn't breathing. Her heart had stopped. But *that's* not the fucked-up part. While she's in Watsonville, she keeps telling her mother some crazy story about mermaids and sea monsters and demons, about these things trying to drag her down to the bottom of the sea and drown her and how it wasn't an undertow at all. She's terrified, convinced that they're still after her, these monsters. Her mother wants to call in a shrink, but her father says no, fuck that, the kid's just had a bad shock, she'll be fine. Then, the second night she's in the hospital, these two nurses turn up dead. A janitor found them in a closet just down the hall from Jacova's room. And here's the thing you're not gonna believe, but I've seen the death certificates and the autopsy reports and I swear to you this is the God's honest truth."

Whatever's coming next, I don't want to hear it. I know that I don't *need* to hear it. I turn my head and watch a sailboat out on the bay, bobbing about like a toy.

"They'd drowned, both of them. Their lungs were full of saltwater. Five miles from the goddamn ocean, but these two women drowned right there in a *broom closet*."

"And you're going to put this in your book?" I ask him, not taking my eyes of the bay and the little boat.

"Hell yeah," he replies. "I am. It fucking happened, man, just like I said, and I can prove it."

I close my eyes, shutting out the dazzling, bright day, and wish I'd never agreed to meet with him.

I close my eyes.

"Down there," Jacova whispers, "you will know nothing but peace, in her mansions, in the endless night of her coils."

We would be warm below the storm

In our little hideaway beneath the waves

I close my eyes. Oh god, I've closed my eyes.

She wraps her strong, suntanned arms tightly around me and takes me down, down, down, like the lifeless body of a child caught in an undertow. And I'd go with her, like a flash I'd go, if this were anything more than a dream, anything more than an infidel's sour regret, anything more than eleven thousand words cast like a handful of sand across the face of the ocean. I would go with her, because, like a stone that has become an incarnation of mystery, she has drawn a circle around me.

CAITLÍN R. KIERNAN is the author of eight novels, including the award-winning *Silk* and *Threshold*, along with *Low Red Moon*, *Daughter of Hounds*, and, most recently, *The Red Tree*. Her short fiction has been collected in *Tales of Pain and Wonder*; *From Weird and Distant Shores*; *To Charles Fort, With Love*; *Alabaster*; and *A is for Alien*. Two volumes of her erotica have been released—*Frog Toes and Tentacles* and *Tales from the Woeful Platypus*—with a third volume, *Confessions of a Five-Chambered Heart*, due out in 2010.

Kiernan lives in Providence, Rhode Island, with her partner, Kathryn.

KIERNAN SAYS: *As an avid reader of HPL since high school, I am pleased to have actually been called "H. P. Lovecraft's spiritual granddaughter" by more than one reviewer. I can easily name a great many authors who have had much more influence on me stylistically, but I think Lovecraft may have had the most influence in terms of theme. His cosmicism is evident in most of what I write, whether it's dark fantasy, science fiction, or erotica. The universe of my fiction is a distinctly Lovecraftian universe, in the fundamental insignificance of humanity, for example, and my recurring focus on deep time. Recently, I appeared in the documentary* Lovecraft: Fear of the Unknown, *and have been asked to be a Guest of Honor at the 2010 HPL Film Festival in Portland.*

MICHAEL CISCO

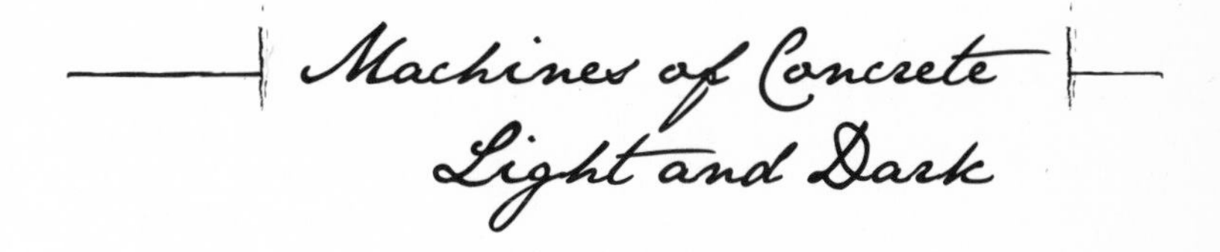

Machines of Concrete Light and Dark

THINGS ALWAYS SEEM closer together on a bad morning. I slept poorly last night, and now the relentless brilliance of the day makes my eyes smart and my face ache with squinting.

Just within the station doors I stop to adjust my bag where it is cutting into my shoulder and I notice at my feet a small piece of black plastic shaped like a capital L, and one end is frayed into a tuft of fibers. What did that come off of—or is it a complete thing?

I check the board and signs and walk hastily to meet my train. A glance to my right tells me that someone has fallen in step with me. I think, *it's Jeanie . . .* but she had one of those faces whose outlines vary so much from one angle to another that she could sometimes be hard to recognize. She always preferred to walk on my right and would keep her head turned to me in just that way, as if she were getting ready to rap me on the scalp with her chin. She's looking at me now with a superior expression, having crept up and fallen in with me, taking me unawares the way she used to do.

Not wanting to acknowledge her, a little frightened, and made blank-minded by surprise, I lower my eyes again on the tile floor ahead of my feet. It's perfectly flat. That would be a pretty pitiful bit of deception, but if it weren't for the weariness I wouldn't be subsiding into myself like this.

Defeated, I turn to her, and she halts with me.

"Jeanie?" I ask, trying to seem to verge on being pleasantly surprised, a fading part of me still en route to my train.

"I thought it was you," she says confidently, her lisp unchanged, her voice much lower now, the hair not much longer, the skin, if anything, paler, flaking a little by her eyes like I'd forgotten it did. She has a bag on her back, too. We always had looked more alike than different, even if she was taller.

"Where are you going?" she asks, a little imperious, looming over me.

I explain disjointedly. The names and places that I belong to now sound as bizarre as if I'd invented them, but they're everything I've loved and built around myself in the nine years since July, the pier or boathouse or whatever it was and the path back through the trees to the street and not looking back and not listening.

"My parents moved back into the old house. That's where I'm going now," she tells me. "Why don't you come along?"

"How long—?" I hear myself ask.

"Just a day. You can spend the night."

"All right," I say. "Sure."

Without smiling, she opens her arms and takes me in them. She is smiling when she releases me.

A thready, faltering sort of voice is chattering to me—it won't take too long, I suppose—I won't be missing anything, and actually I was going back a day early; I could spend the night and go on in the morning. The words skip along the adhesive surface of a black, silent, motionless body of refusal, and its familiar spirit hissing at me, telling me insistently to escape, even if that means turning on my heel and running from her.

The station is vast, the high ceiling above me crawls with a disembodied roar of announcements. Black clocks with shiny plastic faces spell out the time in white points. Cold air gushes from colossal, softly-whirring vents. Everything is new, and spotless, white tile, white plastic, white steel, white air-conditioning tubes, and all manner of gleaming sterility. The air is so cold and dry it hurts my eyes.

Jeanie points the way to her train. One moment it's far off in the distance, and the next moment it's directly in front of us, looking like a prostrate space rocket in a museum, glistening like ice. Its rounded windows and hatches are like frozen wafers of ink. Jeanie is in her clean element; she always hated feeling dirty and derived a great deal of pleasure from the exaggerated measures she took to keep herself clean.

"I think this train is new."

The words drop from my mouth like the lifeless inanities they are. There's something about Jeanie that utterly inhibits idle talk; I never could speak with her unguardedly. I had to watch what I said, vet it, and, as a rule, decide against saying it. It isn't that I wanted to avoid exasperating her with trivia; it's that there is something so relentlessly ultimate about her that I would feel like an ass no matter what I said, and consequently spoke as efficiently as possible.

She nods, looking at the silent train. The muttering under the white ceiling, which seems to hang above us like a luminous cloud, drones on, and somewhere an alarm is buzzing. Another train rumbles away from a nearby platform. Stepping through the hatch, an odor like hospital smell, and new plastic, and bleach, surrounds me.

I'm shocked to see a narrow black passageway in the car, lined with skinny doors of gleaming black acrylic. I was expecting to see rows of ordinary seats.

"Compartment 17C," Jeanie says. "17C."

Suddenly I feel a quick intensification of regret at what I'm doing, now that I know there are compartments instead of open seats and there will be no other people for me to turn to for respite. I didn't realize I would be so completely on my own with Jeanie.

I find a white plastic tab with 17C on it and turn the recessed steel lever, pull the door open, and step back awkwardly to make room for it as it swings out into the corridor. My bag gets caught in the doorway and I have to yank it this way and that behind me to get into the box. Throwing my bag up on the glinting steel rack over the seat, I turn and watch Jeanie coming in, getting jammed a bit and pulling herself free. She has always been taller. Her figure has filled out quite a bit since, much more than mine did, but she's still lean.

It's as acridly cool in the train as it was in the station. Jeanie turns her head toward the platform. Without a sound, the train glides forward, as if at her bidding. Adjusting my bag in the rack, the movement takes me by surprise, and I allow myself to fold onto the seat. The muttering has followed us into the train; the voices are so faint they can't possibly be making announcements—no one would hear. They seem to be murmuring amongst themselves.

Jeanie sits between me and the window, on my right. The train passes a succession of pillars that languidly stroke the station lights, already dimmed by the heavy tinting of the glass. She is looking at me, fixedly, with no expression. I pretend to be more curious about the view through the window than I am. The tunnel covers us like a black cape and we're alone together in a little cell of light, rolling along in the deep. My reflection blocks my view when I try to gaze out directly. I have to look around it, diagonally. Jeanie turns to glance out the window herself, and then becomes still, as if something interesting out there had arrested her attention.

"Darkness—do you ever wonder if darkness is something in itself, and more than just the absence of light?"

"Yes," I say, honestly.

Jeanie was always asking these kinds of questions, without any overture.

I go on, determined not to be cowed by her: "I think that, as a distinct physical sensation in its own right, it's probably no different from light. Just as positive."

Still looking out the window at the tunnel that is presumably conducting us up toward the surface, so that her face is a luminous membrane reflected there, she asks, "Do you think light can be negative?"

" . . . I suppose it could be," I say. "Let me think. It wou—it might be—like a kind of dazzle . . . "

"That's too much of something," she snaps in the old way, peremptory but calm. "I mean a palpable absence."

" . . . if there were no darkness for contrast."

Her tone stirs my defiance; I'm not going to let her have the old ascendancy over me.

"You said you think darkness can be positive as a sensation? I hadn't thought of that."

She smiles at me, as always, without opening her lips.

"It's a good answer, but do you think that a sensation has the same positive essence as an object does?"

"It's just as real," I say, spreading my hands.

"Do you think a sensation has as much reality as a physical object?"

"I don't know. I only say they're both real."

"Yes." She keeps her eyes all but riveted on mine, their focus expands to engulf my whole head. "Can a sensation be outside?"

"Outside the mind?"

I can feel her using me. Wisps of hair escape from the loose ponytail at her neck and waft toward me like gossamer antennae.

"Yes . . ." she draws it out, as if I were being slow.

"That depends," I say. "How would you tell?"

Her eyes slam shut.

"Right," she says briskly. "How would you tell? We should never have parted company. But perhaps this time apart has given us both a chance to learn useful things. We can teach each other."

A glimmer illuminates the walls of the tunnel and the next moment the cape is swept back on buildings that whirl like tops, and trees blackened by a fire spinning as they go by, fragments of daylight twinkle in their charred branches.

I'd known Jeanie since grammar school, and for years we'd been so severely close we'd sealed virtually everyone else out. Now she's asking me about the years of mine she's missed. She gets evasive, vague answers from me. I don't want her to make contact, even secondhand, with the life I lived after I broke with her, and I regret having let slip even the few details I had mentioned back at the station. I feel that I've spoken too freely. But she doesn't seem to be interested in the people I've met or the places I've been; I get the idea she's fishing for something in particular, having to do with abstract ideas.

I can no longer deny I have made a serious mistake.

We had been seated in the same group in second grade. In fourth grade, we hid behind the bungalows lining the lower playground, and I'd joked that she couldn't really be a djinni because she wasn't stuck in a bottle.

"There are all sorts of ways to be confined," she'd replied, a moment later.

Her tone, and her use of the word "confined," sounded precociously adult to me then, and I think that was the moment—the playground visible all around her head, the trees over us, the dark corky ground, dingy white wall of the bungalow, her thin form in shorts and a white t-shirt, hair pulled back as it is now—when I really understood that the strength of her intellect drove her into weird places. Whenever I met her, I was always cutting into a line of reflections that had begun long ago and moved from point to point according to a succession of unpredictable associations.

She was always lecturing me about something. Her father had been a professor, and she'd picked up some of his mannerisms. Adolescence brought us still closer because neither of us were interested in asinine giggling over boys. Jeanie had an affinity for spacious, air-conditioned caverns like museums, libraries, theatres, and train stations. We rode the trains, went exploring in my car, walked together under the stone pylons of the railway trestle that towered over a hundred feet above our heads: the arches cut into the pylons molded space into a tall corridor, like the nave of a ruined cathedral, or a passageway for giants, strewn with their litter, their condoms, their flattened refrigerator boxes, and marked with their graffiti and their urine.

July—when we'd gone to the park together.

There was a pier or a boathouse or something, I can't remember. A splintery old wooden relic by the water in the park. We'd been in there alone, looking out at the broad, green, tepid water, speculating about what invisible thing was causing the circles to spread on its surface. And she'd said something, I don't remember what, that sounded to me like a casual insult. It wasn't the first time that had happened. She often spoke harshly. She had an especially light touch when it came to subtle condescension. But this time I felt my patience completely give way. I was disgusted with her. That disgust grew and grew, was fed by, and opened onto, a long-sealed recess of silent resentment—and *fear.* The feelings showed themselves to me for what they were, then.

I started to walk, following the path through the trees that was the most direct way out of the park, seeing my way home like a map and route. Jeanie came hurrying after me, demanding to know why I'd left that way, without a word.

Turning, I repeated to her whatever it was she'd said. It was an afterthought; she'd said something, and added that I might understand if I were capable of it, something like that.

This made her impatient.

"I didn't mean *that,*" she drawled, rolling her eyes disdainfully. The gesture humanized her too much for her own good, and I felt strengthened. My anger outgrew my fear of her.

"I know," I replied calmly, "but it should have occurred to you—it should have mattered to you—that I might take it that way."

"Don't be stupid!"

"You should express yourself more carefully, Jean."

I didn't think I wanted . . .

I'd grown used to believing I didn't want anything more than to go on with her in the same way forever, and I realized later that that must have been precisely my reason for breaking it off.

Showing her my back, I walked unhurriedly down the path, thinking—is this what I want? Do I just break it all off, just like that? *Now?*

It seemed as though the bond between us had just happened to wear thin, and I had, for the moment, the strength to break it.

Am I really doing it?

I remember feeling her there in the silence behind me as if she were shouting at my back.

Is it happening? Is it?

—I am *doing it!*

For hours afterwards I had to keep on telling myself I'd done it, that I wouldn't go back, and that she wouldn't come after me, before I could believe in it. I pictured a massive, black guillotine blade, as big as a wall, slowly dropping down between us. And there to stay. There never was such a person, I told myself. She never existed. I drove her from my mind.

The sun through the smoky windowpanes gives off a sullen, solarized, leaden light that bursts and flashes over the dusty pines lining the tracks. The rails beneath us make a rheumatic hum, and Jeanie, the window at her back, is nearly a silhouette. That seems to make her more solid, the denseness with which she blocks the light.

Later, I'd heard from someone else who knew her that she'd checked herself into a hospital.

Behind her, rows of massive white globes and pyramids and tall white stacks, billowing clouds of brilliant white steam, float by faster and faster. Slender and lofty tubes tipped with orange fires trail streaks of heat-agitated air, like invisible banners trembling in the wind.

That muttering overhead is more like yammering now, almost like yelps of laughter. Then it cuts off, abruptly.

"God! It's been so long!" Jeanie says, her chin high. I look past the tendons in her neck to the fractured light sluicing by the glass.

The train accelerates to hypnotic speed. With a whisper, it seems to tear the world outside the window to pieces, as if the land and trees and buildings and machinery and sky have all been flung into a blender, and the glass bizarrely separates the stillness of this compartment from the catastrophic violence outside. The sight has a numbing effect on me, and my head is getting heavy.

She used to talk to me about "chafing." The chafing of the arrangements she found herself in was an indication that individual fractions of mind or consciousness created a ghostly tumult around her, making her irritable to the point of desperation. She saw herself caught in the middle of something like a mobile the size of the world. Bigger.

"What do you think of the idea that insanity is a predator or a parasite you see only in its effects on its victims?"

I told her I thought it was a promising idea.

She had been obsessed with the subject of insanity; even then, to an oblivious fool like me, I could tell she was getting to be more and more at home with a tragic idea of herself.

"I close my eyes, look inside, and see the pistons, wheels, gleaming metal," she declared with enthusiasm. "They don't come from inside, or outside, exclusively, but from both at once."

Her words come back to me at random, in a raft of incomplete memories.

"A question of time—if all time is simultaneous—the pieces of mechanized consciousness are drawn into a different . . . *mode* of time, and so they become immanent, which means—old? or do I mean young, or older-younger-older-younger?"

That was her theme: minds devouring each other, taking pieces out of each other. One consuming another. The action was always understood in terms of eating, but the result was something else. Not digestion. Not excretion. Co-optation. Use. Loss.

The idea was that parts of people's minds were being integrated into an interpersonal machine, or more than one. Sometimes these parts were torn out, like chunks of flesh ripped from a carcass, but sometimes they were left in place. Those parts left *in situ* would sometimes be completely inaccessible to the host consciousness, but not always. Quote *insanity* unquote meant one's mind, or part of one's mind, had been lost to, or incorporated into, interpersonal machines, another species of mind following its own scheme of cause and effect—totally, or partially, for an instant, or a while, episodically, or constantly, or forever. Sometimes this could happen so briefly, or on such a small scale, that no one would be aware of it. One would be insane for only a split second. Fractions of consciousness were being used. The predators were the thoughts of other living things being thought with someone else's mind, and minds consisting of pieces of countless minds. Long archipelagoes of insane people, insane animals. Tiny motes of insanity hidden in objects, plants, stones, buildings.

These machines consist of both material and immaterial elements and extend into this dimension from some other. Their tissue is and isn't theirs . . . They don't act according to need—the closest analogy would be sexual, like sex combined with eating. They are machines that build themselves; some parts are gravity; some parts are empty spaces, or light, or even darkness and cold, things that are normally considered strictly negative like death, absence, and silence; colors, gestures, relations of objects in a volume . . . emotions, symbols, and steel and copper and blood and nameless things . . . acts . . . subterranean slime . . . quantities, odors, textures . . . They are bodies seen one way, minds seen another way, and still other things to the infinity of all the ways of seeing. They actually consist in part of the way they are seen, and in relations between the different dimensions, the ways they relate, actually part of them, just like a wheel is part of a car.

"They're organisms," she told me, "but at the same time they're like making a plan, seeing abstract relations . . . like doing calculations in mathematics. They aren't many or one . . . and they have no reasons—they have *no reasons*—" here she spoke with a quickening intensity, almost fiercely. "They're *free!* Really *free!*"

I wake up. Jeanie's eyes are fixed on nothing in particular, not exactly out of the window, but straight ahead. I don't know if I am hearing that yammering again. I don't believe I am. The country outside the window looks narrow, like a medieval landscape painting, crowded and deep. The sun's orange and white octagons keep raking my face. We flash through a station, almost a blink, and I see the faces of the people waiting for the local train all smear together. As I am drooping back into half-sleep, Jeanie turns toward me. Perhaps she wants to sleep with her back to the window.

At dusk we come to the rim of the valley. The ridge line comes rushing toward the train like the edge of the world, crumbling away with terrifying speed.

We've switched seats. I sit by the window. A thrill comes over me—I feel in my chest, in my body, my own life, like light water, a sort of constantly vanishing glory. We're traveling at top speed now. Blue light fills the valley below, and seems to thicken, gathering into a dark, grainy band of deep indigo all around us. Just opposite me, that blue thrusts a shapeless finger high up into the sky, like a plume smoke. A single planet shines at me, almost directly level with my eyes, and I realize that there is a fine mist in the valley, and a thin veil of dim white clouds hanging just above us; the dark indigo band is really a clear gap in between; the "finger" isn't dark blue smoke, but a rent in the white cloud above.

Beneath me, there is the crust of the earth. Beneath that, magma. Go far enough, through the core, eventually there will be crust again, and the bottom of the ocean. Then sea water. Then air. Then the edge of the atmosphere. Then infinite nothingness, directly beneath my feet. The entire earth is a little trapeze, holding me up over yawning emptiness. And space extends to either side of me, in front of me, behind me, and above me as well, forever.

I see the planet out there in the blue the way I might see the porch light at the end of a dark street; I mean, not as a light in a high ceiling or as something in a different plane of existence from me, but as a part the space I occupy. All that there is between that planet and me are this glass, a trivial bit of air, and an inconceivable expanse of empty space. A plummeting fall that would go on for years and years. Innumerable years.

The light changes on the hills all at once. Behind them I imagine clicking gears shimmering with incessant, precise, mindlessly purposive adjustments. The train cants forward and the ridges bound up around us like rigid waves.

My weight shifts oppressively as we begin the long brake into the first station stop.

The air conditioning flutters out, and now the compartment is stuffy. Drowsing, I am dimly aware of a vague outline on the other side of the window and hope that no one wants to share our compartment. The train is so completely silent I can hear a fly buzzing around. It must have wormed its way into the car when the hatches opened and crept under the door, or through the lock. A cold, gelatinous living thing buzzing to and fro above me, and occasionally knocking against the window with a distinct splat.

Jeanie springs up and reaches for her bag.

"We're here," she says, looking down at me from between her upraised arms.

I follow her from the carriage into the stale heat of the open platform. The lights are on in the station, but the curved platform is dark. I can't see either end of the train, only this middle section, white glowing blue. We walk alone into the empty station. The train is gone when we emerge from the other side.

I can hear the rustling of trees and brush far up on the ridges. Behind me, the public announcement system murmurs sleep language, in short, declarative phrases.

Jeanie leads me up a steep sidewalk, lined with old shops in wood-frame houses, curtains drawn across the windows. There are no signs. There are no streetlights, just a porch lamp here and there, throwing distinct circles of wan radiance onto the pavement. Trees dense with leaves tower over the buildings in foamy black heaps and seem to trap the light close to the ground. The town is beautifully eerie, and I begin to feel a pleasurable conspiratorialness with it. Finally, I comment on the quiet.

"That's right," Jeanie says, without really looking back at me. She's walking steadily along and I try to fall in step with her, beginning to breathe hard. It's difficult to shake the jolted-awake feeling. Synchronizing my pace to hers, I suddenly find the effort far less.

After a few moments, I allow myself to drop out of step with Jeanie again. I think I prefer the effort to that strange ease.

As is sensing this, she says, "The town really empties out in the summer."

There are a few streetlights now, like cowled figures dropping cones of heavy light down onto the street. Some are older, simply lamps stuck on poles, and each creates a short halo of foliage around itself where it nestles in the overhanging branches. The houses here are all dark.

We come to the top of the street, where it intersects another that climbs up toward the peak of the hill, to our left. We go down the shoulder. After only a few minutes' descent, Jeanie points to an overhung side street that opens into the darkness like a burrow's mouth. It is illuminated by a solitary lamp at the corner that shines on a crescent of leaves like a stationary wave. A pleasant night wind washes over me as we jolt down the slope toward it.

Turning onto the street is like going under a high archway into another world. Now there's dark blue sky ahead, stars, black ridges jumbled against each other black on black, moving air stirring fragrant brush.

"We're at the edge of town," I remark. My voice sounds strange in the becalmed air.

"M-hm."

She leads me to the silhouette of a roof against the sky.

"Here we are."

Crossing the pale, perfectly new sidewalk, she slips out of her pack and flings it over the high steel fence onto the lawn.

"Let me," she pulls me forward and then takes my pack, throwing it over next to hers.

"You don't have a key?"

"If I had I would have used it," she says bluntly. "You go first."

I pull myself up over the fence and drop next to her, lose my balance and sprawl forward. My outflung hands drive back a mat of newly-laid sod, exposing the coffee-ground topsoil beneath it. We approach the house. The smell of fresh concrete, plaster, and paint mixes with the herby odor from the wild hillside behind the lot. A steel trough, encrusted with dried cement, sits in the driveway like a small boat among heaps of bricks. A shovel leans against the wall of the house, marking it with a dim shadow in the blue. The front door rests on its side against the porch struts. It's the kind you buy at a box store, adorned with a garish window of many small beveled panes radiating from an oval centerpiece. Jeanie walks into the house over a threshold sheeted with clear plastic. I look around. There are other, similar houses there in the dark. I see exposed beams, a cement mixer, tools.

Going inside, I can hear Jeanie moving around in the gloom, her feet making hollow sounds in the empty house. She looks up at me, her eyes dark in her dimly glowing face.

"I guess they're remodeling," she says flatly.

I bend forward to avoid her look and bang my hands against the knees of my pants, leaving faint blackish streaks of topsoil.

When I straighten up again, she has gone through to the next room. I don't follow right away. My mind seems too receptive. I'm no longer tired, but I can't seem to think about what I know is wrong. Jeanie is doing something that involves some scraping and rustling. I go through the doorway.

There's a kitchenette in front of me, a few stray tools, a hammer, caulk gun, boxcutter with a few razors, nails, pins, scattered on the counter. The room beyond the kitchenette is floored with white linoleum, and its sliding glass doors open to the blue backyard. Jeanie crosses toward me naked from the far corner of the room, since I stand by the only door. Brushing by me she sways in my direction and I raise my hand; it streaks her forearm with topsoil.

Her face slackens.

"Dirty. Dirty."

She plucks up one of the loose razors and slices the side of my neck with it. The left side of my head goes cold, and the back of my right knee and right foot instantly go numb. Jeanie cuts my neck first on one side then the other. I twist and flop forward over the counter and I feel her behind me darting her hand in around my shoulder and pushing my arms away. My breath against the counter, and spatter. She pulls me round to face her and keeps cutting at my neck. I watch my arms float up, but there's no strength in them, and she easily bats them back down.

I taste blood. She's gone. I see black streaks everywhere on the white. I am on my back, on the floor. My vision is dim, my eyes are dusty and cold. My neck hurts. I can't tell where my hands and feet are, how I'm lying. My neck hurts worse—impossibly—burning like acid.

They churn avidly, in a trembling, colorless light. I realize they're eating. Rows of pistons, like piano keys, are applauding.

My heat and strength drain onto the linoleum. I tell my heart to stop. It must be made to realize it's pumping my blood out of me, not through me. Each beat hushes in my ear, or the one that doesn't seem to be glued to the floor, and through which the sound of muttering comes to me.

The searing pain in my neck is like a beacon in empty space; it won't let me go. Mindless, automatic greed surrounds it, just out of sight.

My throat is in agony. I want to sob but whatever I do hurts it more. My body is cold, appallingly weak.

I drag myself to my feet. The night is paling. Outside I can hear the coyotes. They must have been on the train the whole time. Barely able to move, I stagger to the sliding glass door. *I need to get out of this house.*

In despair I tug nervelessly at the handle. I make a supreme effort and the rubber seal parts with a kissing sound. Hauling the door out of my way, I nearly throw myself off my feet.

My neck is raw, icy and burning. My shirt is stiff and glued to my body. Slowly I am leaving the house behind. The yammering is all around me, very near. I'm in the back yard. Which way do I go?

I call out.

"I am here!"

My voice is so weak I can hardly hear it.

Why am I calling?

"Here!" I call, fraily, my voice breaking. "I am *here!*"

The ragged whooping erupts on all sides. It rises jubilantly into the sky and dissolves into a swarm of shrill yipes.

The explosion of noise makes me dizzy, I fall at full length on the patio—my wounds are jarred open and bleed again. I gasp, shake. I feel myself nuzzled. For a moment I can almost see myself from a distance—a wild distance.

I turn onto my side. Some part of my mind sees all this, my body outstretched and the coyotes and the grass, house, stars, patio, inside and out, and it's leaving me. A tongue jabs at my neck—I cry out, convulsing with pain and yet not with surprise. I seem to know all this, or part of me does. I taste my own blood in an alien mouth.

From the corner of the house, Jeanie slinks toward me out of the dark, her loose hair frisking her shoulders. They are so precisely coordinated that neither she nor the coyotes take any notice of each other. She kneels beside me and takes my head in her hands, laying it in her lap. This is so painful that I cry out in despair, the churning mutter roaring in my ears and rising to cover the sound of my voice.

Jeanie is bending over me, impassive as a nurse. She lays my arms outspread on the ground to either side of me, her breasts brushing my face. Now she is stroking my forehead.

She whispers to me, "This is necessary," lisping it over and over to the shrinking thing that is still me. "This is necessary."

Jaws sink into my calf and I cry out in pain.

She smiles down at me. Her face becomes part of the sky. She soothes me as they begin eating.

MICHAEL CISCO is the author of four published novels: *The Divinity Student*, *The Tyrant*, *The San Veneficio Canon*, and *The Traitor*, as well as a collection of stories entitled *Secret Hours*. His short fiction has appeared in *The Book of Eibon*, *The Thackery T. Lambshead Pocket Guide to Eccentric and Discredited Diseases*, *Leviathan III*, *Leviathan IV*, *Album Zutique*, *Phantom*, and *Dark Wings*. He is the recipient of the International Horror Writers Guild award for Best First Novel of 1999. Michael Cisco currently lives and teaches in New York. His website is www.prostheticlibido.org.

CISCO SAYS: *Lovecraft's works have consistently provided me with fresh food for thought. Far from reducing his work to a sort of solipsistical monologue with himself, his pointed devotion to his own idiosyncrasies opens his stories and poems outward onto a wider domain of thinking. I wrote this piece to try out a variation on his theme of a lurking power or divinity, and used my own general sensibilities and philosophical outlook in the couching of the story in the same way that Lovecraft used his own.*

MARC LAIDLAW

Leng

EXPEDITIONARY NOTES OF *the Second Mycological Survey of the Leng Plateau Region*

Aug. 3

No adventurer has ever followed lightly in the footsteps of a missing survey team, and today's encounter in the Amari Café did little to relieve my anxiety. Having arrived in Thangyal in the midst of the Summer Grass Festival, which celebrates the harvest of *Cordyceps sinensis*, the prized caterpillar fungus, we first sought a reasonably hygienic hotel in which to stow our gear. Lodging accomplished, Phupten led me several blocks to the café—and what a walk it was! Sidewalks covered with cordyceps! Thousands of them laid out to dry on tarps and blankets, the withered little *hyphae*-riddled worms with their dark fungal stalks outthrust like black mono-antennae, capped with tiny spores (*asci*). Everywhere we stepped, an exotic specimen cried out for inspection. Never have I seen so many mushrooms in one place, let alone the rare cordyceps; never have I visited a culture where mushrooms were of such great ethnic and economic importance. It is no wonder the fungi are beloved and appreciated, and that the cheerful little urchins who incessantly spit in the street possess at their tongue-tips (along with sunflower hulls) the practical field lore of a trained mycologist; for these withered larvae and plump *Tricholoma matsutake* and aromatic *Boletus edulis* have brought revivifying amounts of income to the previously cash-starved locals. For myself, a mere mushroom enthusiast, it was an intoxicating stroll. I can hardly imagine what it must have been like for my predecessors, treading these same cracked sidewalks ten months ago.

Phupten assured me that every Westerner in Thangyal ends up in the cramped café presided over by the rosy-cheeked Mr. Zhang, and this was the main reason for our choice of eatery. Mr. Zhang, formerly of Lhasa, proved to be a thin, jolly restaurateur in a shabby suit jacket, his cuffs protected from sputtering grease by colorful sleeve protectors cut from what appeared to be the legs of a child's pajamas. At first, while we poured ourselves tea and ate various yak-fraught Tibetan versions of American standards, all was pleasant enough. Mr. Zhang required only occasional interpretive assistance from Phupten, and my comment on his excellent command of English naturally led him to the subject of his previous tutors—namely, the eponymous heads of the Schurr-Perry expedition.

Here, at a moment that could have been interpreted as inauspicious by those inclined to read supernatural meaning into random events, the lights dimmed and the power went out completely—a common event in Thangyal, Phupten stressed, as if he thought me susceptible to influence by such auspices. Although the café darkened, Mr. Zhang's chapped cheeks burned brighter, kindling my own excitement as he lit into a firsthand account of the last known days of Danielle Schurr and her husband, Heinrich Perry.

According to Mr. Zhang, Danielle and Heinrich had spent several weeks in Thangyal last October–November, preparing to penetrate the Plateau of Leng (so-called, in fanciful old accounts, the "Forbidden Plateau" (*Journals of the Eldwythe Expedition* (1903)) (which I mistakenly thought I had packed, damn it)). Thangyal still has no airstrip of its own, and like me they had relied on a Land Rover and local drivers to reach it. Upon arrival, they had encountered great difficulty in arranging for guides and packhorses to carry their belongings beyond vehicular routes, and had been obliged to wait while all manner of supplies were shipped in and travel arrangements made. During this wait, Heinrich had schooled our host in English, while Danielle had broadened his American cuisine repertoire. (I have her to thank for the banana pancakes that warm me even now.)

The jovial restaurateur tried many times to talk them out of their foray—and not merely because of winter's onset. Were there political considerations? I asked. For while the Chinese government has relaxed travel restrictions through some border zones of the Tibetan Autonomous Region, stringent regulations are still in effect for Westerners who wish to press into the interior. Many of these stipulations (as I know firsthand) exist mainly to divert tourist lucre into the prefecture's treasury by way of costly travel permits. But in the case of Leng, there seem to be less obvious motives for the restrictions. Despite assurances that I would never repeat his words to any official, Mr. Zhang refused to elaborate on what sort of benefit the Chinese government derived from restricting access. Leng is hardly a mineral rich region; there has been little or no military development there, which indicates it is strategically useless; and recent human rights reports declare it devoid of prisons or other political installations. It remains an area almost completely bypassed by civilizing influences, an astonishing anachronism as China pushes development into every last quarter of Tibet. For a zone set apart from the usual depredations, such resource conservation seems distinctly odd; but perhaps they have other plans for its exploitation. Mr. Zhang's warnings were sufficiently vague that I could easily picture my predecessors brushing them aside. Once he realized that it was my intent to follow them, he directed the same warnings at me. Any request for permission to enter the plateau region would be met with refusal, he said; thus confirming my decision to file no such requests, but depend on the remoteness of the region to lend me anonymity.

When he saw it was my fixed purpose to follow the Schurr-Perry trail, Mr. Zhang got up and shuffled back into the kitchen—now lit solely by a gas stovetop. He returned with a dog-eared ledger and said something in Tibetan which Phupten interpreted as, "Guestbook."

Mr. Zhang opened the ledger, spread it flat on the checkered tablecloth, and guided us backward through the entries—past colorful doodles and excitable notes from the Amari's many international diners—notes in English and German and French. Here were mountaineers bragging of climbs they had just made or climbs just ahead of them, penniless wanderers hoping someone might forward a few million yuan, laments of narrowly missed rendezvous.

Mr. Zhang stopped flipping pages and directed our attention to a ragged strip where one sheet had been ripped from the book.

"Here," he said. "Heinrich and Danielle? They write thank you Mr. Zhang. They say, we go Leng. Bu Gompa. Anyone follow, they read this note, say wait for them in spring. But . . . no come back."

I speak no Tibetan, but I recognized a few words I have heard many times recently, albeit in different context. The locals are always making pilgrimages to their various *gompas*, by which they mean a temple or monastery. And *bu*, I know from *Yartse gunbu*, the local name for the caterpillar fungus. Its precise meaning is "summer grass, winter worm," which is a colorful (if backwards) way of describing the metamorphosis of the cordyceps-inoculated caterpillar, which overwinters as a worm, only to sprout a grasslike fungal stalk—the fruiting body or *stroma*—in early summer (once the fungus has entirely consumed it from within).

I clumsily translated the name as "Temple of the Worm?"

Mr. Zhang said something urgently to Phupten, who listened, nodded, and turned to translate.

"Yes, monastery. Bu Gompa sits in the pass above Leng Plateau. Very old temple, from old religion, pre-Buddhist."

"A Bon temple, you mean?"

"Not Bon-po. Very much older. Bu Gompa for all that time, gateway to Leng. Priests are now Buddhist, but they still guard plateau."

Mr. Zhang was not done with his guest book. "This page, when my friends not return, two men come. Say they look for Heinrich and Danielle. Look for news of expedition."

"This was when?"

"In . . . January? Before they supposed come back. No one worried yet. Tibetan men, say Heinrich friend, ask see guest book. I very busy, many people in restaurant. Think no problem, they look for friends. I go in kitchen, very busy. I come out, they gone. Oh well. Book still here. Later I see page gone!"

"The one Heinrich and Danielle wrote in, you mean? Saying where they were going?"

"Yes."

"These men were Tibetan, you say?"

"Yes. I not see them in Thangyal before, but so many in town. Not only Yartse Festival. Many travelers. I worry they take page, get money from Heinrich and Danielle family."

"Blackmail," said Phupten.

I assured Mr. Zhang that we had heard of no such attempts. I explained that I had followed Heinrich and Danielle's trail after reading a series of letters and articles published in the *Journal of the Mycological Society* in advance of their departure. But all of Mr. Zhang's information was new to me; and that regarding the gompa was particularly interesting, as it suggested where I might next seek news of their whereabouts.

At about this time, the power was restored and a fresh flood of festival attendees pushed into the café. Thinking it right to clear the table for new customers, we bid farewell to Mr. Zhang, thanked him for his kindness, and stepped back out onto a sidewalk now almost completely covered with fungi. I stopped to watch some old gentlemen playing mahjongg on a table they'd set up on the sidewalk, and was hardly surprised to discover that in place of cash or poker chips, they were betting with *Yartse gunbu*.

Aug. 6

This morning, having finally reached the end of the tortuously stony road beyond Thangyal, we climbed from the Land Rovers and found an entire village sitting out in the sun to await our arrival. Our ponies should have been waiting for us, but apparently the drivers had expected us a week ago and had turned them loose to graze in the high meadows. Even so, you might have thought the whole village had sat on the streetside, patiently waiting out the week, as if our arrival were the highpoint of the season and well worth any delay. To mark the moment with a bit of ceremony, I passed around biscuits and let the assemblage pore through my mushroom atlas, which was handed about with amazement and appreciation by the entire community. They pointed out various rare species, giving me the impression that many could be found in the region—however, Phupten was too busy remedying the horse situation to interpret, and I soon reached the limits of my ability to communicate with any subtlety.

Phupten eventually signaled me that immediate arrangements had been made, and that we could set off without further ado. The horses would follow once they had been retrieved and laden with supplies offloaded from the vehicles. With a camp-following of dogs and children, we plunged onto a muddy footpath among the houses. As we passed to the limits of the village, we encountered a number of mushroom hunters returning from their morning labors with plastic grocery bags, wicker baskets, or nylon backpacks bulging with *shamu*—the local term for mushrooms of all varieties. Phupten helped me interview the collectors, making quick inventories of local names, edibility, and market prices they earn from the buyers who scour these remote villages for delicacies. One cannot underestimate the value of mushrooms to these people. Species that grow abundantly here are prized in Japan and Korea, where they absolutely resist cultivation. Although the villagers receive a pittance compared to supermarket prices in Tokyo and Seoul, the influx of cash has completely transformed this previously impoverished land. The mud houses are freshly painted in bright acrylics; solar panels and satellite dishes spring up plentiful as sunflowers. The young men dash about on motorcycles as colorful as their temples. Since a study of mushroom economics had been the announced purpose of the Schurr-Perry expedition (although I suspected the unstated motive was more likely a desire to discover and name some new species found only in Leng), I decided to see if this might be a path already taken. I showed each collector a photograph of Heinrich and Danielle, copied from the dust jacket of their landmark *Fungi of Yunnan*, to see what memories the image might jog loose. One group of giggling youths remembered them well; the adults were harder to pin down. I found reassurance, however, in the innocent recognition of the children, and now feel I am definitely on the right trail—although the chance of losing it remains tremendous in the narrow defiles of the only land route into Leng.

Beyond the village, we crossed a river by way of a swaying cable bridge. Keeping close to the west bank, working our way upriver, we spent the morning traversing damp meadows further dampened by frequent cloudbursts. Our gear, now swaying awkwardly on the backs of four ponies, caught up with us in the early afternoon. Not long after, we crossed back to the east bank, on a much older bridge that put me in mind of a stockade. The blackened timbers were topped with protective shapes that again served as reminders of the mushroom's ancient significance. The more stylized carvings were clearly meant to represent shelf fungi, tree ears, king boletes. The bridge also marked the point at which I felt we had crossed a divide in time. I saw no more hazardous electric lines strung between fencepost and rooftop; no dish antennae were in evidence. The mudbrick walls were topped with mats of cut sod, which made them wide enough that small dogs could run along the heights, barking down at us. Children followed us through streets that ran like muddy streams. Eventually, at the edge of a walled field, we left them all behind, flashing peace signs and shouting after us, "*Shamu-pa! Shamu-pa!*" Phutpen laughed and said, "They call you 'Mushroom Man,'" which sat very well with me. Our guides grinned and set the horses on at greater speed.

After that, all other habitations were simpler and more temporary affairs. Phupten brought us to the black felt tent of a yak herder, where an elderly nomad woman cut squeaking slices of a hard rubbery cheese and sprinkled it with brown sugar; I was grateful for the butter tea that washed it down. But it was the large basket of matsutake that held my interest, each little bud wrapped in an origami packet of rhododendron leaves.

Regretfully, as we ascend we are bound to leave such woodland curiosities behind. The higher elevations are more secretive with their treasures. Consider the elusive cordyceps—notoriously hard to spy, with its one thin filament lost among so many blades of real grass.

Late in the day, we came in sight of the massif that guards the pass into Leng. The late afternoon light made the barrier appear unnaturally close, sharp and serrated as a knife held to my eyes. Such was the clarity of the air that for a moment I felt a kind of horizontal vertigo. I imagined myself in danger of falling forward and stumbling over the rim of the mountains into a deep blue void. When a violet translucence flared above the range, it edged the snowy crests as if auroral lights were spilling up from the plateau hidden beyond them. I suppose this strange, brief atmospheric phenomenon may be akin to the green flash of the equatorial latitudes, but it also made me more aware than ever of the imminent onset of altitude sickness, and the ominous tinge of an incipient migraine. I was grateful when our guides, immediately after this, announced it was time to make camp.

We spread our tents in a wide meadow between two rivers. The rush of rapids was almost deafening. One of our guides, doubling as cook, filled pots and a kettle from one of the streams and soon had tea and soup underway. From a bloody plastic grocery bag, he produced rich chunks of yak and hacked them up along with fresh herbs and wild garlic he had gathered along the trail. I offered several prize boletes of my own finding. We ate and ate well in the shadow of a tall white stupa, also in the shape of a mushroom, adorned with a Buddha's eyes, and I was reminded of another interest of Heinrich's and Danielle's. They had read conjecture in *The Journal of Ethnopharmacology* that the words Amanita and Amrita had their nomenclatural similarity rooted in a single sacred practice. Amrita is the Buddhist equivalent of ambrosia, or the Sanskrit soma, a sacred foodstuff; and it has been suggested that certain Buddhist practices may have been inspired, or at least augmented, by visions following ingestion of the highly psychoactive *Amanita muscaria.* The Schurr-Perrys had stated a desire to be the discoverers (and namers) of *Amanita lengensis*, should such exist. In this way the mycological world resembles the quantum world, in being a realm so rich and various that simply searching for new forms seems to call them into creation; where labels may predate and even prophesy the things to which they are eventually applied; in which scientists now chart out the psychic territory known as *Apprehension.*

When I asked which species we might find beyond the pass, I was surprised to learn from Phupten that our guides had only visited Bu Gompa once or twice in their lifetimes, and had never actually set foot in Leng. Such pilgrimages are not undertaken lightly. Leng is held in such reverence and awe, as a place of supernal power, that they believe it unwise to venture there too often. Sharing our interest in all things mycological, the horsemen related a tale of a stupa-shaped mushroom that had bloated to enormous size and died away to puddled slime in the course of one growing season. This had occurred in their childhoods, but pilgrims still visited the spot in hopes the *Guru Shamu* might reappear. With what in retrospect seems arrogant pedantry, I found myself explaining that the fruiting body they saw, impressive as it might have seemed, was still only a comparatively tiny eruption from a much vaster fungus, the *real* guru, growing unseen and unmeasured beneath the soil. They looked at me with disappointment, as if I had just declared them retarded. In other words, this was hardly news to them. I eventually succeeded, through Phupten, in apologizing. I explained that in the West, extensive knowledge of mushrooms is considered bizarre at worst, the mark of an enthusiast at best. We shared a good laugh. At last I am among kindred spirits. So much about our lives is different, but in our passion for mushrooms we are of one mind.

Aug. 8

A day of astonishment—of revelation. Almost too much to encompass as I sit here typing by the light of my laptop, wrapped up in my sleeping bag as if under the stars, but with my gear pitched instead in a chilly stone cell. I should sleep, I know. I am exhausted and the laptop battery needs charging; but I fear losing track of any detail. I must write while this is all fresh.

After yesterday's slow progress and mounting disappointments, we were relieved to sight the Leng Pass by late morning. We had ascended to such an altitude that even now, in midsummer, snow comes down to the level of the trail in numerous places. Blue deer capered on the steep ragged scree above us, lammergeier were our constant observers, and once we startled a flock of white-eared pheasant, large as turkeys, that hopped rather than flew away through the boulders. The occasional stinkhorn, fancifully obscene, was still to be found among the thinly scattered pine needles, but my desire to forage had receded with the elevation. Grateful to have woken with a clear head, and not at all eager to trigger another migraine, I resolved to conserve my strength. But it was hard to slow down once I saw my view of the sky steadily broadening, with no further mountains moving into the notch above.

We passed cairns of engraved stones and desiccated offerings that seemed neither plant nor animal but something in between, and entered a long flat valley, sinuously curved to match the river flowing through it. The valley floor was high marshland, studded with the medicinal rhubarb we have seen everywhere. This was all picturesque enough, but above it on a slope of the pass, just at the highest point where snow laced the scree, was the most wonderful sight of the journey. Its prayer flags flying against the clouds seemed triumphant banners set out for our welcome. We had reached Bu Gompa, which straddles and guards the entrance to Leng.

Thunder rumbled; rain fell in grey ribbons. Phupten said the monks were bound to read this as an auspicious sign, coupled with our arrival. Our horsemen quickened their steps, and even the ponies hurried as if the object of their own private pilgrimage were in sight. The monastery loomed over us. Above it, among shelves of rock on the steeper slopes, I saw the pockmarks of clustered caves like the openings of beehives. Then we were through a painted gate and the place had consumed us. Happily lost among tall sod-draped walls, I breathed in the musty atmosphere of woodsmoke, rancid butter, and human waste that I have come to associate with all such picturesque scenes in this country.

Several boys, young monks, were first to greet us, laughing and ducking out of sight, then running ahead to alert their elders. We climbed switchback streets, perpetually urged and beckoned to the height of the pass. At last, we entered a walled courtyard. A wide flight of steps soared to a pair of immense doors, presumably the entrance to the main temple. As Phupten conversed with a small contingent of monks, I tried these doors and found them locked. It seemed propitious to leave an offering of ten dollars to show our good intentions and dispose the monks toward our cause. Meanwhile, our horsemen laid themselves repeatedly on the flags of the courtyard in prayerful prostrations, aligned along some faded tracework of symbols so ancient I could detect no underlying pattern. Although the walls were bright with fresh paint, this monastery seemed remote enough to have escaped destruction during the Cultural Revolution.

I retreated down the steps to find Phupten perplexed. The monks, he said, had been expecting us. They led us around the side of the building, skirting the huge locked doors, and entered the main hall by a small curtained passage.

We had seen many fantastically colorful temples along our route, lurid to the point of being day-glo. This one impressed by its warm burnished hues. Rich russets, silvery greys, pallid ivories. Everywhere were exquisite *thangkas*, hand-painted hangings in colors so subdued they evoked a world of perpetual dusk. There was light in these paintings that seemed to emanate from within and could hardly be fully explained by the shifting glow of the numerous butter lamps. Bodhisattvas floated among sharp mountains, hovering cross-legged above vast emerald seas from which radiated gilt filaments painted with such skill that they seemed to vibrate on the optic nerve, creating the illusion of swaying like strands of golden grass. Most of the traditional Buddhas and Bodhisattvas had grown familiar to me after so many recent temple visits, but Phupten pointed out one figure new to me, and quite unusual, which made numerous appearances throughout the room. Pre-Buddhist, and predating even the ancient Bon-po religion of Tibet, Phupten thought this to be the patron of those original priests of Leng. Where Buddhist iconography was highly schematic, drawn according to regular geometric formulae, this figure harkened back to an older style, one unconcerned with distinct form and completely innocent of the rules of perspective: amorphous, eyeless, mouthless, but not completely faceless. Having noticed it once, I began to spy it everywhere, lurking within nearly all the *thangkas*, a ubiquitous shadow beneath every emerald expanse.

I noticed our horsemen moving about the room in clockwise fashion, lighting incense and butter lamps, leaving offerings of currency at several of the shrines. Having taken up this practice myself, as a matter of courtesy rather than devotion, I began to follow their example; but Phupten took my arm and, for the first time in our journey, told me to hang back. When I asked why, he pulled me into a corner of the room and whispered, with curious urgency, "If you look, you see no pictures of His Holiness."

It was true enough, and remarkable, given the common appearance of the Dalai Lama in every temple we had visited across the eastern fringe of Tibet.

"Not good. Old disagreement. They do practice here, very old, from Leng. His Holiness say very bad. Three years ago, the priests of Leng, they speak out against Dalai Lama, that he is suppressing their religion. He says their protector deity is like a demon—"

"I thought all the old Bon spirits were demons once."

"Yes, but this one never enlightened. False wisdom. So, a very big fight, and even a man who try to kill his Holiness in Dharamsala. They said it was Chinese assassin behind it, but many believe it was ordered by monks of Leng."

"So . . . no offerings," I finished.

"Yes."

"But what about our guides? Don't they know?"

Before he could answer, our inspection of the temple was interrupted by the arrival of several more monks. Two were elders, dignified men, strong but gentle seeming. The third was younger, with strongly Caucasian features. In his monastic garb, with head shaved, and given the fact I had only seen him as a lecturer, at a distance, at one or two mycological conferences, I suppose I can be forgiven for not having recognized him until he came up to me, put out his hand, and said, "You don't recognize me, do you? Heinrich Perry!"

Ten minutes later, we were seated in the courtyard enjoying a sun break, sipping tea and chewing dumplings of tea-moistened *tsampa*. It seemed that all the monks of Bu Gompa had turned out to get a look at me. They laughed and posed for photographs until their various duties took them off again, for meditation or debate. Heinrich said news of our coming had preceded us up the passes; he had been expecting us since our visit to Mr. Zhang, although he was surprised anyone would have followed in his footsteps. The Schurr-Perry expedition was anything but lost. He had already found more than he ever expected to find, without even crossing into Leng. His wife had ventured onto the plateau and made discoveries of her own, but Heinrich had not set foot across the threshold.

"And where is Ms. Schurr?" I asked.

Heinrich gestured airily in the direction of the surrounding slopes. "She is in retreat." Leaving me to infer some transcendental meaning in this statement, he must have seen my glazed expression, for he laughed and elaborated: "Above the monastery are many old caves used for meditation. She has been there since her return from the plateau." He leaned forward and said confidentially, "She has been recognized as a superior practitioner, while I scrub pots and chop wood!"

So our predecessors, far from lost, had simply gone native. And their mycological survey? Their dreams of discovering new species in Leng? It was hard to believe they had given up on their passion.

Heinrich said, "Not at all. I would say we have embraced it. The Leng Plateau is a treasure chest of rarities, previously unknown. Once you attain the plateau, it is impossible to describe the wealth of discovery that awaits. But . . . once I reached this spot, such things lost their importance. Danielle has never been one to hold back, but I . . . I feel fulfilled as a porter at the gate. All Leng lies before me, but I know myself not yet ready for what it has to offer."

This seemed like a shame, and I said as much, for Perry's reports had always been received eagerly by mycological society. In a profession which had yearly become more and more the domain of geneticists, more partitioned into microscopic domains, Perry and Schurr had been unafraid of bold strokes and sweeping statements. Their papers, while thoroughly grounded in empirical observation, never shied from leaning out over the thrilling edge of speculation. Their gift of synthesis was to couple personal reportage with

ecological insight; their reports, while botanically rigorous, o
neglect the social and economic implications of their finds. Ye
parently the line between devout ethnomycology and monastic a
similation had been porous. I considered it a shame, but then felt awkward and ashamed of myself for harboring critical thoughts of this pair, whom I knew not at all. If they had found personal fulfillment in casting aside purely academic concerns and embracing the spiritual, then who was I to judge them? If anything, I felt a keen resolve to work even harder in order to compensate for the loss of Schurr-Perry's ongoing contributions to the field. The success of my foray into Leng seems more crucial than ever.

By now it was early evening, and we walked out to stand on a temple balcony, looking out across the very threshold of Leng. The serried peaks opened before us like a curtain of violet ice pulled back to reveal a sea of rolling green that broke against the misty edges of infinity. The most evocative passages of the literature of Leng came rushing back to me—from the lush descriptions of Gallardo's *Folk and Lore of the Forbidden Plateaux* (1860) to the spare journal entries of the tragic Eldwythe misadventure of 1903, made all the more macabre and ironic by its innocence of the repercussions it would inevitably have on British and Russian relations. " . . . lost land of unnameable mysteries . . . beauty beyond reach and beyond utterance . . . effulgent as the evenstar's radiance alight on the breast of earth, enflaming the mind and senses . . ." Although I had always thought such descriptions must have been flights of fancy, my first sight of Leng simply made me sympathetic to the self-avowed descriptive failings of all previous writers.

It was no wonder Perry had stopped here, I thought, for to descend into that remote wilderness was to risk stripping it of the intense mystery that gave rise to its fantastic beauty. While I knew that on the morrow we would put one foot before the other and gradually make our way down to that strange green plain, I regretted the thought of taking any action that would lessen Leng's magic while heightening its reality. It struck me as a dreamland, suspended in its own hallucination of itself, impervious to the senses. And yet such bubbles—how readily they burst. I feared this was a delusion of the evening, of the twilight air, doomed by the threat of morning. But there was nothing for it. I tried to hold on to a sense of anticipation, reminding myself of what Perry had hinted: that new discoveries awaited us below.

Horns resounded deep within the monastery, amid the clanging of cymbals and bells, and several boys came to fetch us back. Just before we turned away, the first stars appeared above the misty plains, and I sent up a fervent wish that I would never forget the feelings that had accompanied their arrival. Needless to say, these impressions will make no appearance in my published survey notes. In fact, I hope I can word my reports in such a way that none of my colleagues feel compelled to follow my trail and impinge upon this mystic land. It is such a strange feeling, as if I have been entrusted with a secret rare and exquisite, one that seems to blow up from the plateau on scented winds. I feel it would be wrong, shameful, to blunt it with too many perceivers. I am of course committed to sharing the knowledge I find here, and in no danger of falling into the trap that claimed the Schurr-Perry party. But I find myself certain that those Tibetans who visited Mr. Zhang and tore the entry from his guestbook must have been sent at Heinrich Perry's request, in an understandable attempt to cover up his trail.

During dinner, we spoke only of plans for the journey ahead. Phupten dined with the drivers, so I relied on Perry for interpretation. It seemed strange to me that they would have embraced him as a lama when his only real expertise, to my knowledge, was in the area of mycology. Likewise, how had Danielle managed to distinguish herself so swiftly among this group of lifelong spiritual practitioners? It was one thing to rush ahead fearlessly, as Heinrich had suggested was her wont—and quite another to convert that mortal zeal into an act of transcendence.

These questions were hard to frame while my hosts plied me with such a remarkable meal. Knowing my interest in local mushrooms, the monk chefs contrived a meal of savories that grew within range of the temple, prime among them a delectable red fly agaric, or chicken egg mushroom—*Amanita hemibapha* (once incorrectly known as Caesar's mushroom (or, I would imagine, 'Gesar's mushroom' in these lands), viz., *Amanita caesarea*, but delightful whatever its name). In my tea I found a special additive—a wrinkled grub, perhaps three inches long, like a sodden medicinal root. Heinrich confirmed my suspicion that it was nothing less than cordyceps, and a most prized variety, being collected along the edges of the grasslands that blanket the plateau. Like the worm in a bottle of tequila, it bobbed against my lips as I drank. In tropical climes, where insects are rife, the invasive cordyceps comes in many forms, to encompass the wild variety of insect hosts; but in these high cold climes, its hosts are few and unprepossessing. Whatever traits might have distinguished *Cordyceps lengensis* from the more common variety were not at all obvious to my eye; in fact, soaked and swimming in tea, it looked more like a shred of ginseng than anything else. Heinrich said the monks called it *phowa bu*, which I hesitate to translate. "Death Worm" gives the wrong impression altogether, and "Transcendence Worm" is not much better. Phowa is a ritual done at the moment of death, intended to launch its practitioner cleanly into the Pure Lands through his crown—to be more precise, through the fontanelle at the top of the skull. Heinrich claims that in true practitioners of phowa, a blood blister forms at the top of one's head, and a hole opens there. This channel is just wide and deep enough to hold a single stalk of grass—and in fact, this is the traditional test used by lamas to gauge an initiate's readiness. With its single grasslike stalk, the shriveled cordyceps serves as a humble reminder of the sacred practice.

I asked Heinrich if I might see fresh specimens of *Cordyceps lengensis* before my departure, but he demurred—and there I caught a glimpse of the old academic, cagey and wary with his findings. "Of course," I quipped, "you have yet to publish!" And was gratified to hear him laugh. I'd struck truth! For all his monastic garb, he is still a mushroom hunter through and through—protective of his private foraging grounds!

Although the sun had barely set, I found the cumulative exertions of the last few days and the effects of the altitude had overcome me. The cordyceps infusion seems to have some medicinal properties, for tonight as I lay down to make these entries, I found my breathing easy. Normally, these past few nights, I have felt a crushing weight on my chest, exaggerated when I recline, and I wake many times before dawn, gasping for breath. Something tells me that tonight I will sleep well.

Stray thought—Heinrich's research re Amanita/Amrita. Must ask in the morning. Where that led him; what he found, if anything. Cordyceps aplenty, but no sign of *Amanita lengensis*. I'd like to charge the laptop before I go, but I couldn't ask them to run the generator all night. Low on power.

Undated Entry

Phupten is dead. Or worse.

I believe our guides may have met a similar fate—I cannot call it an end, although it might be that. I will do my best to explain while I still have power, in hopes this laptop may be found by someone who may benefit by my warnings. I cannot flee back across the pass. The only other path is a trackless one, forward across the plateau. Leng. There are good reasons not to know it any better than I do already.

Two nights ago? Three? Phupten woke me in the dark monastic cell, with a flashlight in my eyes and fear in his voice. He said we were at risk of losing our guides to the gompa. Whether they had planned it from the start, or merely found themselves seduced by the monastic order upon arrival, he was unsure. They had mentioned childhood vows that needed renewing, but apparently things had gone too far.

I was already dressed inside my sleeping bag, so I scrambled out and followed him along dark halls, taking nothing but the few valuables in my backpack. We passed under timbered passages and starry gaps, and eventually came to the side door of the great hall. Inside, the monks sat chanting in row upon row with our guides now among them. Phupten held me back, as if I would have plunged among them—but I was not inclined to interrupt that ceremony.

Both guides stood at the head of the temple, close to the central altar. Incense fumes shrouded them, as if they were being fumigated, purified in sacred smoke. The smoke rose from a fat grey mass, as large as a man's torso, that smoldered but did not seem to burn. A lama stood near the men, his face hidden behind a richly embroidered veil of yellow cloth shot through with gold and red. He held a long wooden wand, possibly a yarrow stalk, which he used to softly prod and poke at the lump, stirring up thick billowing clouds of the odorless incense with each touch. I realized I was seeing a tangible version of the icon featured in so many *thangkas*—the local protector deity made manifest, squatting in the place that should have been occupied by a Buddha or Bodhisattva.

Sensing our arrival, the lama laid down his wand and walked toward us, stripping off his veil as if it were a surgeon's mask. I was much surprised to find Heinrich leading a ceremony of such obvious importance. Without a word, he took me by the arm and steered me toward the side door. I looked around and discovered that Phupten had already crept away.

"Your guides have elected to stay," he said.

"If they wish to take monastic vows it's no business of mine," I said. "But they should first fulfill their obligation to the survey. You know the importance of our work, Heinrich. Once you were as devoted to mycology as anyone on earth. Can't you ask them to postpone this sudden bout of spirituality for a few weeks? I'll be happy to leave them with you on my return from the plateau."

Rather than argue, Heinrich led me away with a gentleness that later seemed more forceful than sympathetic.

"I understand your point of view, but there is another," he said patiently. "When Dani and I first arrived here, our survey seemed more pressing than anything on earth. I remember my eagerness to catalog the contents of Leng. But there is a faster way to that knowledge. A richer and deeper kind of knowing."

We were moving up the mountainside along a rough path. The hollow eye sockets of caves peered down without seeing us. The cloistered buildings fell below.

"Speak with Danielle," Heinrich said. "She can explain better than I."

Starshine through the frayed clouds was all the light we had, but on the snowy flanks of the mountains, it was almost dazzling. Heinrich brought me to a black throat of darkness. Small icons sculpted of butter and barley flour were arranged at its mouth; there were shapes like spindles, bulbs, ears. We stepped inside. My first impression was of choking dryness and dust. I saw a grey knot, far back in the cave, bobbing in the guttering light of a single butter lamp that burned on the ground before it. I could make out a figure wrapped in robes, with head bowed slightly forward. All was grey—the face, the long hair cleanly parted down the middle. I supposed it was a woman, but she did not speak, nor stir to greet us.

"This is Danielle," Heinrich said. "She has answers to all your questions."

I was not sure what to ask, but I swore I heard her answering already. Deeper into the cave I went, stooping as the ceiling lowered, until my ears were very near her mouth. The sound of speech was louder now but still indecipherable, like mumbles inside which something was gnawing. Thinking it might help to match mouth to syllable, I watched her face until I was certain her mouth never moved. When I stepped back, a faint grey filament stirred in the breeze I'd made. It jutted from her scalp like a stalk of straw. The mark of the *phowa* adept. It seemed incredible she could have attained such a transcendent state in so little time. Was this why they had decided to remain? Could the monks of Bu Gompa offer a short path to enlightenment? Was there something about Leng itself, something in the rarified air, in the snowy mountains and the rolling misty grasslands, that provoked insight? I thought of how I had felt looking out over the fields—as if perpetually on the verge of understanding, of merging with a mystery that underlay all existence. But I had hesitated then and I hesitated now, even as I teetered on the brink. Doubt assailed me, and I have been trained to rely on doubt. Was enlightenment invariably good and wise? Was it possible that some forms of enlightenment, more abrupt than others, might be more than a weak mind could encompass? Were there not perhaps monks who, at the moment of insight, simply went mad? Or, in a sense, shattered?

Heinrich had been joined by others. Dark shapes clustered outside the cave, with the stars beyond them looking infinitely farther than stars had ever looked to me before. There was some aspect of menace in the silent arrival of the monks, and I suddenly felt myself the victim of a fraud. Doubt drove me entirely now. In a last bid to assert my rationality, to make all this as real as I felt it needed to be, I turned back to Danielle Schurr. It was time to end all deception. My fingers closed on the blade that jutted from her crown. Far from a dry grassy stalk, it proved to be pliable, rubbery, tough. I thought of the lure of a benthic anglerfish—something that belonged far deeper than this cave extended. As I pulled it from her scalp, or tried to, the top half of her head tore away in my hand, hanging from the end of the stalk in shreds, like a wet paper bag. The rest of her, what was left of her, exploded like a damp tissue balloon packed with grey dust. If you have ever kicked a puffball fungus, you might have some idea of the swirling clouds of spores that poured like scentless incense from the soft grey body—in such quantity that the dry husk was instantly emptied and lay slumped across the floor, inseparable from its robes.

I knew I must not breathe till I was far from the cave, but of course I already had gasped. Thus the shock of terror plays a critical role in the inoculation. I backed away, expecting to be caught by Heinrich and his cohorts. But no one stopped me. All stood aside.

My descent was a desperate and precarious one, especially once I abandoned the trail and cut off along the only available route—the pass leading down into Leng. The thought that I might accidentally blunder back into the monastery filled me with terror. By starlight, and some miracle, I found my way off the treacherous rocks and onto a stable path. An enormous clanking shape lurched toward me, matching my wild imaginings of some shaggy supernatural guardian that had descended to track me down. It proved to be one of the pack horses, bearing an ungainly bundle quickly assembled from our belongings, and led by none other than Phupten. He was as startled to see me as I was to meet him, for he had understandably thought only of saving himself. He said the path in the other direction had been gated off, the far side of the monastery impassable; so he'd had no choice but to flee toward Leng.

Behind us came the drone of horns, and I half expected the baying of hounds in pursuit. But though cymbals clashed and bells clanged and chanting rose up to the stars, nothing but sound pursued us down through the pass toward the unknown plateau of Leng, which became less unknown with each step. We fled through icy mountain fogs so luminous that I thought several times the sun must be rising, but each time found myself deceived.

At last, in exhaustion, Phupten pegged the ponies and dragged down blankets, and built a fire among the roots of a tree to give us some shelter against a miserable rain. We made plans for the morning, plans that have since evaporated. We debated whether we should wait till the following night to try and sneak back the way we had come. I dreaded the thought of returning to the monastery; it seemed impossible that we could ever creep unseen through the narrow maze of lanes; and who knew what the monks would do if they apprehended us? But Phupten insisted this was the only way back. For ages, it had been the one route into and out of Leng. There in the cold night, knowing that Leng was close,

I regretted ever seeking it out. I wanted nothing more than to have remained ignorant of its mystery.

We slept there fitfully, shivering, and I dreamt fearful dreams of something wary and watchful toward which we fled. Small white buds were stirring among the roots of the tree, growing swiftly, like *plasmodium* in a stop-motion film; they bulged from the soil and then opened, staring at me, a cluster of bloodshot eyes.

I jerked awake in a frozen dawn, hearing Phupten calling my name. But he was nowhere to be seen. The ponies waited where he had tethered them, so I thought he must have gone off for water or more wood.

I waited there all morning.

The mist veiled the mountains as if urging me to forget them. In the other direction, endless rolling hills of grass emerged. Alluring terrain, yet the notion of venturing there seemed madder than going to sea without a compass or the slightest knowledge of celestial navigation. I clung to the misty margin and watched the grasslands through much of the day, noting the way the light shifted and phantom sprites sometimes moved through the air above the rippling strands, auroral presences like the vaporous dreams of things hidden below the soil. I wondered if the Chinese suspected what dreamed there—if they hoped to harness it somehow, to tame or oppress it. Or had it managed to hide itself from them—from all controlling powers? Was it not itself an agent of utter control? Maddening insights flowered perpetually within me, the merest of them impervious to transcription. I wondered if there were degrees of immersion . . . or infection. Danielle had rushed out to meet the powers of the plateau . . . I continued to hold back . . . I felt on the verge of exploding with insight; as my mind quickened, I felt it ever more incumbent upon me to hold very still. A horrid wisdom took hold. These thoughts were only technically my own. Something else had planted them. In me, they would come to fruit.

I realized my eyes had closed, rolling back in my skull to point at a hidden horizon. With an effort of recall that felt like lurching disappointment, I disgorged a memory of Danielle Schurr's final, meditative posture. This drove me to my feet. I stamped about, remembering how to walk. I felt emptied out. Cored. I foraged among the packs for food, hoping nourishment would abate my unaccustomed sense of lightness. Altitude still explained a great deal, I told myself. But something else was wrong. Almost everything.

In the afternoon, I finally saw Phupten, far out on the sea of grass. He would not come close enough for me to read his features, nor did I dare walk out to greet him. Maybe he had been there all along. He stood with his face turned in my direction, and I began to hear mumbling like that which had filled the space in Danielle's cave. I could not resolve words. The tone was plaintive, pleading, then insistent. Phupten walked off some distance, sat down, and grew very still. I believe night came again, although it might have been a different kind of darkness falling. My head swarmed—swarms—with dreams not my own. Leng stretches out forever, and beneath its thin skin of grass and soil waits a presence vast and ancient but hardly unconscious. It watches with Phupten's eyes, while he still has them. I dreamt it spoke to me, promising I would understand all. It would hold back nothing. I would *become* the mystery—the far-off allure of things just beyond the horizon. The twilight hour, the gate of dreams. All these would be all that is left of me, for all these things are Leng of the violet light. I felt myself spread to great immensity. Only the smallest leap was needed—only the softest touch and form would no longer contain me.

I woke to find myself walking out onto the plateau. Onto the endless green where Phupten waited. I crossed the threshold. The veil parted. I beheld Leng.

The plateau spread to infinity before me, but it was bare and horrible, a squirming ocean beneath a gravelled skin, with splintered bones that tore up through the hide, rending the fleshy softness that heaved in a semblance of life. A trillion tendrils stirred upon its surface, antennae generating the illusion that protected it, *configuring the veil.* This was Leng. *Is!* A name and a place and a thing. Leng is what dreams at the roof of the world and sends its relentless imaginings to cover the planet. The light that shines here is not the violet and orange of twilight or dusk. It is the grey of a suffocating mist, a cloud of obscuring putrefaction, full of blind motes that cannot be called living yet swarm like flies and infest every pore with grasping hunger. A vastness starving and all-consuming that throws up ragged shadows like clots of tar to flap overhead in the form of the faceless winged creatures that wheel away from the plateau to snatch whatever hapless souls they find beyond the gates of nightmare and carry them back here, toward a pale grey haze of shriveled peaks so lofty that even though they rise at an infinite distance, still they dwarf everything. And having glimpsed the impossible temple upon those improbable peaks, I know I can never return. Even though I took but the one step across the threshold and then fell back, I cannot unsee what I have seen. There is no unknowing. The veil is forever rent. I cannot wake. And though I write these words because I am compelled, because Leng's spell is such that others will read this and be drawn to it, I pray for an end to wakefulness and sleep. I cannot stop my ears or eyes or mind from knowing what waits. Leng's vision for Earth is a blind and senseless cloud that spreads and infects and feeds only to spread, infect and feed. And its unearthly beauty—we are drawn to it like any lure. I pray you have not touched me. I pray the power has

---

MARC LAIDLAW explored Tibetan themes and settings in his 1988 novel *Neon Lotus* and again in the short story, "The Vulture Maiden" (1992), but it was not until 2007 that he finally traveled in Tibet. "Leng" is therefore the first of his Tibetan stories to draw on direct experience rather than research. The Lovecraftian influence on his work is more pervasive (see *The 37th Mandala*) but no less the result of experience: Every day can be an exercise in cosmic dread.

LAIDLAW SAYS: *There is no author whose work has meant more to me than Lovecraft's, but I temper my devotion with caution. The risk of losing one's auctorial identity through obsessive impersonation was impressed on me early by the late James Turner, erstwhile editor of Arkham House, who received a number of my insipid Lovecraft pastiches in the mid-1970s and pointedly advised me to find other outlets of expression. I consider this fine advice. For a certain breed of budding writer, imitating HPL is an occupational hazard. Learning from Lovecraft, without leaning on him, is the challenge. Returning to the core principles that motivated him, we may eschew arbitrary tentacles and embrace his passion for the role of the amateur in science; put aside R'lyeh and elevate Kadath; and remember that as he beat the twilit byways of New England, looking for insights that must remain nameless and ineffable, to be spied just beyond the limits of our capacity for knowledge, he found not only horror but beauty.*

MICHAEL CHABON

In the Black Mill

IN THE FALL of 1948, when I arrived in Plunkettsburg to begin the fieldwork I hoped would lead to a doctorate in archaeology, there were still a good number of townspeople living there whose memories stretched back to the time, in the final decade of the previous century, when the soot-blackened hills that encircle the town fairly swarmed with savants and mad diggers. In 1892 the discovery, on a hilltop overlooking the Miskahannock River, of the burial complex of a hitherto-unknown tribe of Mound Builders had set off a frenzy of excavation and scholarly poking around that made several careers, among them that of the aged hero of my profession who was chairman of my dissertation committee. It was under his redoubtable influence that I had taken up the study of the awful, illustrious Miskahannoks, with their tombs and bone pits, a course that led me at last, one gray November afternoon, to turn my overladen fourthhand Nash off the highway from Pittsburgh to Morgantown, and to navigate, tightly gripping the wheel, the pitted ghost of a roadbed that winds up through the Yuggogheny Hills, then down into the broad and gloomy valley of the Miskahannock.

As I negotiated that endless series of hairpin and blind curves, I was afforded an equally endless series of dispiriting partial views of the place where I would spend the next ten months of my life.

Like many of its neighbors in that iron-veined country, Plunkettsburg was at first glance unprepossessing—a low, rusting little city, with tarnished onion domes and huddled houses, drab as an armful of dead leaves strewn along the ground. But as I left the last hill behind me and got my first unobstructed look, I immediately noted the one structure that, while it did nothing to elevate my opinion of my new home, altered the humdrum aspect of Plunkettsburg sufficiently to make it remarkable, and also sinister. It stood off to the east of town, in a zone of weeds and rust-colored earth, a vast, black box, bristling with spiky chimneys, extending over some five acres or more, dwarfing everything around it. This was, I knew at once, the famous Plunkettsburg Mill. Everything was coming on, and in the half-light its windows winked and flickered with inner fire, and its towering stacks vomited smoke into the autumn twilight. I shuddered, and then cried out. So intent had I been on the ghastly black apparition of the mill that I had nearly run my car off the road.

"'Here in this mighty fortress of industry,'" I quoted aloud in the tone of a newsreel narrator, reassuring myself with the ironic reverberation of my voice, "'turn the great cogs and thrust the relentless pistons that forge the pins and trusses of the American dream.'" I was recalling the words of a chamber of commerce brochure I had received last week from my hosts, the antiquities department of Plunkettsburg College, along with particulars of my lodging and library privileges. They were anxious to have me; it had been many years since the publication of my chairman's *Miskahannock Surveys* had effectively settled all answerable questions—save, I hoped, one—about the vanished tribe and consigned Plunkettsburg once again to the mists of academic oblivion and the thick black effluvia of its satanic mill.

"So, what is there left to say about the pointy-toothed crowd?" said Carlotta Brown-Jenkin, drawing her glass of brandy. The chancellor of Plunkettsburg College and chairwoman of the antiquities department had offered to stand me to dinner on my first night in town. We were sitting in the Hawaiian-style dining room of a Chinese restaurant downtown. Brown-Jenkin was herself appropriately antique, a gaunt old girl in her late seventies, her nearly hairless scalp worn and yellowed, the glint of her eyes, deep within their cavernous sockets, like that of ancient coins discovered by torchlight. "I quite thought that your distinguished mentor had revealed all their bloody mysteries."

"Only the women filed their teeth," I reminded her, taking another swallow of Indian Ring beer, the local brew, which I found to possess a dark, not entirely pleasant savor of autumn leaves or damp earth. I gazed around the low room with its ersatz palm thatching and garlands of wax orchids. The only other people in the place were a man on wooden crutches with a pinned-up trouser leg and a man with a wooden hand, both of them drinking Indian Ring, and the bartender, an extremely fat woman in a thematically correct but hideous red muumuu. My hostess had assured me, without a great deal of enthusiasm, that we were about to eat the best-cooked meal in town.

"Yes, yes," she recalled, smiling tolerantly. Her particular field of study was great Carthage, and no doubt, I thought, she looked down on my unlettered band of savages. "They considered pointed teeth to be the essence of female beauty."

"That is, of course, the theory of my distinguished mentor," I said, studying the label on my beer bottle, on which there was printed Thelder's 1894 engraving of the Plunettsburg Ring, which was also reproduced on the cover of *Miskahannock Surveys*.

"You do not concur?" said Brown-Jenkin.

"I think that there may in fact be other possibilities."

"Such as?"

At this moment the waiter arrived, bearing a tray laden with plates of unidentifiable meats and vegetables that glistened in garish sauces the colors of women's lipstick. The steaming dishes emitted an overpowering blast of vinegar, as if to cover some underlying stench. Feeling ill, I averted my eyes from the food and saw that the waiter, a thickset, powerful man with bland Slavic features, was missing two of the fingers on his left hand. My stomach revolted. I excused myself from the table and ran directly to the bathroom.

"Nerves," I explained to Brown-Jenkin when I returned, blushing, to the table. "I'm excited about starting my research."

"Of course," she said, examining me critically. With her napkin she wiped a thin red dribble of sauce from her chin. "I quite understand."

"There seem to be an awful lot missing limbs in this room," I said, trying to lighten my mood. "Hope none of them ended up in the food."

The chancellor stared at me, aghast.

"A very bad joke," I said. "My apologies. My sense of humor was not, I'm afraid, widely admired back in Boston, either."

"No," she agreed, with a small, unamused smile. "Well." She patted the long, thin strands of yellow hair atop her head. "It's the *mill*, of course."

"Of course," I said, feeling a bit dense for not having puzzled this out myself. "Dangerous work they do there, I take it."

"The mill has taken a piece of half the men in Plunkettsburg," Brown-Jenkin said, sounding almost proud. "Yes, it's terribly dangerous work." There had crept into her voice a boosterish tone of admiration that could not fail to remind me of the chamber of commerce brochure. *"Important work."*

"Vitally important," I agreed, and to placate her I heaped my plate with colorful, luminous, indeterminate meat, a gesture for which I paid dearly through all the long night that followed.

I took up residence in Murrough House, just off the campus of Plunkettsburg College. It was a large, rambling structure, filled with hidden passages, queerly shaped rooms, and staircases leading nowhere, built by notorious lady magnate, "the Robber Baroness,

"Philippa Howard Murrough, founder of the college, noted spiritualist and author and dark genius of the Plunkettsburg Mill. She had spent the last four decades of her life, and a considerable part of her manufacturing fortune, adding to, demolishing, and rebuilding her home. On her death the resultant warren, a chimera of brooding Second Empire gables, peaked Victorian turrets, and baroque porticoes with a coat of glossy black ivy, passed into the hands of the private girls' college she had endowed, which converted it to a faculty club and lodgings for visiting scholars. I had a round turret room on the fourth and uppermost floor. There were no other scholars in the house and, according to the porter, this had been the case for several years.

Old Halicek, the porter, was a bent, slow-moving fellow who lived with his daughter and grandson in a suite of rooms somewhere in the unreachable lower regions of the house. He too had lost a part of his body to the great mill in his youth—his left ear. It had been reduced, by a device that Halicek called a Dodson line extractor, to a small pink ridge nestled in the lee of his bushy white sideburns. His daughter, Mrs. Eibonas, oversaw a small staff of two maids and a waiter and did the cooking for the dozen or so faculty members who took their lunches at Murrough House every day. The waiter was Halicek's grandson, Dexter Eibonas, an earnest, good-looking, affable redhead of seventeen who was a favorite among the college faculty. He was intelligent, curious, widely if erratically read. He was always pestering me to take him out to dig in the mounds, and while I would not have been averse to his pleasant company, the terms of my agreement with the board of the college, who were the trustees of the site, expressly forbade the recruiting of local workman. Nevertheless I gave him books on archaeology and kept him abreast of my discoveries, such as they were. Several of the Plunkettsburg professors, I learned, had also taken an interest in the development of his mind.

"They sent me up to Pittsburgh last winter," he told me one evening about a month into my sojourn, as he brought me a bottle of Ring and a plate of Mrs. Eibonas's famous kielbasa with sauerkraut. Professor Brown-Jenkin had been much mistaken, in my opinion, about the best-laid table in town. During the most tedious, chilly, and profitless stretches of my scratchings-about in the bleak, flinty Yuggoghenies, I was often sustained solely by thoughts of Mrs. Eibonas's homemade sausages and cakes. "I had an interview with the Dean of Engineering at Tech. Professor Collier even paid for a hotel for Mother and me."

"And how did it go?"

"Oh, it went fine, I guess," said Dexter. "I was accepted."

"Oh," I said, confused. The autumn semester at Carnegie Tech, I imagined, would have been ending that very week.

"Have you—have you deferred your admission?"

"Deferred it indefinitely, I guess. I told them no thanks." Dexter had, in an excess of nervous energy, been snapping a tea towel back and fourth. He stopped. His normally bright eyes took on a glazed, I would almost have said dreamy, expression. "I'm going to work in the mill."

"The *mill?*" I said, incredulous. I looked at him to see if he was teasing me, but at that moment he seemed to be entertaining only the pleasantest imaginings of his labors in that fiery black castle. I had a sudden vision of his pleasant face rendered earless, and looked away. "Forgive my asking, but why would you want to do that?"

"My father did it," said Dexter, his voice dull. "His father, too. I'm on the hiring list." The light came back into his eyes, and he resumed snapping the towel. "Soon as a place opens up, I'm going in."

He left me and went back into the kitchen, and I sat there shuddering. *I'm going in.* The phrase had a heroic, doomed ring to it, like the pronouncement of a fireman about to enter his last burning house. Over the course of the previous month I'd had ample opportunity to observe the mill and its effect on the male population of Plunkettsburg. Casual observation, in local markets and bars, in the lobby of the Orpheum on State Street, on the sidewalks, in Birch's general store out on Gray Road where I stopped for coffee and cigarettes every morning on my way up to the mound complex, had led me to estimate that in truth, fully half of the townsmen had lost some visible portion of their anatomies to Murrough Manufacturing, Inc. And yet all my attempts to ascertain how these often horribly grave accidents had befallen their bent, maimed or limping victims were met, invariably, with an explanation at once so detailed and so vague, so rich in mechanical jargon and yet so free of actual information, that I had never yet succeeded in producing in my mind an adequate picture of the incident in question, or, for that matter, of what kind of deadly labor was performed in the black mill.

What, precisely, was manufactured in that bastion of industrial democracy and fount of the Murrough millions? I heard the trains come sighing and moaning into town in the middle of the night, clanging as they were shunted into the mill sidings. I saw the black diesel trucks, emblazoned with the crimson initial *M*, lumbering through the streets of Plunkettsburg on their way to and from the loading docks. I had two dozen conversations, over the endless mugs of Indian Ring, about shift schedules and union activities (invariably quashed) and company picnics, about ore and furnaces, metallurgy and turbines. I heard the resigned, good-natured explanations of men sliced open by Rawlings divagators, ground up by spline presses, mangled by steam sorters, half-decapitated by rolling Hurley plates. And yet after four months in Plunkettsburg I was no closer to understanding the terrible work to which the people of that town sacrificed, with such apparent goodwill, the bodies of their men.

I took to haunting the precincts of the mill in the early morning as the six o'clock shift was coming on and late at night as the graveyard men streamed through the iron gates, carrying their black lunch pails. The fence, an elaborate Victorian confection of wickedly tipped, thick iron pikes trailed with iron ivy, enclosed the mill yard at such a distance from the mountainous factory itself that it was impossible for me to get near enough to see anything but the glow of huge fires through the begrimed mesh windows. I applied at the company offices in town for admission, as a visitor, to the plant but was told by the receptionist, rather rudely, that the Plunkettsburg Mill was not a tourist facility. My fascination with the place grew so intense and distracting that I neglected my work; my wanderings through the abandoned purlieus of the savage Miskahannocks grew desultory and ruminative, my discoveries of artifacts, never frequent, dwindled to almost nothing, and I made fewer and fewer entries in my journal. Finally, one exhausted morning, after an entire night spent lying in my bed at Murrough House staring out the leaded window at a sky that was bright orange with the reflected fire of the mill, I decided I had had enough.

I dressed quickly, in plain tan trousers and a flannel work shirt. I went down to the closet in the front hall, where I found a drab old woolen coat and a watch cap that I pulled down over my head. Then I stepped outside. The terrible orange flashes had subsided and the sky was filled with stars. I hurried across town to the east side, to Stan's Diner on Mill Street, where I knew I would find the day shift wolfing down ham and eggs and pancakes. I slipped between two large men at the long counter and ordered coffee. When one of my neighbors got up to go to the toilet, I grabbed his lunch pail, threw down a handful of coins, and hurried over to the gates of the mill, where I joined the crowd of men. They looked at me oddly, not recognizing me, and I could see them murmuring to one another in puzzlement. But the earliness of the morning or an inherent reserve kept them from saying anything. They figured, I suppose, that whoever I was, I was somebody else's problem. Only one man, tall, with thinning yellow hair, kept his gaze on me for more than a moment. His eyes, I was surprised to see, looked very sad.

"You shouldn't be here, buddy," he said, not unkindly.

I felt myself go numb. I had been caught.

"What? Oh, no, I-I—"

The whistle blew. The crowd of men, swelled now to more than a hundred, jerked to life and waited, nervous, on the balls of their feet, for the gates to open. The man with the yellow hair seemed to forget me. In the distance an equally large crowd of men emerged from the belly of the mill and headed toward us. There was a grinding of old machinery, the creak of stressed iron, and then the ornamental gates rolled away. The next instant I was caught up in the tide of men streaming toward the mill, borne along like a cork. Halfway there our group intersected with the graveyard shift and in the ensuing chaos of bodies and hellos I was sure my plan was going to work. I was going to see, at last, the inside of the mill.

I felt something, someone's fingers, brush the back of my neck, and then I was yanked backward by the collar of my coat. I lost my footing and fell to the ground. As the changing shifts of workers flowed around me I looked up and saw a huge man standing over me, his arms folded across his chest. He was wearing a black jacket emblazoned on the breast with a large *M*. I tried to stand, but he pushed me back down.

"You can just stay right there until the police come," he said.

"Listen," I said. My research, clearly, was at an end. My scholarly privileges would be revoked. I would creep back to Boston, where, of course, my committee and, above all, my chair would recommend that I quit the department. "You don't have to do that."

Once more I tried to stand, and this time the company guard threw me back to the ground so hard and so quickly that I couldn't break my fall with my hands. The back of my head slammed against the pavement. A passing worker stepped on my outstretched hand. I cried out.

"Hey," said a voice. "Come on, Moe. You don't need to treat him that way."

It was the sad-eyed man with the yellow hair. He interposed himself between me and my attacker.

"Don't do this, Ed," said the guard. "I'll have to write you up."

I rose shakily to my feet and started to stumble away, back toward the gates. The guard tried to reach around Ed, to grab hold of me. As he lunged forward, Ed stuck out his foot, and the guard went sprawling.

"Come on, professor," said Ed, putting his arm around me. "You better get out of here,"

"Do I know you?" I said, leaning gratefully on him.

"No, but you know my nephew, Dexter. He pointed you out to me at the pictures one night."

"Thank you," I said, when we reached the gate. He brushed some dust from the back of my coat, handed me the knit stocking cap, then a black bandana from the pocket of his dungarees. He touched a corner of it to my mouth, and it came away marked with a dark stain.

"Only a little blood," he said. "You'll be all right. You just make sure to stay clear of this place from now on." He brought his face close to mine, filling my nostrils with the sharp medicinal tang of his aftershave. He lowered his voice to a whisper. "And stay off the beer."

"What?"

"Just stay off of it." He stood up straight and returned the bandanna to his back pocket. "I haven't taken a sip in two weeks." I nodded, confused. I had been drinking two, three, sometimes four bottles of Indian Ring every night, finding that it carried me effortlessly into profound and dreamless sleep.

"Just tell me one thing," I said.

"I can't say nothing else, professor."

"It's just—what is it you do, in there?"

"Me?" he said, pointing to his chest. "I operate a sprue extruder."

"Yes, yes," I said, "but what does a sprue extruder *do*? What is it *for*?"

He looked at me patiently but a little remotely, a distracted parent with an inquisitive child.

"It's for extruding sprues," he said. "What else?"

Thus repulsed, humiliated and given good reason to fear that my research was in imminent jeopardy of being brought to an end, I resolved to put the mystery of the mill out of my mind once and for all and get on with my real business in Plunkettsburg. I went out to the site of the mound complex and worked with my brush and little hand spade all through that day, until light failed. When I got home, exhausted, Mrs. Eibonas brought me a bottle of Indian Ring and I gratefully drained it before I remembered Ed's strange warning. I handed the sweating bottle back to Mrs. Eibonas. She smiled.

"Can I bring you another, professor?" she said.

"No, thank you," I said. Her smile collapsed. She looked very disappointed. "All right," she said. For some reason the thought of disappointing her bothered me greatly, so I told her, "Maybe one more."

I retired early and dreamed dreams that were troubled by the scratching of iron on earth and by a clamoring tumult of men. The next morning I got up and went straight out to the site again.

For it was going to take work, a lot of work, if my theory was ever going to bear fruit. During much of my first several months in Plunkettsburg I had been hampered by snow and by the degree to which the site of the Plunkettsburg Mounds—a broad plateau on the eastern slope of Mount Orrett, on which there had been excavated, in the 1890s, thirty-six huge molars of packed earth, each the size of a two-story house—had been picked over and disturbed by that early generation of archaeologists. Their methods had not in every case been as fastidious as one could have hoped. There were numerous areas of old digging where the historical record had, through carelessness, been rendered illegible. Then again, I considered, as I gazed up at the ivy-covered flank of the ancient, artificial hillock my mentor had designated B-3, there was always the possibility that my theory was wrong.

Like all the productions of academe, I suppose, my theory was composed of equal parts of indebtedness and spite. I had formulated it in kind of rebellion against that grand old man of the field, my chairman, the very person who had inculcated in me with a respect for the deep, subtle savagery of the Miskahannock Indians. His view—the standard one—was that the culture of the builders of the Plunkettsburg Mounds, at its zenith, had expressed, to a degree unequaled in the Western Hemisphere up to that time, the aestheticizing of the nihilist impulse. They had evolved all the elaborate social structures—texts, rituals, decorative arts, architecture—of any of the world's great religions: dazzling feats of abstract design represented by the thousands of baskets, jars, bowls, spears, tablets, knives, flails, axes, codices, robes, and so on that were housed and displayed with such pride in the museum of my university, back in Boston. But the Miskahannocks, insofar as anyone had ever been able to determine (and many had tried), worshiped nothing, or, as my teacher would have it, Nothing. They acknowledged neither gods nor goddesses, conversed with no spirits or familiars. Their only purpose, the focus and the pinnacle of their artistic genius, was the killing of men. Nobody knew how many of the unfortunate males of the neighboring tribes had fallen victim to the Miskahannocks' delicate artistry of torture and dismemberment. In 1903 Professor William Waterman of Yale discovered fourteen separate ossuary pits along the banks of the river, not far from the present site of the mill. These had contained enough bones to frame the bodies of seven thousand men and boys. And nobody knew why they had died. The few tattered, fragmentary blood-on-tanbark texts so far discovered concerned themselves chiefly with the recurring famines that plagued Miskahannock civilization and, it was generally theorized, has been responsible for its ultimate collapse. The texts said nothing about the sacred arts of killing and torture. There was, my teacher had persuasively argued, one reason for this. The deaths had been purposeless; their justification, the cosmic purposelessness of life itself.

Now, once I had settled myself on spiteful rebellion, as every good pupil eventually must, there were two possible paths available to me, The first would have been to attempt to prove beyond a doubt that the Miskahannocks had, in fact, worshiped some kind of god, some positive, purposive entity, however blood-thirsty. I chose the second path. I accepted the godlessness of the Miskahannocks. I rejected the refined, reasoning nihilism my mentor had postulated (and to which, as I among very few others knew, he himself privately subscribed). The Miskahannocks, I hoped to prove, had had another motive for their killing: they were hungry; according to the tattered scraps of the Plunkettsburg Codex, very hungry indeed. The filed teeth my professor subsumed to the larger aesthetic principles he elucidated thus had, in my view, a far simpler and more utilitarian purpose. Unfortunately, the widespread incidence of cannibalism among the women of a people vanished four thousand years since was proving rather difficult to establish. So far, in fact, I found no evidence of it at all.

I knelt to untie the canvas tarp I had stretched across my digging of the previous day. I was endeavoring to take an inclined section of B-3, cutting a passage five feet high and two feet wide at a 30-degree angle to the horizontal.

This endeavor in itself was a kind of admission of defeat, since B-3 was one of two mounds, the other being its neighbor B-5, designated a "null mound" by those who studied the site. It had been thoroughly pierced and penetrated and found to be utterly empty; reserved, it was felt, for the mortal remains of a dynasty failed. But I had already made careful searches of the thirty-four other tombs of the Miskahannock queens. The null mounds were the only ones remaining. If, as I anticipated, I found no evidence of anthropophagy, I would have to give up on the mounds entirely and start looking elsewhere. There were persistent stories of other bone pits in the pleats and hollows of the Yuggoghenies. Perhaps I could find one, a fresh one, one not trampled and corrupted by the primitive methods of my professional forebears.

I peeled back the sheet of oiled canvas I had spread across my handiwork and received a shock. The passage, which over the course of the previous day I had managed to extend a full four feet into the side of the mound, had been completely filled in. Not merely filled in; the thick black soil had been tamped down and a makeshift screen of ivy had been drawn across it. I took a step back and looked around the site, certain all at once that I was being observed. There were only crows in the treetops. In the distance I could hear the Murrough trucks on the tortuous highway, grinding gears as they climbed up out of the valley. I looked down at the ground by my feet and saw the faint imprint of a foot smaller than my own. A few feet from this, I found another. That was all.

I ought to have been afraid, I suppose, or at least concerned, but at this point I confess, I was only angry. The site was heavily fenced and posted with NO TREPASSING signs, but apparently some local hoodlums had come up in the night and wasted all the previous day's hard work. The motive for this vandalism eluded me, but I supposed that a lack of any discernible motive was in the nature of vandalism itself. I picked up my hand shovel and started in again on my doorway into the mound. The fifth bite I took with the little iron tooth brought up something strange. It was a black bandanna, twisted and soiled. I spread it across my thigh and found the small, round trace of my own blood on one corner. I was bewildered, and again I looked around to see if someone were watching me. There were only the laughter and ragged fingers of the crows. What was Ed up to? Why would my rescuer want to come up onto the mountain and ruin my work? Did he think he was protecting me? I shrugged, stuffed the bandanna into a pocket and went back to my careful digging. I worked steadily throughout the day, extending the tunnel six inches nearer than I had come yesterday to the heart of the mound, then drove home to Murrough House, my shoulders aching, my fingers stiff. I had a long, hot soak in the big bathtub down the hall from my room, smoked a pipe, and read, for the fifteenth time at least, the section in *Miskahannock Surveys* dealing with B-3. Then at 6:30 I went downstairs to find Dexter Eibonas waiting to serve my dinner, his expression blank, his eyes bloodshot. I remember being surprised that he didn't immediately demand details of my day on the dig. He just nodded, retreated into the kitchen and returned with a heated can of soup, half a loaf of white bread, and a bottle of Ring. Naturally after my hard day I was disappointed by this fare, and I inquired as to the whereabouts of Mrs. Eibonas.

"She had some family business, professor," Dexter said, rolling up his hands in his tea towel, then unrolling them again. "Sad business."

"Did somebody—die?"

"My uncle Ed," said the boy, collapsing in a chair beside me and covering his twisted features with his hands. "He had an accident down at the mill, I guess. Fell headfirst into the impact mold."

"What?" I said, feeling my throat constrict. "My God, Dexter! Something has to be done! That mill ought to be shut down!"

Dexter took a step back, startled by my vehemence. I had thought at once, of course, of the black bandanna, and now I wondered if I was not somehow responsible for Ed Eibonas's death. Perhaps the incident in the mill yard the day before, his late-night digging in the dirt of B-3 in some kind of misguided effort to help me, had left him rattled, unable to concentrate on his work, prey to accidents.

"You just don't understand," said Dexter. "It's our way of life here. There isn't anything for us but the mill." He pushed the bottle of Indian Ring toward me "Drink your beer, professor."

I reached for the glass and brought it to my lips but was swept by a sudden wave of revulsion like that which had overtaken me at the Chinese restaurant on my first night in town. I pushed back from the table and stood up, my violent start upsetting a pewter candelabra in which four tapers burned. Dexter lunged to keep it from falling over, then looked at me, surprised. I stared back, chest heaving, feeling defiant without being sure of what exactly I was defying.

“I am not going to touch another drop of that beer!” I said, the words sounding petulant and absurd as they emerged from my mouth.

Dexter nodded. He looked worried.

“All right, professor,” he said, obligingly, as if he thought I might have become unbalanced. “You just go on up to your room and lie down. I’ll bring you your food a little later. How about that?”

The next day I lay in bed, aching, sore and suffering from that peculiar brand of spiritual depression born largely of suppressed fear. On the following morning I roused myself, shaved, dressed in my best clothes, and went to the Church of St. Stephen, on Nolt Street, the heart of Plunkettsburg’s Estonian neighborhood, for the funeral of Ed Eibonas. There was a sizable turnout, as was always the case, I was told, when there had been a death at the mill. Such deaths are reportedly uncommon; the mill was a cruel and dangerous but rarely fatal place. At Dexter’s invitation I went to the dead man’s house to pay my respects to the widow, and two hours later I found myself, along with most of the other male mourners, roaring drunk on some kind of fruit brandy brought out on special occasions. It may have been that the brandy burned away the jitters and anxiety of the past two days; in any case, the next morning I went out to the mounds again, with a tent and a cookstove and several bags of groceries. I didn’t leave for the next five days.

My hole had been filled in again, and this time there was no clue to the identity of filler, but I was determined not to let this spook me, as the saying goes. I simply dug. Ordinarily I would have proceeded cautiously, carrying the dirt out by thimblefuls and sifting each one, but I felt my time on the site growing short. I often saw cars on the access road by day, and headlight beams by night, slowing down as if to observe me. Twice a day a couple of sheriff’s deputies would pull up to the Ring and sit in their car, watching. At first whenever they appeared, I stopped working, lit a cigarette, and waited for them to arrest me. But when after the first few times nothing of the sort occurred, I relaxed a little and kept on with my digging for the duration of their visit. I was resigned to being prevented from completing my research, but before this happened I wanted to get to the heart of B-3.

On the fourth day, when I was halfway to my goal, George Birch drove out from his general store, as I had requested, with cans of stew, bottles of soda pop and cigarettes. He was normally a dour man, but on this morning his face seemed longer than ever. I inquired if there were anything bothering him.

"Carlotta Brown-Jenkin died last night," he said. "Friend of my mother's. Tough old lady." He shook his head. "Influenza. Shame."

I remembered that awful, Technicolored meal so many months before, the steely glint of her eyes in their cavernous sockets. I did my best to look properly sympathetic.

"That is a shame," I said.

He set down the box of food and looked past me at the entrance to my tunnel. The sight of it seemed to disturb him.

"You sure you know what you're doing?" he said.

I assured him that I did, but he continued to look skeptical.

"I remember the last time you archaeologist fellows came to town, you know," he said. As a matter of fact I did know this, since he told me almost every time I saw him. "I was a boy. We had just got electricity in our house."

"Things must have changed a great deal since then," I said.

"Things haven't changed at all," he snapped. He was never a cheerful man, George Birch. He turned, hitching up his trousers, and limped on his wooden foot back to his truck.

That night I lay in my bedroll under the canvas roof of my tent, watching the tormented sky. The lantern hissed softly beside my head; I kept it burning low, all night long, advertising my presence to any who might seek to come and undo my work. It had been a warm, springlike afternoon, but now a cool breeze was blowing in from the north, stirring the branches of the trees over my head. After a while I drowsed a little; I fancied I could hear the distant fluting of the Miskahannock flowing over its rocky bed and, still more distant, the low, insistent drumming of the machine heart in the black mill. Suddenly I sat up: the music I had been hearing, of breeze and river and far-off machinery, seemed at once very close and not at all metaphoric. I scrambled out of my bedroll and tent and stood, taut, listening, at the edge of Plunkettsburg Ring. It *was* music I heard, strange music, and it seemed to be issuing, impossibly, from the other end of the tunnel I had been digging and redigging over the past two weeks—from within the mound B-3, the null mound.

I have never, generally, been plagued by bouts of great courage, but I do suffer from another vice whose outward appearance is often indistinguishable from that of bravery: I am pathologically curious. I was not brave enough, in that eldritch moment, actually to approach B-3, to investigate the source of the music I was hearing; but though every primitive impulse urged me to flee, I stood there listening, until the music stopped, and hour before dawn. I heard sorrow in the music, and mourning, and the beating of many small drums. And then in the full light of the last day of April, emboldened by bright sunshine and a cup of instant coffee, I made my way gingerly toward the mound. I picked up my shovel, lowered my foolish head into the tunnel, and crept carefully into the bowels of the now-silent mound. Seven hours later I felt the shovel strike something hard, like stone or brick. Then the hardness gave way, and the shovel flew abruptly out of my hands. I had reached, at last, the heart of mound B-3.

And it was not empty; oh no, not at all. There were seven sealed tombs lining the domed walls, carved stone chambers of the usual Miskahannock type, and another ten that were empty, and one, as yet unsealed, that held the unmistakable, though withered, yellow, naked and eternally slumbering form of Carlotta Brown-Jenkin. And crouched on her motionless chest, as though prepared to devour her throat, sat a tiny stone idol, hideous, black, brandishing a set of wicked ivory fangs.

Now I gave in to those primitive impulses; I panicked. I tore out of the burial chamber as quickly as I could and ran for my car, not bothering to collect my gear. In twenty minutes I was back at Murrough House. I hurried up the front steps, intending only to go to my room, retrieve my clothes and books and papers, and leave behind Plunkettsburg forever. But when I came into the foyer I found Dexter, carrying a tray of eaten lunches back from the dining room to the kitchen. He was whistling lightheartedly and when he saw me he grinned. Then his expression changed.

"What is it?" he said, reaching out to me. "Has something happened?"

"Nothing," I said, stepping around him, avoiding his grasp. The streets of Plunkettsburg had been built on evil ground, and now I could only assume that every one of its citizens, even cheerful Dexter, had been altered by the years and centuries of habitation. "Everything's fine. I just have to leave town."

I started up the wide, carpeted steps as quickly as I could, mentally packing my bags and boxes with essentials, loading the car, twisting and backtracking up the steep road out of this cursed valley.

"My name came up," Dexter said. "I start tomorrow at the mill."

Why did I turn? Why did I not keep going down the long, crooked hallway and carry out my sensible, cowardly plan?

"You can't do that," I said. He started to smile, but there must have been something in my face. The smile fizzled out. "You'll be killed. You'll be mangled. That good-looking mug of yours will be hideously deformed."

"Maybe," he said, trying to sound calm, but I could see that my own agitation was infecting him. "Maybe not."

"It's the women. The queens. They're alive."

"The queens are alive? What are you talking about, professor? I think you've been out on the mountain too long."

"I have to go, Dexter," I said. "I'm sorry. I can't stay here anymore. But if you have any sense at all, you'll come with me. I'll drive you to Pittsburgh. You can start at Tech. They'll help you. They'll give you a job . . ." I could feel myself starting to babble.

Dexter shook his head. "Can't," he said. "My name came up! Shoot, I've been waiting for this all my life."

"Look," I said. "All right. Just come with me, out to the Ring." I looked ay my watch. "We've got an hour until dark. Just let me show you something I found out there, and then if you still want to go to work in that infernal factory, I'll shake your hand and bid you farewell."

"You'll really take me out to the site?"

I nodded. He set the tray on a deal table and untied his apron.

"Let me get my jacket," he said.

I packed my things and we drove in silence to the necropolis. I was filled with regret for this course of action, with intimations of disaster. But I felt I couldn't simply leave town and let Dexter Eibonas walk willingly into that fiery eructation of the evil genius, the immemorial accursedness, of his drab Pennsylvania hometown. I couldn't leave that young, unmarked body to be broken and split on the horrid machines of the mill. As for why Dexter wasn't talking, I don't know; perhaps he sensed my mounting despair, or perhaps he was simply lost in youthful speculation on the unknown vistas that lay before him, subterranean sights forbidden and half-legendary to him since he had first come to consciousness of the world. As we turned off Gray Road on to the access road that led up to the site, he sat up straight and looked at me, his face grave with the consummate adolescent pleasure of violating rules.

"There," I said. I pointed out the window as we crested the rise. The Plunkettsburg Ring lay spread out before us, filled with jagged shadows, in the slanting, rust red light of the setting sun.

From this angle the dual circular plan of the site was not apparent, and the thirty-six mounds appeared to stretch from one end of the plateau to the other, like a line of uneven teeth studding an immense, devouring jawbone.

"Let's make this quick," I said, shuddering. I handed him a spare lantern from the trunk of the Nash, and then we walked to the edge of the aboriginal forest that ran upslope from the plateau to the wind-shattered precincts of Mount Orret's sharp peak. It was here, in the lee of a large maple tree, that I had set up my makeshift camp. At the time the shelter of that homely tree had seemed quite inviting, but now it appeared to me that the forest was the source of all the lean shadows reaching their ravening fingers across the plateau. I ducked quickly into my tent to retrieve my lantern and then hurried back to rejoin Dexter. I thought he was looking a little uneasy now. His gait slowed as we approached B-3. When we trudged around to confront the raw earthen mouth of the passage I had dug, he came to a complete stop.

"We're not going inside there," he said in a monotone. I saw come into his eyes the dull, dreamy look that was there whenever he talked about going to work in the mill. "It isn't allowed."

"It's just for a minute, Dexter. That's all you'll need."
I put my hands on his shoulders and gave him a push, and we stumbled through the dank, close passage, the light from our lanterns veering widely around us. Then we were in the crypt.

"No," Dexter said. The effect on him of the sight of the time-ravaged naked body of Carlotta Brown-Jenkin, of the empty tombs, the hideous idol, the outlandish ideograms that covered the walls, was everything I could have hoped for. His jaw dropped, his hands clenched and unclenched, he took a step backward. "She just died!"

"Yesterday," I agreed trying to allay my own anxiety with a show of ironic detachment.

"But what . . . what's she doing out here?" He shook his head quickly, as though trying to clear it of smoke or spiderwebs.

"Don't you know?" I asked him, for I still was not completely certain of his or any townsman's uninvolvement in the evil, at once ancient and machine-age, that was evidently the chief business of Plunkettsburg.

"No! God, no!" He pointed to the queer, fanged idol that crouched with a hungry leer on the late chancellor's hollow bosom. "God, what is that thing?"

I went over to the tomb and cautiously, as if the figure with its enormous, obscene tusks might come to life and rip off a mouthful of my hand, picked up the idol. It was as black and cold as space, and so heavy that it bent my hand back at the wrist as I hefted it. With both hands I got a firm grip on it and turned it over. On its pedestal were incised three symbols in spiky, complex script of the Miskahannocks, unrelated to any other known human language or alphabet. As with all of the tribe's inscriptions, the characters had both a phonetic and a symbolic sense. Often these were quite independent of one another.

"Yu . . . yug . . . gog," I read, sounding it out carefully. "Yuggog."

"What does it mean?"

"It doesn't mean anything, as far as I know. But it can be read another way. It's trickier. Here's tooth . . . gut—that's hunger—and this one—" I held up the idol toward him. He shield away. His face had gone completely pale, and there was a look of fear in his eyes, of awareness of evil, that I found, God forgive me, strangely gratifying. "This is a kind of general intensive, I believe. Making this read, loosely rendered, hunger . . . itself. How odd."

"Yuggog," Dexter said softly, a thin strand of spittle joining his lips.

"Here," I said cruelly, tossing the heavy thing toward him. Let him go into the black mill now, I thought, after he's seen *this.* Dexter batted at the thing, knocking it to the ground. There was a sharp, tearing sound like matchwood splitting. For an instant Dexter looked utterly, cosmically startled. Then he, and the idol of Yuggog, disappeared. There was a loud thud, and a clatter, and I heard him groan. I picked up the splintered halves of the carved wooden trapdoor Dexter had fallen through and gazed down into a fairly deep, smooth-sided hole. He lay crumpled at the bottom, about eight feet beneath me, in the light of his overturned lantern.

"My God! I'm sorry! Are you all right?"

"I think I sprained my ankle," he said. He sat up and raised his lantern. His eyes got very wide. "Professor, you have to see this."

I lowered myself carefully into the hole and stared with Dexter into a great round tunnel, taller than either of us, paved with crazed human bones stretching far beyond the pale of our lanterns.

"A tunnel," he said. "I wonder where it goes."

"I can only guess," I said. "And that's never good enough for me."

"Professor! You aren't—"

But I had already started into the tunnel, a decision that I attributed not of courage, of course, but to my far greater vice. I did not see that as I took those first steps into the tunnel I was in fact being bitten off, chewed, and swallowed, as it were, by the very mouth of the Plunkettsburg evil. I took small queasy steps along the horrible floor, avoiding, insofar as I could, stepping on the outraged miens of human skulls, searching the smoothed, plastered walls of the tunnel for ideograms or other hints of the builders of this amazing structure. The tunnel, or at least this version of it, was well built, buttressed regularly by sturdy iron piers and lintels, and of chillingly recent vintage. Only great wealth, I thought, could have managed such a feat of engineering. A few minutes later I heard a tread behind me and saw the faint glow of a lantern. Dexter joined me, favoring his right ankle, his lantern swinging as he walked.

"We're headed northwest," I said. "We must be under the river by now."

"Under the river?" he said. "Could Indians have built a tunnel like this?"

"No, Dexter, they could not."

He didn't say anything for a moment as he took this information in.

"Professor, we're headed for the mill, aren't we?"

"I'm afraid we must be," I said.

We walked for three quarters of an hour, until the sound of pounding machinery became audible, grew gradually unbearable and finally exploded directly over our heads. The tunnel had run out. I looked up at the trapdoor above us. Then I heard a muffled scream. To this day I don't know if the screamer was one of the men up on the floor of the factory or Dexter Eibonas, a massive hand clapped brutally over his mouth, because the next instant, at the back of my head, a supernova bloomed and flared brightly.

I wake in an immense room, to the idiot pounding of a machine. The walls are sheets of fire flowing upward like inverted cataracts; the ceiling is lost in shadow from which, when the flames flare brightly, there emerges the vague impression of a steely web of girders among which dark things ceaselessly creep. Thick coils of rope bind my arms to my sides, and my legs are lashed at the ankles to those of the plain pine chair in which I have been propped.

It is one of two dozen chairs in a row that is one of a hundred, in a room filled with men, the slumped, crew-cut, big-shouldered ordinary men of Plunkettsburg and its neighboring towns. We are all waiting, and watching, as the women of Plunkettsburg, the servants of Yuggog, pass noiselessly among us in their soft, horrible cloaks stitched from the hides of dead men, tapping on the shoulder of now one fellow, now another. None of my neighbors, however, appears to have required the use of strong rope to conjoin him to his fate. Without a word the designated men, their blood thick with the dark earthen brew of the Ring witches, rise and follow the skins of miscreant fathers and grandfathers down to the ceremonial alter at the heart of the mill, where the priestesses of Yuggog throw oracular bones and, given the result, take hold of the man's ear, his foot, his fingers. A yellow snake, its venom presumably anesthetic, is applied to the fated extremity. Then the long knife is brought to bear, and the vast, immemorial hunger of the god of the Miskahannocks is assuaged for another brief instant. In the past three hours on this Walpurgis Night, nine men have been so treated; tomorrow, people in this bewitched town that, in a reasonable age, has learned to eat its men a little at a time, will speak, I am sure, of a series of horrible accidents at the mill. The women came to take Dexter Eibonas an hour ago. I looked way as he went under the knife, but I believe he lost the better part of his left arm to the god. I can only assume that very soon now I will feel the tap on my left shoulder of the fingers of the town librarian, the grocer's wife, of Mrs. Eibonas herself. I am guiltier by far of trespass than Ed Eibonas and do not suppose I will survive the procedure.

Strange how calm I feel in the face of all this; perhaps there remain traces of the beer in my veins, or perhaps in this hellish place there are other enchantments at work. In any case, I will at least have the satisfaction of seeing my theory confirmed, or partly confirmed, before I die, and the concomitant satisfaction, so integral to my profession, of seeing my teacher's theory cast in the dustpan. For, as I held, the Miskahannocks hungered; and hunger, black, primordial, unstaunchable hunger itself, was their god. It was indeed the misguided scrambling and digging of my teacher and his colleagues, I imagine, that awakened great Yuggog from its four-thousand-year slumber. As for the black mill that fascinated me for so many months, it is a sham. The single great machine to my left takes in no raw materials and emits no ingots or sheets. It is simply an immense piston, endlessly screaming and pounding like the skin of an immense drum the ground that since the days of the Miskahannocks has been the sacred precinct of the god. The flames that flash through the windows and the smoke that proceeds from the chimneys are bits of trickery, mechanical contrivances devised, I suppose, by Philippa Howard Murrough herself, in the days when the revived spirit of Yuggog first whispered to her of its awful, eternal appetite for the flesh of men. The sole industry of Plunkettsburg is carnage, scarred and mangled bodies the only product.

One thought disturbs the perfect, poison calm with which I am suffused—the trucks that grind their way in and out of the valley, the freight trains that come clanging in the night. What cargo, I wonder, is unloaded every morning at the docks of the Plunkettsburg Mill? What burdens do these trains bear away?

MICHAEL CHABON is a novelist, screenwriter, columnist and short story writer. His first novel, *The Mysteries of Pittsburgh*, was his master's thesis. He followed it with a second novel, *Wonder Boys* (made into a movie), and two short-story collections. His third novel, *The Amazing Adventures of Kavalier & Clay*, was critically acclaimed and was awarded the Pulitzer Prize for Fiction in 2001.

His most recent novel, *The Yiddish Policemen's Union*, an alternate-history mystery novel, was published in 2007 and won The Hugo Award, the Nebula Award, and the Sidewise Award; his serialized novel *Gentlemen of the Road* appeared in book form in the fall of that same year.

Chabon has written two Lovecraftian tales so far in his career: "The Gods of Dark Laughter" and "In the Black Mill," the latter published here.

CHABON SAYS: *At a certain point in my reading life—around the age of twelve or thirteen—I became fascinated by global abstracts, maps, if you will, of writers' work. It started with my copy of* The Wizard of Oz, *which had a detailed summary at the back of all of LFB's other books. From there I moved on to the "biographical essay" on Conan, Philip José Farmer's* Doc Savage *book, the Yoknapatawpha Chronology in* The Portable Faulkner, *and at some point found my way to Derleth's essay on the Cthulhu mythos. I guess I was interested in saving time! Or maybe it was just that it fired my imagination to think about a writer creating an entire parallel universe along with his or her lifelong work. The first actual Lovecraft story I remember reading and loving, shortly thereafter, is "The Music of Erich Zann." When I go to Paris, I'm still searching maps for the "Rue d'Auseil."*

LAVIE TIDHAR

One Day, Soon

THE PAGES OF the book felt unpleasantly moist. They were yellowing and yet *alive*, like human skin that had been hung up to dry in the Mediterranean sun, yet never quite did. Somehow, the book repulsed him just as it aroused a strange excitement in him, which he couldn't quite place, couldn't quite give a name to. It was leather bound. At first it seemed like a cheap paperback, but that was just a trick of the eye or the nerve ends at the tips of his fingers. The leather was black. There was no title on the spine or front. When he leafed through the book there were merely names, in tidy columns, and beside each name a number. Some of the names had comments beside them, in many hands, all in the same black ink. He didn't know the language, but he thought it could have been German.

The book sat on the third shelf from the top in Mr. Rosenfeld's shop in Hadar, towards the back, where Mr. Rosenfeld used to dump those books that, at his considered glance, would be a hard sell. When Benjamin came to the shop he always looked through those shelves (they comprised the top three levels), once finding a Hungarian cookbook with the covers missing, an illegible inscription and the drawing of a heart on the flyleaf; once finding a *siddur minyan*, a book of prayers, printed in Yiddish, published in Warsaw at the closing days of the nineteenth century; once he found an illustrated guide to the frogs of Palestine, paintings of green amphibians on the backgrounds of deserts and camels and tents, by an English painter he had never heard of; the project commissioned by the Bible Society of Great Britain and titled, simply, *The Second Plague.*

This was just another one of those lost books, those homeless wandering volumes that all, inevitably, ended up in the ghetto of the top three shelves at the back of Mr. Rosenfeld's shop. And yet it felt different to the others, but he couldn't quite articulate why. It felt, he thought at last, as he paid the modest sum scribbled in pencil on the flyleaf and refused the offer of a plastic bag—"It's only a paperback," Mr. Rosenfeld had said, inexplicably—as if it did not belong. Not here. And it occurred to him—and for some reason he felt a shiver, despite the hot sunshine that came streaming down the Carmel—that everything belongs somewhere.

The worst kind of dream is a jail, and you can't wake up. I think that's where it began, in that time of the morning when dreams encroach the closest on the waking world, and the mind lies vulnerable, in a liminal state. In the dream I wore dirty pajamas. I was walking down a mountain and gradually it became apparent to me that I was marching inside a mass of bodies, all dressed the same, all heading in the same direction. I became aware that all around us there were evergreen trees, and I remember thinking how well they resembled the forests of the Carmel. I tried to make that observation to those near me, but when I turned to them I saw that none wore a face. I remember not being especially surprised by it, though it did make me uneasy. Also, I don't usually dream smell, but I remember very distinctly the taste of smoke in the air, and that the air was cool and that it was a bright morning. I also remember music playing, something like a marching song. I don't know at what point I became acutely uncomfortable. There was a moment when we passed a puddle on the road, and I remember thinking it must have rained the night before, and when I looked down into the pool of water I saw I too had no face. I remember thinking this must be a dream, and feeling very much comforted by the thought, and willing myself to wake up from it. But I couldn't wake up. That must have been the moment I became frightened, though there was nothing actually very frightening about the dream. I remember thinking it was a beautiful morning, and I saw a pinecone lying by the side of the road and I picked it up to check if there were any nuts inside it, the way we did when we were children, but then I realized it wasn't a pinecone at all, it was a hip bone, and it still had bits of flesh attached to it, which I might have mistaken for pine nuts though I don't see how. I think at that point Mira woke me up. She said I'd been screaming, though I don't recall. By then it was already fading. Mira said, Are you feeling okay? And I said, sure, it was only a bad dream. The only thing I could remember about the dream afterwards was that it was about a pinecone, and it made me feel a little embarrassed. There's nothing scary about pinecones, is there?

He left the book untouched for quite a while. For some reason the book made him uncomfortable, and he hid it from his wife, as if it were a dirty magazine. It was only columns and numbers, but somehow he knew Mira would not approve, and he put it in the toolshed, which was what he called the small room facing the mountain that he had converted into his little study-slash-workshop, though it was mainly and simply his place of refuge, a small space all to himself with a door to close behind him, where even Mira left him alone. From his desk he could look up the slopes of the Carmel, beyond the houses which every year sprouted higher up, but still higher were the evergreen forests. Benjamin remembered childhood walks through the trees, following the hiking trails, and the guide talking about the birds and their different calls, and then there would be a bonfire and they would cook potatoes in the coals until the crust was ash, but when you broke it open the inside was steaming and soft and burned your fingers when you tried to extract it too soon. That had been a long time ago.

He liked the old stories best. How his grandfather, when he was eighteen, left his home in Marosvasarhe, the small town in the Carpathian Mountains of Transylvania, where it snowed every winter and the family owned a small holding outside the town. Benjamin had a picture of his grandfather—only a boy, really—saying goodbye to his own father, the old man wearing a wide-brimmed hat and a long coat, both posing formally for the camera. Benjamin's grandfather traveled by train from Brasov to Bucharest and fell asleep as it passed through the mountains, and when he woke up his coat was gone. It had been stolen. From Bucharest by train to the coast, and from there by boat to Haifa in Palestine, where he remained until he died. He never saw his father again.

Now he himself was a father and his two children were grown up and he did not see much of them either. His books, the secrets they contained, were his solace, and the view of the mountain rising above him, a feeling of security, a knowledge that this ancient port town had always been there, will always be there: it gave him hope.

Benjamin was different after he came back from the shop, though for a long time afterwards I didn't quite realize it. I guess, once you've been married for some time, you tend to give each other space, you know? A quiet place for all the little eccentricities. I have them too, of course, but . . . it took me a while to realize something was wrong.

I saw the book, naturally, but, you know, even though for a long time I blamed it for what happened, I realize now that that's ridiculous. It was only a book. A fiction book! One of those cheap tatty paperbacks like you can pick up for ten shekels in those dingy shops in Hadar. You can't blame *books* for people's actions, or their state of mind. Can you?

It was a paperback, one of those pocket books, with cheap yellowing paper and—well, it wasn't much. One of those cheap bright covers with too much color—I used to be an art student, back before we had Pnina. It showed a group of people in these kind of gray pajamas, like mushroom-gray, marching down a hill. There were forests on either side, very vivid greens, and the road—I remember it wasn't paved, it was a dirt track, like you used to get down the Carmel before the municipality grew, and there was a very bright yellow sun in a deep blue sky—you see what I mean, almost like a picture from a children's book. And there was—now that I think about it, you know, I don't think I even consciously noticed it, but there was smoke.

Rising ahead of them. You couldn't see where it originated from, only that it was there. Come to think of it, I can't remember what it looked like. I mean, I would have thought the artist would have used pencil lines, maybe, or—but I can't think of what it actually *looked* like. It just . . .

It was just there.

It was as he walked along the promenade, high on the mountain, from where one can look down and see the Baha'i temple rising amidst the extensive gardens, that it happened for the first time. He loved to come up there to admire the gardening, the profusion of flowers, the orderly way in which they were arranged. When the sun was high overhead, the golden dome of the temple would blaze with light, and the Mediterranean would sparkle a deep blue beyond it. He had the book with him; he didn't know why. He had taken to carrying it around with him. Sometimes it seemed to him that the book changed in his hands, the hard leather binding changing into a picture, bright and yet somehow terrifying, like something out of a dream one no longer remembered but which lingered still. Sometimes it felt light, sometimes heavy. That day, as he looked down on the gardens, his hand rested on the binding, which felt warm, warmer than another person's touch, almost burning, like an oven. He had to blink back tears from the sun, and when he looked down, the gardens were no longer there—or rather, something had happened to them, and at first he did not understand it.

The temple was in ruins. The golden dome lay on its side, and it seemed to him its circumference was melting. There were craters everywhere, and as he looked, he thought he saw something like a corpse lying in one of the craters, one hand reaching out to a place where a single red flower was still growing, but never quite reaching it. The lying figure only had one arm. It had no head. He coughed then, his whole body shaking, and when he breathed it seemed to him it was smoke he was breathing, and he heard whistling noises overhead, and it reminded him of the Yom Kippur War, when he was a young soldier: it sounded like mortars.

It must have been only his imagination, because when his cough stopped and he looked back, the temple was there as always, and the gardens were as well tended and as pretty as before. He shook his head slowly and realized his hand was still holding the book, and so he pulled it out, and as he did so, a small piece of paper fell to the ground. When he picked it up, he saw someone had scribbled a date on it: 5 November 1942.

I dreamed of a swastika sprayed against the wall of the Technion building.

He became very withdrawn. He would sit in his little study for hours, the door closed, and when I'd come in he'd be staring out of the window, not talking, and I could see his hands in his lap. He had an old, dirty coat across his knees—I don't know where he got it from—and he was hiding something there.

Of course I looked at the book. When he wasn't there. It wasn't hard to find the first time, but after that he took to carrying it with him. Still, I saw it.

Like I said, it was just a paperback. I remember he taught me how to look at the publication information, the copyright information, but I couldn't find it anywhere—it must have been torn off at some point. I started reading it—just the first few pages. I can't say this sort of writing is my thing, really; it was very—melodramatic, you know—not very well written. There was no art to it. What it was, it was the writer sitting down and telling a story—almost, now that I think about it, like it was a testimony, and not a story at all. You know, like they gave at the Eichmann trial. We used to listen to that on the radio. Only this was just cheap fiction. It was, how do you say? Fanciful.

Oh, it was about the war. Maybe that's why I was just thinking of Eichmann. The war in Palestine. It was set in '42, when Rommel was advancing through Egypt with his Afrika Korps. If he had reached the Suez Canal, then he could have taken Palestine. Which, in the book, is what happened. Rommel wins El-Alamein in '42, and keeps going.

I remember my father telling me—he came to Haifa before the war; we've been here a long time—he told me that back then, when they thought the Nazis might reach Palestine, the British and the Jewish leadership formed a plan. In the case of a German invasion the Carmel would have become the last bastion, a new Masada. There was even—the Haganah had this German unit who were preparing for it—I remember reading about them in the newspaper a few years back, and the article said that, really, it was just a bunch of guys in a cave down in the valley, speaking German amongst themselves, practicing Nazi salutes—they all *looked* German, at least the way Germans were supposed to look, blond and blue eyed and all that—basically getting ready for a German invasion. So in the book there *was* a German invasion. I thought it was silly.

It was worse the next few times he stepped out of the house. Once, as he passed by the old harbor, he heard the sound of guns, and, turning, saw vast troop carriers floating on the sea, and the old British flag above the harbor was burning. When he looked again the flag was the same blue and white it should have been, and the guns were merely the honking of passing cars. Another time, as he drove past the Stella Maris Monastery high above the sea on the ridge of the Carmel, he saw uniformed men streaming out of the ancient building, shouting in a language he didn't understand; as he stopped the car and watched, a group of people arrived over the road, men and women in strange, old-fashioned clothes, and children, and they were herded into the monastery by the soldiers, and, as he drove away, he heard the sound of shots from inside the enclave, and a solitary scream, cut short.

It was only inside his toolshed that he felt safe. It was his hiding hole, and they would never find him there. The way his aunt Susana had hidden in Budapest all those years ago, spending months inside an abandoned apartment in the city, never going out, a friend bringing her what water and food could be found.

He took to consulting the book for hours at a time, sitting in front of the window, not seeing the bright sunny world outside, his attention focused on the leather-bound book in his hands. He held it open in his lap and went through it one page at a time, his finger running down the endless list of names, searching—but what he was searching for he couldn't quite say, not then. He would fall asleep in the chair, the book still open in his lap, the door safely locked, and wake up startled with early morning light, gasping for air, not knowing where he was.

I dreamed the soldiers were coming and there was no escape. I didn't know what soldiers these were, or where I was, but I knew I was trapped. There was no way out. A part of me knew it was a dream, but there was no waking from it. I could hear them coming along the road, hundreds of them, marching in a perfect beat, the sound of hundreds of pairs of heavy boots echoing through the old streets. I tried to say, Won't anyone help me? But there was no one to answer. Somewhere nearby, I think there were other people. I heard a whimpering in the dark. Minute sounds of shifting, like old bodies trying not to move in a confined space. But I knew they were coming. I could hear them marching closer, and as they did I heard doors banging open, and shouts, a baby crying, someone talking in a high, angry voice that did no good, no good at all. I knew then what the world is like: it is like an egg. Outside it is smooth, and beyond its shell there is sunlight, and grass, and white clouds in a deep blue sky. But inside it there is nothing, only a viscous darkness, a space that confines, that binds, an imprisonment from which there can be only birth, or death. The approaching boots came closer and closer. They were one door down the street. Then I heard my own door break open, and a voice barked commands in a foreign tongue, and then they came for me.

Where is he? I wish I knew. I spoke to the police, and the officer was very sympathetic, and he said sometimes it happens, more often than you think, when people get old and they no longer think right, even if you can't tell at first, they still look the same but inside something breaks. Like a perfect egg that, only when you crack it, you smell the rot inside. He said of course they would do their best to find him, and he was very reassuring. It's a small country, people can't just disappear.

I dreamed about him that night. In the dream he was walking down a dirt road on the Carmel, between the trees. He was wearing pajamas. That's funny, isn't it? He was with a lot of other people, but I couldn't see their faces. The sun was very bright, and I remember there was smoke in the distance. It had a very strong taste. It felt like it had been burning for a long time. I tried to pull him away, but he couldn't see me. I don't know why I did that. It seemed like a happy enough scene, like a memory of a childhood hike, but somehow I was afraid. Then I woke up, and I was crying, but I didn't know why I did that either, and I felt silly.

I still have the book, though recently it seems heavier, and the cover has faded, and the face of the book is featureless, and sometimes when I open it I see not the story I thought was in there, but names, just names, an endless list of them, and sometimes I start reading them, searching for something, though I'm not quite sure what. I have the strangest conviction I might find my own name in there, one day, soon.

LAVIE TIDHAR is the author of the linked-story collection *HebrewPunk*; the novellas *An Occupation of Angels* and *Cloud Permutations*; and, with Nir Yaniv, a short novel called *The Tel Aviv Dossier*, as well as many stories in various anthologies and magazines. He grew up on a kibbutz in Israel and has since lived on three continents and one island nation; he currently lives in Southeast Asia.

TIDHAR SAYS: *The real horror of Lovecraft comes from futility. You find it in Larkin too: that realization that death is not a gateway to another world but an end—nothing more terrible than an absence. The universe appeared, the solar system formed, we evolved, death by countless death—and one day, soon, the sun will die and the universe will follow. We can rage against the dying of the light, but I think Lovecraft understood best of all the futility of that grand gesture—and that, to me, is the real horror.*

JOYCE CAROL OATES

Commencement

THE SUMMONS. Commencement! Bells in the Music College on its high hill are ringing to summon us to the Great Dome for the revered annual ceremony!

This year, as every year, the University's Commencement is being held on the last Sunday in May; but this year will be the two hundredth anniversary of the University's founding, so the occasion will be even more festive than usual and will attract more media attention. The Governor of the State, a celebrated graduate of the University, will give the Commencement address, and three renowned Americans—the Poet, the Educator, and the Scientist—will be awarded honorary doctorates. Over four thousand degrees—B.A.'s, M.A.'s, Ph.D.'s—will be conferred on graduates, a record number. As the University Chancellor has said, "Every year our numbers are rising. But our standards are also rising. The University is at the forefront of evolution."

And so here we are on this sunny, windy May morning, streaming into the Great Dome, through Gates 1–15. Thousands of us! Young people in black academic gowns, caps precariously on their heads; their families, and friends; and many townspeople associated with the University, the predominant employer in the area. We're metal filings drawn by a powerful magnet. We're moths drawn to a sacred light. The very air through which we make our way crackles with excitement, and apprehension. Who will be taken *to the Pyramid*, how will the *ceremony of renewal* unfold? Even those of us who have attended Commencement numerous times are never prepared for the stark reality of the event, and must witness with our own eyes what we can never quite believe we've seen, for it so quickly eludes us.

The Great Dome! We're proud of our football stadium, at the northern, wooded edge of our hilly campus; it seats more than thirty thousand people, in steeply banked tiers, a multimillion-dollar structure with a sliding translucent plastic roof, contracted in fair weather. The vast football field, simulated grass of a glossy emerald green, has been transformed this morning into a more formal space: thousands of folding chairs, to accommodate our graduates, fan out before a majestic speakers' platform raised six feet above the ground, and at the center rear of this platform, festooned in the University's colors (crimson, gold) is the twelve-foot Pyramid (composed of rectangles of granite carefully set into place by workmen laboring through the night) that is the emblem of our University.

A crimson satin banner unfurled behind the platform proclaims in gold letters the University motto: NOVUS ORDO SECLORUM. ("A New Cycle of the Ages.")

It has been a chilly, fair morning after a night of thunderstorms and harsh pelting rain, typical in this northerly climate in the spring; the Chancellor, having deliberated with his staff, has decreed that the Great Dome be open to the sun. The University orchestra, seated to the left of the platform, on the grass, is playing a brisk, brassy version of the stately alma mater, and as graduates file into the stadium many of them are singing:

Where snowy peaks of mountains
Meet the eastern sky,
Proudly stands our Alma Mater
On her hilltop high.

Crimson our blood,
Deep as the sea.
Our Alma Mater,
We pledge to thee!

These words the Assistant Mace Bearer believes he can hear, a mile from the University. A sick, helpless sensation spreads through him. "So soon? It will happen—so soon?"

The Robing. In the Great Dome Triangle Lounge where VIPs assemble before Commencement, as before football games, the Chancellor's party is being robed for the ceremony. Deans of numerous colleges and schools, University marshals, the Governor, the Poet, the Educator, the Scientist, the Provost, the President of the Board of Trustees, the President of the Alumni Association, and the Chancellor himself—these distinguished individuals are being assisted in putting on their elaborate robes, hoods, and hats, and are being photographed for the news media and for University archives. There's a palpable excitement in the air even among those who have attended many such ceremonies during their years of service to the University. For something can always go wrong when so many people are involved, and in so public and dramatic a spectacle. The retiring Dean of Arts and Sciences murmurs to an old colleague, "Remember that terrible time when—" and the men laugh together and shudder. Already it is 9 AM; the ceremony is scheduled to begin promptly at 10 AM. Already the University orchestra has begun playing "Pomp and Circumstance," that thrilling processional march.

Declares the Chancellor, "Always, that music makes me shiver!"

Surrounded by devoted female assistants, this burly, kingly man of youthful middle age is being robed of magnificent crimson gown with gold-and-black velvet trim; around his neck he wears a heavy, ornate medallion, solid gold on a gold chain, embossed with the University's Pyramid seal and the Latin words *NOVUS ORDO SECLORUM.* The Chancellor has a broad buff face that resembles a face modeled in clay and thick, leonine white hair; he's a well-liked administrator among both faculty and students, a graduate of the University and one-time all-American halfback on the University's revered football team. Each year the Chancellor is baffled by which side of his crimson satin cap the gold tassel should be on, and each year his personal assistant says, with a fondly maternal air of reproach, "Mr. Chancellor, the *left.* Let me adjust it." Such a fury of activity in the Triangle Lounge! A TV crew, photographers' flashes. Where is the Dean of the Graduate School, in charge of conferring graduate degrees? Where is the Dean of the Chapel, the minister who will lead more than thirty thousand people in prayer, in less than an hour? There's the University Provost, the Chancellor's right-hand man, with a sharp eye on the clock; there's the newly appointed Dean of Human Engineering, the most heavily endowed (and controversial) of the University's school, talking and laughing casually with one of his chief donors, the billionaire President of the Board of Trustees; there's the President of the Alumni Association, another University benefactor whose gift of $35 million will be publicly announced at the luncheon following Commencement, talking with his old friend the Governor. And there's the University Mace Bearer, one of few women administrators at the University, with a helmet of pewter hair and scintillant eyes, frowning toward the entrance—"Where's my assistant?"

The Assistant Mace Bearer, the youngest member of the elite Chancellor's party—*where is he?*

In fact, the Assistant Mace Bearer is only now entering the Great Dome, at Gate 3. Hurrying! Breathless! Amid an ever-thickening stream of energetic, fresh-faced young men and women in black gowns and mortarboards, flanked by families and relatives, being directed by ushers into the immense stadium. "Show your tickets, please. Tickets?" The Assistant Mace Bearer has a special crimson ticket and is respectfully directed upstairs to the Triangle Lounge. How has it happened, he's late. . . . Traffic was clogging all streets leading to the University, he hadn't given himself enough time, reluctant to leave home, though, of course, he had no choice but to leave his home and to join the Chancellor's party as he'd agreed he would do; this is his first Commencement *on the Pyramid.* He's a recent faculty appointment, after only three years of service he's been promoted to the rank of associate professor of North American history; for a thirty-four-year-old, this is an achievement. His students admire him as Professor S——, soft-spoken and reserved but clearly intelligent; not vain, but ambitious; eager to perform well in the eyes of his elders.

"Still, I could not turn back now." As he ascends the cement stairs to Level 2. "Even now." As he makes his way in a stream of strangers along a corridor. "It isn't too late. . . ." Those smells! His stomach turns, he's passing vendors selling coffee, breakfast muffins, bagels, even sandwiches and potato chips, which young people in billowing black gowns are devouring on their way into the stadium. You would think that the occasion wasn't Commencement but an ordinary sports event. The Assistant Mace Bearer nearly collides with a gaggle of excited girls carrying sweet rolls and coffee in Styrofoam cups; he feels a pang of nausea, seeing a former student, a husky boy with close-cropped hair, wolfing down a Commencement Special—blood sausage on a hot-dog roll, with horseradish. At this time of morning!

Even as the Chancellor, the Governor, and the honorary degree recipients, the Poet, the Educator, and the Scientist are being photographed, and the Mace Bearer and the head University marshal are checking the contents of the black lacquered box that the Assistant Mace Bearer will carry, the Assistant Mace Bearer enters the Triangle Lounge. At last! Cheeks guiltily heated, he stammers an apology, but the Mace Bearer curtly says, "No matter; you're here, Professor S——." Chastened, he reports to the robing area where an older, white-haired assistant makes a check beside his name on a list and helps outfit him in his special Commencement gown, black, but made of a synthetic waterproof fabric that will wipe dry, with crimson-and-gold trim, and helps him adjust his black velvet hat. . . . "Gloves? Don't I wear—gloves?" There's a brief flurried search; of course the gloves are located: black to match the gown, and made of thin, durable rubber. When Professor S—— thanks the white-haired woman nervously, she says, with an air of mild reproach, "But this is our responsibility, Professor." She's one of those University "administrative assistants" behind the scenes of all Commencements, as of civilization itself. With a dignified gesture she indicates the boisterous Triangle Lounge in which the Chancellor's party, predominantly male, gowned, resplendent, and regal, is being organized into a double column for the processional. "This is our honor."

The Processional. At last! At 10:08 AM, almost on time, the Chancellor's party marches into the immense stadium, eye-catching in their elaborate gowns and caps: faculty and lesser administrative officers first, then the Mace Bearer and the Assistant Mace Bearer (who carries in his slightly trembling black-gloved hands the black-lacquered box), the deans of the colleges and the Dean of the Chapel, the Chancellor and his special guests. As they march, the orchestra plays "Pomp and Circumstance" ever louder, with more rhythmic emphasis. "Thrilling music," the Chancellor says to the Governor, "even after so many Commencements." The Governor, who has been smiling his broad public smile at the gowned young people seated in rows of hundreds on the stadium grass in front of the speakers' platform, says, "How much more so, Mr. Chancellor, it must be for those whose first Commencement this is, and last." The elderly Poet marches at the side of the Provost, who will present him for his honorary degree; the Poet, long a revered name in American literature, was once a tall, eagle-like imposing presence, now of less than moderate height, with slightly stooped shoulders and a ravaged yet still noble face; where lines of poetry once danced in his head, unbidden as butterflies, now he's thinking with a dull self-anger that he should be ashamed to be here, accepting yet another award for his poetry, when he hasn't written anything worthwhile in years. ("Still, I crave recognition. Loneliness terrifies me. How will it end!") Blinking in the pale, whitely glaring light of the stadium, the Poet wants to think that these respectfully applauding young people—some of them alarmingly young—in their black gowns and mortarboards, gazing at him and the other elders as they march past, know who he is, and what his work has been—a fantasy, yet how it warms him! Behind the Poet is the Educator, a heavy, flush-faced woman in her early sixties; unlike the tormented Poet, the Educator is smiling happily, for she's proud of herself, plain, big-boned, forthright, beaming with health and American optimism after decades of professional commitment; never married—"Except to my work," as she says. The Educator is one of the very first women to be awarded an honorary doctorate by the University, and so it's appropriate that she's being escorted into the stadium by the Dean of the Education School, another woman of vigorous middle age, who will present the Educator for her award. This is the Educator's first honorary doctorate; she's thinking that her years of industry and self-denial have been worth it. ("If only my parents were alive to see me! . . .")

Behind the Educator is the Scientist, a long-ago Nobel Prize winner, with gold-glinting glasses that obscure his melancholy eyes; another ravaged elderly face, rather equine, with tufted gray eyebrows, a long hawkish nose and enormous nostrils; unlike the Educator, the Scientist can't summon up much enthusiasm for this ceremony and can't quite recall why he'd accepted the invitation. ("Vanity? Or—loneliness?") For, after the Nobel, which he'd won as a brash young man of thirty-seven, what do such "honors" mean? The scientist, in his ninth decade, has come to despise most other scientists and makes little effort to keep up with new discoveries and developments, even in his old field, biology; especially, he loathes publicity-seeking idiots in fields like human genetics and "human engineering"; he believes such research to be immoral, criminal; if he had his way, it would be banned by the U.S. government. (However, the Scientist keeps such views to himself. He knows better than to say such inflammatory things. And he has to admit that, yes, if he were a young man again, very possibly he'd be involved in such research himself, and to hell with the views of his elders.) Marching into the stadium, past the rows of gowned young people, so fresh-faced, so expectant, blinking at their revered elders and intermittently applauding, the Scientist oscillates between a sense of his own considerable worth and the fact that, to all but a handful of the many thousands of men and women in this ghastly open space, he's a name out of the distant past, if a "name" at all; younger scientists in his field are astonished, if perhaps not very interested, to hear that he's still alive. Such a fate, the Scientist thinks, is a kind of irony. And irony has no place on Commencement day, only homilies and uplifting sentiments. "The young know nothing of irony, as they know nothing of subtlety or mortality," the Scientist observes dryly to his escort, the Dean of the Graduate School, who inclines his head politely but murmurs only a vague assent. With "Pomp and Circumstance" being played so loudly, as the processional of dignitaries passes close by the orchestra, very likely the Graduate Dean can't hear the Scientist.

As the Mace Bearer and the Assistant Mace Bearer ascend the steps to the platform, there's rippling applause from graduates assembled on the grass. "With young people, you can't tell: are they honoring us, or mocking us?" the Mace Bearer observes with a grim smile to her silent assistant. Professor S——, who has attended a number of Commencements at the University, as a B.A. candidate (summa cum laude, history) and more recently as a young faculty member, would like to assure the Mace Bearer that the applause is genuine, but it isn't for them as individuals: the applause is for their function, and more specifically for the contents of the black-lacquered box. Taking his seat beside the Mace Bearer, to the immediate right of the Pyramid, the Assistant Mace Bearer glances out at the audience for the first time and swallows hard. So many! And what will they expect from him! (For the nature of the Assistant Mace Bearer's task is that it cannot be rehearsed, only "premeditated," according to tradition.) A thrill of boyish excitement courses through him. He's breathing quickly, and grateful to be finished with the procession. Nothing went wrong; he hadn't stumbled on any steps, hadn't become lightheaded in the cool, white-tinged air. The thought has not yet come to him, sly as a knife blade in the heart: *But now you can't escape.* By his watch the time is 10:17 AM.

The Invocation. The Dean of the Chapel, an impressive masculine figure in a black gown trimmed with crimson-and-gold velvet, like the Chancellor a former University athlete (rowing), comes forward to the podium, in front of the Pyramid, to lead the gathering in a prayer. "Ladies and gentlemen, will you please rise?" Despite its size, the crowd is eager to obey as a puppy. The gowned graduates, and the spectators in the steeply banked stadium, all rise to their feet at once and lower their eyes as the Dean of the Chapel addresses "Almighty God, Creator of Heaven and Earth," alternately praising this being for His beneficence and asking of Him forgiveness, inspiration, imagination, strength to fulfill the sacred obligations prescribed by "the very presence of the Pyramid"; to enact once again the sacred "ceremony of renewal" that has made this day, as "all our days," possible. The Poet is thinking how banal, such words; though they may be true, he isn't listening very closely; in a lifetime one hears the same words repeated endlessly, in familiar combinations, for the fund of words is finite while the appetite for uttering them is infinite. (Is this a new idea? Or has the Poet had such a thought numerous times, while sitting on stages, gazing out into audiences with his small fixed dignified-elder smile?) The Educator, seated beside the Poet, listens to the chaplain's invocation more attentively; she can't escape feeling that this Commencement revolves somehow around *her*, there are few women on the platform, and it's rare indeed that any woman, however deserving, has received an honorary doctorate from the University. She imagines (not for the first time!) that, in any gathering, young women are admiring her as a model of what they might accomplish with hard work, talent, and diligence. ("And self-sacrifice. Of course.") The Scientist is shifting restlessly in his chair, which is a folding chair, and damned hard on his lean haunches. Religious piety! The appeal to mass emotions! Thousands of years of "civilization" have passed, and yet humankind seems incapable of transcending its primitive origins. . . . The Scientist oscillates between feeling despair over this fact, which suggests a fundamental failure of science to educate the population, and simple contempt. The Scientist resents that he has been invited to this Commencement only to be subjected to the usual superstitious rhetoric in which (he would guess!) virtually no one on the speakers' platform believes; yet the chaplain is allowed to drone on for ten minutes while thousands of credulous onlookers gaze up at him. ". . . we thank You particularly on this special day, the two hundredth anniversary of the University's Commencement, when Your generosity and love overflow upon us, and our sacrifice to You flows upward to be renewed, in you, as rainfall enriches the earth. . . ." So the broad-shouldered Dean of the Chapel intones, raising his beefy hands aloft in an attitude of, to the Scientist, outrageous supplication. There's a brisk, chilly breeze; the sky overhead is no longer clear, but laced with cloud-like frost on a windowpane; the crimson banners draped about the platform stir restlessly, as if a god were coming to life, rousing himself awake.

The Poet opens his eyes wide. Has he been drifting off into sleep? Or—has he been touched by inspiration, as he has rarely been touched in recent years? (In fact, in decades.) He smiles, thinking yes he is proud to be here, he believes his complexly rhyming, difficult poetry may be due for a revival.

Presentation of Colors. Here's a welcome quickening of spirit after the solemnity of the chaplain's prayer! Marching army and air force cadets in their smart uniforms, three young men and two young women, bear three colorful flags: the U.S. flag, the state flag, and the University's crimson and gold. The army cadets flanking the flag bearers carry rifles on their shoulders. A display of military force, in this peaceful setting? The Educator, a pacifist, disapproves. The Scientist gazes on such primitive rituals with weary scorn. Display of arms! Symbolizing the government's power to protect, and to destroy, human life in its keeping! A crude appeal to the crude limbic brain, yet as always, it's effective. The Poet squints and blinks and opens his faded eyes wider. Flapping flags, shimmering colors, what do these things mean? In the past, such moments of public reverie provided the Poet with poetry: mysterious lines, images, rhythms came fully formed to him as if whispered into his ear. Now he listens with mounting excitement, and hears—what? ("The God of the Great Dome. Stirring, waking.") In his deep well-practiced baritone voice the Chancellor addressed the audience from the podium: "Ladies and gentlemen, will you please rise for the national anthem?" Another time the great beast of a crowd eagerly rises. More than thirty thousand individuals are led in the anthem, a singularly muscular, vulgar music (thinks the Scientist, who plays violin in a string quartet, and whose favorite music is late Beethoven) by a full-throated young black woman, one of this year's graduates of the Music School. *O say can you see . . . bombs bursting in air.* Patriotic thrill! The Educator, though a pacifist, finds herself singing with the rest. Her voice is surprisingly weak and uncertain for a woman of her size and seeming confidence, yet she's proud of her country, proud of its history; for all our moral lapses, and an occasional overzealousness in defending our boundaries (in Mexico in the mid-nineteenth century, in Vietnam in the mid-twentieth century, for instance), the United States is a *great nation*. . . . ("And I am an American.") The Poet is thinking: Blood leaps!—like young trout flashing in the sun. ("Of what dark origins, who can prophesy?") The Poet cares nothing, truly, for what is moral, what is right, what is decent, what is good; the Poet cares only for poetry; the Poet's heart would quicken, except its beat is measured by a pacemaker stitched deep in his hollow chest. This is the first poetic "gift" he's had in years, he could weep with gratitude.

The Assistant Mace Bearer, standing beside the Mace Bearer in the pose of a healthy young warrior-son beside his mother, tall and imposing in her ceremonial attire, clenches his fists to steady his trembling. But is he nervous, or is he excited? He's proud, he thinks, of his country; of those several flapping flags; to each, he bears a certain allegiance. As a professor of North American history he would readily concede that "nations"—"political entities"—are but ephemeral structures imposed upon a "natural" state of heterogeneous peoples, and yet—how patriotism stirs the blood, how real it is; and how reassuring, this morning, to see such impressive masculine figures as the Chancellor, the Dean of the Chapel, the Provost, the President of the Board of Trustees, and others are on the platform, praying, singing the national anthem, in the service, as he is, of the Pyramid. Even if strictly speaking Professor S—— isn't a believer, he takes solace in being amid believers. . . . The Assistant Mace Bearer is particularly proud of the burly, authoritative figure of the Chancellor; though he has reason to believe that the Dean of Arts and Sciences invited him to assist the Mace Bearer, and not the Chancellor, he prefers to think that the Chancellor himself knew of young Professor S——'s work and singled him out for this distinction.

The national anthem is over, the young black soprano has stepped back from the microphone, the thousands of graduates and spectators in the stadium are again seated, with a collective sigh. Such yearning, suddenly! And the spring sun hidden behind a bank of clouds dull as scoured metal.

Commencement Address. Now comes the Governor to the podium amid applause to speak to the Class of —— in an oiled, echoing voice. Like his friend the Chancellor, the Governor has a large face that resembles an animated clay mask; he's bluff, ruggedly handsome, righteous. He speaks of a "spiritually renewed, resolute future" that nonetheless "strengthens our immortal ties with the past." His words are vague yet emphatic, upbeat yet charged with warning—"Always recall: moral weakness precedes political, military, sovereign weakness." With practiced hand gestures the Governor charges today's graduates with the mission of "synthesizing" past and future communities and "never shrinking from sacrifice of self, in the service of the community." The Poet wakes from a light doze, annoyed by this politician's rhetoric. Why has *he*, a major figure of the twentieth century, been invited to the University's Commencement, to endure such empty abstractions? If the Governor speaks of ideals, they are "selfless ideals"; if he speaks of paths to be taken, they are "untrod paths." The Governor is one who leaves no cliché unturned, thinks the Poet, with a small smile. (This is a clever thought, yes? Or has he had it before, at other awards ceremonies?) Minutes pass. Gray-streaked clouds thicken overhead. There's a veiled glance between the Chancellor and the Provost: the Governor's speech has gone beyond his allotted fifteen minutes, the more than four thousand black-gowned graduates are getting restless as young animals penned in a confined space. When the Governor tells jokes ("my undergraduate major here was political science with minors in Frisbee and Budweiser"), the audience groans and laughs at excessive length, with outburst and applause. (The beaming Governor doesn't seem to catch on, this mocking, not appreciative, laughter.) A danger sign, thinks the Assistant Mace Bearer, who recalls such whirlpools of adolescent-audience rebellion from his own days, not so very long ago, as an undergraduate at the University.

So it happens: at the center of the traditionally rowdiest school of graduates, the engineers, of whom ninety-nine percent are male, what looks like a naked mannequin—female?—suddenly appears, having been smuggled into the stadium beneath someone's gown. There are ripples of laughter from the other graduates as the thing is tossed boldly aloft and passed from hand to hand like a volleyball. University marshals in their plain black gowns are pressed into immediate service, trying without success to seize the mannequin; such juvenile pranks are forbidden at Commencement, of course, as students have been repeatedly warned. But the temptation to violate taboo and annoy one's elders is too strong; many graduates have been partying through the night and have been waiting for just such a moment of release. As the governor stubbornly continues with his prepared speech, in which jokes are "ad-libbed" into the text, there are waves of tittering laughter as a second and a third mannequin appear, gaily tossed and batted about. One of these is captured by a red-faced University marshal, eliciting a mixed response of boos and cheers. The mood in the Great Dome is mischievous and childish, not mutinous. This is all good-natured—isn't it? Then another mannequin is tossed up, naked, but seemingly male; where his genitals would have been there are swaths of red paint; on his back, flesh-colored strips of rubber have been glued which flutter like ribbons to be torn at, and torn off, by grasping male fingers. There's an intake of thousands of breaths; not much laughter; a wave of disapproval and revulsion, even from other graduates. A sense that *this has gone too far, this is not funny.*

What a strange, ugly custom, thinks the Educator, polishing her glasses to see more clearly, if it is a custom? Are those young people *drunk?*

Primitives! Thinks the Scientist, his deeply creased face fixed in an expression of polite disdain. In situations in which there are large masses of individuals, especially young males poised between the play of adolescence and the responsibilities of adulthood, it's always risky to court rebellion, even if it's playful rebellion, beneath the collective gaze of elder family members. (Long ago, the Scientist did research in neurobiology, investigating the limbic system, the oldest part of the brain; the ancient part of the brain, you might say; his focus was a tiny structure known as the amygdala. The amygdala primes the body for action in a survival situation, but remains inoperative, as if slumbering, otherwise. In his ninth decade, the Scientist thinks wryly, his amygdala might have become a bit rusty from disuse.)

A spirit of misuse! Thinks the Poet, smiling. Despite his age, and the dignity of his position on the platform, the Poet feels by nature, or wants badly to feel, a tug of sympathy for those blunt-faced grinning young men. For the Governor, that ass of a politician, *is* an oily bore. At the luncheon following Commencement, the Poet presumes that he, and the other honorary award recipients, will be called upon to speak briefly, and he will proclaim to the admiring guests—"The spirit of poetry is the spirit of youthful rebellion, the breaking of customs, and, yes, sometimes the violation of *taboo*."

But the offensive bloody mannequin is quickly surrendered to an indignant University marshal, who folds it up (it appears to be made of inflatable rubber) and quickly trundles it away. The other mannequins disappear beneath seats as the now frowning Governor concludes his remarks with a somber charge to the graduates to "take on the mantle of adulthood and responsibility"—"put away childish things, and give of yourself in sacrifice, where needed, in the nation's—and in the species'—service." These are rousing words, if abstract, and the audience responds with generous applause, as if to compensate for the rudeness of the engineers. The Governor, again beaming, even raises his fist aloft in victory as he steps from the podium.

("What a fool a politician is," thinks the Poet smugly. "The man has not a clue, how the wayward spirit of the god, inhabiting that crowd, could have destroyed him utterly.")

Recognition of Class Marshals and Scholars. Conferring of Ph.D. Degrees. Now follows a lengthy, disjointed Commencement custom, in which numerous graduates in billowing black gowns and mortarboards, smiling shyly, stiffly, at times radiantly as they shake hands with their respective deans, the Provost, and the Chancellor, proceed across the platform from left to right. For these scholars, Commencement is the public recognition of years of hope and industry; many of them are being honored with awards, fellowships, grants to continue their research in postdoctoral programs at the University or elsewhere. Many of the scientists have received grants from private corporations to sponsor their research in biogenetics, bioengineering, bioethics. The Poet, the Educator, and the Scientist, sobered by the number of "outstanding" individuals who must pass across the stage as their names are announced, shake hands with administrators, and receive their diplomas, and descend the stage, are nonetheless impressed by this display of superior specimens of the younger generation. So many! Of so many ethnic minorities, national identities, skin colors! The University seems to draw first-rate students from many foreign countries. And all are so hopeful, shaking hands with the Chancellor, glancing with shy smiles at the revered dignitaries on the platform. The Poet, the Educator, and the Scientist suddenly feel—it's quick as a knife blade to the heart, so swift as to be almost painless—that these young people will soon surpass them, or have already surpassed them, not defiantly, not rebelliously, but simply as a matter of course. *This is their time. Our time is past. Yet, here we are!* The Poet tries to fashion a poem out of this revelation, which strikes him as new, fresh, daunting, though (possibly!) it's a revelation he has had in the past, at such ceremonies. The Educator smiles benignly, a motherly, perhaps grandmotherly figure in her billowing gown, for, as an educator, she expects her work, her theories, her example to be surpassed by idealistic young people—of course. The Scientist is aghast, and fully awakened from his mild trance, to learn that his own area of biological research, for which he and two teammates were awarded their Nobel Prizes, seems to have been totally revolutionized. "Cloning"—a notion of science fiction, long ridiculed and ethically repugnant—is now a simple matter of fact: five young scientists are receiving postdoctoral grants from private corporations to continue their experiments, which seem to have resulted in the actual creation, in University laboratories, of successfully cloned creatures. ("Though no *Homo sapiens*," the Graduate Dean remarks, no doubt for the benefit of wealthy alumni who disapprove of such science.) There are Ph.D.'s who seem to have experimented successfully in grafting together parts of bodies from individuals of disparate species; there are Ph.D.'s who seem to have altered DNA in individuals; an arrogant-looking young astrophysicist has received a postdoctoral fellowship to continue his exploration into the "elasticity of time" and the possibility of "sending objects through time." There's an obese, in fact grotesquely deformed female in a motorized wheelchair whom the Graduate Dean describes (unless the Scientist mishears?) as a "colony of grafted alien protoplasm." There's an entirely normal-appearing young man in black cap and gown who moves phantomlike across the stage, seeming to shake hands with the Graduate Dean but unable to accept his diploma; the audience erupts into applause, informed that this is a "living hologram" of the scientist himself, who is thousands of miles away. ("But his diploma is thoroughly 'real,'" the Graduate Dean says with a wink.)

Most repulsive, but stirring even more applause from the audience, is a human head on a self-propelled gurney! This head is of normal size and dimensions, with a normal if somewhat coarse female face; there's a mortarboard on the head and bright lipstick on the mouth of the face. Evidently, this is an adventurous young scientist whose experimental subject was herself! The technical description of this "extraordinary, controversial" neurophysiological project in detaching a head from a body and equipping it with computer-driven autonomy is so abstruse, even the Scientist can't grasp it, and the Poet and the Educator are left gaping.

Other projects include minute mappings of distant galaxies, "reengineering" of repressed memory in brain tissue, computational mathematics in fetal research, "game theory" and sensory transduction, "viral economics" in west Africa, computational microbial pathogenesis! By the time this portion of Commencement ends, with tumultuous applause and cheers, even the younger members of the Chancellor's party, like the Assistant Mace Bearer, are feeling dazed.

The Pyramid. The Ceremony of Renewal. Conferring of Honorary Degrees. The orchestra plays the alma mater now in a slower rhythm, eerily beautiful, nostalgic, not a brisk march but an incantatory dirge, featuring celli, oboes, and harp, as the somber Dean of the Music College leads thousands of voices in a song that thrills even the Poet, the Educator, and the Scientist, who are new to this University's Commencement and unfamiliar with the song before today.

Where snowy peaks of mountains
Meet the eastern sky,
Proudly stands our Alma Mater
On her hilltop high.

Crimson our blood,
Deep as the sea.
Our Alma Mater,
We pledge to thee!

(The Poet shivers, in his light woolen gown. Abysmal rhyming, utterly simple and predictable verse, and yet—! This, too, is poetry, with a powerful effect upon these thousands of spectators.)

The ceremony *on the Pyramid* is the climax of Commencement, and through the stadium, as well as on the platform, anticipation has been steadily mounting. There's an electric air of unease, apprehension, excitement. The Assistant Mace Bearer, too, shivers in his gown, though not for the reason the Poet has shivered.

For nearly an hour he has sat beside the Mace Bearer, close by the Pyramid, the black-lacquered box on his lap, firmly in his gloved fingers. His heartbeat is quickening, there's a swirl of nausea in his bowels. *No, I should not be here, this is a mistake.*

Yet, here he is! Escape for him now, as for the Poet, the Educator, and the Scientist, is not possible.

For the Chancellor has resumed his place at the podium to speak, in a dramatic voice, of the "oldest, most mysterious" part of Commencement; the "very core, of the Pyramid," of Commencement; a "precious fossil of an earlier time"—hundreds of thousands of years before *Homo sapiens* lived. "Yet our ancestors are with us; their blood beats proudly in our veins. We wed their strength to our neuro-ingenuity. We triumph in the twenty-first century because they, our ancestors, prevailed in their centuries." There's a flurry of applause. The uplifted faces among the young graduates are rapt in expectation, their eyes widened and shining.

The Assistant Mace Bearer finds himself on his feet. His entire body feels numb. There's a roaring in his ears. The Mace Bearer nudges him gently, as if to wake him from a trance. "Professor S——! Just follow me." Like an obedient son the Assistant Mace Bearer follows this tall, capable woman with the steely eyes who carries the University's ceremonial mace (a replica of a medieval spiked staff, approximately forty inches in length, made of heavy, gleaming brass) as he, the young professor of North American history, bears the black-lacquered box in his gloved hands; together they march to the base of the Pyramid as the Chancellor intones in his sonorous baritone, "Candidates for honorary doctorates will please *rise*." And so the Poet, the Educator, and the Scientist self-consciously stand, adjusting their long robes, and are escorted to the base of the Pyramid by the Provost, the Dean of the Education School, and the Dean of the Graduate School respectively; in the buzzing elation of the moment it will not occur to these elders that their escorts are gripping them firmly at the elbow, and that the Mace Bearer and her able young assistant are flanking them closely. As the Chancellor reads citations for "these individuals of truly exceptional merit . . . " thousands of eyes are fastened avidly upon the Poet, the Educator, and the Scientist; even as there are a perceptible number of individuals, almost entirely female, who turn aside, or lower their eyes, or even hide behind their Commencement programs, unable to watch the sudden violent beauty of the *ceremony of renewal.*

The University orchestra is playing the alma mater more urgently now. The tempo of Commencement is quickening, like a gigantic pulse. Only just beginning to register uncertainty, the Poet, the Educator, and the Scientist are being escorted up the inlaid granite steps of the Pyramid, to the sacred apex; ascending just before them are the Mace Bearer and the Assistant Mace Bearer, taking the steps in measured stride. There's a collective intake of breath through the stadium. The sacred moment is approaching! A glimmer of pale sun is seen overhead, bordered by massive clouds. The Poet stammers to the Provost, whom he had mistaken as a loyal companion through the ritual of Commencement, "W-what is happening? Why are—?" The Educator, a stout woman, is suddenly short of breath and smiles in confusion at the sea of faces below, greedily watching her and the other honorees; she turns to her escort, to ask, "Excuse me? Why are we—?" when she's abruptly silenced by a tight black band wrapped around the lower part of her face, wielded by the Dean of Education and an assistant. At the same time, the Poet is gagged, flailing desperately. The Scientist, the most suspicious of the three elders, resists his captors, putting up a struggle—"How dare you! I refuse to be—!" He manages to descend several steps before he, too, is caught, silenced by a black gag and his thin arms pinioned behind him.

In the wild widened eyes of the honorees there's the single shared thought. *This can't be happening! Not this!*

As these distinguished elders struggle for their lives at the apex of the Pyramid, the vast crowd rises to its feet like a great beast and sighs; even the rowdiest of the young graduates quiver in sudden instinctive sympathy. There's a wisdom of the Pyramid, well known to those who have attended numerous Commencements: "Life honors life"—"The heart of one call to the heart of many."

The Chancellor continues, raising his voice in recitation of the old script: "By the power invested in me Chancellor of this University, I hereby confer upon you the degrees of Doctor of Humane Letters, *honoris causa* . . ." The elders' robes have been torn open; their faces, deathly white, distended by the tightly wrapped black bands, register unspeakable terror, and incredulity. *This can't be happening! Not this!* Through the stadium, spectators are swaying from side to side, some of them having linked arms; it's a time when one will link arms with strangers, warmly and even passionately; more than thirty thousand people are humming, or singing, the alma mater, as the orchestra continues to play sotto voce, with a ghostly predominance of celli, oboes, and harp. *Crimson our blood, deep as the sea* . . . Many in the audience are openly weeping. Even among the dignitaries on the platform there are several who wipe at their eyes, though the wonders of Commencement are not new to them. There are some who stare upward at the ancient struggle, panting as if they themselves have been forcibly marched up the granite steps from which, for the *honorees of sacrifice*, there can be no escape.

(It's a theory advanced by the Dean of the Graduate School, who has a degree in clinical psychology, that to experience the ritual of Commencement is to experience, again and again, one's first Commencement, so that intervening years are obliterated—"In the *ceremony of renewal*, Time has ceased to exist. On the Pyramid we are all immortal, and we weep at the beauty of such knowledge.")

The *moment of truth* is imminent. The Dean of the Chapel, an imposing manly figure in his resplendent gown and velvet cap, climbs the granite steps like one ascending a mountain. The orchestra is now playing the alma mater at double time; it's no longer a dirge but a fevered tarantella. The tight-lipped Mace Bearer makes a signal to her trembling assistant, and the Assistant Mace Bearer opens the black-lacquered box and presents to the Mace Bearer the *instrument of deliverance*, which she bears aloft, toward the sun. This appears to be a primitive stone dagger but is in fact a sharply honed stainless steel butcher's knife with an eighteen-inch blade. The Mace Bearer holds it above her head, solemnly she "whirls" it in one direction, and then in another; this gesture is repeated twice; for every inch of the *instrument of deliverance* must be exposed to the sun, to absorb its blessing. The dagger is then sunk deep into the chests of the honorees; it's used to pry the rib cages open and to hack away at the flesh encasing the still-beating hearts, which emerge from the lacerated chests like panicked birds. These, the Dean of the Chapel must seize bare-handed, according to custom, and raise skyward as high as he is capable.

Led by the Chancellor's deep baritone, the vast crowd chants: "*Novus ordo seclorum.*"

(A lucky coincidence! A pale, fierce sun has nearly penetrated the barrier of rain clouds, and within seconds will be shining freely. Though the ceremony of renewal has long been recognized as purely symbolic, and only the very old or the very young believe that it has an immediate effect upon the sun, yet it's thrilling when the sun does emerge at this dramatic moment. . . . Cries of joy are heard throughout the stadium.)

The hearts, no longer beating, are placed reverently on an altar at the Pyramid's apex.

Next, the *ceremony of the skin*. The Mace Bearer and her assistant are charged with the difficult task of flying the bodies; it's a task demanding as much precision as, or more precision than, removing the beating hearts. Now mere corpses, the bodies of the Poet, the Educator, and the Scientist would sink down lifeless, and fall to the base of the Pyramid, but are held erect as if living. Blood flows from their gaping chest cavities as if valves have opened, into grooves that lead to a fan-shaped granite pool beneath the speakers' platform. By tradition, the Mace Bearer flays two of the bodies, and the Assistant Mace Bearer flays the third, for the *ceremony of renewal* also involves, for younger participants, an initiation. ("One day, you will be Mace Bearer, Professor S——! So watch closely.") Under enormous pressure, knowing that the eyes of thousands of people are fixed upon him, still more the eyes of the Chancellor and his party, the Assistant Mace Bearer makes his incision at the hairline of his corpse, with the blood-smeared dagger; it's slippery in his fingers, so he must grip it tight; and delicately, very slowly peels the skin downward. The ideal is a virtually entire, perfect skin but this ideal is rarely achieved, of course. (Tradition boasts of a time when "perfect skins" were frequently achieved, but such claims are believed to be mythic.) Both the Poet and the Educator yield lacerated skins, and the Scientist yields a curiously translucent skin, like the husk of a locust, which is light and airy and provokes from the crowd, as the skins are held aloft and made to "dance" to the tarantella music, an outburst of ecstatic cries and howls.

The Assistant Mace Bearer, exhausted by his ordeal, hides his face in his hands and weeps, forgetting that his gloved hands are sticky with blood, and will leave a blood-mask on his heated face.

Conferring of Baccalaureate and Associate Degrees. Three graduates of the Class of ——, two young men and one young woman, with the highest grade point averages at the University, are brought to the platform to bear aloft the skins, and to continue the "dance" while the deans of various schools present their degree candidates and confer degrees upon them. (By tradition, these young people once stripped naked and slipped into the flayed skins, to dance; but nakedness would be considered primitive today, if not repulsive, in such a circumstance. And the skins of elder honorees surely would not fit our husky, healthy youths.) One by one the University's schools are honored. One by one the deans intone, "By the authority invested in me . . ." Hundreds of graduates leap to their feet as their schools are named, smiling and waving to their families in the bleachers. College of Arts and Sciences. School of Architecture. School of Education. School of Engineering and Computer Science. School of Social Work. Public Affairs. Speech and Performing Arts. Environmental Studies. Nursing. Agricultural Sciences. Human Engineering. Hotel Management. Business Administration . . . There are prolonged cheers and applause. Balloons are tossed into the air. Champagne bottles, smuggled into the Great Dome, are now being uncorked, University marshals are less vigilant, the mood of the stadium is suffused with gaiety, release. The Chancellor concludes Commencement with a few words—"Congratulations to all, and God be with you. I now declare the University's two hundredth Commencement officially ended."

The University orchestra is again playing "Pomp and Circumstance" as the Chancellor's party descends from the platform.

(And what of the pulpy, skinned bodies of the honorees? Now mere garbage, these have been allowed to tumble behind the Pyramid into a pit, lined with plastic, and have been covered by a tarpaulin, to be disposed of by the groundskeepers when the stadium is emptied. By tradition, such flayed bodies, lacking hearts, are "corrupted, contaminated" meat from which the mysterious spark of life has fled, and no one would wish to gaze upon them.)

Recessional. The triumphant march out! Past elated, cheering graduates, whose tassels are now proudly displayed on the left side of their mortarboards. The pale fierce sun is still shining, to a degree. It's a windy May morning, not yet noon; the sky is riddled with shreds of cloud. The Chancellor's party marches across the bright green AstroTurf in reverse order of their rank, as they'd entered. Familiar as it is, "Pomp and Circumstance" is still thrilling, heartening. "We tried Commencement with another march," the Dean of Music observes, "and it just wasn't the same." The Mace Bearer and the Assistant Mace Bearer march side by side; the Assistant Mace Bearer is carrying the black-lacquered box, in which the *instrument of deliverance* is enclosed. (It was a thoughtful maternal gesture on the part of the Mace Bearer to wet a tissue with her tongue and dab off the blood smears on her assistant's face, before they left the platform.) In fact the Assistant Mace Bearer is feeling dazed, unreal. His eyes ache as if he has been gazing too long into the sun and he feels some discomfort, a stickiness inside one of his gloves, which must have been torn in the ceremony; but his hands are steadier now, and his fingers grip the black-lacquered box tight. Marching past rows of gowned graduates he sees several former students, some of them cheering wildly; their glazed eyes pass over his face, and return, with looks of shocked recognition and admiration. ("Prof. S——!" yells a burly young man. "*Cool.*") A number of the bolder young people have slipped past University marshals to dip their hands and faces in the pool of warm blood at the base of the platform. Some are even kneeling and lapping like puppies, muzzles glistening with blood.

"Am I happy? It's over, at least."

The Assistant Mace Bearer stumbles midway across the field, but regains his balance quickly, before the Mace Bearer can take hold of his arm; he dreads the woman's touch and his own eager response to it. "Professor S——! Are you all right?" Certainly he's all right, the cheering of thousands of spectators is buoyant, like water bearing him up; he would sink, and drown, except the passion of the crowd sustains him. He would choke, except the crowd breathes for him. He would stumble and fall and scream, a fist jammed against his mouth, except the crowd forbids such a display of unmanly behavior. . . . He perceives that his life has been cut in two as with an *instrument of deliverance.* His old, ignorant, unconscious life, and his new, transformed, conscious life. Yes, he's happy! *I am among them now. I have my place now.*

The Graduate Dean observes, passing by graduates clustered excitedly at the foot of the platform, "So encouraging! You can forgive these kids almost anything, at Commencement."

The Chancellor observes, "It's a sight that makes me realize, we are our youth, and they us."

Disrobing. Returned to the Triangle Lounge, the Chancellor's party is disrobing. What relief! What a glow of satisfaction, as after a winning football game. The Chancellor, the Governor, and the President of the Board of Trustees, three beaming individuals of vigorous middle age, are being interviewed by a TV broadcaster about the "special significance" of the two hundredth anniversary. Everywhere in the lounge there's an air of festivity. Flashbulbs are blinding, greetings and handshakes are exchanged. The Assistant Mace Bearer enters shyly, to surrender his blood-dampened gown and torn rubber gloves, and immediately he's being congratulated on a "job well done." The Graduate Dean himself shakes his hand. The Provost! "Thank you. I—I'm grateful for your words." More photographers appear. A second TV crew, hauling equipment. Bottles of champagne are uncorked. The Assistant Mace Bearer would accept a glass of champagne but doesn't trust his stomach, and his nerves.

Is he envious? Shortly after the disrobing there will be a lavish luncheon for most of the Chancellor's party at the University Club, but Professor S—— is not invited; the Assistant Mace Bearer is too minor an individual to have been included with the others. Another year, perhaps!

He has exited the room, eager to be gone. Makes his way along a corridor like a man in a dream. Without his Commencement costume, he feels exposed as if naked to the eyes of strangers; yet, paradoxically, he's invisible; in ordinary clothes he's of no extraordinary importance; he hopes no former students will notice him. . . . He's passing swarms of graduates, still in their robes, and their families and relatives, all smiles. Small children are running feverishly about. The smell! Professor S——'s mouth waters furiously. Food is again being sold, everywhere customers are queuing up to buy.

Minutes later he's devouring a Commencement Special. Horseradish and sausage juice dribble down his hands, he's famished.

JOYCE CAROL OATES is one of the most prolific and respected writers in the United States today. Oates has written fiction in almost every genre and medium. Her keen interest in the Gothic and psychological horror has spurred her to write dark suspense novels under the name Rosamond Smith, to write enough stories in the genre to have published five collections of dark fiction—the most recent are *The Museum of Dr. Moses: Tales of Mystery and Suspense* and *Wild Nights!: Stories about the Last Days of Poe, Dickinson, Twain, James, and Hemingway*—and to edit *American Gothic Tales.* Oates's short novel *Zombie* won the Bram Stoker Award, and she has been honored with a Life Achievement Award by the Horror Writers Association.

Oates's most recent novels are *Blood Mask, The Gravedigger's Daughter,* and *My Sister, My Love: The Intimate Story of Skyler Rampike.* She has been living in Princeton, New Jersey, since 1978, where she teaches creative writing. She and her husband Raymond J. Smith ran the small press and literary magazine *Ontario Review* for many years, until he died in 2008.

OATES SAYS: *When I was eleven or twelve years old, I discovered H. P. Lovecraft in the Lockport Public Library, in upstate New York—the collection of Lovecraft stories was large and unwieldy with a distinctive font, which I can "see" vividly if I shut my eyes. The stories that riveted me immediately were "The Rats in the Walls" and "The Dunwich Horror." At once I fell under the Lovecraftian spell—subsequently I have reprinted Lovecraft tales in anthologies of "literary" stories in the hope of breaking down the artificial barriers and unfortunate prejudices between genres.*

SIMON KURT UNSWORTH

Vernon, Driving

VERNON DROVE.

He did not drive with a destination in mind, but let the roads and traffic choose for him. Along with one stream of cars, across another, stopping here and going there, just driving and yet leaving nothing behind. Around in circles. At first, he had tried to drive with the radio on, but its chatter became wearing so he turned it off. Then, however, the silence allowed his thoughts to swell, fill the car and press against his skin like thorns, so he turned it back on and found a classical music station with little talk. That kept the thinking at bay.

Vernon had first met Jay, and introduced him to Scott, at a reading in the library's committee room late the previous year. It was one of the few perks of Vernon's job: working in the library was rarely exciting, but occasionally local authors would agree to attend groups or give readings, and then Vernon would experience a small break with his established routines, and could have fun. Jay's reading was actually shared with two other up-and-coming local literary figures, a poet whose poems had won small-press rave reviews and a novelist whose intense, angry prose alienated as many people as it impressed. The three had amused Vernon, although he had not let it show. They looked similar, all in jeans and jackets and boots and T-shirts with political slogans or band photographs printed on them, and they had acted as though what they were reading, what they had written, was going to shake the pillars of the earth.

Eventually, the constant circling grated on Vernon's nerves and he began to follow a route rather than simply driving. He started to make decisions, making choices and following roads, although he still did not know exactly where he was going. Out, certainly. Out of the town. Somewhere. Anywhere. *Away.* As he drove, he wished that he could shed the hurt behind him in chunks, discarding it out of the window like old cigarette butts and the empty chocolate bar and prepackaged food wrappers that lined the sides of the road wherever he went these days, but it was not to be. It stayed, clinging with fingers like old clicking bone and growing like some malignant ulcer in his belly that pressed up against his solar plexus and compressed his breathing into hard little bullets.

The poet and the other novelist, who made little impression on the assembled crowd in the library, were soon finished and then it was Jay's turn. Vernon had to admit he was a good-looking boy, even if he wasn't Vernon's type: tall but not too skinny, his hair long and pushed back from a smooth forehead. His black jeans and jacket hung nicely about him, framing rather than hiding his figure, and his smile, which he did too rarely, was open and engaging. He had introduced himself briefly and then, leaning over the lectern casually and looking down at his typed sheets only once or twice, started to read.

The denser buildings of the city center finally fell away and became the more widely spaced homes and shops of suburban living, the gardens and houses chained and docile behind fences that crept up in height each year as the world became a less friendly place. Vernon had lived out here once, but had moved at Scott's behest, transplanting them to an apartment high in a building that had no garden, surrounded by other buildings that had no gardens, but did have underground parking and CCTV in the lobby, monitored twenty-four hours by faceless security firms. Vernon had hated it really, but had coped because of Scott. Because he loved Scott, loved him for his energy and youth and passion, for the way he talked about each day as though it were something special, had some new gift just ready to unfurl for him, for the way he kissed Vernon goodbye whenever he left and hugged him hello when he returned. Vernon tried to approach things the same way Scott did, but never felt he managed it; his age, his attitude, seemed to prevent him, made him slower, always behind Scott, encouraging and loving but never partaking. Now, the spaces between the houses seemed to mock him for ever leaving, for ever thinking that someone like him could exist happily in the claustrophobic depths of the city. In their open, capricious shadows, Vernon saw a mockery of the space he thought he and Scott had carved for themselves and the pain bloomed, bitter and raw.

"They came," Jay read, "from their places on the far side of reality, tearing open the thin barrier between their vast, cold plane of existence and ours and dragging themselves towards us and they were as inexorable as the movement of the abyssal oceans or the final setting of a sun gone hidden and dark. As they passed, the walls were sucked free of life and grew brittle and were marked with their text, words written in blood and unreadable by any human eye. Their bodies filled the streets and their foul, flailing limbs clutched at any place they could gain hold, clutched and held so that they could not be dislodged. Men went mad at the sight of them, their hair becoming white as ash as they gazed upon their faces and at their bloated flesh. Terrible and ancient and scarred with the endless cold of space, the terrible and ancient things glistened with frozen moisture and colors played across the surface of their skin, colors that were never meant to be seen on earth. Before them, humankind could not stand and instead fled or fell beneath claws or teeth or arms that had no bones and yet a million grasping limbs, were taken into the shadows of the world where the gnashing things could feed, twisting and writhing about the ripped and torn flesh of men and the opened bellies of women. On the other side of the shadows more of them gathered, waiting for their time, for the moment when the world would open itself to them like a gutted thing, rolling and submissive in its own horrors and the stench of its own defeat. They came, and more came after, wearing the night's darkness like a cape."

Vernon grimaced as he drove, remembering Jay, remembering his intensity and the way he leaned over the podium like a preacher in a revivalist meeting. It was undeniable that he had charisma, had dominated the room. He had, at that moment, taken all of Vernon's life in his hand.

Jay had read more in this vein that night, but Vernon thought it was terrible, overwritten and preposterous. Scott, however, loved it, said later that he loved Jay's reading and the way his voice filled the domed room until it sounded like echoes of other, more distant voices. Vernon watched his partner, rapt as Jay read, and felt a swell of emotion. He had arranged this; Scott's pleasure was Vernon's pleasure, and he had pride that he had a hand in it.

Driving through the night, Vernon tried to pinpoint where things had started to go wrong. When he had asked Scott if he wanted to attend the reading? When he had first sent the tentative e-mail to Jay to ask if he would be interested in doing the reading? When he had first read about Jay in a local writers' magazine? When he had first met Scott and opened himself to this terrible, aching hurt? No. Not then. Whatever the end result, he must never think of Scott as a mistake, never think of Scott as something that shouldn't have happened. Scott was the high point in a life that had been lived along staid, repeating lines for its entire length, was the one genuine passion that Vernon could lay claim to. Not blameless, to be sure, Scott was at least not a regret. This ache in his soul Vernon could place squarely at one person's feet: Jay.

Following the reading, Scott became one of Jay's biggest fans. He would tell Vernon in breathless, excited tones about Jay's progress. Not about the stories themselves, which Scott seemed to consider a private pleasure, but about the writer's progress. How he had sold a story to this magazine or that anthology, how his work was building on ideas of earlier writers but would soon eclipse them entirely, how he had been nominated for this award or how that magazine had given Jay a glowing review. Vernon had listened to it all, happy that Scott had something to enjoy. Even when Scott and Jay began to converse more and more frequently via e-mail and then started to meet, he had no concerns. Scott came back from the meetings, if it was possible, even more excited and started talking about setting up a website for Jay, somewhere to collate all the good news and give his fans somewhere to talk no matter where in the world they were. He would work late into the night, no longer coming to bed with Vernon and appearing only late in the mornings, bleary eyed and grumpy until he checked his e-mails and found a new message from Jay.

Gradually, the urban landscape changed, shifted. The roads narrowed and began to climb over hills whose grass seemed bleached to gray in the darkness. The valleys between the hills were pools of inky shadow and the reception on the car radio worsened slightly, overlaying the music with a light cobweb of static and interference. Vernon turned his lights to full beam, seeing how they splashed over the dry stone walls that lined the edges of the fields about him, picking out some details and losing others in the gloom, and was reminded horribly of how the photographs had looked.

It was oddly exciting. He never really believed that Scott was having an affair with Jay, but it was fun acting as though he was. It was his imagination; it had to be, didn't it? He and Scott were in love, were a couple, and had been for years. Why would Scott need to have an affair? Surely Vernon gave him everything he needed and wanted? But still, those tiny suspicions moved wormlike in him. Why did Scott, a longtime opponent of mobile phones, suddenly get one, and why was he so secretive about the texts and calls he received on it? Why was he meeting Jay so often, and why did he come home so late and so tired after the meetings? Vernon acted like a cuckolded husband in a bad drama, looked through Scott's things and letters when he was out, tried to listen in on his calls, and once he even tried to follow him but lost him in the bustle of the shopping center. When Scott was at home, Vernon would drop references to Jay in the conversation to see how he would react, secretly pleased when Scott did nothing suspicious. In the end, he had no evidence but a heart full of suspicions, and it ceased to be fun, ceased to feel an enjoyable role-play and became sour and grim. He turned to a professional.

Once he started thinking about the pictures, reminded himself of them, Vernon couldn't stop seeing them. They played out across the overlapping circles of the headlights and slipped among the trunks of the trees that sometimes stood sentinel at his sides as he drove. He turned up the radio, trying to force the visual from him with the auditory but could not. He pressed down harder on the accelerator, letting the car leap forward and feeling the throb of the engine travel through the pedal and seat itself in his body, and, hating himself, he thought of the pictures.

"I'm sorry," said the man quietly as he passed over the brown envelope. Vernon felt the world tilt and whirl under him in that moment, heard in the man's tone the cracking and splintering of the thin veneer of the reality that he had built over the years and had held on to so strongly for these past weeks. "Oh Scott," he murmured because if he had let his voice out louder than a murmur he felt it would grow and grow until it was filling his skin and tearing his throat. The man, a private investigator that Vernon had hired never expecting him to find anything, rose delicately and left Vernon's office. Vernon, his hands shaking, opened the envelope and let its contents fall across his desk. There were so many, most taken at a distance and with their edges blurring: Scott and Jay in a café innocently sitting apart and drinking coffee or tea in white cups; Scott and Jay walking in some nondescript street, their arms around each other; Jay leaning against a wall as Scott took money from an ATM; Scott driving as Jay leaned against him and both smiling. So many, and most of the pictures, and there were dozens, could be explained innocently. Except for the last three. Scott and Jay, in a room somewhere, fucking.

Faster and faster, Vernon let the car suck the road into itself and spew it out behind. What fragile control he had was splintering, was failing, and he had a sudden image of glass falling into an abyss, its sharp edges catching the light as it fell, turning and turning and turning and turning and never stopping. It welled up within him, this blackness and the pain, until he was moaning as he drove, an animal cry of misery that drowned the already-loud radio and gibbered like some living thing alongside him in the car.

Of the three, the worst picture was the first. In it, Scott lay on a bed in only his underwear. The picture was taken from a vantage point, presumably a window, to the side, so that Vernon could see all of Scott as he lay. Jay stood at the foot of the bed, visible in profile, naked. He was grinning and his erection jutted out in front of him. His cock was big, bigger than Vernon's, and the look on Scott's face was one of terrible, animal anticipation. His own erection was visible inside his pants, straining against the tight cotton. The digital time printed in the corner of the photograph showed that it was the middle of the afternoon, and every detail in the photograph was clear and incontrovertible. Vernon and Scott had never made love in the middle of the afternoon; Vernon could not ever remember Scott having that expression on his face when he was with Vernon. Until he saw the photographs, he would have said that Scott, his sensitive and beautiful love, was incapable of making that face.

Finally, Vernon tore at the wheel of the car and dragged it off the road and onto one of the single-lane tracks that splintered out across the fields from time to time. Ahead was a small forest scattered with picnic areas and deserted clearings, and he came to a halt in one of them, switching off the engine and taking the key from the ignition so that the car and radio both fell silent. The only sounds were the ticking of the engine as it cooled and the warring whoop of his own breath and anguish in his ears. He understood now that he had not been driving entirely randomly, but that some long-distant memory had been setting out his path, pressuring him to come to this place, and he knew why. He had brought Scott here early in their relationship, hoping to show him the beauty of these wide-open spaces, but it had not been a good day. Scott had been bored and frustrated, and Vernon could not properly communicate how glorious this landscape was, how with the solid earth underneath and the vast and impersonal sky above he gained a sense of perspective and felt humbled and within the grasp of the infinite. He simply had not the language for it, nor the imagination to do it justice. They had come home early and not spoken to each other during the journey. And yet, here he was. The night gathered about the car.

Vernon had left work early; the pictures had affected him like a punch to the stomach, left him feeling sick and hollow. Oh God, for that feeling to have been all he felt that day! But as he walked the streets, unsure of anything in his world anymore, the hollow space in him filled with the poisonous burn of grief and fury and helplessness, and Vernon had known then that everything had changed. He wondered how unseemly it was for middle-aged men to cry as they walked the streets and found he didn't care. He walked, initially slowly and without purpose, and then faster and faster, speeding up as though he could outrun his feelings. Of course, he found he could not, that they came with him and smothered him so that he lost himself for a time, regaining his hold to find himself in his car and driving. He had little sense of the previous hours, of the sound of something terrible happening, of seeing flesh torn and battered and the barriers between worlds falling. He was simply driving.

The picnic table sagged gently in the middle, the wood beaten into submission by countless hard winters and wet autumns. Vernon ran his finger along the grooved wood and let his nail carve into the bloating surface. Why had he come here? Because it was a place he had been hurt in before? What did he hope to gain? He did not know. Sighing, he looked up at the clear sky above him. Jay was a fool, he thought; it looked nothing like a cape. Instead, it was as though he had thrust his face through the surface of some great inky pool and was looking into its chill depths. The stars glittered, sharp and impersonal like the eyes of sulking dolls. He let its weight bear down on him for a moment, letting its cold seep through the thin material of his shirt, and then he returned to the car and opened the boot.

At some point on the journey, Jay had choked to death. Crumpled in the small space, he had vomited behind the gag that Vernon had drawn about his head and into his mouth, and the vomit had escaped around the edges of the material and spattered across his face in long tendrils. They had dried into pale things, like the scurf of some writhing, bilious snake, and the smell was sharp and sour.

Blood had soaked down from his nose and then dried to a hard, brittle shell that flaked as Vernon pulled at Jay's stiffening flesh. He saw that Jay's hands were still bound, but that where they had simply been turning blue when Vernon had pushed the unconscious boy into the car, now they were torn and bloody. Looking at the underside of the boot lid, he saw smears and spots of blood, pieces of torn skin clinging to the dried liquid like tiny insects feeding. Grinning, Vernon said aloud, "There's your unreadable text, Jay! What last message where you trying to send?" and then he was on his knees behind the car and crying, his bruised hands clutching at the metal rim of the boot and his head against the cold kiss of the bumper. He screamed, hating Jay even more—if that were possible—for the alien world he brought Vernon to the edge of, made him enter.

Eventually, he stood. His cries trailed off, lost and pointless and dying in the darkness. He dragged Jay from the car, dropping him to the earth where he lay like so much spoiled meat. Vernon looked down, filled with a sudden wave of sadness. "Oh, Jay," he said softly, "you never understood, did you? They're not coming from any far place. They've been here as long as we have."

SIMON KURT UNSWORTH lives in the north of England, somewhere between Lancaster and Morecambe, with his gorgeous wife, exuberant son, and two dogs rescued from the local dogs' home; he used to have fish, but they let him down by dying. By profession, he's a freelance consultant and trainer working across the whole of the UK (which gives him plenty of time on trains to write stories), but by inclination he's a writer of essentially grumpy fiction. His work has previously been published by the BBC and the Ash-Tree Press, in their anthologies *At Ease with the Dead* and *Shades of Darkness*. His story from *At Ease with the Dead*, "The Church on the Island," was reprinted in Stephen Jones's *The Mammoth Book of Best New Horror #19* and was nominated for a 2008 World Fantasy Award for best short story. He has more short fiction in the anthologies *Exotic Gothic 3* and *Gaslight Grotesque*, both published in 2009.

UNSWORTH SAYS: *I'm not sure I'm particularly influenced by Lovecraft above any other author, and it seems to me that the abyssal depths and writhing terrors he created and wrote about, those places beyond forever trying to broach our walls, are just as likely to be found within us as they are without. However, his ideas and the fevered claustrophobia of his writing, I think, continue to exert a huge influence on the genre, and I was interested with "Vernon, Driving" to see if I could do something that blended my approach to writing with his.*

MICHAEL SHEA

The Recruiter

But the wakened dead's doorways, once opened, gape wider.
Through these you may go where the galaxies sprawl,
And up through the star-web dance sprightly as spiders,
And dart quick as rats through Time's ceilings and walls.

LATE IN THE DAY, old Chester Chase walks down the hall from his room, headed for the stairs. His legs have seventy-five years on them, but normally he's not as tottery as this. Today he must walk wide-legged, as if the danger of falling has suddenly increased.

He passes the barred window of the cage. Elmer, the day clerk, is in there, lying on the couch and watching TV.

" 'Lo, Chester." Elmer's a scrawny old rooster in an undershirt, with thick goggle-glasses and a phlegmy voice, but he's not old like Chester, not near-the-end-of-it old.

"Hi, Elmer." Chester's own voice sounds far and faint to him, like dead leaves blown down a sidewalk. Creaking down the two flights of stairs to the street, he's seized by sorrow. All the funky details—this carpet runner, these banisters—seem to glow, perilously precious. In the bubble mirror at the stairs' turning, he sees himself, big-headed, skinny, an old man on his way out. He pauses to confront the steel-framed street door, battered and shabby, but implacable when you're shut outside it. Stepping through, he stands outside of the Hyperion Hotel, his home for the last five years.

The homeless are in evidence on this busy street in San Francisco's Mission district. A pair of them—smudged, multisweatered shapes—sit on a porch stoop just down the block. Normal folk know the sociobabble explaining these roofless souls, but when viewing the vagabonds, their eyes betray a more limbic response: that these dirty squatters are a kind of spontaneous alien growth. Chester has long known that many of them make their debuts on the streets from the doors of shabby old residence hotels just like the Hyperion. Even he, once so carelessly strong, has just crossed that threshold.

He worked shipyard for years after he and Emily got married, and for decades after that, he drove tour buses. He'd had a touchy side, had fought with officious bosses now and then, but he also had a gift for the work, loved sharing the world's most beautiful bay with his passengers.

For the worst years following Emily's passing, the driving was an anesthetic for her absence. A few years after that, BayScape Tours laid him off, and he couldn't get hired by anyone else. Their various so-sorries meant simply that he was too old.

Since then, even if he doesn't eat at all, his social security can't quite make his rent. The past three years now, his elder sister Samantha up in Portland has sustained him with her slender checks, but he's just learned that she died two weeks ago. The last installment of her pension bought the coffin she was buried in.

Chester walks and walks, and it seems to him his only countrymen out here are the ones on stoops, in doorways, in alley mouths. They are snug for now in blankets of pills and Night Train, or, like fanatics, they radiate a fierce insistence that they *do* exist, despite not owning one square foot of roof or wall. Laired everywhere they are, in little nooks of nowhere they've staked out.

Block after block he walks as the dark settles down, and with the work of it, a memory of his old strength comes back to his legs, he breathes a tonic in the night air. But still there is only nowhere after nowhere that this strength can take him to. He's always loved the Mission's nightfall, with its neons blossoming everywhere, but now that it has fallen on him, he's reminded that night is the biggest Nowhere of all.

Just past midnight, Chester drops onto a bus-stop bench. Be a man! Here's where he'll sleep tonight. Try the night on for size, before being thrown into it. He lies on his side, knees drawn into the skirts of his coat, upturned collar his pillow, trying to ignore how hungry he is, and wishing for the vanished muscle, the sheathed chest and shoulders that could wield a rivet gun long hours, that might have made the bench slats softer. *Cold.* If he sinks into sleep in this cold, is there a chance it will painlessly take him? Like Scott, near the Pole?

Huddled, he feels a prayer fighting its way up into his throat. All the neons are dead now, but as he walked they made him think fleetingly of the stained-glass windows in church when he was a kid. My God, that Place where they used to send up their prayers to—whatever happened to it? Right now, there's just the roofless October night above him, mist-drenched by the bay. He manages a brief, embarrassed mutter: *Help me somehow. Somehow, please help me . . .*

He must have half-dozed, is awakened by a sound, a faint friction behind him . . . a stealthy sound. From a streetlamp around the corner, light pools on the sidewalk, and as he looks, the tip of a shadow inches into view. A narrow prow of shadow, and slow, rather than sneaking.

A fellow denizen of Nowhere, whose shape's low-slung it seems, for the scuffle is near, and yet the outline is squat and long . . . And, complicating the silhouette, a skinny foreleg carefully advances. A dog, he thinks. A big old decrepit dog.

But no, it's a man who rounds the corner. Bent almost in half, and plying a cane. A man Chester recognizes from the Hyperion. It's old Mr. what's-his-name . . . Canning?

Here now, *this* is age—old, old age indeed. Chester's seen him inching down the halls, his frosty eye peeping up from his grotesque stoop, crudely printed tracts protruding from the side pocket of his shabby coat. He's creeping right towards Chester's bench, arthritically extracting something from his pocket.

An answer to his unaccustomed prayer? Chester almost smiles. The sidewalk evangelist crouches at the end of the bench, his oblique eye an ice chip. His grizzled jaw grins almost merrily. Such joie de vivre, so evidently near life's end. Chester can only admire, and smile back. A long moment they gaze at each other. No sound from the whole wide city arises, not even a far whisper of tires.

And then, "Aaartah!"

"I'm sorry. What?" Chester realizes that the man can barely speak.

"Nnnn-yarrrrtah!" And then, turning to pantomime, Mr. Canning extends in display not a tract, but a wad of bills. Places the money on the bench, and next indeed draws forth a tract, and holds it up. Gestures at the cash, and brandishes his leaflet, a brow cocked in query.

"You're . . . giving me *that* . . . if I take *that*?"

Vigorous assenting growls and nods. Chester is stunned. Actual tears fill his eyes. The evangelist again extends the paper, and Chester receives it. In large, crude type:

OUR GOD

SHALL RAISE

THE DEAD

He looks at the stooped ancient, whose frosty eye seems to wink. Now it's the cash Mr. Canning hands him, and the instant Chester takes it, turns and creeps caning away. Awed, Chester watches him vanish. Luck! He walked out at random to face his fate, and met Luck. Walked out . . . and *prayed*? Can he believe that? Maybe he can . . . His heart sends a tender salute to his sister, to her affection, to her faith.

He gazes on the cash. Now anything seems possible. For starters, he can eat. The dark is just beginning to pale. The sidewalk's emptiness feels friendlier; now he has a pleasant destination, the all-night Silver Dragon Cafeteria.

Turkey and potatoes and beans are his again! Hot coffee and cold milk! Hello, world—I'm back at the table. Five hundred dollars. A month's rent, and plenty in pocket.

There's almost a spring in his step as he climbs the Hyperion's stairs. Elmer, though groggy at sunrise, seems pleased by Chester's payment. Elmer would have been the one to take his key, to shepherd him out the door with his things.

Though dead for sleep, Chester lingers in the halls, trading shoulder-thwacks with morning-shifters on their way out to work, leaning at the bars of the cage for a while, commiserating with Elmer about alimony payments and his relentless ex. By God, how lucky he was to have his own Emily. There was something to him after all, to have won and kept a woman like her. Maybe enough left in him still, to win a bit more luck before the end.

Back to his room. Bright morning fills his air-shaft window. He gets his shoes and coat off, gives up on the rest. Sighs and falls back on his bed, into sleep.

When he opens his eyes, the wan light of late day fills the shaft. He goes for a shower, and in clean sweats and socks, lies back down on his bed. Emergency has yielded to a faintly melancholy ease. Has he really prayed, and been answered? Did that kind, crazed old preacher receive on his spiritual antennae the intercession of dear Emily, sweet Samantha, on his behalf?

Chester will go to St. Anthony's tomorrow. Ask to volunteer. It might even lead to some paid work. He must answer mercy with action. Is a God who RAISES the DEAD really impossible? Wasn't he feeling almost dead last night?

If he has been helped, his life has not merited it. He guesses that his life has in fact been pretty selfish. *Remember driving over to the city that night? You'd dropped in on Charles and Frances and their new baby, and crossing the Bay Bridge back over, you suddenly knew you would never be a father.*

He remembers the afternoon when he first made love to Emily. Still only engaged, they did it on her parents' couch. Though her parents were away, the couch seemed less sinful, more provisional than one of the beds. Remembers how they both cried out in surprise and delight.

All those times all those years you could have been kinder. Your three nights a week at the bar because your work had earned them! All those hours of hers you could have made less lonely, all those hours you could have had closeness and sweetness together.

He remembers all the ships he worked on, fantasizing how he and Em would see the places they'd been . . . remembers a couple women he'd had on the side, in his still-swaggering middle age. Did she know, and love him anyway? . . .

Has he been dozing again? Deep night fills the air shaft, yet the human traffic in the halls and on the floors above him is only now starting to dwindle, and he realizes that it's Friday night. Realizes too that for some time he's been hearing another kind of movement.

Not hearing, exactly. It's more like feeling. A faint, tactile ripple that draws his awareness slowly up stairwells, up air shafts, and down along hallways throughout the big, rambling, century-old box of a building.

He's never felt any sensation quite like this and expects it to subside into the mere metabolic buzz of his own uneasy nerves. But no. Losing none of its furtive sublety, it grows more distinct. He can discern now that its movement ripples not just along the floors of the hallways, but across their walls and ceilings as well. And it has a familiarity, this movement, a quality both pizzicato and fluid. A childhood memory teases him, something about summer afternoons hiking in the hills around Mount Diablo . . . Those big green centipedes and the tarantulas they hunted on those hikes, the ripple of their little hooked feet across the ground . . . that's what these movements recall.

Chester gazes around the familiar room, stunned that he lies here surrounded by this sudden strangeness. His eyes fall on Mr.

Canning's tract, and he sees that it is not a single sheet, but a folded one, and is open, with lines of smaller print on the inside. He takes it up, and within that faint seethe of movement all around him, reads:

Where the lich in the loam has lain mouldering long
And the maggoty minutes gnaw meat off his bones,
There Time is a monster that mows down the throng
Of once-have-been, gone-again, featureless drones
And that lich's coffin to me is a door
Through which I go nosing Eternity's spoor.

But the wakened *dead's doorways, once opened, gape wider.*
Through these you may go where the galaxies sprawl,
And up through the star-web dance sprightly as spiders,
And dart quick as rats through Time's ceilings and walls!
There we go feasting and rutting at will,
Where time is a wine we imbibe when we kill!
There we conjoin with Gods older than All,
And preside with them over the Eons' slow crawl!

It's like melting, what Chester feels lying there, not understanding these lines themselves, but sensing that accepting them from that old man's hand . . . was a mistake. Surely there is this soft stir, this seething surrounding him now. It is a simmering of expectation. Whatever moves within these walls is welcoming a thing greater than itself. Something else is coming.

For a heavier, more deliberate footfall is moving down a nearby stairwell. Its tread is massive, though padded—a sinewy quadruped, he senses it to be.

Its big forepaw crackles on the hall's plastic runner. Chester's floor. Its muscled stealth moves up the corridor to Chester's turning . . . and down it. A faint click as of blunt claws staccatos its advance. The hotel is otherwise utterly silent.

Galvanized, he sits up to swing his legs off the bed—discovers a terror that dwarfs what he's already feeling: his body has not stirred. Violently, he again exerts his will . . . and his frame lies untouched by it, calm as sleep.

The visitor has stopped outside the door. Sharp-fingered cold starts touching Chester here and there.

Hello in there. Not heard. Directly understood within his mind.

Hello in there.

Time to prepare.

You and I must go somewhere.

The sly lyric drifts into his floating consciousness . . . But not just floating, for Chester is pulled; a kind of gravitation draws him upward. Gently, insistently, something is tugging the spiritous roots of his soul from his body.

He rises clear, a little knot of conscious atmosphere, and drifts towards the wall, trailing, it seems, only faint tendrils of body memory, misty wisps of limbs. Is this death? This Someone with him now, tugging him away, murmuring in his mind?

Faster, Chester! Chase, make haste!
Let's go where they rest and fester,
the hustlers finished with the race.
All lie low now, slow with faster.
Let's fly down and scope the place!

If this is Death's voice, this sneering jollity, why is Chester's body still breathing down there on the bed? He cries out voicelessly, *Emily!*—as if she still lived to take hold of. Pulled more powerfully, he impacts the wall and pierces it, experiences chalky plaster and splintery laths. Next door, his neighbor Karl lies below, snoring in the dark. This room too he crosses, this wall pierces.

And is accelerating, till succeeding walls are rungs of a ladder of sleepers, each in his own dark. Last, he penetrates the hotel's outer wall, and plunges out into the night air, the chill drench of mist.

Evicted. In a way he never dreamed of dreading. *Is* this Death? Buildings are pouring past him, the street a black river beneath. The Mission blurs under him, until it yields to vast pavements of rooftops spangled with streetlamps, sweeping downslope to the bay. He too angles downwards, towards a highway flanked by great trees. Chester recognizes this neighborhood. Colma. Cemetery City. Death *must* have him. Death beyond doubt.

Look where they moulder and crumble away
—how rank-and-file orderly is their array!
An army of underlings, mine to control.
Let's do some recruiting! Come down! Lend a soul!

Still diving, now much faster than before, beneath him a tombstone-studded lawn grows large, grows huge, becomes one grave to which alone he plunges, arrowing through sod, through soil, through wood and metal . . .

Once more, he inhabits a body. A body in a box, in a suit, and within that suit clothed in a withered garment shrunken to the bone. If his terror had the least leverage at its command, this coffin and the earth atop it would explode into the moonlight, but his terror's the tenant of unmoving meat.

Unmoving . . . but unquiet. Someone shares this envelope with Chester. Tendrils of memory haunt the cadaver's parched terrain. Chester encounters scents he never knew, snatches of music he never heard, the terror of clutching a rifle under whistling bullets, hugging the sand in a desert war he never fought. The corpse's spirit threads through the bones he lies in. Those bones *stir.*

I bid thee to a journey, lich.
This is an invitation which
thou'lt not refuse. Within this hour

thou'lt know thy Master, and his power!
Now let reanimation start! The butting skull's the bulky part.
So let it, Chester, lead the way,
and ram your passage through the clay!

The skull leaps, Chester himself a foggy commotion within it. The cranium, like a slo-mo fist, drives a sinus up through the stubborn soil.

Now from its rack unjoint each bone
and climb the rat hole one by one.
Each rib and radial, ulna, femur,
scuttle limber as a lemur!
What rags of flesh that may remain,
worm after in a snaky train!

Chester pops into moonlight, his vessel the empty-windowed skull, hanging in air while the body joins him piecemeal from below. Soon his skull crowns a tall scaffolding. He has dangling arms, and hands which tatters of sinew and skin are bandaging. This reknit body still prickles with memories; they trickle into his hands like strays to a shelter, the feel of a sun-warmed kitten stroked, of a loved breast gripped almost too hard, of fingertips picking foxtails from an itchy sock. His legs too remember, treading concrete, and the weary work of sand dunes climbed, and the silvery feel of scissoring in the bright blue water of a public pool, while the summer clamor of a hundred splashing kids teases the tattered remnants of his ears.

Captain Chester! Ten-shun.

A chaotic tremor through the borrowed body, and it comes to a swaying straightness.

Let's all stroll down to the bus stop, old buddy!
No one will squawk that you're smelly and muddy.

It's your own private coach, and your fare is prepaid,
and no one will notice you're slightly decayed.
Let's give them the signal, Ches! Lead the parade!

Only now does Chester grasp—vertebrae crackling as he scans the field—that in the stone-studded acres a dozen *other* shapes stand, crooked shadows like himself, teetering here and there, while the towering eucalypti shudder and whisper in the breeze above them. Give them the signal? He gropes for the memory of his own arms. Up comes his host's creaking arm, and waves those others forward.

Tottering, drunken-footed, they move down the gently sloping grass, their march at first so feeble it seems accidental, while the starlit trees whisper, *Yess. Yessss.*

Ahead, a big shape squats on a ribbon of pavement: an old yellow bus with a jutting hood, doors folded open—the kind he remembers from school days.

Chester's lich mounts, and takes the driver's seat. The wheel that meets his tattered grip feels like an eon-dead sorcerer's bone, necromancy burning like ice in it. The lich produces a gasping jest, mocking Chester's captive soul:

All aboard for the Bay Tour . . .

His slat-ribbed, staggery soldiers mount and file past him, gaunt jaws hanging agape, in awe at a world regained. Their stark, thin fingers touch the air before them, feeling it like some long-forgotten fabric, while in the gulfs of their eye holes, memories glint like the dim stars that are suns to distant planets . . . They settle to their seats with an arid whisper, gaunt shapes rustling like dead leaves.

Filled with his Possessor's joy in this vehicle's power, he slips the clutch, and treads the gas. The bus surges down the graveyard's laneways, and swoops out onto the highway. Oh, this is flight! No less majestic than a hawk's! Tilting the wheel is like banking their wings—they soar up onto the Bayshore Freeway.

Plunging through long graceful curves, the vehicle lofts into view of the dreaming metropolis. The empty freeway lies like the spine of a black dragon draped on that city, and down along that spine they run.

He dares not know where he is driving. Like a man on the roof of his flooded house, he dares not to descend into his captured mind, but undeniably he feels a great dread of the bay, and a *pull* from its glinting black plain.

They swing down an exit, through two swift turns, and here is Sixteenth. North they take it—baywards.

Rolling down a corridor of lonely lamps and black windows, he is touched by his cohorts' wonder as they gaze on the emptied theater of the living, their wakened memories haunting his own.

Rocketing across Third, they turn onto the empty shoreside drive, wrench the bus crosswise to the street, and idle. Their prow is aimed at an open stretch between two little forests of eroded pier legs.

He tromps the gas. The bus jolts over the curb and through the fencing, jouncing at full drive down into the water.

Though muted under the sea's dark weight, their engine's roar thrums on, drags them unfaltering downward, the tires somehow biting the cottony silt, lifting its inky shroud around them, impelling their slow-motion descent of the bay floor. Down here, the wide unpartitioned reach of the Undersea embraces his smallness, and he knows, *feels* that these deeps are inhabited. A shape half fills them, an alert colossus of cold intent . . . and *this* is their Summoner. He knows now what he dreaded from the bay: his being taken by this sunken thing.

But the seizure that comes is not what he is dreading. He's snatched up out of his host. Climbs the water in a roiling bubble. Erupts into night air and rises, rises . . .

The bay's grand constellated rim below him now, his flight has paused. Chester hears again his Taker's thought.

Its Rule is thus: once served, released.
You've raised my quota of Deceased.
Obedient, I now thee dismiss,
And let thy life go where it lists.
But how thou goest's not prescribed—
Thine own path take where thou'd'st abide!

Time to get back to your meat rack, ol' Ches!
You've been parted from him quite a span.
Can you make three miles' trek through the air, more or less?
I fervently pray that you can.

This mockery is his Taker's farewell. Chester is alone now, he is free. Free to hang here, high in the night, a knot of being with not a muscle to command. How can he move? Will the next gust of wind blow him out like a candle? The whole world rolls on its mighty axis under his naked life, and he can't touch it.

Rage and bitterness rack him. On that bus-stop bench, in his extremity, he raised his voice in unaccustomed prayer. And now, behold Prayer's answer: the presence, in that water, of a something mightier than death. Not only his own life to gutter out in the air, not only himself to be taken from the world, but the world itself to be taken . . .

Up on the low hills, there is the red neon circle of a rooftop Target sign. Chester yearns to be there with it, a mile inland, a mile closer to his stolen body . . . yet he is only a yearning that cannot move. His yearning becomes desolation, desolation becomes rage, becomes despair, becomes a fiercer rage that *wills* that distant red radiance nearer.

But . . . has it grown fractionally *larger*?

He struggles to grasp his will again, wrestles in rage with its elusiveness, wrestles the rage itself towards that purer will . . . and again, so slightly, that bull's eye nears.

It is such labor at first, lensing his longing into a beam as pure as a laser, pulling the whole shore under him, a block at a time. His mind like a muscle cramps with the toil, till he learns that the inertia he struggles with is himself, is the clutter of his rage and fear. Though desperate, he must somehow will *calmly* . . . And ever more smoothly, the red ring grows, till he has pierced its center like an arrow.

It is well that he is learning this tricky art of focus, for again and again he loses it and must struggle to find it anew. Because his cohorts still remotely share his mind, and they take it from him now and then. Still they lurch and dive, in a smoke of silt, down that drowned terrain. And now it is not quite ink black, that storm of murk their journey raises. A purplish luminescence begins to limn the muddy roil. And he feels with his gravemates that they are all *beheld*, can feel the touch of a gaze possessing them. The light they approach is its darkly radiant awareness, and their journey is at its command . . .

Each time he fights off this knowledge, he focuses, drags himself onward landmark by landmark across the City. Nevertheless, at length with his gravemates he meets their Summoner, and at the last, he learns that which he has so urgently wished not to know.

Still his own extremity commands him to his work. When finally he reaches the Hyperion, approaches the black Z's of its fire escape, he has thinned to a terrifying faintness, his spirit like a crumbling TV image sprayed out by a faltering cathode ray. But just the walls now, just the rooms full of sleep to be pierced, the rooms full of sleep . . .

But when he arrives at his own body on its bed, here at the end he's defeated. His body is too dense a mass to enter, and himself too frail and patchy to force his way in. Surrendering at last, he thinks of Emily, and says his farewell to her. Remembers her touch on that body of his, how she held it, and kindled it, how she made him feel in it . . . and suddenly, he is inside it.

Sleep engulfs him. Through the next day and into the following night it holds him, a cherishing hand in whose grip he's regathered, a kernel kindling in its healing closure. His dreams are not his own. The dead he wakened live again in him, their hours beneath the sun and stars, the treasures that their eyes and hearts collected on their paths: neon jewels reflected on a rain-wet street, the buttery ripple of foliage in a summer breeze, a hawk's calm crucifixion in the clouds, a love song echoed in a young child's eyes . . .

He wakes bolt upright, and is sitting in a building once more sunk in silence. Nothing protects Chester now from seeing again what his gravemates encountered at their journey's end last night. He remembers the bus slowing, and stopping on the sunken plain . . .

A storm of silt roiled around them, gorgeous billows of a purple glow. So slowly it resettled! But as it did, a revelation dawned. The subsidence was unveiling some kind of drowned Sun that lay on the sea floor. The fog thinned away, and It towered before them, Its somber radiance shafting down through the bus windows. A titanic eye. Deep-strewn stars wheeled within Its gulf. It knew them. It summoned them. They rose . . . and obeyed.

Chester is up, and dressing. Glad of his good tough running shoes, his stout warm coat. Doubtfully, he draws from his pocket the substantial remnant of Mr. Canning's cash. He is struck with dread of the link it might form if he uses it. But at length he says, "No! I earned it," and tucks it away.

Once again Chester walks the empty night streets. Staggery at first, at length he gains purpose, and strides. Tired he admittedly is, and old, near the end of his life. Terrified, too, he most surely is, and, even as his strength regathers, it is not what it was.

But he is fierce-eyed too, and by-God angry at his core, an anger to answer the dread that provokes it. He means to live all right, has found this will clear and strong in himself for the first time in years. He means to live and means to fight, means to find allies if he can, knowing as he does what fills the great bay, what embraces himself and his species in Its ageless, cold attention.

All he hopes for is a little luck.

MICHAEL SHEA was born in Venice, California, and began writing as a poet at the age of thirteen. This devotion to (strictly metric) verse lasted through his college years at UC Berkeley. Years of travel followed, hitchhiking all over the U.S., Canada, and western Europe, during which time he became literate in French, Spanish, and German. Influenced by Borges, Shakespeare, and Jack Vance, he turned to fantastic prose, while never wholly abandoning verse.

His first published novel was a Vancean pastiche (with that author's kind permission), *A Quest for Simbilis*. Novels set in Shea's own world followed: *In Yana, the Touch of Undying*, *Nifft the Lean* (winner of the World Fantasy Award), *The Mines of Behemoth*, *The A'Rak*, *The Color out of Time* (an HPL pastiche); a collection, *Polyphemus*; some two dozen novellas, including the World Fantasy Award–winning *The Growlimb*; and a more comprehensive collection just out from Centipede Press, *The Autopsy and Other Tales.*

Shea lives with his wife, the artist and writer Lynn Cesar, in northern California.

SHEA SAYS: *I always return to Mythos because it is, in its essence, apocalyptic, or more precisely, preapocalyptic. And that seems to me to be the most natural way to view our universe.*

GEMMA FILES

Marya Nox

INTRODUCTORY NOTES:

In March of 2006, after the accidental discovery of spectral evidence apparently linking the deaths of medium Emma Yee Slaughter and Freihoeven Institute intern Eden Marozzi (see related materials, file #FI5556701), Institute Director Dr. Guilden Abbott requested that ParaPsych Department intern Sylvester Horse-Kicker have the Institute "psychically cleansed." Horse-Kicker therefore contacted Father Wale Oja, S.J. (probably best known for his participation in 1999's notorious "exorcism girl" case (see attached file)), and a buildingwide blessing was carried out on March 23.

Pleased with the results, Dr. Abbott then invited Fr. Wale to lecture on a subject of personal interest ("Spiritual Warfare: Some Notes on the Difficult History of Demonic Possession at the Celebration of Christ's Millennium") at the Institute's Jay and Jay Memorial Theatre. This event, hosted by Horse-Kicker, also included an interview with Fr. Wale, followed by questions from the audience. A partial transcript of that interview (coded as file #FI0007695) begins here.

HORSE-KICKER: . . . but I don't think I've ever heard that term before.

FR. WALE: No? You must have had a very secular education.

HORSE-KICKER: Well, um . . . yeah. I guess.

FR. WALE: Obviously! [Laughs] I apologize—I actually meant to be making a joke, some sort of light, amusing chitchat, but no matter how long I stay in Canada, I don't think my English is ever going to be quite up to pulling other people's legs. [Beat] That doesn't sound quite right either, does it?

HORSE-KICKER: No, I'm sorry too, I know what you mean. You were talking about—

FR. WALE: Mmm, yes, *acheiropoieta*—in other words, I wrote my seminary dissertation on the study of icons which came into existence miraculously.

HORSE-KICKER: Like the Shroud of Turin.

FR. WALE: Well, that's debatable; I would say more like the Mandylion of Edessa, an image of Jesus's face which somehow reached King Abgar in AD 384, without ever having been commissioned or, apparently, painted by anyone. These objects are called "true images not made by human hands" . . . the "true" part being often deemed more important than their definitive source. We are still very afraid of "false images" in the Church, you see—and rightly so.

HORSE-KICKER: Why?

FR. WALE: This is what the iconoclasts of the Byzantine Empire asked themselves. They believed, as Muslims do today, that to portray the face of God, His saints, His mother, was an imposition, a heresy in itself. How can we know that the face of *a* Jesus is the face of Jesus? Human artists are inspired by many things. A man may see what he thinks is the face of the Madonna on a whore, and paint it into his study of the classic *pietà*; his perfect Jesus could be a drunk, his St. Peter a criminal. To the artist, it's all a valid interpretation.

But to those who believe God has, *can* have, only one true face, it's blasphemy—literal idolatry. If what you're worshiping isn't a true depiction of God, then where do the prayers you address to it end up? You might think you were worshiping Almighty God, legitimate Creator of Heaven and Earth, source of every good thing in existence, only to later find out you were . . .

HORSE-KICKER: . . . worshiping someone else? Some*thing*—?

FR. WALE: [A pause. Then] . . . Mistaken. Yes, I think that would be the appropriate English word. Mistaken.

HORSE-KICKER: Is that why Father Mihaly Doncheff asked you to go to Macedonia with him?

FR. WALE: In a way. You know where I come from, originally?

HORSE-KICKER: Uh, yes, I think—Dr. Abbott said Nigeria.

FR. WALE: Offa, that's where I was born . . . a little village, near the border. My father was a doctor, a very smart man, very scientific—he was educated in Lagos—but he was also Yoruba, and of course he told me many strange things that were specific to our area, many . . . tribal things. But there were always refugees coming in from other areas, trying to leave through the ports, to go to England or America and claim political asylum—fleeing from wars and famines in Sierra Leone, Liberia, Côte d'Ivoire. And once I remember a Temne woman passing through, and she was pregnant, with twins . . .

Now, you have to understand that the Temne have very specific cults and beliefs around the birth of twins: They think all twins are river demons who have somehow managed to enter the mother's womb while she was bathing, and so they are related to every type of reptile, and they can live on land or in the water. They also believe that if a child is born deformed, that child should be returned to the bush—but if the deformed child is a twin, you must treat it with great respect, and do many rituals while exposing it. Because you don't want to take the chance, obviously, that the child's relatives—the reptiles—might be insulted by the way you treat it when you are . . .

HORSE-KICKER: . . . *killing* it? This—helpless, deformed baby?

FR. WALE: It seems cruel, I know. It *is* cruel. But these people we're talking about haven't accepted Christ yet. They see things in a completely different way than we do.

Anyhow, this Temne woman had her babies, and my father delivered them. One of them was clearly megacephalic, with a huge, misshapen head; the other was fine, perfect. And because my father knew what the woman would want to do with the deformed baby, he made plans to send both children to the hospital in Lagos . . . But before he could, there was an outbreak of sleeping sickness, which is spread by a very pernicious waterborne parasite. He was called away.

So that night, the woman and another so-called "doctor"—a tribal medicine worker, a male witch—snuck out of my father's surgery, leaving the "good" baby behind with the nurses. They carried the deformed twin to a cotton tree in the bush, and they dressed the baby and the "doctor" in red, and they made the usual offerings: A bottle of wine, rice flour, some chicken's eggs. They started to sing some songs.

HORSE-KICKER: Then what happened?

FR. WALE: It's hard to say . . . I wasn't there. But the woman said the baby started to change his shape from a person to a demon; his head became the head of a snake, and he ate all the rice flour, then burrowed down into a hole at the tree's base and was lost from sight. And at this point the "doctor" told her they should run back to town, because soon the place would become too terrible, and if they stayed there, they would both die.

By the time they came back, having walked all that way, they were both sick—my father said the Temne woman, who you'll remember had just given birth, had peritonitis. And later, the "doctor" *did* die.

HORSE-KICKER: Wait. She walked how many miles, just after having had twins?

FR. WALE: [Laughs] Believe me, it's not impossible! Especially if, like many people from my country, you're used to physical labor . . . and pain. And if you *really* think you need to.

HORSE-KICKER: So . . . then what happened?

FR. WALE: Well, my father thought for certain that the Temne woman would die as well—but instead, she got better. She said it was because she had asked her sister to bring her certain leaves, then made a broth and washed with them, which had changed her scent so that if her demon baby came sniffing back around, he wouldn't be able to recognize her as his mother.

HORSE-KICKER: Did anyone ever find the baby's corpse, where they left it? Out in the bush?

FR. WALE: No, but that doesn't mean much—anything might have taken it from under the tree, eaten it, buried it. But to the mother, she'd done exactly what she needed to, and indeed, her other baby—the "good" baby—was absolutely fine, after that . . . It thrived. And when she moved on, finally, she took that baby with her.

Now, who actually knows what happened, out there in the bush? Not me; like I said, I wasn't there. But the reason I told you that story is for a bit of . . . context, I suppose.

In Nigeria, we don't have a tradition of making false images, so much, as renaming the ones we already have. The *orishas*, our local gods, have come to be identified with various Catholic saints, just as in Santeria and Vodoun traditions—it's a sort of protective coloration many pagan cults take on, for purposes of survival, after an area has fallen to Christ. And that was certainly what I found in Macedonia, when I went there—something, some*one*, who had been renamed, possibly in an attempt to . . . understand her? Control her?

HORSE-KICKER: But there was an image involved, too. Right?

FR. WALE: Yes.

HORSE-KICKER: Of what?

FR. WALE: I don't know. Not even now, not really. I don't . . . [A longer pause]

After I came to the Church and realized my vocation, I attended the seminary in Lagos, and eventually, I was ordained. This was in 1990. And following my ordination, my first real mission was to accompany another priest out into the field, on a sort of an internship; Fr. Mihaly, like you said, from the former Socialist Republic of Macedonia. He had been my Comparative Theology teacher—I remember he once gave me a failing grade on a paper about St. Augustine, and underneath it he wrote, "You argue your points very well. If I thought you actually believed any of what you said, I would have given you an A."

He took me home, to a very small village near Lake Ohrid, probably the oldest lake in Europe, with a unique endemic ecosystem that has come under attack recently because of human encroachment—it used to be full of eels that migrated to spawn in the Sargasso Sea, whose children then returned afterward. But because of hydroelectric dams which have been built near the lake, this is no longer possible, so the eels are kept stocked, instead. That's a whole subculture in Macedonia, or was when I was there: Eel farming.

It was just after *perestroika*, and Fr. Mihaly and I were supposed to open a school, instituting an explicitly Bible-based curriculum—cooperate with the local Orthodox Church in order to bring religion "back" to the region, which we all knew meant helping it resurface from where it had been hiding underground, almost since the Revolution. Of course, Macedonia is a place where things are very easy to hide: it's rough, beautiful country, rugged, full of mountains and very cold, very inaccessible. Completely unlike Nigeria. But I was busy there, helping Fr. Mihaly—so much so, I didn't even have time to get homesick . . .

Around the same time our school finally opened its doors, a group of fortune hunters unearthed a buried Byzantine church nearby, on a shelf overlooking the pass our children had to climb through in order to attend preclass services. They said they were archaeologists, but everyone knew they were really after Scythian gold. It's a very seismic region, so at first, they thought the church had simply been covered over during an avalanche. But the more they studied it, the more they came to believe it had been buried deliberately—probably sometime between the seventh century, when the Byzantines lost control over Macedonia, and the eleventh century, when it became a holding of the First Bulgarian Empire.

Since it must have happened during a period of Byzantine iconoclasm, they further theorized the church might have been deemed heretical because it was an iconodule church—it dared to contain an image of the Virgin Mary carrying the Christ Child, surrounded by a train of other children who seemed to be either holding up or sheltering beneath the train of her cloak. I can still see it now, as freshly as the day we entered that church's doors for the very first time . . .

HORSE-KICKER: Tell me about it, Father.

FR. WALE: I wish I could, truly. Words . . . fail me whenever I think of that place, in Yoruba *or* English.

As with most churches of the era, we approached through a dim vestibule called a *narthex*, a narrow passageway meant to move us from one world into another. This is the "fennel stalk" or perfume box, the road to Paradise—the place, traditionally, where unbaptized *catechumens* would be required to stand during services until they had become true converts, finally able to enter and take communion.

But neither Fr. Mihaly nor I had that problem anymore, while those of us who still did weren't about to let it slow them down. So we entered, and looked up . . .

HORSE-KICKER: What did you see?

FR. WALE: Stars.

[Pause]

Surprisingly small, the space inside. There were catacombs below, or so the "archaeologists" told us—a stairway leading downward was concealed under the altarpiece's cover, easily accessible by rolling away the stone, like Christ's tomb. Above us, however, we saw only an *apse* that enfolded the altar and its canopy, providing the church with its centralized *axis mundi*, the Christian world's turning point. And that entire *apse*, its whole hollow, upreaching expanse, was covered with a glass mosaic made from millions of tiny *tesserae*, colored tiles.

I've never seen anything like it, before or since. Most iconographic mosaics position their figures in front of either a gold screen (to represent Heaven's glory) or a clear blue screen (to represent the daytime sky); this whole half dome was obviously supposed to represent the night . . . dark and deep, a rich indigo blue, almost navy. And stars, everywhere stars, sprinkled like little white eyes made from fire. They hung above us, peering down pitilessly, watching our every move.

The blue of the night sky around her and the blue of her cloak, her veil, were almost indistinguishable from each other; only the way the stars set behind her, winking out at they touched her shoulders and outlining her with darkness, showed you where they ended and she began. And though she held a baby in her arms—the Christ Child, we assumed—she was, indeed, surrounded by a crowd of other children, all of whom seemed to be shrouded by the bulk of her outflung cloak. But they didn't seem to me as though they were happy or reverent so much as weepy and afraid, transfixed and large eyed, even by Byzantine standards.

But the strangest thing was her face . . .

HORSE-KICKER: Her face?

FR. WALE: Well, to begin with, it wasn't made of glass tiles, like the rest of the mosaic; it was carved from some sort of stone, maybe basalt, something shiny and volcanic, so that it pushed forward from the wall in *bas-relief.* Cast its own shadows, seemed to loom over you, in a ghostly sort of way. And—it was black.

She was a black woman, this Virgin. Very smooth, very regular, very beautiful. She looked like a perfect amalgam of all the most beautiful women I might have ever seen at home, before I was ordained . . . in Nigeria.

HORSE-KICKER: In *Macedonia.*

FR. WALE: Exactly. A black Madonna carved from obsidian, presiding over a congregation of small, scared, white-faced, obviously Macedonian children.

Oh, and one last thing: The baby? It definitely had a halo of some sort, a thin crown made of stars like the ones above and around her. But she held it *towards* her, cradling it close and fiercely to her breast, so you couldn't see its face. Most Virgins hold the Christ Child *outward*, for worshipers to adore—because our Lady, more than anyone else, understands that she is only the caretaker of this infant, our one true Redeemer, who must by His very nature belong to the entire world.

As we stood there, I heard Fr. Mihaly draw his breath, slow and horrified. He said, "It's as I thought: This is not the Virgin. This place is not a Church. This place . . . is cursed."

HORSE-KICKER: Cursed how?

FR. WALE: That's what the "archaeologists" wanted to know. Of course, Fr. Mihaly was in no hurry to tell *them*—he thought they'd spent far too much time inside the Church as it was, that they might already be . . . contaminated.

But later that night, when we were safely back in our lodgings, he told me about a story his grandmother had passed on to him, growing up—not as a legend, a mere fairy tale, but as an entirely practical warning. Apparently, she believed that up in the mountains . . . somewhere above that same pass where the church had been discovered, in fact . . . lived a very sad, very beautiful woman who only came out at night, who loved all children and should be respected by them in turn—yet avoided at all costs, nevertheless.

Fr. Mihaly's grandmother had taught him a song to sing if he ever met this woman, and he translated its words for me—said they praised her for "protecting" the village children, though in language which could also be interpreted as meaning "for not killing them," or "for not taking them away." He said she was identified with dream and sleep and the sky, like the Egyptian goddess Nut, but that she was just as often identified with disease, in the same way the Bengals consider Sitala Ma—smallpox—a seductive, maternal female deity. The Bengals bribe and flatter Sitala Ma to *not* visit their homes in the middle of the night, to *not* caress their children with her many-spotted hands . . .

HORSE-KICKER: Did this woman—this goddess—have a name?

FR. WALE: Fr. Mihaly couldn't remember. The next day, however, the "archaeologists" uncovered a ring of Roman lettering around the baptismal font. It said, ORA PRO NOBIS MARYA NOX, "Our Lady of Night."

[A pause]

Though it excuses nothing, it must be remembered I wasn't long in Christ's active service, at this point. Yes, my instructors had all told me that the church was founded as a supernatural society—but how could I possibly know what that meant, really, beyond a metaphor here and a lofty phrase there? It all just seemed so ridiculous.

Yes, the church was unique, singular, even off putting. But the more passionate Fr. Mihaly became in his belief that it was—*polluted*, somehow—the more it seemed as though nothing untoward at all had come from finding it, let alone opening it. Our school flourished, prospering. I taught all day while Fr. Mihaly grew increasingly frantic, interviewing every village elder he could find, looking for even one amongst them who knew the same tales as his grandmother.

Then a group of die-hard Communists broke in while the "archaeologists" were following up another report of nearby Scythian burial mounds. They desecrated the church as a "nonutilitarian remnant of a decadent age."

The next night, twenty children went to sleep, as usual . . . and never woke up again.

HORSE-KICKER: Because of—?

FR. WALE: Nobody knew. The village doctor was baffled. Eventually, he started talking about *Encephalitis lethargica* . . . Again, sleeping sickness, which is unfortunately fairly normal in Nigeria, but . . . not in Macedonia.

HORSE-KICKER: This crowd that broke into the church . . . what did they do, when they were in there?

FR. WALE: Oh, painted party slogans, stole things. Tried to wrench the Virgin's face out of the wall, which proved impossible. But they also managed to damage several of the individual children in her train, erasing their faces. And . . . they broke off the Christ Child's head.

Interestingly, the desecrators were very easy to find later, since most of them turned up at a clinic operated by Doctors Without Borders, twenty miles away. They complained of tinnitus and auditory hallucinations—tolling bells, babies crying, a woman's angry whisper. One man, perhaps the ringleader, developed inoperable cataracts on both corneas; he told Fr. Mihaly that when he touched the Virgin's face, she opened her eyes, and looked at him.

HORSE-KICKER: Did you ever find out exactly how many of the children's figures were destroyed?

FR. WALE: Yes, certainly. Nineteen.

HORSE-KICKER: And her baby . . .

FR. WALE: . . . makes twenty, yes.

By this point, I thought I knew what to do—what I would have done in Nigeria, at any rate. We all know what to do when things like this happen: Leave. That was my first impulse—this is witchcraft! How insane, how arrogant, to even attempt to fight it! Just bury the church again, and go. Only Father Mihaly kept me from getting on a plane back to Lagos, back to transplanted gods and goddesses whose rules I could at least understand. No, he said, we must do something. Okay, I said, finally—let's go and pray for guidance. Let's pray for a plan.

And soon enough, we had one.

We came back the next day, because the area remained rugged and difficult to travel, and no one wanted to go with us during the night. I remember my eyes felt as though they'd been boiled. We'd been up late, blessing enough water to reconsecrate the entire sacristy, which we did . . . That took some time. Then we went along the whole processional of her children, one by one, and we baptized the ones who'd been damaged, reclaiming them in Christ's name. The rest . . . we left to her.

While we were doing all this, meanwhile, the local police had been searching every inch of the surrounding area—scouring the bushes, feeling through crevices in the rocks, dragging the creeks. Incredibly grueling work! Finally, they found what they were looking for, in the pit underneath the "archaeologists' " outhouse; one of the desecrators had thrown it down there, as a final insult. But its face was still clean, miraculously enough, and its halo of stars was intact.

I used concrete to reattach the Christ Child's head, turned back to its mother's breast, where it was always meant to be. The sun was going down, by then. We lit the candles, and we left.

[A long pause]

HORSE-KICKER: So . . . what happened afterwards?

FR. WALE: To Fr. Mihaly and I?

HORSE-KICKER: To the village? The children?

FR. WALE: Six of them had been in danger of respiratory failure, attached to life-support machines. They began to breathe on their own again, and the machines were removed. But only one of them ever woke up, a little girl, if that's what you're asking—the rest are still asleep, in a hospital in Skopje, one of Macedonia's finest chronic-care facilities. I think the oldest has just turned twenty-seven.

It's a good city, Skopje. Mother Teresa was born there.

But now you're looking at me, Mr. Horse-Kicker, wondering how to ask the questions you obviously want to . . . those hard questions about faith, about salvation. Was it really all for nothing, with no happy ending in sight? Was this goddess, this creature, this . . . Marya Nox . . . really so strong? Is *God* really so weak?

HORSE-KICKER: [After a moment] Well, obviously, I don't want to . . . insult you, Father . . .

FR. WALE: Oh, don't worry about that; I don't feel insulted. We did what we could: Those children are alive. She does not have them, not anymore; God holds them in the hollow of his hands, their sins forgiven, their suffering over. And one day they *will* wake, in a far better place than this—a place that you and I may see too, one day, eventually. If we keep faith.

Sometimes I still think about that buried Church . . . Marya Nox's sanctuary. I think about who must have designed it, who oversaw the laying of its foundations, or gave the orders to raise it. About who, exactly, carved the face for that mosaic altarpiece. A priest, probably—maybe two priests, even. An old one, perhaps, like Fr. Mihaly, secure in his faith even against this mystery they faced, Biblically versed enough to use tradition against tradition—yet wily and insane enough, as well, to dare reframe this savage, nameless goddess as the Mother of God, half in heresy, half in hope—to give her a child of her own at last, the Christ Child Himself, who redeems the whole world. Yet not to thereby redeem *her* so much as to protect others—the innocent, the unwary. The as-yet unborn.

And a young one like me, too, as I was then: Not quite so sure, not quite so fore-armed . . . never quite so sure, not even at the end.

But it is ended. Marya Nox has what is due to her once more, and her place remains hers, sacrosanct. It is over . . . or as over as it ever can be, at least, given the circumstances.

I'm a bit uncomfortable even now, actually, saying the name out loud. But then again, it's only what the Byzantines called her.

Her true name, the one they tried so hard to erase by making her into a variation on our Lady—perhaps only those children she touched know that. Or Fr. Mihaly.

HORSE-KICKER: Excuse me?

FR. WALE: Yes, him too. A month later, after we had returned to Lagos, he too went to sleep one night, and never woke up.

HORSE-KICKER: Jesus! [Embarrassed] Uh, um. Sorry, Father.

FR. WALE: Don't be. That's a name I *like* to hear.

As for me, I left Nigeria, came here, to Toronto. I never went back. Not yet, anyhow.

HORSE-KICKER: Mind if I ask you how you sleep?

FR. WALE: Me? Pretty well. Most nights.

[Pause]

She was very beautiful, you know.

HORSE-KICKER: I can imagine.

FR. WALE: [After a long pause] No. You really can't.

Transcript excerpt ends here. See full file for further details.

Born in England and raised in Toronto, Canada, **GEMMA FILES** has been a film critic, teacher, and screenwriter, and is currently a wife and mother. She won the 1999 International Horror Guild Best Short Fiction Award for her story "The Emperor's Old Bones," and the 2006 *ChiZine*/Leisure Books Short Story Contest for her story "Spectral Evidence." Her fiction has been published in two collections (*Kissing Carrion* and *The Worm in Every Heart*, both from Prime Books), and five of her stories were adapted into episodes of *The Hunger*, an anthology TV show produced by Ridley and Tony Scott's Scot Free Productions. She has also published two chapbooks of poetry. In 2009, Dark Arts Publications' yearly anthology will feature three of her stories (two new, one reprint). Her first novel, *A Book of Tongues*, will be released by ChiZine Publications in 2010.

FILES SAYS: *The key fascination of Lovecraft lies, to me, in his least quantifiable quality—not the big words (nethescurial!) or the made-up ones (Nyarlathotep!), the limited point of view, the overexposition and lack of dialogue; but that idea of empty metaphysical space, the lag between immediate perception . . . maybe safe and happy, but not necessarily . . . and a choice of equally horrid realities. This is where he crosses over with people like Arthur Machen and M. R. James (or, more contemporarily, Joyce Carol Oates and Susan Hill), whose best tales carry a clear subtext: "I can't tell you WHY this happened, only that it did." So: that's what I was trying for here—Lovecraft in miniature, since I'm certainly not qualified to attempt the epic. I hope it came across.*

SARAH MONETTE & ELIZABETH BEAR

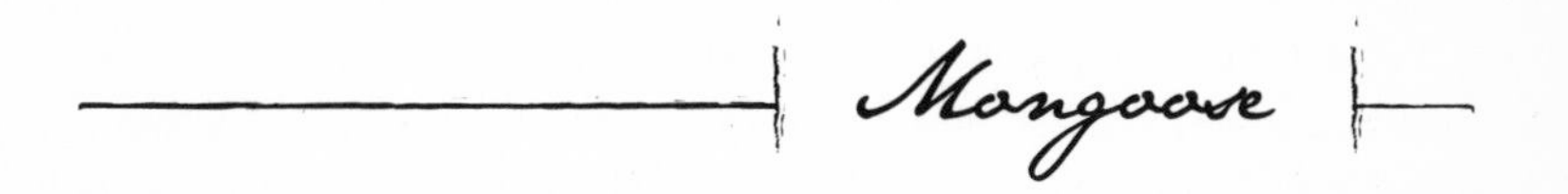

IZRAEL IRIZARRY STEPPED through a bright-scarred airlock onto Kadath Station, lurching a little as he adjusted to station gravity. On his shoulder, Mongoose extended her neck, her barbels flaring, flicked her tongue out to taste the air, and colored a question. Another few steps, and he smelled what Mongoose smelled, the sharp stink of toves, ammoniac and bitter.

He touched the tentacle coiled around his throat with the quick double tap that meant *soon*. Mongoose colored displeasure, and Irizarry stroked the slick velvet wedge of her head in consolation and restraint. Her four compound and twelve simple eyes glittered, and her color softened but did not change, as she leaned into the caress. She was eager to hunt and he didn't blame her. The boojum *Manfred von Richthofen* took care of its own vermin. Mongoose had had to make do with a share of Irizarry's rations, and she hated eating dead things.

If Irizarry could smell toves, it was more than the "minor infestation" the message from the stationmaster had led him to expect. Of course, that message had reached Irizarry third or fourth or fifteenth hand, and he had no idea how long it had taken. Perhaps when the stationmaster had sent for him, it *had* been minor.

But he knew the ways of bureaucrats, and he wondered.

People did double takes as he passed, even the heavily modded Christian cultists with their telescoping limbs and biolin eyes. You found them on every station, and steelships, too, though mostly they wouldn't work the boojums. Nobody liked Christians much, but they could work in situations that would kill an unmodded human or a even a gilly, so captains and stationmasters tolerated them.

There were a lot of gillies in Kadath's hallways, and they all stopped to blink at Mongoose. One, an indenturee, stopped and made an elaborate hand-flapping bow. Irizarry felt one of Mongoose's tendrils work itself through two of his earrings. Although she didn't understand staring exactly—her compound eyes made the idea alien to her—she felt the attention and was made shy by it.

Unlike the boojum-ships they serviced, the stations—Providence, Kadath, Leng, Dunwich, and the others—were man made. Their radial symmetry was predictable, and to find the stationmaster, Irizarry only had to work his way inward from the *Manfred von Richthofen*'s dock to the hub. There he found one of the inevitable safety maps (you are here; in case of decompression, proceed in an orderly manner to the life vaults located here, here, or here) and leaned close to squint at the tiny lettering. Mongoose copied him, tilting her head first one way, then another, though flat representations meant nothing to her. He made out STATIONMASTER'S OFFICE finally, on an oval bubble, the door of which was actually in sight.

"Here we go, girl," he said to Mongoose (who, stone deaf though she was, pressed against him in response to the vibration of his voice). He hated this part of the job, hated dealing with apparatchiks and functionaries, and of course the stationmaster's office was full of them, a receptionist, and then a secretary, and then someone who was maybe the *other* kind of secretary, and then finally—Mongoose by now halfway down the back of his shirt and entirely hidden by his hair and Irizarry himself half stifled by memories of someone he didn't want to remember being—he was ushered into an inner room where Stationmaster Lee, her arms crossed and her round face set in a scowl, was waiting.

"Mr. Irizarry," she said, unfolding her arms long enough to stick one hand out in a facsimile of a congenial greeting.

He held up a hand in response, relieved to see no sign of recognition in her face. It was Irizarry's experience that the dead were best left to lie where they fell. "Sorry, Stationmaster," he said. "I can't."

He thought of asking her about the reek of toves on the air, if she understood just how bad the situation had become. People could convince themselves of a lot of bullshit, given half a chance.

Instead, he decided to talk about his partner. "Mongoose hates it when I touch other people. She gets jealous, like a parrot."

"The cheshire's here?" She let her hand drop to her side, the expression on her face a mixture of respect and alarm. "Is it out of phase?"

Well, at least Stationmaster Lee knew a little more about cheshire cats than most people. "No," Irizarry said. "She's down my shirt."

Half a standard hour later, wading through the damp bowels of a ventilation pore, Irizarry tapped his rebreather to try to clear some of the tove stench from his nostrils and mouth. It didn't help much; he was getting close.

Here, Mongoose wasn't shy at all. She slithered up on top of his head, barbels and graspers extended to full length, pulsing slowly in predatory greens and reds. Her tendrils slithered through his hair and coiled about his throat, fading in and out of phase. He placed his fingertips on her slick-resilient hide to restrain her. The last thing he needed was for Mongoose to go spectral and charge off down the corridor after the tove colony.

It wasn't that she wouldn't come back, because she would—but that was only if she didn't get herself into more trouble than she could get out of without his help. "Steady," he said, though of course she couldn't hear him. A creature adapted to vacuum had no ears. But she could feel his voice vibrate in his throat, and a tendril brushed his lips, feeling the puff of air and the shape of the word. He tapped her tendril twice again—*soon*—and felt it contract. She flashed hungry orange in his peripheral vision. She was experimenting with jaguar rosettes—they had had long discussions of jaguars and tigers after their nightly reading of Pooh on the *Manfred von Richthofen*, as Mongoose had wanted to know what jagulars and tiggers were. Irizarry had already taught her about mongooses, and he'd read *Alice in Wonderland* so she would know what a cheshire cat was. Two days later—he still remembered it vividly—she had disappeared quite slowly, starting with the tips of the long coils of her tail and tendrils and ending with the needle-sharp crystalline array of her teeth. And then she'd phased back in, all excited aquamarine and pink, almost bouncing, and he'd praised her and stroked her and reminded himself not to think of her as a cat. Or a mongoose.

She had readily grasped the distinction between jaguars and jagulars, and had as quickly decided that she was a jagular; Irizarry had started to argue, but then thought better of it. She was, after all, a Very Good Dropper. And nobody ever saw her coming unless she wanted them to.

When the faint glow of the toves came into view at the bottom of the pore, he felt her shiver all over, luxuriantly, before she shimmered dark and folded herself tight against his scalp. Irizarry doused his own lights as well, flipping the passive infrared goggles down over his eyes. Toves were as blind as Mongoose was deaf, but an infestation this bad could mean the cracks were growing large enough for bigger things to wiggle through, and if there were raths, no sense in letting the monsters know he was coming.

He tapped the tendril curled around his throat three times, and whispered, "Go." She didn't need him to tell her twice; really, he thought wryly, she didn't need him to tell her at all. He barely felt her featherweight disengage before she was gone down the corridor as silently as a hunting owl. She was invisible to his goggles, her body at ambient temperature, but he knew from experience that her barbels and vanes would be spread wide, and he'd hear the shrieks when she came in among the toves.

The toves covered the corridor ceiling, arm-long carapaces adhered by a foul-smelling secretion that oozed from between the sections of their exoskeletons. The upper third of each tove's body bent down like a dangling bough, bringing the glowing, sticky lure and flesh-ripping pincers into play. Irizarry had no idea what they fed on in their own phase, or dimension, or whatever.

Here, though, he knew what they ate. Anything they could get.

He kept his shock probe ready, splashing after, to assist her if necessary. That was sure a lot of toves, and even a cheshire cat could get in trouble if she was outnumbered. Ahead of him, a tove warbled and went suddenly dark; Mongoose had made her first kill.

Within moments, the tove colony was in full warble, the harmonics making Irizarry's head ache. He moved forward carefully, alert now for signs of raths. The largest tove colony he'd ever seen was on the derelict steelship *Jenny Lind*, which he and Mongoose had explored when they were working salvage on the boojum *Harriet Tubman*. The hulk had been covered inside and out with toves; the colony was so vast that, having eaten everything else, it had started cannibalizing itself, toves eating their neighbors and being eaten in turn. Mongoose had glutted herself before the *Harriet Tubman* ate the wreckage, and in the refuse she left behind, Irizarry had found the strange starlike bones of an adult rath, consumed by its own prey. The bandersnatch that had killed the humans on the *Jenny Lind* had died with her reactor core and her captain. A handful of passengers and crew had escaped to tell the tale.

He refocused. This colony wasn't as large as those heaving masses on the *Jenny Lind*, but it was the largest he'd ever encountered not in a quarantine situation, and if there weren't raths somewhere on Kadath Station, he'd eat his infrared goggles.

A dead tove landed at his feet, its eyeless head neatly separated from its segmented body, and a heartbeat later, Mongoose phased in on his shoulder and made her deep clicking noise that meant, *Irizarry! Pay attention!*

He held his hand out, raised to shoulder level, and Mongoose flowed between the two, keeping her bulk on his shoulder, with tendrils resting against his lips and larynx, but her tentacles wrapping around his hand to communicate. He pushed his goggles up with his free hand and switched on his belt light so he could read her colors.

She was anxious, strobing yellow and green. *Many*, she shaped against his palm, and then emphatically, *R*.

R was bad—it meant rath—but it was better than *B*. If a bandersnatch had come through, all of them were walking dead, and Kadath Station was already as doomed as the *Jenny Lind*. "Do you smell it?" he asked under the warbling of the toves.

Taste, said Mongoose, and because Irizarry had been her partner for almost five solar, he understood: the toves tasted of rath, meaning that they had recently been feeding on rath guano, and given the swiftness of toves' digestive systems, that meant a rath was patrolling territory on the station.

Mongoose's grip tightened on his shoulder. *R*, she said again. *R. R. R.*

Irizarry's heart lurched and sank. More than one rath. The cracks were widening.

A bandersnatch was only a matter of time.

Stationmaster Lee didn't want to hear it. It was all there in the way she stood, the way she pretended distraction to avoid eye contact. He knew the rules of this game, probably better than she did. He stepped into her personal space. Mongoose shivered against the nape of his neck, her tendrils threading his hair. Even without being able to see her, he knew she was a deep, anxious emerald.

"A rath?" said Stationmaster Lee, with a toss of her head that might have looked flirtatious on a younger or less hostile woman, and moved away again. "Don't be ridiculous. There hasn't been a rath on Kadath Station since my grandfather's time."

"Doesn't mean there isn't an infestation now," Irizarry said quietly. If she was going to be dramatic, that was his cue to stay still and calm. "And I said raths. Plural."

"That's even more ridiculous. Mr. Irizarry, if this is some ill-conceived attempt to drive up your price—"

"It isn't." He was careful to say it flatly, not indignantly. "Stationmaster, I understand that this isn't what you want to hear, but you have to quarantine Kadath."

"Can't be done," she said, her tone brisk and flat, as if he'd asked her to pilot Kadath through the rings of Saturn.

"Of course it can!" Irizarry said, and she finally turned to look at him, outraged that he dared to contradict her. Against his neck, Mongoose flexed one set of claws. She didn't like it when he was angry.

Mostly, that wasn't a problem. Mostly, Irizarry knew anger was a waste of time and energy. It didn't solve anything. It didn't fix anything. It couldn't bring back anything that was lost. People, lives. The sorts of things that got washed away in the tides of time. Or were purged, whether you wanted them gone or not.

But this was . . . "You do know what a colony of adult raths can do, don't you? With a contained population of prey? Tell me, Stationmaster, have you started noticing fewer indigents in the shelters?"

She turned away again, dismissing his existence from her cosmology. "The matter is not open for discussion, Mr. Irizarry. I hired you to deal with an alleged infestation. I expect you to do so. If you feel you can't, you are of course welcome to leave the station with whatever ship takes your fancy. I believe the *Arthur Gordon Pym* is headed in-system, or perhaps you'd prefer the Jupiter run?"

He didn't have to win this fight, he reminded himself. He could walk away, try to warn somebody else, get himself and Mongoose the hell off Kadath Station. "All right, Stationmaster. But remember that I warned you, when your secretaries start disappearing."

He was at the door when she cried, "Irizarry!"

He stopped, but didn't turn.

"I can't," she said, low and rushed, as if she was afraid of being overheard. "I can't quarantine the station. Our numbers are already in the red this quarter, and the new political officer . . . It's my head on the block, don't you understand?"

He didn't understand. Didn't want to. It was one of the reasons he was a wayfarer, because he never wanted to let himself be like her again.

"If Sanderson finds out about the quarantine, she finds out about you. Will your papers stand up to a close inspection, Mr. Irizarry?"

He wheeled, mouth open to tell her what he thought of her and her clumsy attempts at blackmail, and she said, "I'll double your fee."

At the same time, Mongoose tugged on several strands of his hair, and he realized he could feel her heart beating, hard and rapid, against his spine. It was her distress he answered, not the station-master's bribe. "All right," he said. "I'll do the best I can."

Toves and raths colonized like an epidemic, outward from a single originating point, Patient Zero in this case being the tear in space-time that the first tove had wriggled through. More tears would develop as the toves multiplied, but it was that first one that would become large enough for a rath. While toves were simply lazy—energy-efficient, the Arkhamers said primly—and never crawled farther than was necessary to find a usable anchoring point, raths were cautious. Their marauding was centered on the original tear because they kept their escape route open. And tore it wider and wider.

Toves weren't the problem, although they were a nuisance, with their tendency to use up valuable oxygen, clog ductwork, eat pets, drip goo from ceilings, and crunch wetly when you stepped on them. Raths were worse; raths were vicious predators. Their natural prey might be toves, but they'd take small gillies—or small humans—when they could get them.

But even they weren't the danger that had made it hard for Irizarry to sleep the past two rest shifts. What toves tore and raths widened was an access for the apex predator of this alien food chain.

The bandersnatch: *Pseudocanis tindalosi.* The old records and the mendicant Arkhamers called them hounds, but of course they weren't, any more than Mongoose was a cat. Irizarry had seen archive video from derelict stations and ships, the bandersnatch's flickering angular limbs appearing like spiked mantis arms from the corners of sealed rooms, the carnage that ensued. He'd never heard of anyone left alive on a station where a bandersnatch manifested, unless they made it to a panic pod damned fast. More importantly, even the Arkhamers in their archive ships, breeders of Mongoose and all her kind, admitted they had no records of anyone *surviving* a bandersnatch rather than *escaping* it.

And what he had to do, loosely put, was find the core of the infestation before the bandersnatches did, so that he could eradicate the toves and raths and the stress they were putting on this little corner of the universe. Find the core—somewhere in the miles upon miles of Kadath's infrastructure. Which was why he was in this little-used service corridor, letting Mongoose commune with every ventilation duct they found.

Anywhere near the access shafts infested by the colony, Kadath Station's passages reeked of tove—ammoniac, sulfurous. The stench infiltrated the edges of Irizarry's mask as he lifted his face to a ventilation duct. Wincing in anticipation, he broke the seal on the rebreather and pulled it away from his face on the stiff elastic straps, careful not to lose his grip. A broken nose would not improve his day.

A cultist engineer skittered past on sucker-tipped limbs, her four snake arms coiled tight beside her for the narrow corridor. She had a pretty smile, for a Christian.

Mongoose was too intent on her prey to be shy. The size of the tove colony might make her nervous, but Mongoose loved the smell—like a good dinner heating, Irizarry imagined. She unfolded herself around his head like a tendriled hood, tentacles outreached, body flaring as she stretched towards the ventilation fan. He felt her lean, her barbels shivering, and turned to face the way her wedge-shaped head twisted.

He almost tipped backwards when he found himself face to face with someone he hadn't even known was there. A woman, average height, average weight, brown hair drawn back in a smooth club; her skin was space pale and faintly reddened across the cheeks, as if the IR filters on a suit hadn't quite protected her. She wore a sleek space-black uniform with dull silver epaulets and four pewter-colored bands at each wrist. An insignia with a stylized sun and Earth-Moon dyad clung over her heart.

The political officer, who was obviously unconcerned by Mongoose's ostentatious display of sensory equipment.

Mongoose absorbed her tendrils like a startled anemone, pressing the warm underside of her head to Irizarry's scalp where the hair was thinning. He was surprised she didn't vanish down his shirt, because he felt her trembling against his neck.

The political officer didn't extend her hand. "Mr. Irizarry? You're a hard man to find. I'm Intelligence Colonel Sadhi Sanderson. I'd like to ask you a few quick questions, please."

"I'm, uh, a little busy right now," Irizarry said, and added uneasily, "ma'am." The *last* thing he wanted was to offend her.

Sanderson looked up at Mongoose. "Yes, you would appear to be hunting," she said, her voice dry as scouring powder. "That's one of the things I want to talk about."

Oh, *shit*. He had kept out of the political officer's way for a day and a half, and really that was a pretty good run, given the obvious tensions between Lee and Sanderson, and the things he'd heard in the transient barracks: the gillies were all terrified of Sanderson, and nobody seemed to have a good word for Lee. Even the Christians, mouths thinned primly, could say of Lee only that she didn't actively persecute them. Irizarry had been stuck on a steelship with a Christian congregation for nearly half a year once, and he knew their eagerness to speak well of everyone; he didn't know whether that was actually part of their faith or just a survival tactic, but when Elder Dawson said, "She does not trouble us," he understood quite precisely what that meant.

Of Sanderson, they said even less, but Irizarry understood that, too. There was no love lost between the extremist cults and the government. But he'd heard plenty from the ice miners and dock-workers and particularly from the crew of an impounded steelship who were profanely eloquent on the subject. Upshot: Colonel Sanderson was new in town, cleaning house, and profoundly not a woman you wanted to fuck with.

"I'd be happy to come to your office in an hour, maybe two?" he said. "It's just that—"

Mongoose's grip on his scalp tightened, sudden and sharp enough that he yelped; he realized that her head had moved back toward the duct while he fenced weakly with Colonel Sanderson, and now it was nearly *in* the duct, at the end of a foot and a half of iridescent neck.

"Mr. Irizarry?"

He held a hand up, because really this wasn't a good time, and yelped again when Mongoose reached down and grabbed it. He knew better than to forget how fluid her body was, that it was really no more than a compromise with the dimension he could sense her in, but sometimes it surprised him anyway.

And then Mongoose said, *Nagaina*, and if Colonel Sanderson hadn't been standing right there, her eyebrows indicating that he was already at the very end of the slack she was willing to cut, he would have cursed aloud. Short of a bandersnatch—and that could still be along any time now, don't forget, Irizarry—a breeding rath was the worst news they could have.

"Your cheshire seems unsettled," Sanderson said, not sounding in the least alarmed. "Is there a problem?"

"She's eager to eat. And, er. She doesn't like strangers." It was as true as anything you could say about Mongoose, and the violent colors cycling down her tendrils gave him an idea what her chromatophores were doing behind his head.

"I can see that," Sanderson said. "Cobalt and yellow, in that stippled pattern—and flickering in and out of phase—she's acting aggressive, but that's fear, isn't it?"

Whatever Irizarry had been about to say, her observation stopped him short. He blinked at her—*like a gilly*, he thought uncharitably—and only realized he'd taken yet another step back when the warmth of the bulkhead pressed his coveralls to his spine.

"You know," Sanderson said mock confidentially, "this entire corridor *reeks* of toves. So let me guess: it's not just toves anymore."

Irizarry was still stuck at her being able to read Mongoose's colors. "What do you know about cheshires?" he said.

She smiled at him as if at a slow student. "Rather a lot. I was on the *Jenny Lind* as an ensign—there was a cheshire on board, and I saw . . . It's not the sort of thing you forget, Mr. Irizarry, having been there once." Something complicated crossed her face—there for a flash and then gone.

"The cheshire that died on the *Jenny Lind* was called Demon," Irizarry said, carefully. "Her partner was Long Mike Spider. You knew them?"

"Spider John," Sanderson said, looking down at the backs of her hands. She picked a cuticle with the opposite thumbnail. "He went by Spider John. You have the cheshire's name right, though."

When she looked back up, the arch of her carefully shaped brow told him he hadn't been fooling anyone.

"Right," Irizarry said. "Spider John."

"They were friends of mine." She shook her head. "I was just a pup. First billet, and I was assigned as Demon's liaison. Spider John liked to say he and I had the same job. But I couldn't make the captain believe him when he tried to tell her how bad it was."

"How'd you make it off after the bandersnatch got through?" Irizarry asked. He wasn't foolish enough to think that her confidences were anything other than a means of demonstrating to him why he could trust her, but the frustration and tired sadness sounded sincere.

"It went for Spider John first—it must have known he was a threat. And Demon—she threw herself at it, never mind it was five times her size. She bought us time to get to the panic pod and Captain Golovnina time to get to the core overrides." She paused. "I saw it, you know. Just a glimpse. Wriggling through this . . . this *rip* in the air, like a big gaunt hound ripping through a hole in a blanket with knotty paws. I spent years wondering if it got my scent. Once they scent prey, you know, they never stop . . ."

She trailed off, raising her gaze to meet his. He couldn't decide if the furrow between her eyes was embarrassment at having revealed so much, or the calculated cataloguing of his response.

"So you recognize the smell, is what you're saying."

She had a way of answering questions with other questions. "Am I right about the raths?"

He nodded. "A breeder."

She winced.

He took a deep breath and stepped away from the bulkhead. "Colonel Sanderson—I have to get it *now* if I'm going to get it at all."

She touched the microwave pulse pistol at her hip. "Want some company?"

He didn't. Really, truly didn't. And if he had, he wouldn't have chosen Kadath Station's political officer. But he couldn't afford to offend her . . . and he wasn't licensed to carry a weapon.

"All right," he said and hoped he didn't sound as grudging as he felt. "But don't get in Mongoose's way."

Colonel Sanderson offered him a tight, feral smile. "Wouldn't dream of it."

The only thing that stank more than a pile of live toves was a bunch of half-eaten ones.

"Going to have to vacuum scrub the whole sector," Sanderson said, her breath hissing through her filters.

If we live long enough to need to, Irizarry thought, but had the sense to keep his mouth shut. You didn't talk defeat around a politico. And if you were unfortunate enough to come to the attention of one, you certainly didn't let her see you thinking it.

Mongoose forged on ahead, but Irizarry noticed she was careful to stay within the range of his lights, and at least one of her tendrils stayed focused back on him and Sanderson at all times. If this were a normal infestation, Mongoose would be scampering along the corridor ceilings, leaving scattered bits of half-consumed tove and streaks of bioluminescent ichor in her wake. But this time, she edged along, testing each surface before her with quivering barbels so that Irizarry was reminded of a tentative spider or an exploratory octopus.

He edged along behind her, watching her colors go dim and cautious. She paused at each intersection, testing the air in every direction, and waited for her escort to catch up.

The service tubes of Kadath Station were mostly large enough for Irizarry and Sanderson to walk through single file, though sometimes they were obliged to crouch, and once or twice Irizarry found himself slithering on his stomach through tacky half-dried tove slime. He imagined—he hoped it was imagining—that he could sense the thinning and stretch of reality all around them, see it in the warp of the tunnels and the bend of deck plates. He imagined that he glimpsed faint shapes from the corners of his eyes, caught a whisper of sound, a hint of scent, as of something almost there.

Hypochondria, he told himself firmly, aware that that was the wrong word and not really caring. But as he dropped down onto his belly again, to squeeze through a tiny access point—this one clogged with the fresh corpses of newly slaughtered toves—he needed all the comfort he could invent.

He almost ran into Mongoose when he cleared the hole. She scuttled back to him and huddled under his chest, tendrils writhing, so close to out of phase that she was barely a warm shadow. When he saw what the access point had led them to, he wished he'd invented a little more.

This must be one of Kadath Station's recycling and reclamation centers, a bowl ten meters across sweeping down to a pile of rubbish in the middle. These were the sorts of places you always found minor tove infestations. Ships and stations were supposed to be kept clear of vermin, but in practice, the dimensional stresses of sharing the space lanes with boojums meant that just wasn't possible. And in Kadath, somebody hadn't been doing their job.

Sanderson touched his ankle, and Irizarry hastily drew himself aside so she could come through after. He was suddenly grateful for her company.

He really didn't want to be here alone.

Irizarry had never seen a tove infestation like this, not even on the *Jenny Lind*. The entire roof of the chamber was thick with their sluglike bodies, long lure tongues dangling as much as half a meter down. Small flitting things—young raths, near transparent in their phase shift—filled the space before him. As Irizarry watched, one blundered into the lure of a tove, and the tove contracted with sudden convulsive force. The rath never stood a chance.

Nagaina, Mongoose said. *Nagaina, Nagaina, Nagaina.*

Indeed, down among the junk in the pit, something big was stirring. But that wasn't all. That pressure Irizarry had sensed earlier, the feeling that many eyes were watching him, gaunt bodies stretching against whatever frail fabric held them back—here, it was redoubled, until he almost felt the brush of not-quite-in-phase whiskers along the nape of his neck.

Sanderson crawled up beside him, her pistol in one hand. Mongoose didn't seem to mind her there.

"What's down there?" she asked, her voice hissing on constrained breaths.

"The breeding pit," Irizarry said. "You feel that? Kind of a funny, stretchy feeling in the universe?"

Sanderson nodded behind her mask. "It's not going to make you any happier, is it, if I tell you I've felt it before?"

Irizarry was wearily, grimly unsurprised. But then Sanderson said, "What do we do?"

He was taken aback and it must have shown, even behind the rebreather, because she said sharply, "*You're* the expert. Which I assume is why you're on Kadath Station to begin with and why Stationmaster Lee has been so anxious that I not know it. Though with an infestation of this size, I don't know how she thought she was going to hide it much longer anyway."

"Call it sabotage," Irizarry said absently. "Blame the Christians. Or the gillies. Or disgruntled spacers, like the crew off the *Caruso*. It happens a lot, Colonel. Somebody like me and Mongoose comes in and cleans up the toves, the station authorities get to crack down on whoever's being the worst pain in the ass, and life keeps on turning over. But she waited too long."

Down in the pit, the breeder heaved again. Breeding raths were slow—much slower than the juveniles, or the sexually dormant adult rovers—but that was because they were armored like titanium armadillos. When threatened, one of two things happened. Babies flocked to mama, mama rolled herself in a ball, and it would take a tactical nuke to kill them. Or mama went on the warpath. Irizarry had seen a pissed-off breeder take out a bulkhead on a steelship once; it was pure dumb luck that it hadn't breached the hull.

And, of course, once they started spawning, as this one had, they could produce between ten and twenty babies a day for anywhere from a week to a month, depending on the food supply. And the more babies they produced, the weaker the walls of the world got, and the closer the bandersnatches would come.

"The first thing we have to do," he said to Colonel Sanderson, "as in, *right now*, is kill the breeder. Then you quarantine the station and get parties of volunteers to hunt down the rovers, before they can bring another breeder through, or turn into breeders, or however the fuck it works, which frankly I don't know. It'll take fire to clear this nest of toves, but Mongoose and I can probably get the rest. And *fire*, Colonel Sanderson. Toves don't give a shit about vacuum."

She could have reproved him for his language; she didn't. She just nodded and said, "How do we kill the breeder?"

"Yeah," Irizarry said. "That's the question."

Mongoose clicked sharply, her *Irizarry!* noise.

"No," Irizarry said. "Mongoose, don't—"

But she wasn't paying attention. She had only a limited amount of patience for his weird interactions with other members of his species and his insistence on *waiting*, and he'd clearly used it all up. She was Rikki-tikki-tavi, and the breeder was Nagaina, and Mongoose knew what had to happen. She launched off Irizarry's shoulders, shifting phase as she went, and without contact between them, there was nothing he could do to call her back. In less than a second, he didn't even know where she was.

"You any good with that thing?" he said to Colonel Sanderson, pointing at her pistol.

"Yes," she said, but her eyebrows were going up again. "But, forgive me, isn't this what cheshires are for?"

"Against rovers, sure. But—Colonel, have you ever seen a breeder?"

Across the bowl, a tove warbled, the chorus immediately taken up by its neighbors. Mongoose had started.

"No," Sanderson said, looking down at where the breeder humped and wallowed and finally stood up, shaking off ethereal babies and half-eaten toves. "Oh. *Gods*."

You couldn't describe a rath. You couldn't even look at one for more than a few seconds before you started getting a migraine aura. Rovers were just blots of shadow. The breeder was massive, armored, and had no recognizable features, save for its hideous, drooling, ragged-edged maw. Irizarry didn't know if it had eyes, or even needed them.

"She can kill it," he said, "but only if she can get at its underside. Otherwise, all it has to do is wait until it has a clear swing, and she's . . ." He shuddered. "I'll be lucky to find enough of her for a funeral. So what *we* have to do now, Colonel, is piss it off enough to give her a chance. Or"—he had to be fair; this was not Colonel Sanderson's job—"if you'll lend me your pistol, you don't have to stay."

She looked at him, her dark eyes very bright, and then she turned to look at the breeder, which was swinging its shapeless head in slow arcs, trying, no doubt, to track Mongoose. "Fuck that, Mr. Irizarry," she said crisply. "Tell me where to aim."

"You won't hurt it," he'd warned her, and she'd nodded, but he was pretty sure she hadn't really understood until she fired her first shot and the breeder didn't even *notice.* But Sanderson hadn't given up; her mouth had thinned, and she'd settled into her stance, and she'd fired again, at the breeder's feet, as Irizarry had told her. A breeding rath's feet weren't vulnerable as such, but they were sensitive, much more sensitive than the human-logical target of its head. Even so, it was concentrating hard on Mongoose, who was making toves scream at various random points around the circumference of the breeding pit, and it took another three shots aimed at that same near front foot before the breeder's head swung in their direction.

It made a noise, a sort of *wooaaurgh* sound, and Irizarry and Sanderson were promptly swarmed by juvenile raths.

"Ah, fuck," said Irizarry. "Try not to kill them."

"I'm sorry, try *not* to kill them?"

"If we kill too many of them, it'll decide we're a threat rather than an annoyance. And then it rolls up in a ball, and we have no chance of killing it until it unrolls again. And by then, there will be a lot more raths here."

"And quite possibly a bandersnatch," Sanderson finished. "But—" She batted away a half-corporeal rath that was trying to wrap itself around the warmth of her pistol.

"If we stood perfectly still for long enough," Irizarry said, "they could probably leech out enough of our body heat to send us into hypothermia. But they can't bite when they're this young. I knew a cheshire man once who swore they ate by crawling down into the breeder's stomach to lap up what it'd digested. I'm still hoping that's not true. Just keep aiming at that foot."

"You got it."

Irizarry had to admit, Sanderson was steady as a rock. He shooed juvenile raths away from both of them, Mongoose continued her depredations out there in the dark, and Sanderson, having found her target, fired at it in a nice steady rhythm. She didn't miss; she didn't try to get fancy. Only, after a while, she said out of the corner of her mouth, "You know, my battery won't last forever."

"I know," Irizarry said. "But this is good. It's working."

"How can you tell?"

"It's getting mad."

"How can you *tell*?"

"The vocalizing." The rath had gone from its *wooaaurgh* sound to a series of guttural huffing noises, interspersed with high-pitched yips. "It's warning us off. Keep firing."

"All right," Sanderson said. Irizarry cleared another couple of juveniles off her head. He was trying not to think about what it meant that no adult raths had appeared in response to the breeder's distress. How far had they ranged through Kadath Station? How much of it did they consider their hunting grounds, and was it enough yet for a second breeder? Bad questions, all of them.

"*Have* there been any disappearances lately?" he asked Sanderson.

She didn't look at him, but there was a long silence before she said, "None that *seemed* like disappearances. Our population is by necessity transient, and none too fond of authority. And, frankly, I've had so much trouble with the stationmaster's office that I'm not sure my information is reliable."

It had to hurt for a political officer to admit that. Irizarry said, "We're very likely to find human bones down there. And in their caches."

Sanderson started to answer him, but the breeder decided it had had enough. It wheeled toward them, its maw gaping wider, and started through the mounds of garbage and corpses in their direction.

"What now?" said Sanderson.

"Keep firing," said Irizarry. *Mongoose, wherever you are, please be ready.*

He'd been about 75 percent sure that the rath would stand up on its hind legs when it reached them. Raths weren't sapient, not like cheshires, but they were smart. They knew that the quickest way to kill a human was to take its head off, and the second quickest was to disembowel it, neither of which they could do on all fours. And humans weren't any threat to a breeder's vulnerable abdomen: Sanderson's pistol might give the breeder a hot foot, but there was no way it could penetrate the breeder's skin.

It was a terrible plan—there was that whole 25 percent where he and Sanderson died screaming while the breeder ate them from the feet up—but it worked. The breeder heaved itself upright, massive, indistinct paw going back for a blow that would shear Sanderson's head off her neck and probably bounce it off the nearest bulkhead, and with no warning of any kind, not for the humans, not for the rath, Mongoose phased viciously in, claws and teeth and sharp-edged tentacles all less than two inches from the rath's belly and moving fast.

The rath screamed and curled in on itself, but it was too late. Mongoose had already caught the lips of its—oh gods and fishes, Irizarry didn't know the word. Vagina? Cloaca? Ovipositor? The place where little baby raths came into the world. The only vulnerability a breeder had. Into which Mongoose shoved the narrow wedge of her head, and her clawed front feet, and began to rip.

Before the rath could even reach for her, her malleable body was already entirely inside it, and it—screaming, scrabbling—was doomed.

Irizarry caught Sanderson's elbow and said, "Now would be a good time, *very slowly*, to back away. Let the lady do her job."

Irizarry almost made it off of Kadath clean.

He'd had no difficulty in getting a berth for himself and Mongoose—after a party or two of volunteers had seen her in action, after the stories started spreading about the breeder, he'd nearly come to the point of beating off the steelship captains with a stick. And in the end, he'd chosen the offer of the captain of the *Erich Zann*, a boojum; Captain Alvarez had a long-term salvage contract in the Kuiper belt—"cleaning up after the ice miners," she'd said with a wry smile—and Irizarry felt like salvage was maybe where he wanted to be for a while. There'd be plenty for Mongoose to hunt, and nobody's life in danger. Even a bandersnatch wasn't much more than a case of indigestion for a boojum.

He'd got his money out of the stationmaster's office—hadn't even had to talk to Stationmaster Lee, who maybe, from the things he was hearing, wasn't going to be stationmaster much longer. You could either be ineffectual *or* you could piss off your political officer. Not both at once. And her secretary so very obviously didn't want to bother her that it was easy to say, "We had a contract," and to plant his feet and smile. It wasn't the doubled fee she'd promised him, but he didn't even want that. Just the money he was owed.

So his business was taken care of. He'd brought Mongoose out to the *Erich Zann*, and insofar as he and Captain Alvarez could tell, the boojum and the cheshire liked each other. He'd bought himself new underwear and let Mongoose pick out a new pair of earrings for him. And he'd gone ahead and splurged, since he was, after all, *on* Kadath Station and might as well make the most of it, and bought a selection of books for his reader, including *The Wind in the Willows*. He was looking forward, in an odd, quiet way, to the long nights out beyond Neptune: reading to Mongoose, finding out what she thought about Rat and Mole and Toad and Badger. Peace—or as close to it as Izrael Irizarry was ever likely to get.

He'd cleaned out his cubby in the transient barracks, slung his bag over one shoulder with Mongoose riding on the other, and was actually in sight of the *Erich Zann*'s dock when a voice behind him called his name.

Colonel Sanderson.

He froze in the middle of a stride, torn between turning around to greet her and bolting like a rabbit, and then she'd caught up to him. "Mr. Irizarry," she said. "I hoped I could buy you a drink before you go."

He couldn't help the deeply suspicious look he gave her. She spread her hands, showing them empty. "Truly. No threats, no tricks. Just a drink. To say thank you." Her smile was lopsided; she knew how unlikely those words sounded in the mouth of a political officer.

And any other political officer, Irizarry wouldn't have believed them. But he'd seen her stand her ground in front of a breeder rath, and he'd seen her turn and puke her guts out when she got a good look at what Mongoose did to it. If she wanted to thank him, he owed it to her to sit still for it.

"All right," he said, and added awkwardly, "Thank you."

They went to one of Kadath's tourist bars: bright and quaint and cheerful and completely unlike the spacer bars Irizarry was used to. On the other hand, he could see why Sanderson picked this one. No one here, except maybe the bartender, had the least idea who she was, and the bartender's wide-eyed double take meant that they got excellent service: prompt and very quiet.

Irizarry ordered a pink lady—he liked them, and Mongoose, in delight, turned the same color pink, with rosettes matched to the maraschino "cherry." Sanderson ordered whisky, neat, which had very little resemblance to the whisky Irizarry remembered from planetside. She took a long swallow of it, then set the glass down and said, "I never got a chance to ask Spider John this: how did you get your cheshire?"

It was clever of her to invoke Spider John and Demon like that, but Irizarry still wasn't sure she'd earned the story. After the silence had gone on a little too long, Sanderson picked her glass up, took another swallow, and said, "I know who you are."

"I'm *nobody*," Irizarry said. He didn't let himself tense up, because Mongoose wouldn't miss that cue, and she was touchy enough, what with all the steelship captains, that he wasn't sure what she might think the proper response was. And he wasn't sure, if she decided the proper response was to rip Sanderson's face off, that he would be able to make himself disagree with her in time.

"I promised," Sanderson said. "No threats. I'm not trying to trace you, I'm not asking any questions about the lady you used to work for. And, truly, I'm only *asking* how you met *this* lady. You don't have to tell me."

"No," Irizarry said mildly. "I don't." But Mongoose, still pink, was coiling down his arm to investigate the glass—not its contents, since the interest of the egg whites would be more than outweighed by the sharp sting to her nose of the alcohol, but the upside-down cone on a stem of a martini glass. She liked geometry. And this wasn't a story that could hurt anyone.

He said, "I was working my way across Jupiter's moons, oh, five years ago now. Ironically enough, I got trapped in a quarantine. Not for vermin, but for the black rot. It was a long time, and things got . . . ugly."

He glanced at her and saw he didn't need to elaborate.

"There were Arkhamers trapped there, too, in their huge old scow of a ship. And when the water rationing got tight, there were people that said the Arkhamers shouldn't have any—said that if it was the other way round, they wouldn't give us any. And so when the Arkhamers sent one of their daughters for their share . . ." He still remembered her scream, a grown woman's terror in a child's voice, and so he shrugged and said, "I did the only thing I could. After that, it was safer for me on their ship than it was on the station, so I spent some time with them. Their professors let me stay.

"They're not bad people," he added, suddenly urgent. "I don't say I understand what they believe, or why, but they were good to me, and they did share their water with the crew of the ship in the next berth. And of course, they had cheshires. Cheshires all over the place, cleanest steelship you've ever seen. There was a litter born right about the time the quarantine finally lifted. Jemima—the little girl I helped—she insisted they give me pick of the litter, and that was Mongoose."

Mongoose, knowing the shape of her own name on Irizarry's lips, began to purr, and rubbed her head gently against his fingers. He petted her, feeling his tension ease, and said, "And I wanted to be a biologist before things got complicated."

"Huh," said Sanderson. "Do you know what they are?"

"Sorry?" He was still mostly thinking about the Arkhamers, and braced himself for the usual round of superstitious nonsense: demons or necromancers or whatnot.

But Sanderson said, "Cheshires. Do you know what they are?"

"What do you mean, 'what they are'? They're cheshires."

"After Demon and Spider John . . . I did some reading and I found a professor or two—Arkhamers, yes—to ask." She smiled, very thinly. "I've found, in this job, that people are often remarkably willing to answer my questions. And I found out. They're bandersnatches."

"Colonel Sanderson, not to be disrespectful—"

"Subadult bandersnatches," Sanderson said. "Trained and bred and intentionally stunted so that they never mature fully."

Mongoose, he realized, had been watching, because she caught his hand and said emphatically, *Not.*

"Mongoose disagrees with you," he said and found himself smiling. "And really, I think she would know."

Sanderson's eyebrows went up. "And what does Mongoose think she is?"

He asked, and Mongoose answered promptly, pink dissolving into champagne and gold: *Jagular.* But there was a thrill of uncertainty behind it, as if she wasn't quite sure of what she stated so emphatically. And then, with a disdainful twist of her head at Colonel Sanderson, like any teenage girl: *Mongoose.*

Sanderson was still watching him sharply. "Well?"

"She says she's Mongoose."

And Sanderson really wasn't trying to threaten him, or playing some elaborate political game, because her face softened in a real smile, and she said, "Of course she is."

Irizarry swished a sweet mouthful between his teeth. He thought of what Sanderson had said, of the bandersnatch on the *Jenny Lind* wriggling through stretched rips in reality like a spiny, deathly puppy tearing a blanket. "How would you domesticate a bandersnatch?"

She shrugged. "If I knew that, I'd be an Arkhamer, wouldn't I?" Gently, she extended the back of her hand for Mongoose to sniff. Mongoose, surprising Irizarry, extended one tentative tendril and let it hover just over the back of Sanderson's wrist.

Sanderson tipped her head, smiling affectionately, and didn't move her hand. "But if I had to guess, I'd say you do it by making friends."

ELIZABETH BEAR was born on the same day as Frodo and Bilbo Baggins, and very nearly named after Peregrin Took. She is a recipient of the John W. Campbell, Locus, and Hugo Awards, as well as multiple British Science Fiction Awards, as well as a Dick nominee. She currently lives in southern New England with a famous cat. Her hobbies include murdering inoffensive potted plants, ruining dinner, and falling off rock faces.

Her most recent books are a space opera, *Chill*, from Bantam Spectra, and a fantasy, *By the Mountain Bound*, from Tor.

BEAR SAYS: *My introduction to Lovecraft came, strangely enough, through the non-Mythos story "Cool Air," which remains my favorite.*

I feel moved to explore his work in part because it's such an uncomfortable blend of the unsettling and the problematic. I feel moved to question the boundaries of Lovecraft's (often uncomfortably racist and misogynist) biological determinism, and find that his own metaphors of alienation and internalized inhumanity make an excellent tool for doing so.

SARAH MONETTE wanted to be an author when she grew up, and now she is. She lives and writes in a 103-year-old house in the upper Midwest with four cats, one husband, and an albino bristlenose plecostomus. She writes novels and short stories, and sometimes does both with Elizabeth Bear. Her short stories have appeared in *Lady Churchill's Rosebud Wristlet*, *Weird Tales*, and *Strange Horizons*, among other venues; her novels, *Melusine*, *The Virtu*, *The Mirador*, and *Corambis*, have been published by Ace Books. Her collaboration with Elizabeth Bear, *A Companion to Wolves*, was published in 2007. Visit her online at www.sarahmonette.com

MONETTE SAYS: *I found Lovecraft in graduate school and fell instantly in love, not only with his darkly elaborate cosmology, his ghouls and shoggoths and Elder Gods, but also with his own love affair with the English language. And somehow, for Lovecraft and for me, the two things go together: the words and the monsters, the monsters and the words.*

LAIRD BARRON

Catch Hell

FOR YEARS SHE awakened in the darkest hours to a baby crying. She finally accepted the nursery they'd sealed like a tomb was really and truly empty, that the crib was empty. She learned to cover her ears until the crying stopped. It never stopped.

2

Olde Towne lay forty miles east of Seattle in hill country, a depressed region populated by poor rural folk who worked the ranches, dairies, and farms. Forests, deep and forbidding, swept along the hem of tilled land. Farther on, the terrain rose into a line of mountains that divided the state.

The town's streets were bracketed by houses with peaked roofs. The houses were made of brick or stone with tall brick chimneys. People had settled here long ago; many homes bore bronze plates designating them as historic landmarks. Shops squeezed tight, fronted by wooden awnings and boardwalks; signs were done in gilt script over double-paned glass, or etched into antique shingles. Ancient magnolias and chestnuts reared at intervals to shade the sidewalks and the lanes. The police station, firehouse, and city hall occupied the far end of Main Street; art deco structures bordered by lawns, hedgerows, and picket fences.

One could imagine the police gunning down the McCoys on the courthouse steps.

Sonny and Katherine Reynolds waited for the light to change at the intersection of Main Street and Wright. Options at the airport had been limited, so they rented a sedan—a blocky gas guzzler that swallowed most of its lane, but, happily enough, possessed far more than sufficient trunk space to accommodate their luggage and Sonny's carton of research texts and notes. He told her several times during the drive it was like steering a boat. Katherine wanted a chance behind the wheel. Sonny laughed and said he'd let her drive it on the return leg of their journey. She called him a liar, but the ease of his humor, so removed from his usual melancholy, surprised her into a smile and she reached across and clasped his hand. Their hands on the wheel caught fire and burned orange, then red, as if they'd renewed an unspoken blood compact.

"Wow, a real live soda shop," she said. The sign outside of town claimed a population of three thousand. She estimated two or three times that number seeded throughout the surrounding countryside. Such a small, insular community—no wonder it clung to its heyday.

"Stuck in the '50s," he said. "Cripes—is that a wooden Indian in front of the barber shop?"

"Yes indeedy."

"You gotta be kidding."

"I've never seen so many weathervanes in one place," she said. This was true; she spied one on nearly every roof, lazily revolving in the westerly breeze. Most were iron roosters.

"Wisconsin it's cheese," he said. "Here, the fascination seems to be with cock. Gotta watch out for them cock fetishists."

"It's a left. Up ahead past that pink building." She shook her road map open.

"Looks like the set of a modern gothic. I read there's a big institution just down the road with the lights still on and everything. Guess they weren't *all* closed in the '80s."

Katherine immediately withdrew from him, embittered by his indifference, his callous disregard for her aversion to such places. "You fuck," she said and turned away and rested her forehead against the window.

"Yeah, I'm a fuck," he said cheerfully and played with the radio dial. The local station crackled in. Apparently the afternoon DJ was a transcendentalist; she spoke in the monotone of an amateur hypnotist and played recordings of wind chimes and the periodic rattle of what might've been gravel shaken in a jar.

The street narrowed to a bumpy stretch of country road, and climbed a series of bluffs that gave them a view of the entire valley. Sonny turned onto a blacktop drive that made a shallow, quarter-mile curve through a field of wildflowers and blackberry thickets and overgrown wooden fences, until it ended in a lot before the Black Ram Lodge. The building sat at the edge of a forest: brick and mortar and half-timber; three floors with a long, sloping tile roof, flanked by hedges and a stand of enormous magnolia trees. The windows were dark and impenetrable.

"Nothing looks the same in real life," he said.

"It seemed way smaller in the pictures," Katherine said, even though she'd suspected otherwise all along. She'd taken the brochure from her purse, comparing black-and-white photographs against the real artifact. "God, I hope this place isn't as empty as it looks." *Why'd I have to say that? Another excuse for him to think of me as a needy little bitch? Being alone isn't so bad. Not like I'm alone, anyway. I got you, babe, ha.* She glanced sidelong at her husband, checking for the oblique signs of contempt. *Maybe I* am *a needy little bitch. I'll say something stupid just to get a reaction. Some attention.*

There was no denying her dread of aloneness. She'd made peace with loneliness and sorrow, become accustomed to her own bleak thoughts, her recriminations and regrets. True isolation was a different proposition entirely. It seemed as if she'd dozed off during the drive from shiny, metropolitan Seattle and woken to find herself lost in a green wasteland. The town wasn't even comfortably picturesque anymore. Far below in the deepening gulf, lamps blinked on like the running lights of a seagoing vessel in fog. Sunset wasn't for another hour, yet a soft curtain of twilight had settled over the land. This was nowhere. *I hate you, Sonny. Selfish asshole.*

"I hope it is," Sonny said.

"Huh? Hope it's what?"

"Empty."

A wooden garage lay a hundred yards or so off in what had once likely been a cow pasture. Perhaps the garage was built from the bones of a massive barn, the place where they'd milked the cows, or slaughtered them. According to the pamphlet, more buildings were hidden beyond the central structure: a series of bungalows, a walled garden, a small distillery.

Two men stood in conversation on the cement steps of the main building. One was tall and lean, an older gentleman whose snowy hair touched the shoulders of his gray suit. The other man was a bit younger and heavier and dressed in slacks and a dark polo shirt.

"Welcome to Fantasy Island," Sonny said, and laughed. He put on his sunglasses and climbed out of the car. Katherine watched him approach the men on the steps. Exhaustion had stolen her will, melted her into the seat. She chafed at his ability to adopt a genial demeanor with such casual efficacy, like a chameleon brightening to match the foliage.

"Mr. Reynolds," the taller man said as he shook hands with Sonny. His voice was dampened by glass. "I'm Kent Prettyman, humble steward of the Black Ram. This is my accomplice, Derek Lang." As a group, they glanced at the car as Katherine emerged, a badger driven from her burrow. "Ah, Mrs. Reynolds! I'm Kent Prettyman. Call me Kent, please. And this is—"

Her sunglasses were the oversized variety worn by actresses and battered wives. "Kat. Just Kat."

"Meow," Mr. Lang said. His face was almost as dark as his shirt and he was brutishly muscular beneath the softness of his shoulders and belly.

Mr. Prettyman explained that Mr. Lang managed the grounds. There was a significant measure of yearly upkeep on the buildings and environs, a monetary burden divided between the state, the county, and the owners of the estate. When Katherine inquired who these owners were, he said the landlords, a family of hereditary nobility, resided in Europe. The family possessed numerous holdings and cared little for the lodge, leaving its management to intermediaries, most lately (as of 1995) a nonprofit foundation for the preservation of historical sites. All rather boring, he assured them. Did they have many bags? One of the boys would fetch their luggage and park the car.

The lodge predated Olde Towne and the very weight of its history settled upon Katherine's shoulders when she followed Mr. Prettyman through the double doors of age-blackened oak into the grand foyer. The Black Ram had been established as a trading post in the 1860s, doing a brisk business with settlers from Seattle and tribes from neighboring Snohomish Valley. The post was expanded and refurbished as the manse of the Welloc family, the very same who carried the deed to this day, until it finally became an inn directly following the Great Depression, and thus remained. Slabbed beams crisscrossed the upper vault and glowed gold-black from the light passing through leaded glass. Katherine squinted to discern the shadowed forms of suits of armor and weapons on display, moldering tapestries of medieval hunts, and large potted plants of obscure genuses that thrived in gloom. The flavor was certainly far more Western European than Colonial America, or America of any other era, for that matter.

She stood in the semicircle of men, oversized shades dangling from her fingers. Her arm brushed Sonny's and each of them instinctively flinched. She opened her mouth to mutter an apology and saw the gesture would be fruitless; he'd already forgotten her. His white shirt shone in the encroaching darkness and it illuminated his inscrutable, olive face, lent it the illusion of life. Mr. Prettyman said something to Mr. Lang, and Mr. Lang slunk away.

"No phones?" Sonny said, incredulous enough to drop his fake smile for a moment.

"There is a house phone," Mr. Prettyman said. He pointed to a wooden-paneled booth across from the front desk. Another bit of bric-a-brac from a dusty period in European history. Doubtless the lodge sported a billiards room, a smoking den, tables for baccarat and canasta. "And another in my office. No wireless Internet, I'm afraid. We make every attempt to foster an atmosphere of seclusion and relaxation here at the Black Ram. Guests needn't trouble themselves with intrusions from the city while in our care."

"A *house* phone . . ."

"It's all in the brochure," Katherine said. "Didn't you read the brochure, honey? It'll be an adventure, like the hotel we stayed at in Croatia, or the other one in Mexico." Remote, decrepit half-star hotels, the pair of them. It rained torrentially during their stay in Mexico and the roof leaked in a half-dozen places, water fairly poured in, truth be told, and sent cockroaches skittering across the bed sheets in search of high ground. "Who cares. I'm sure we've got plenty of bars on this hill." She flipped open her cell phone and checked.

"Are we the only guests?" Sonny asked.

"Oh, well, there are several others. Fewer than a dozen, at the moment. Midsummer doldrums," Mr. Prettyman said. He rubbed his hands together when he spoke, absently polishing the malachite ring on the third finger of his left hand—Katherine couldn't make out the symbol embossed upon the onyx; a star, perhaps. "At our peak we can host on the order of eighty or so guests. I'll give you a tour of the property—tomorrow morning, say? Allow me to introduce the staff." Even as he spoke, a pair of strapping boys laboriously rolled a baggage cart overstuffed with the Reynolds' belongings through the lobby and onto the elevator at the opposite end of the room. The elevator was flanked by a pair of marble rams and appeared as ancient as everything else, a wide platform caged in wrought iron. It lifted almost silently, except for the soft ding of a bell and the hum and slide of well-oiled gears.

As promised, Mr. Prettyman walked them through the lodge, and Katherine smugly noted there was indeed a den containing card and billiard tables, an abundance of big-game trophies, and the largest stone fireplace she'd ever seen—larger than the ones found in the proud old rustic ski lodges in Italy they'd frequented before Sonny broke his knee and gave up skiing altogether.

"Naturally it gets rather soggy during the winter, but summer storms are also fierce in these parts," Mr. Prettyman said. "A front will roll down out of the mountains and positively deck us with thunder and lightning. Nothing like a roaring fire and hot cocoa to steel a soul against the weather. . . ."

The proprietor oversaw a chef and bartender and their requisite assistants, a handful of maids and custodial personnel, two porters (Billy and Zack, the burly farm boys), a maintenance man, and the concierge, a gaunt, clerkish gentleman named Kristoff. Kristoff had jaundiced eyes and old-fashioned false teeth that didn't quite fit his mouth. He smelled sharply of alcohol. Katherine thought the dour fellow probably kept a flask of something strong under the desk. As Mr. Prettyman swept them along to the upper floors, he mentioned Mr. Lang was responsible for nearly a dozen carpenters, laborers, and gardeners. In addition, Mr. Lang stood in as the de facto chief of security—he handled the infrequent trespasser; hunters, mainly. Poachers who slipped into the wooded preserve beyond the lodge in hopes of bagging a deer or one of the wild boars or black bears that roamed the hills. The land had once doubled as a private wildlife preserve.

"Wild boar? Bears?" Katherine wasn't happy with this revelation. "Is that even . . . well, legal?"

"I don't think the family concerned itself with the niceties back then," Mr. Prettyman said. "They stocked their game in the '20s, I believe. Possibly earlier. Money talks, as the saying goes. Local law enforcement was frequently invited to hunt with the, ah, royalty, as it were. Oh, and there's a small cougar population. Indigenous."

"So much for nature walks."

"Nonsense, Mrs. Reynolds! Don't bother them, they won't bother you. Very few of the big animals venture close to the lodge proper. Besides, if you'd care to explore the region, sightsee the ruins and whatnot, I'm sure Mr. Lang would be happy to organize a day trip. He's a dead shot. Small likelihood of your being eaten by bears, I promise."

She pictured Mr. Lang's sadistic grin, his sweaty hands caressing a hunting rifle. "I think I'd like to lie down now."

Their suite occupied the second floor of the southern wing. It consisted of a living room, kitchenette, bedroom, and one and a half baths. The pine bureaus and armoire were antiques. A tapestry depicting a stag hunt hung over the bed, some pastoral oil paintings were scattered elsewhere, and in the living area was a Philco radio that must've been popular in the 1940s, but no television. The living-room window commanded a view of the forested hills.

Katherine eyed the stag hunt. The vision of the stag, rearing before frothing mastiffs and men on horses, all eyes black and wild, the horns and the spears—this visceral image looming over the bed was a disquieting prospect.

"First no phones, now no television." Sonny rummaged through the drawers of a small writing desk. A kerosene lamp perched atop the hutch of the desk, bookending a handful of cloth-bound volumes so decrepit, humidity had sloughed the titles from their spines. He sniffed the sooty glass. "Makes you wonder how often they lose power. Prettyman says there's a coal furnace in the boiler room."

"Maybe it's part of the ambience. Lamps, rose petals—"

"Yep, and a romantic game of cribbage. Or dominoes." He rattled a velvet bag and she laughed.

A few minutes later they argued, an indication things were back to normal, or what passed for normalcy here in the lucky thirteenth year of their union. She'd made reference to Mr. Prettyman's offhand comment regarding ruins and Sonny immediately clammed up. He leaped to his feet and began pacing the bedroom. Then he grabbed his coat. Katherine asked where he was going, alarmed at the prospect of being deserted in this place, surrounded by strangers, one of whom gave her the serious creeps. "Out," he said.

"But where?" By an act of supreme will she kept her voice level.

"Don't worry about it. Take a nap. Whatever." He was on his way, face set, a man in action.

Jesus, and I thought the alpha-male routine was sexy, once. "We're in this together. This leaky ol' rowboat. Right?"

"I'll see you for supper." His demeanor was that of a man announcing to his family he was running to the corner store for cigarettes. *I'll be right back!* He turned away, snuffing the conversation.

"Yeah, sure." She wanted to stick her nail file in his ass cheek.

"Kitchen's open till ten. Put on something nice. You look good in the taffeta." He walked out, shutting the door carefully behind him.

Katherine flipped him the bird with both hands and slumped on the bed and seethed. She hated him, not because he'd dismissed her as one dismisses an inferior, a child, although certainly that was a portion. Her rage sprang from the simple fact that he always seemed to know so much more than she did.

She went to the window and stared out at a landscape growing soft and shapeless as light slipped away. Toward the horizon and closing fast came a towering storm cloud, a death's-head lit by internal fires. Her eyes grew heavy. She swallowed a couple of pills from one of multiple bottles that comprised her daily regimen of behavioral equalization, and fell asleep. Wind clattered the shutters and the last bit of evening sun faded and died.

— 3 —

Katherine had spent six years dwelling on the accident, yet she seldom pictured Janie. Baby clothes, the odor of formula and spittle, but not the baby herself. In retrospect, the pregnancy, the seven months that had followed, were dreamlike; they left an impression that she'd engaged in a protracted struggle with some indefinable illness or injury. Yes, it seemed the stuff of dreams. There *were* scars: her vertigo persisted, and too, her phobia of bridges and overpasses. Sometimes the cry of an infant caused her to lactate. Sometimes it elicited a flood of tears and inconsolable sobbing. She'd screamed at a hapless mother in a coffee shop; told her to *shut up her squalling brat* and was instantly mortified at the lady's expression of shock and fear. Thankfully, the fits of lunacy had ebbed.

Sonny had wanted another child right away. A few months after the dust of the tragedy settled, he insisted they try again. His desire developed into an unequivocal force, an implacable usurper of their life aspirations, of all they'd planned during their days as romantic conspirators.

Katherine's mother pulled her aside at the family Christmas dinner—she recalled her father's and Sonny's laughter echoing from the living room, how it transcended the boom and roar of a football game on TV. Sonny hated football, sneered at the preening athletes, their "bling" and arrogance; he pretended to enjoy sports to bond with her father, who'd been a devout booster of his own hometown high-school team since forever.

Are you sure you're ready? Mom said. *Is it what you want?* And what Mom meant was, *Are you still the kind of bitch who eats her own puppies?* Katherine smiled brightly and bore down on the potato peeler. She said, *Yes, yes, of course we're ready. I want this.* Mom's eyes hinted at a profound unhappiness born of doubt that abruptly submerged to be replaced by her songbird cheer. Mom was a survivor, too. Everyone had a nice, fattening dinner and far too many Irish coffees. While they watched one of Pop's moldy old VCR tapes of a Bob Hope special, Katherine thought, *What I really want is to be punished. That's why I can't get well. Why I stay married to the sonofabitch.*

When a year passed without a positive result, they, or Sonny, to be specific, grew concerned. It developed his sperm count was merely adequate. The specialists were at a loss in her case: she tested fertile; nonetheless, her insides had lapsed into a peculiar dormancy. Adoption was out of the question; Sonny would accept no less than his own image in miniature. This went on and on. Then the desperate act—the surrogacy. They borrowed money, they recruited a volunteer, and the volunteer miscarried. Their marriage plunged into the Dark Ages.

It wasn't the end, though; there's no end to hell.

4

Katherine and Sonny arrived in time for a late supper in the dining room. Sonny had apparently stopped off at the hotel bar and made the acquaintance of three fellow guests whom he invited to join Katherine and himself for supper. She instantly recognized that her husband had indulged in several drinks from his slightly disheveled hair, the width of his smile, the shine of his eyes. As he flushed, the old patina of acne scars became fiercely evident and roughened his cheeks, lending his expression a coarseness one might glimpse in a mug shot. Not good—Sonny's wit became caustic when he drank overmuch. Luckily, he didn't indulge frequently, preferring to focus upon less hedonistic pursuits. Katherine wondered if she might prefer an alcoholic husband to a morbidly obsessive one.

Gary Woodruff was a retired investment banker on vacation from Manhattan. He wore a suit out of place in their rustic surroundings. Lyle Cockrum neglected to divulge his occupation. Katherine pegged him for a playboy. His hands were fragile, his black hair expensively styled, his boredom complete and genuine.

His designer clothes were loose and a compellingly tasteless shade of lime. He'd arrived with a frail blonde woman who'd immediately professed awful allergies and retreated to her room. The third guest, Melvin Ting, served as assistant curator of Olde Towne's most venerable repository of historical artifacts, the Welloc-Devlin Museum. Of evident Eurasian lineage, he struck Katherine as much too young for such a post: thirty years old at most, and clad in a turtleneck and slacks, a gold hoop in his left ear. He would've fit right in at a trendy coffeehouse slinging lattes or reciting the poetry of the disaffected. He also smiled too much for her taste. This, of course, was the very individual they'd traveled from California to meet. However, since the rendezvous was intended to be clandestine, neither she nor Sonny gave any hint.

The chef personally introduced the courses, which included salmon and truffles, and sorbet for dessert. Afterward, they ordered drinks and lounged near the softly crackling hearth, their conclave presided over by an enormous black ram's head on the mantle. Buzzed from several glasses of red wine and somewhat disarmed by her cozy surroundings, Katherine nonetheless wished they'd chosen to call it a night. The lights flickered and died to a chorus of gasps and mild curses. The group sat in tense silence, listening to grand old beams shift and creak, and rain slash against the windows while hotel staff bustled about lighting lanterns and refreshing drinks.

"So, what's your line?" Mr. Cockrum said. He studied Sonny over the rim of a brandy snifter.

"Until recently I taught cultural anthropology at a little college in Pasadena. Folklore. I've dabbled in archaeology. Now I write for travel journals." And, in a perfunctory gesture to his wife, "Kat is vice president of communications for the Blessingham Agency. They design colors."

"For marketing strategies, I presume," Woodruff said.

"If you've ever wondered where Super Burger restaurants got that color scheme, or why Tuffenup Buddy pain reliever comes in a Day-Glo pink box, I'm the one to ask." She smiled faintly.

There was a long, dead pause.

"How does one become an expert in folklore?" Woodruff's tone suggested vast condescension. He exaggerated the syllables of "expert."

"His father was a famous primatologist," she said in automatic defense of her husband's pride. Whether it would bolster his confidence or annoy him was a gamble. She couldn't help herself.

"Ah, not really famous," Sonny said. "He read traditional fairy tales to us kids every night. The unvarnished ones where Cinderella's sisters cut off pieces of their feet to fit the glass slipper. Sex and cannibalism—all the good stuff modern publishers whitewash. It stuck."

"He researched ape languages at Kyoto University." Katherine tried her wine, determined to slug it out now that she'd gone this far. It had grown unpleasantly warm. "Sonny won't tell you this, but his father, Quentin, did a lot of important work for the Primate Research Group in the 1950s. A very prestigious organization. The Japanese thought so highly of him they bought him a house."

"He left the university long ago," Sonny said. "I'm sure you've never heard of him—"

"What kind of folklore do you study?" Mr. Ting asked. He'd remained silent during dinner while chain-smoking and sipping espresso.

"Japanese mythology. I've some facility with Chinese and Indian oral traditions, a smattering of others." This was exceptionally modest of Sonny. He'd acquired extensive knowledge of several dozen mythological traditions.

"You get into the scary shit, I see," Mr. Cockrum said. Katherine wondered how much the man knew about the subject. Cliffs Notes and Penguin Abridged Classics, most likely. He hardly seemed the type to pore over scholarly treatises.

"Eh, the *really scary shit* would be the Slavic mythos. Or Catholicism, ha-ha," Sonny said.

"He's written books." Katherine stared at her glass. The vein in her temple began to pulse.

"Oh, more than magazine features? You mean real books?" Mr. Woodruff said.

"Ah, of course he has," Mr. Cockrum said. "Publish or perish; is this not the academic way, Mr. Reynolds?"

What the fuck do you know about academia, Cock Ring?

"Damned straight it is." Sonny swallowed a half glass of whiskey and signaled the cocktail waitress for another. His ruddy flush deepened and crept beneath his open collar. He was growing bellicose and reckless, and Katherine decided she'd best figure a graceful way to maneuver them away from the dinner party before things got truly ugly.

"Well, if you want spooky, get Prettyman or Lang to tell you about the local legends," Cockrum said. "An associate of mine spent his honeymoon here a couple of years ago. They sat right here in this den and swapped ghost stories. Prettyman and Lang had some doozies about the Old Man of the Wood."

"Oooh! The Old Goat!" Mr. Woodruff chortled at his own wit.

"I read about that," Sonny said. "The locals used to think he stole their livestock and seduced their womenfolk—"

"—and granted wishes," Mr. Ting said.

"For a price, no doubt." Mr. Cockrum had lighted a cigarette. Its cherry illuminated the panes of his face.

"He has colorful appellations—Wild Bill, Splayfoot Bill, Billy the Black—"

"—Mr. Bill," said Mr. Cockrum to Mr. Ting's pained smile.

"Hear, hear!" Woodruff said. "Seducer of women? A satyr."

Cockrum winked at Sonny. "Not a satyr. Not a randy flautist, not Pan incarnate. The legends around here are darker than that."

"The Old Man of the Wood is a devil," Sonny said. "One of Lucifer's circle."

"Or Satan Hisownself. Isn't that right, Mr. Ting?" Mr. Cockrum exhaled toward the curator.

Mr. Ting shrugged. "Admittedly, in the olden days many an unfortunate event was laid at the feet, erm, hooves, of the Old Man."

"I'd say rape, murder, mutilation, the kidnapping of wee children qualifies as *unfortunate*, all right." Mr. Cockrum leaned toward Katherine. "You wanna see what I mean, there's a painting of the old boy down the hall on the way to the stairs. Curl your toes." Then, he lowered his voice to a stage whisper, "Prettyman says the Goat Lord still blunders through the darkest woods, that occasionally he meets up with a lost hiker, or a kiddie, pardon the pun. . . . On nights such as these it almost seems plausible."

On her way to dinner, Katherine had stopped to view the painting of the so-called Old Man of the Wood. The oils were old and blurry, yet the depiction of the naked figure in a grove was oddly disquieting. One could discern, obscured by shadow, massive horns; a sinister smile; a beckoning hand, elongated and strange. The painting possessed a quality of tainted eroticism, the fanciful and unnerving impression of a piece of ancient history leaked into the present. It gleamed darkly from its alcove, insinuating the permanence of lust and wickedness and the mortal fascination with such corruption.

"Let us not forget, our esteemed proprietor was once a man of the cloth," Mr. Ting said. "A good Lutheran minister descended from the Olde Towne tradition of such men. Understandably his conjecture would veer to the ecclesiastical."

"Really?" Sonny said. "He appears a bit, I dunno, wild, to be a minister."

"*Former* minister," Mr. Ting said.

"I say, whoever named this lodge certainly possessed a fiendish sense of humor," Mr. Woodruff said. "*Black Ram* is a tad obvious, though."

"Placation," Sonny said. "One must give the Devil his due."

"Puhleeze!" Katherine reached over and smacked his arm to the accompaniment of groans and chuckles.

Lights sputtered and fizzed in their sockets and power was restored to a round of tipsy applause. There came a brief lull, and when people began yawning, she seized the opportunity to proclaim road exhaustion, and soon the party drifted to their respective quarters.

— 5 —

Mr. Ting knocked on the door after a discreet period. Sonny poured nightcaps from a complimentary bottle of vodka management had stored in the icebox. Ting drew a leather packet from his valise and set it on the table and clicked on the lamp. The leather had paled to yellow and was bound with rawhide strings. The curator undid the knots and delicately spread several sheets of ancient, curling parchment. The papers were written in Latin, and decorated with alchemical annotations and cryptic diagrams. Ting explained that the materials had once been the property of the Welloc-Devlin Museum via the estate of Johansen Welloc, one of Olde Towne's self-styled nobles during the early 1900s. Welloc was a trained archaeologist and noted collector of antiquities, the latter including a preoccupation with manuscripts and art objects certain to have gotten him burned at the stake during quainter times.

"Olde Towne is a rather fascinating case," Mr. Ting said. "Reading between the lines, one might surmise its founding fathers were predominantly occultists. Witchcraft, hermetic magic, geomancy . . . the gentry pursued knowledge of all manners of superstitious methodology. A veritable goldmine for an anthropologist."

"A wet dream," Katherine said. Clearly the town hadn't escaped the eccentricities of its founders—a flock of Golden Dawn–style crackpots who'd transmitted their kookiness down through the generations.

While Sonny studied the papers, Ting made himself another drink. "You realize, I assume, this is all rubbish." He produced a battered geophysical map of Olde Towne and environs. Red Xs marked several locations.

"Yes, yes. Rubbish." Sonny didn't bother to glance up. His eyes were slits twinkling with lamplight. He licked his lips.

Mr. Ting smiled dryly. "Nor should I need to warn you about the legality of traipsing across sites of cultural import . . . much less tampering with anything you might find. The locals frown upon tourists pocketing arrowheads and such as souvenirs. Mr. Lang keeps a sharp eye on the grounds, I might add."

"Not to worry, Ting. That's a contemptible sport." Sonny's grin wasn't his most convincing.

Mr. Ting nodded and dragged on his cigarette. He exhaled and his shrewd expression was partially screened by the blue cloud, the back of his hand. "You have to be cautious," he said. He gestured at the discarded leather case, the survey map. "A word to the wise, my friends: there are those in Olde Towne who enjoy meeting nice people such as yourselves. These parties I mention are possessed of selfish interests and curious appetites. That's all I'll say."

"Um, thanks," Sonny said.

"Forgive my crassness, but the fee. . . . Regrettable; however, my acquisition of your papers was not without some jeopardy to my position."

"Forgive you?" Sonny scribbled a check for a sum that made him wince, and sent the fellow on his way.

"Finally," Katherine said. She thought of the rotting grimoires with titles in Latin, German, and Greek, the mandrake roots and moon dust, and the other items stowed among their suitcases and bags. What would the unflappable Mr. Ting think of those? *He'd probably think we're just two more loons in a long line.*

Sonny locked the door. He went to the bed and dragged it about eighteen inches away from the wall. He'd purchased crimson chalk from a witch in Salem, Massachusetts. The witch was the real deal, he said, and he only tracked her down after many weeks of legwork. The crone dwelt in a shack in a bog, like all authentic witches did. She sold him the chalk, a dirty nub allegedly preserved from the collection of a Renaissance sorcerer who dabbled in the summoning of various entities best not mentioned, and candles made from the tears of freshly hanged men and babies' fat. Katherine refused to ask what the so-called witch had wanted in exchange for her services. The possibilities induced a shudder.

He drew a pentagram around the bed, and another on the ceiling directly above, all the while muttering a Latin incantation. When he'd finished, he dusted off his hands and surveyed his work. The pentagrams were protective circles designed to repel negative forces that crept upon hapless sleepers: the night hags, the succubae and incubi, whatever unnamed demons that made feasts of a dreamer's spirit. "Be sure to step carefully when you get into bed. Smudge the line and it's useless."

"The maid is gonna love this," she said. Probably Sonny had arranged for them to be left undisturbed, however. He thought of everything. "Maybe we should sacrifice a goat. Yeah, ram's blood. And a virgin."

"You're drunk. Go to sleep," he said.

— 6 —

Katherine lay sleep drugged and passive while Sonny fucked her. His face always changed during sex. His eyes narrowed, his teeth shone like tarnished gemstones; he seemed dangerous and she occasionally fantasized he was a criminal, maybe a gangster who'd decided to have his way with her.

She turned her cheek against the coolness of her pillow while he grunted in her ear. The room was dark, but by the glow of the guttering candles, she slowly realized Mr. Lang stood in the doorway, watching. She groaned, and Sonny put his hand over her mouth, as he'd gotten in the habit of doing back when they were young and lusty and dwelt in an apartment with paper-thin walls. She struggled and that excited him and he moved faster, pressed her so hard the mattress formed a cave around them. Mr. Lang sidled from the doorway and toward the bed and slipped from her field of view. All she could hear was Sonny panting like a dog, her own muffled moans and cries. She panicked and thrashed against him and then she came and moments later he finished and collapsed upon her like a dead man.

Gasping and sobbing, Katherine shoved him until he rolled over. She frantically looked around, but Mr. Lang was nowhere to be seen. Her chest squeezed so tight her vision twinkled with motes and stars. Then, the urge to pee came over her. She was terrified to walk across the floor and into the pit of darkness that was the bathroom.

She lay awake, curled tight as a spring until morning light slowly pushed the shadows away and into the corners of the room. By then she'd half convinced herself Mr. Lang's appearance was that of an apparition. She chuckled wryly: what if Sonny's pentagram had kept them safe?

Good as his word, following breakfast Mr. Prettyman gathered a party, which included Mr. Cockrum and his girlfriend Evelyn Fabini, and squired his guests around the expansive property on foot. The morning was damp. Golden light fell over the leaves and grass. It was a hushed and sacred moment before reaping time. The world was balanced on the edge of a scythe.

Mr. Lang, accompanied by a scruffy field-hand type, shadowed them. Katherine's flesh crawled, and she endeavored to walk so one or more of her companions blocked Mr. Lang's view of her backside. On several instances she'd begun to broach the subject of the man's intrusion into their bedroom, but Sonny ignored her this morning, submerged in one of his moods. He wouldn't have believed her anyway. She took her fair share of pills, and that wasn't something he let her forget. The accident had destroyed his trust in her judgment, perhaps her rationality.

Their tour skirted the outlying forest. Katherine, a veteran hiker, was nonetheless impressed with the girth of the trees, the brooding darkness that lurked within their confines. Periodically, well-beaten paths diverged and disappeared into the dripping trees. Mr. Prettyman led them past a tract of stone bungalows and into a cluster of decrepit outbuildings. The distillery was in the middle stages of collapse, its equipment quietly rusting amidst the rye and blackberry brambles. A stream clogged with brush gurgled nearby. He claimed that one of the state's only functioning windmills, a stone-and-timber replica of the famous Dutch models, had long dominated the rolling fields. Storms had destroyed it decades prior, but its foundation could probably still be located should an intrepid soul assay chopping back mountains of Scotch broom and weedy sycamore.

It had grown hot. She stared into the distance where the tall grass had begun to turn yellow and brown, and felt an urge to fly pell-mell into the field and roll in the grass, to burrow and hide in the soft, damp earth, to stare at the sky through a secret lattice.

"What's that?" asked Ms. Fabini, Mr. Cockrum's pale young mistress. "Over there."

Katherine had previously noted a copse of rather deformed oak trees that crowned a low rise in the otherwise flat field. She counted five trees, each heavily entwined in hawthorn bushes to roughly waist height. The thorn bushes made a sort of arched entrance to the hollow interior. Shadows and foliage obscured what appeared to be large pieces of statuary.

Mr. Prettyman said, "Ah, that would be one of several pagan shrines scattered across this region. They're no secret, but we keep mention of them to a minimum. The edification of our esteemed guests is one thing. Wouldn't do to stir up a swarm of crass tourists, on the other hand."

"Of course, of course, my good man," Mr. Cockrum said, to which the rest of the party members added their semirticulate concurrence.

"Indian totems?" Mr. Woodruff asked, shading his eyes. "Shall we nip over and take a closer look?"

"Celtic," Sonny said.

"Quite right," Mr. Prettyman said. "You've done your homework. The details are sketchy, but Mr. Welloc and those of his inner circle imported various art objects from Western Europe and installed them in various places—some obvious, others not so. Allegedly, this piece was recovered in Wales."

"In other words, robbed from the peasants," Mr. Cockrum said to his girlfriend from behind his hand.

They filed into the copse, where it was cool and dim.

"My word," Mr. Woodruff said.

The stone effigy of a muscular humanoid with ram horns reared some eight or so feet and canted sharply to one side. It radiated an aura of unspeakable antiquity, its features eroded, its form shaggy with moss that issued from countless fissures. Pieces of broken masonry jutted from the bed of dead leaves at the statue's foot—the remnants of a marble basin lay shattered and corroded. Even in its ruin, Katherine recognized the sacrificial altar for what it was. Heat and chill cycled through her. Blue sky peeped through a notch in the canopy and it seemed alien.

"Exactly like the painting," Sonny said, his voice hushed.

"It's . . . ghastly," Ms. Fabini said, white-gloved hand fluttering near her mouth as she stared in awe and horror at the statue's prodigious endowment.

"Oh, honey, control yourself." Cockrum squatted to examine the base of the statue, which had sunk to its calves in the dark earth. Sonny joined him, dusting here and there in a fruitless search for an inscription. From Kat's vantage, their heads obscured the Goat Lord's genitals. It struck her as a disquieting tableau, and without thinking, she raised her camera and snapped a picture an instant before they rose, dusting off their hands.

Katherine toed the ashes of a small fire pit, stirred sand and charred bits of bone. She said to Mr. Prettyman, "Who comes here? Besides your guests."

"Only guests. No one else is permitted access to the property."

Mr. Prettyman stood beside her. He'd tied his long, white hair in a ponytail. It matched the severity of his expression. "There are those who pay for the privilege of borrowing the shrine. They hold services, observe vigils."

"You find it distasteful," she said.

He laughed coldly. "I understand the will to madness that is faith."

"You say they imported this from Wales."

"Yes, from a ruined temple."

"But, isn't this a pagan god? It resembles—"

"Old Nick. Of course. Don't you suppose the Prince of Darkness transcends religion? The true Man of a Thousand Faces. He's everywhere, no matter what one may call him."

"Or nowhere," she said.

"Ah. You have a scientific mind."

"What's left of it. Not much room for superstition."

"He doesn't require much," Mr. Prettyman said. "A fly will lay eggs on the smallest morsel."

8

They lay in bed in the darkness of their small Pasadena home. He spooned her, his arm across her shoulder. The weight of his arm used to be a comfort; now it frightened her somehow. She knew he was awake because he wasn't snoring. A fan revolved somewhere above them. The room broiled. Her skin was cold and slick. She trembled.

Katherine?

She held her breath, waiting for his hand to slide from her breast to her belly, to push her legs apart and begin stroking her pussy. This was how it started, if it started at all. The hairs on her neck stood and she felt sick, flush with precognition that sent a wave of queasiness through her.

Did you do it on purpose? His whisper came low and harsh. It might've been the voice of a perfect stranger.

She cried then. Her entire body shook, wracked with shame and grief and guilty terror. His hand fell from her and he began to snore.

— 9 —

It wasn't a bad week. Sonny drank more than usual, which worried her at first. This seemed to improve his mood, however. Between his daylong excursions into the countryside and midnight sessions poring over ye archaic tomes by candlelight in the far corner of the suite, he was utterly preoccupied. He acted euphoric, which was his custom when approaching the solution to some particularly thorny problem. He kissed her gently in the morning before his departure, and when they shared dinners on the deck overlooking the valley, he was absentminded, yet sweet. She warmed to her independence, lounging with a book in the shade of the yard trees, walking the grounds as she pleased, hopping rides with Mr. Cockrum and Ms. Fabini for day trips into town.

One late morning, she and Ms. Fabini contrived to ditch Mr. Cockrum when he nipped into the Haymaker Tavern to slum with the plebeians. The women explored, although there wasn't much to see after one had taken in the Main Street shops and the museum. The abbreviated center of town lay cupped by gently rising hillsides. Industry was relegated to the eastern edge, beyond the deep, quick waters of Belson Creek, where dwelt the junkyards, auto shops, tattoo parlors, taverns, and the brewery, a monument which had been installed shortly after the end of Prohibition. Most everything else had withered on the vine over the years, leaving a series of darkened warehouses, the shuttered bulk of an old mill, and a defunct textile factory. These last loomed in steadfast isolation like headstones.

Ms. Fabini spotted a decent antique shop and they spent an hour browsing through Depression-era furniture and bric-a-brac. Katherine had wandered into a cluttered aisle in a gloomy corner of the shop when she came across several framed photographs taken in the late 1800s. Most were bubbled and faded, but one stood in stark contrast, albeit yellow at the edges. A group of men in greatcoats and dusters stood around a wagon freighted with hay. The farmers were stoic as per the custom of pioneer America; even the youngest of them wore a thick, handlebar mustache. A blot of discoloration caught her glance. A person lay in the shadows beneath the wagon axle and leered between wheel spokes at the photographer, at her. She recognized the face.

10

Katherine went for a stroll along the grounds in the afternoon. She reached the second gate and kept walking, kept treading the path until she'd come to the bungalows, all of them locked, drapes drawn tight: a cluster of family tombs.

Mr. Lang reclined in a wicker chair on the grass. He set a bottle of beer on the table near his elbow. "Hello," he said. His smile was insolent.

She hesitated, then walked directly to his chair and stood nearly looming over him, fists set into her hips. "What do you want?"

"I live here."

"This one?" She gestured.

"The Goat's Head Bungalow," he said. His face was a dark moon. "Thinking of dropping in for a beer later?"

"No, Mr. Leng—"

"Lang. Call me Derek."

"I want you to stay far away from us, Mr. Lang. I don't like you."

Mr. Lang raised an eyebrow and took a pull from his beer. "Yesterday, your husband went into the country, to a farm I told him about. He bought himself a cute little nanny goat. Pure, virginal white. Paid me a hundred bucks to help him smuggle the critter onto the property. We took the goat to that shrine in the field. Man, that's one nasty dagger your husband's got. Said he picked it up in India from some real live cultist types. Some screws rattling around in there, you ask me."

She stared, dumbfounded. *He's not lying. Sweet baby Jesus, he's not lying.*

"I charged him an extra C-note to dump the goat in the woods. I've done it before for a few other wackos—usually cats and rabbits, but hey."

"Screw you. Jesus, you're insane. You'd best stay clear of us." She hoped she sounded brave. She wanted to vomit. *God damn you, Sonny.*

"If you say so. I'm not the one slaughtering farm animals to get his kicks."

"I should march right into Mr. Prettyman's office and tell him what kind of psycho he's turned loose on the public."

"Should you?"

"Yeah. We'll see how smug you are when you're sent packing."

"And I should be reporting your husband."

That stopped her in her tracks. "About what? The goat? Go to hell. We're leaving on Monday. Frankly, it suits me if we blow this freak circus a couple of days early."

Mr. Lang's smile faded. He said with mock gravity, "Interesting hobby he's got, hiking in the hills, digging up things that don't belong to him. Probably thinks he hit the mother lode. I could just shoot him. The sheriff would thank me."

"What? No. Sonny doesn't . . . He takes notes for his articles. Sketches, sometimes. That's it." Her guts felt like they were sliding toward her shoes.

"That's it? That's all?"

"Yeah. Just sketches." She bit her lip until sparks shot through her vision and her eyes watered.

"Oh." He nodded as if her explanation was eminently reasonable. "You're a funny one, Mrs. Reynolds. Give me these come-hither looks all week, and now you get coy."

"You're deluded. Frankly, I can't believe you dare to threaten my husband. Mr. Prettyman will—"

"I know you," Mr. Lang said. "I check all the guests. That's *my* hobby."

She breathed heavily, her lungs thick as wet cotton. "You're a peeping Tom, too."

"You were in the papers. The Associated Press. You're kind of famous, Mrs. R."

"What's wrong with you?"

"With me? With me, you ask." He chuckled, a soft wheeze that originated from the depths of him. "They let you walk. We're so sympathetic these days. Throw your baby off a bridge and everybody gives you a hug and sends get-well cards. So, Kat. Are you well? Those doctors fix your poor brain? Do those plainclothes detectives still follow you around, watching to see what 'that crazy Reynolds woman' is going to do next?"

She gagged on her tongue, choked when she tried to speak.

"Okay, darling. I'm not completely heartless. A cool grand, I forget to mention your hubby's hijinks to the good sheriff. Hell, bring it over personally and I'll take half in trade."

Her arm swung wide, as if connected to someone else, and her fist crashed into his mouth. He slumped, arms hanging slack, as she stumbled backward. Blood poured over his chin. His sides shook and that wheezing laughter followed her as she lifted her skirt and fled.

Katherine made it to the suite. She leaned over the toilet and dry heaved. Nothing came out. Her knuckles bled where she'd sliced them against Mr. Lang's teeth. Numbly, she washed her hand and pressed a washcloth against the cuts until the bleeding stopped. *Christ, what now? What am I going to tell Sonny?* Who knew what Sonny would do. He'd probably accuse her of leading the bastard on. Not that he'd say it aloud. His disgusted expression would do the talking. She was the millstone around his neck. *Why, oh why don't you just leave? Why not fuck your secretary, why not run away with one of those nubile coeds who are eager to throw themselves at you? Surely you could knock up one of those bitches and solve all of our problems.*

A better question might be: If she must stay, why didn't she have an affair of her own? Mr. Lang's bloody grin flickered in her mind and she realized her left hand had drifted to her inner thigh, that her fingers stroked softly, almost imperceptibly. "Oh, my God," she said and jerked her hand away. Her face burned.

She collapsed into a chair near the window. The light shifted to orange. A breeze swirled the leaves of the magnolias. What she saw then, with cold, pitiless clarity, was an overpass, a woman carrying a pink bundle above a stream of headlights. The woman's face was blank and cold as plaster. The woman opened her arms. "Yes. I think I did it on purpose," she said to the empty room, and wished she had a gun to put against her head.

II

Sonny stumbled in well after dark. He'd been clambering through hill and dale by the look of him—his hair was mussed, pine needles and leaves clung to his jacket, gathered in the cuffs of his muddy pants. He said hello and began to undress. Katherine still sat in the oversized chair in the gloom. She turned on the lamp so they could see one another. He glanced at her hand without comment and tossed his clothes in a pile near the foot of the bed.

"Sonny?"

"Yeah?" He regarded himself in the mirror. "Did you do anything today?"

"I walked around. Read a bit." They'd been sharing a couple of the amusing potboilers from the reading shelves in the lodge's den. Sonny *had* been pleased to discover titles by Machen and Le Fanu among the dreck.

"That's nice."

"Find anything?"

He shook his head. He rubbed his arm where a bruise flowered, dark and angry. "It's like a jungle. Thorns everywhere. I could spend a whole summer in there with a chainsaw and not find anything. Sheesh."

"Oh?"

He smiled briefly and took off his watch and set it on the dresser.

"Sonny."

"Hmm?"

"You're being careful." When he didn't answer, she cleared her throat. "No one's following you, or anything. You'd know, wouldn't you?"

"I'm just taking pictures."

"Okay," she said.

He walked into the bathroom and the shower started.

12

Sonny had tried to summon the Devil once. He'd drawn a complicated pentacle in the basement, lit some candles, and slaughtered a stray cat with a ceremonial dagger. Satan was lord of all flesh; pay Him some blood and maybe he'd give them the means to make a child. It was the kind of stunt dumb, oversexed teenagers pulled to impress their friends and scare themselves. Sonny admitted such rituals were essentially powerless; on the other hand, mind over matter—spiritual placebo—was another beast entirely. She had almost left him then. Only her numb guilt, her essential apathy kept her yoked to him. Later, she stayed because at its worst, their relationship served as her self-inflicted flagellation, her penance.

It all started innocently enough.

In high school and college Katherine had played with tarot cards and Ouija boards—the weird roommate with the weirder off-campus-friends syndrome. Drink a bit of wine, take a few hits, and the next thing she knew she'd be having an unexpected quasi-lesbian experience, or would find herself smack in the middle of an amateur thaumaturgy session, or, on one infamous Halloween night, a botched séance. When she'd first dated Sonny it had come as no surprise he dabbled in native rituals; this *was* his area of expertise.

One didn't keep a stack of books on the nightstand such as the ubiquitous *The Golden Bough* and *The Key of Solomon the King*, and treatises by Agrippa, Bruno, and Mathers, among a host of others, without dipping one's toe in on occasion. They practiced feng shui after a half-assed fashion; it was all the rage with their postcollege associates, like so many westerners' fleeting dalliances with Buddhism and Kabala. Nothing serious; more a casual pastime akin to some couples' weekend canasta games. And if Sonny happened to study what he called "hoodoo" to a great degree, that was because his job depended on the research.

Then the accident. Matters had become bizarre. Kafka and William Burroughs–type bizarre. At least Sonny hadn't tried to blast a glass off her head. He'd done other things, however. A quiet, festering resentment bubbled to the surface in a glance, a smile, the subtle tightening of his grip on her wrist, the way he hurt her in bed, though never beyond the pale, just enough to let her feel his animosity. She feared that's what they'd gradually become—a pair of mated animals who snapped and snarled at one another, who remained together due to instinct, to pure expediency.

His sophomoric attempt to raise hell, as it were, signaled a sharp descent.

Mind over matter, he said when first introducing her to the ebon figurine of some dead tribe's fertility god, a trinket he acquired during his travels abroad; he clutched the fetish in his left hand whenever they fucked—and, oh, hadn't sex become a choreographed event. He tried to put the fetish in her until she slapped him hard enough to leave a mark. *Mind over matter*, he said the next time from behind a Celtic mask while painting her with red ochre, and the time after that when feeding her peyote buttons while shaking voodoo rattles in her face. Once, they'd visited the wreckage of a church sunk beneath projects in Detroit, and a priest in black robes had killed a chicken and anointed her in blood as a circle of bare-breasted acolytes howled. The unholy congregation had melted away and Sonny had mounted her, his expression twisted, a mirror of her own insides, and after, neither could look the other in the eye. Riding the empty late-night bus back to their hotel, they had huddled near the rear, she wrapped in a blanket, staring at her reflection, staring into and past her own dead eyes at block after block of urban blight; there had been no streetlights, no blue-flickering television screens or reading lamps, only the blackness.

No baby was forthcoming, either.

— 13 —

The next morning, after Sonny slipped away, she took a long hot shower and was drying her hair when she heard a door shut in the other room.

Someone left an envelope addressed to her on the table. Her name was printed in a loose, sloppy hand. The envelope contained two dozen photographs. Several were shots of Sonny digging up artifacts. Ten or so were close-ups of arrowheads, pottery, figurines and the like. All were quite damning in their clarity. An itemized list documented various pieces, where they'd been acquired and who had purchased them. Some of the photos were fifteen or more years old, dating back to Sonny's graduate days. Katherine knew about his compulsive theft, but she'd not allowed herself to dwell upon how long he'd engaged in his habits.

The list was signed, *Meet me, tonight. Witching Hour.* Mr. Lang was indeed wily, leaving her to infer his identity and where to rendezvous. Her hands shook as she tossed the envelope and its contents into the fireplace. She hugged herself and watched the packet curl and burn. Only much later, after she'd called Ms. Fabini to cancel their luncheon plans and burrowed under the covers to hibernate, did she recall that there were no ashes from the impromptu fire, only a fine tracing of soot that swirled and disappeared into the chimney.

In her dreams, Sonny called from the recesses of the chimney while she started a fire from his papers and books and a pile of his muddy clothes. She'd collected a sack of his clipped hair and threw it on for kindling. He screamed at her, but she didn't stop. She ripped off her wedding dress and added it to the blaze. A baby shrieked as it cooked and sizzled. She tossed on pieces of the old crib and watched them burn.

14

At first, she tried to convince herself this would be about rescuing Sonny from the clutches of crazy, vindictive Mr. Lang. Except, that didn't fly—there was no way to avoid the reality that Sonny getting caught and jailed for a few years would be a relief from tension and satisfying to boot. Truthfully, his getting nailed for a career of misdeeds appealed to her on several levels.

Regardless of Sonny's legal hassles or potential financial ruin, it was really his problem alone. Her face hadn't been photographed. Her name hadn't appeared on any lists. In any event, no matter how dire the circumstances, she could run home to mama; a girl could always do that. No, there were other deeper, less rational motives for keeping the rendezvous. She just refused to face them directly.

Katherine crumbled sleeping pills and Valium into two consecutive glasses of vodka and watched Sonny gulp them down. He was already a bit drunk, so it was almost like the movies, frighteningly easy. For all she knew, she'd dealt him an elephant's dose that might stop his heart. He fell asleep in his chair, snoring gently into his scattered notes. She blew out the candles.

The hour was late.

The moon hung cold and yellow behind a gossamer scrim. Her shoes crunched against the path that wound from the lodge and its attendant structures. Katherine arrived on the doorstep of the Goat's Head Bungalow at the appointed time and was slightly surprised to find it dark. She rapped on the door and waited. Her left hand dug into her jacket pocket and tightened around the can of mace attached to her keychain. In her right pocket was an envelope stuffed with twenty-dollar bills she'd withdrawn from an ATM in Olde Towne earlier that day. The mace was a decade old: Sonny bought it for her after a guy mugged them in Venice. The thug gave her a shiner and a sprained neck in the process of yanking away her camera. Stunned, Sonny had stood there while it happened. That evening in the hotel, he berated her for carrying the camera, attracting trouble. Later, he apologized by handing her the mace and some flowers. When they returned to the states, he enrolled in karate lessons and attended classes religiously until he quietly dropped them in a few weeks.

No one stirred within the bungalow; it squatted dead and cold as a husk, tenanted by silence so palpable it throbbed in her ears. Clouds slid across the face of the moon, and its yellow light curdled, reddened into the eye of a drunk. The temperature had dipped, and her breath streamed from her mouth. She stepped off the porch and surveyed the empty field. Fire briefly shone within the distant oak grove.

She walked the path to the very shadow of the grove, hesitated before the briar arch. A figure barred the way, a black form silhouetted by the dim illumination from coals dying in the pit. "Mr. Lang," she said, knowing in that instant her mistake, experiencing the sweet, horrific bloom of understanding that accompanies waking to a nightmare within a nightmare.

He laughed. His laugh was similar to Mr. Lang's, but deeper, darker. Hearing it was like hearing blood rush over pebbles. Red shadows crawled from the fire pit and enlarged him. His outline flickered, suggestive of manifold possibilities.

"I'm here," she said.

"Yes, you are," he said in a voice that whispered as from a distance. A familiar voice, but clotted with an excess of saliva and eagerness. She thought if some ancient creature of the wood could form words this would be their shape. "Bravery born of damnation isn't courageous, is it, lovely one?"

"You're Bill," she said.

"If you'd like."

"I brought money."

"But I don't want that."

"Four hundred and sixty dollars. That's all I could get. Take it . . . I'll write you a check when we get back home. I'll be wanting the negatives."

"Negatives? Negatives for pictures that never were? I wouldn't worry about them."

"Take the money—let's not play games, okay?"

"Yes, yes. It's time to quit pretending," he said.

"I don't understand."

He laughed again. The coals hissed and his silhouette became a lump of utter darkness. "These woods are very old."

"And dark; I know," she said. She could no longer see him. His presence magnified in her mind; it obliterated everything else.

"These woods are dear to me."

"It's right here. Please." She brandished the envelope in defiant supplication. The envelope absorbed the starlight, gleamed like a tooth. "Here. I swear, my husband won't trespass into the woods again."

"Yet, he's the fool who called me," he said. "What of you, sweet?"

Her arm shook from extending the envelope, so she folded her hands at her waist. "I've never gone into the forest."

"Pity, pity." He laughed again and now she imagined a hyena with an overdeveloped skull regarding her from the darkness, a stag crowned by tiers of crooked and decaying antlers. There was a terrible sickness in that laughter. "What of you? Tell me what *you* need."

"Nothing."

"Best wish for something," he said. "I could lie with you until you shrieked fair to drive the pheasants from their nests. Then I could split you open on the altar and have you to the fullest."

"Oh." The stars began to flash and she allowed her jelly legs to fold. She bowed her head, aware of the obscenity of this pseudo-genuflection. "Not that."

"Then speak your desire."

Her mouth opened and she blurted, "You fucking well know, don't you?" Tears dripped from the end of her nose. She dared to raise her gaze, lips curled to bare her teeth in an expression of abject self-loathing. “Give me that. It’s what I deserve, isn’t it.”

“I think you are both richly deserving.”

“What . . . what must I do?”

“Why, pet, it’s done. All these years I’ve been waiting to hold up my end of the bargain.”

He emerged from the curtain of darkness and it stretched to limn him, to halo him in a writhing, black nimbus. She looked upon him and gave forth an involuntary moan of terror. For a moment, it was who she expected, the huntsman, florid and smug in triumph. The moonlight brightened and his face waxed ordinary—the face of a lover, the man who reads the meter, a blank-eyed passenger sharing a bus seat; a face mundane in its capacity for cruelty or avarice. Then he smiled and fulfilled every dreadful image conceived in a thousand plates in a thousand hallowed tomes, and woodblock illustrations and overwrought cinema. Corrupt heat pulsed from his flesh; his breath stunned her with its foul humidity. Yet, the impulse to clutch his lank beard, to twine her tongue in his, consumed her will. Her thighs trembled and she moistened. She wept as she pressed her lips against his muscular thigh and inhaled the reek of sulfur, bestial sweat, and rank, over-ripe sex.

His fingers tangled in her hair, long nails like hooks pricking at her scalp. He whispered, “Ask and ye shall receive.”

The sulfurous moon had almost dissolved into the horizon.

Katherine returned to the suite and stood for a while as a shadow among shadows, watching Sonny. He groaned in his sleep and called a name she couldn’t recognize for his slurring. She erased a section of the ridiculous chalk pentagram with her bare foot, then went to him and murmured in his ear and coaxed him to bed. They fell across it and she undressed him. She sweated. The fierceness of her need was an agony, a pressure of such magnitude it eclipsed reason, caused the room to spin around her. The painting of the stag hunt caught her glance for a moment, its detail obscured and grainy, but—the mastiffs sat on their haunches and the stag towered on its hind legs, and the entire dark company gazed down upon the couple on the bed.

She caressed him, licked his ear and kissed his neck until he stirred and woke. It didn't take much more. Her heat was contagious and he made a sound in his chest and rolled atop her. She closed her eyes and arched, hooked her calves over his hips, pinned him to her with all her strength.

Motes and sparks behind her eyelids stuttered with her pulse. Pleasure shot through her brain and unfolded a kaleidoscope. She saw the white nanny goat bound at the foot of the statue. It bleated, then the knife and a fan of blood, her husband, his face one of legion, exultant and savage.

He drove into her without love, merciless; and in her skull, rockets. *Sonny, what did you wish?* She knew, oh, yes, but the question lingered, bored into her just as he did, and she trembled violently. *What did you wish?* The nanny goat rolled its head on the altar and its eyes flared red to a surge of panpipes, an offstage Gregorian liturgy, thunderous laughter.

She came, and, simultaneously, he rocked with a powerful spasm and bellowed. Her eyes snapped open. His face was a white mask, flesh stretched so tight his mouth pulled sharply upward at the corners. He vibrated as if he'd grabbed a high-voltage wire. Something cracked, a tendon, a bone, and he shoved away from her, flew from the bed and crashed to the floor. She managed to right herself. Her belly felt overfull. It was the strangest sensation, this ballooning inside, the sudden rush of nausea.

Sonny thrashed against the floorboards and continued to ejaculate. In the near darkness, she became confused by what she saw—the short, quick spurts that arced across his body were neither ropes nor strands, but thick and segmented. She'd seen a dead bird in the garbage and what had feasted upon it in it oozing carpets, and her mental equilibrium wobbled mightily. He squealed as his rigid muscles softened and sloughed. He rapidly diminished and became physically incomprehensible, emptied of substance. What remained of him continued to flow in seeping tributaries toward the bed, and her. It happened very fast; a time-lapse photo of an animal decomposing in the forest.

Sticky things squirmed upon her thighs and loins, and when she registered the flatworm torsos and embryonic faces, she screamed, was still screaming long after people finally came through the door and everything was over.

They couldn't find a trace of Sonny anywhere.

16

The pregnancy wasn't complicated. The hospital staff (they called it a "home") gave her a single-occupancy room with a lovely view of the grounds. A squirrel lived in the chestnut tree near the window, and the nurses let her feed him breadcrumbs over the sill. Nurse Jennifer gave her medicine in the morning. Nurse Margaret tucked her in at night. Dr. Green visited daily and gave her peppermint candies, which she'd loved since childhood.

She slept a lot. She ate Jell-O cups whenever she liked, and watched *The 700 Club* on the television hanging in the corner. Occasionally, after dark, it'd be something nasty with bare tits and gouts of gore, children with withered faces who glared hatefully, and priests walking with their heads on backwards, but she didn't panic, the screen always went blank then returned to regularly scheduled programming when a nurse came in to check on her. Sometimes she watched the reverend Jerry Falwell or Benny Hinn. She followed their sermons from a new King James Bible her father brought after an incident he'd jokingly referred to as an "exorcism" when she first came to the home. Admittedly, she had had issues in the beginning, some outbursts. There hadn't been an incident in months, and she'd practically blacked out entire sections of the Old Testament by underlining. She knew what to expect. She was ready. Things had gone so smoothly, so dreamily, it had scarcely felt like being pregnant at all.

It happened in the middle of the night, and she didn't feel anything after the epidural except sweet, bright oblivion. They removed the baby before she revived. Nurse Jennifer told her she'd given birth to a healthy boy and they'd bring him around soon. Several days later, they wheeled her into the sunshine and parked her on the patio by the fountain. She loved this spot. The grounds were decorated with manicured hedges and plum trees, and, obscured by the trees, a high stone wall topped with wrought-iron spikes.

Dr. Green, Nurse Jennifer, and one of the big male attendants brought the baby wrapped in a yellow blanket. The doctor and the nurse seemed reserved, disquieted despite their friendly greetings, and they exchanged looks. She'd heard them whispering about progeria while they thought she was asleep. They probably weren't sure what to tell her, were doubtless loath to upset her at this delicate juncture.

Dr. Green cleared his throat. "So, have you decided what you're going to call him?" He watched carefully as the attendant put the boy in her arms.

"Baby *has* a name," she said, staring with wonder and terror at her child's face. *You'll be talking in a few months. Oh, sweet Lord, won't that be interesting?* His smooth, olive skin was pitted by a faint scatter of acne scars. His eyes were alive with a dreadful knowingness. He already resembled his driver's-license photo.

LAIRD BARRON'S work has appeared in such publications as *The Magazine of Fantasy and Science Fiction*, *Sci Fiction*, *Inferno: New Tales of Terror and the Supernatural*, *Poe: 19 New Tales Inspired by Edgar Allan Poe*, and *The Del Rey Book of Science Fiction and Fantasy.* It has also been reprinted in numerous *Year's Best* anthologies. His debut collection, *The Imago Sequence and Other Stories*, was the winner of the inaugural Shirley Jackson Award. Barron is an expatriate Alaskan currently at large in Washington State.

BARRON SAYS: The Shadow out of Time *remains one of my favorite pieces of dark fantasy—a sublime melding of horror and science fiction, and one that opened my mind to depicting terror on a cosmic scale. As much as I savor a good pastiche, Lovecraft's visionary narratives interest me more as a doorway to exploring other modes of the weird and the fantastic.*

NICK MAMATAS

That of Which We Speak When We Speak of the Unspeakable

IT WAS AUGUST. Everything was going to change. They could feel it. Jase was a prophet and prophets like to talk, so he did. He was talking about the end of all things and how great it was going to be.

They were sitting—Jase and Melissa and Stephan—near the mouth of a cave, around a rock shaped conveniently like a coffee table. The kerosene lamp flickered and stank up the place a little bit. Stephan could taste it in his whisky.

"And you can forget about love," Jase said. Jase wasn't into love, and really he wasn't even into sex anymore, though he'd had plenty, he told his friends. Even just on the way up to the cave to wait for the end, he'd hired a girl and then later stopped at the bus station. Anything, anytime, anywhere, he said. Stephan thought that Jase was just going on about sex because Melissa was right there, catty-corner to him, on the side of the rock deeper in the mouth of the cave.

"Why do you even bring up love?" Stephan asked. Then Melissa said that she thought the conversation was already about sex, as it would have to be once the Missoula bus-station bathroom was brought up as a setting, if not the main topic. She gulped her Teacher's right after that, and Stephan took a sip of his and then reached for the bottle.

"Love is that supposed all-powerful, all-encompassing force. You know, a dog gets lost on vacation with its owners and then four months later shows up on the doorstep, covered in twigs and with its fur all matted up, but in fine shape and with a big panting smile."

"Yeah, I saw that on television," Stephan said. "Dog follows owners home on a three-thousand-mile beam of love."

"Beam of love, exactly," said Jase.

"So how do you think the dog got home?" asked Melissa. "Luck?" Stephan guessed aloud that Jase didn't believe in luck either, or maybe just bad luck, or that luck was running out for everyone.

"No, not at all. I consider myself very lucky." Jase poured himself another drink. He waved his plastic cup of Teacher's under his chin like he was sniffing at a fine wine or some Italian grandma's Sunday meat sauce. "Lucky to be here for the end. To see the sky when the stars blink out, to watch the seas boil and the Elder Gods crush us all."

"That's him," Melissa said to Stephan. "Jase is all about the tentacles and the worship. He likes the drama. He's a drama king."

Stephan said, "There's a sucker born every minute." He tried to keep it going, extend it into a joke. Suckers and tentacles, something like that, but the whisky took the joke away from him even as it had helped him open his mouth for the windup. "Suckers," he repeated, just like that.

Jase stood up, dusted off his ass and teetered toward the mouth of the cave. Stephan thought Jase might start urinating, sending a stream down into the valley below the cave, into the colorless grass. Instead Jase just threw up his arms and shouted, "Fuck love!" If he was hoping for an echo, he didn't get one—not even a cricket cricketed in response. "I'm lucky," he said, turning back to Stephan and Melissa, "because I've never had a thing to do with love. You know what my childhood was like?"

"Same as anyone else's," Melissa said.

"Exactly, yeah, exactly," Jase said. "Sitting on a couch. Doing stuff, growing up. I catch a ball, my father's proud. I hurt my foot, my mother clucks her tongue and pulls out the splinter with a pair of tweezers."

"Sounds dreadful," said Stephan. He squinted his eyes to keep the flicker of the lamp away, turning Jase into a little buzzing kaleidoscope. "Sounds just like being raped twice a day, every day, for fourteen years or something."

"Well, here's the thing," Jase said. He stomped back up the rock and kicked at it twice, knocking the mud from his heels. "It's boring. Everything gets boring."

"Yeah," said Melissa. "I had a boyfriend once who ended up doing some time in prison." Stephan and Jase both got quiet at that. "Nothing bad . . . well, nothing that bad. It was just a fight, but he knew some stuff, judo, and the guy he was fighting ended up in a coma. Anyway, he went to prison for ninety days and he was mostly very bored. He said everyone else was eager for their hour of exercise, even if it meant getting shived or raped by three guys because otherwise it was just boring."

Jase snorted. "You probably loved him too, eh? Waited for him to get out of prison."

"It was only three months," Stephan said. Stephan wondered if someone would wait for him for three months if he ended up in prison for accidentally putting some guy into a coma. Not that he knew how to put anyone into anything, not even a headlock. Maybe he could run somebody down with a car. He could go to prison and be bored except for the hour of raping every day.

"Yeah, I guess I did. I loved him more when he wasn't around." She looked a little anxious, or maybe she was just chilly. She was deeper in the cave, where it was wet, on the lip of the dark. "You know, when someone is around you remember the bad breath and the rolls of fat hanging over the elastic of his underwear and that annoying way he winks when he's saying something he isn't sure about. So I broke up with him, but I waited until he was out of prison."

"Because you loved him?" Stephan said.

"Because you were bored?" Jase said.

"Because I didn't know what else to do. It's hard to break up with someone in prison. The phone calls are monitored. You have to wait for certain days to go visit, and it's not a place for a real conversation. You can taste metal on your tongue; it's like being sick or allergic to everything."

"Allergic to everything, yeah," Jase said. "I feel a prophecy coming on." He shook out his hair. There was a leaf in it.

Stephan leaned back, his arms behind him, a finger brushing against Melissa's jeans.

Jase trembled, his arms wide, and started doing his tongues trick. Melissa scooted forward and shifted on her hips to keep from making contact with Stephan. She reached for the Teacher's and took a pull from the bottle, then put it back on the rock and held her cup to her lips, tilting it backwards to get some last drop she had forgotten before. There was still almost a third left in the bottle so Stephan poured some more into his cup too and said, "What do you think of all the yoobalalala stuff," which was a pretty good impression of Jase right then.

"I don't know."

"Is it real?"

"I don't know if he's real, but it's sure real," Melissa said. "No denying that now. Not after New York and not after the Mississippi River."

"And China." It annoyed Stephan that everyone forgot about China, how they tried to nuke the thing when it appeared, all hungry eyes and inside-out angles, and the bomb wiped out half of Shenzen and flooded Hong Kong and then the thing just rematerialized in the same spot the next day, but radioactive. One time Jase just laughed and said that in China everyone forgot about New York, but Stephan doubted it.

"You see, that's the thing," said Jase. He was on the ground, arms and legs swaying like he was making a grass-and-leaf-and-twig angel. "Everyone thinks love is the answer. You look at someone and say 'I love you' and the cancer gets better, or 'I love you' and they'll love you back, or 'I love you' and the decades they spend in shitty jobs to buy shitty food mean something, or 'I love you' and you're not a fat drunk anymore." Stephan wondered if Jase's mother had been a fat drunk.

"Is this still prophecy?" asked Melissa.

"Can't you tell yet?" asked Stephan. Melissa had been following Jase around for longer than Stephan had, for two months, since the Mississippi started swimming with the carpets of tadpoles with the faces of men. Stephan had just wandered up to the cave with them the night before.

"Not prophecy, baby, reality. That's just a story. My story. My folks said they loved me, and showed it by buying me fish sticks and a Christmas present and then they died after a car wreck. You know, not in one, after one. Months later, in traction, their skin all shriveled and burnt. Nothing but screaming pain for the both of them, the pain of sponges and businesslike nurses with thick shoulders going at them, just to keep them alive and in more pain."

"Sorry," Stephan said.

"Are you really?" Jase said.

Stephan thought about it for a second and decided that he wasn't sorry. He said that mostly he just hoped that saying sorry would get Jase to move on to another topic.

"Yeah, that's what we do, right? We move on. I loved my parents too—they trained me to love them with food and physical contact. My brain developed under the tyranny of love. And you know what? After they died and I cried and all that and I still had to figure out how to keep the lights on and the fridge running and the love didn't matter anymore. And when I took off and hit the road people asked about my parents, but just in general. 'Where are your parents? Why are you out here on the streets?' I was just a broken tooth on an otherwise functional cog in a great big machine. There was no love out there, and I moved on. I don't even love my parents anymore. Love fades, like a rash." That last made Stephan laugh.

"Keep laughin', laughing boy," Jase said. He was up on one elbow now, another arm stretched toward the rock. "Whisky," he said and Stephan leaned over and gave him the bottle of Teacher's and he took a sip and scowled. "Well, so much for all that, eh? Forget cogs, we got crazy backwards ninth-dimensional geometry in the machines now. Can't you see 'em in the sky, when you look up and squint and concentrate on the anja chakra? The dark tentacles in a sky just as dark—"

"Yeah, the end of the universe and it's a whistling squid. Greeeeat," said Melissa. Stephan looked at her. Her hair was stringy and slick from the road and the woods. She smiled tightly over her teeth and fiddled with her thumbnails. "Ah, here they come," she said, more quietly, to Stephan. She pointed with her chin to the dark patch of woods. If there was something moving or crawling or oozing out there Stephan couldn't see. Stephan often couldn't see much anyway. Jase didn't seem to notice either, because he was still talking about the sky tentacles.

"This is truly, you know . . ." Stephan said, then he stopped talking. He held out his arms and waved them around a bit. Jase's talk had devolved back into the thrashy gibbering.

"Yeah, it is," said Melissa. The shoggoths oozed into the clearing like an oil slick, filmed and then projected backwards, sliding uphill. It seemed to take them a long time to do. "You know, I got into this sort of thing a long time ago, before the Mississippi, before New York. When it was all just hints and footnotes in history. It felt good, really. I was just a kid. I went to the mall, painted my nails, drank Orange Juliuses." Stephan took the hint and jogged around the rock to pick up the bottle from next to where Jase lay and brought it back into the cave. Melissa had both hands up and fingers outstretched, like she was waiting for a baby to be passed to her. She drank, then said, "It just felt good, that there was something bigger than yourself out there. To think you knew something that other people didn't know. Well, everybody knows now."

"Yeah, and mostly people got used to it. We didn't go insane or anything. Not more crazy than people get in some war or during some epidemic. Well, except for Jase, maybe. Are you in love with him?"

"I dunno. Kinda. He's like looking in the mirror. 'So that's what would have happened,' I think when I look at him, 'if I never really grew up, never got used to the idea of doing the dishes even though they'd just get dirty again—' "

At the last minute, Jase broke. He stopped his twisting around and babbling and tried to run back to the cave. A shoggoth drew itself high and came down on him like a wave. Stephan heard a hard crunch. He looked over to Melissa, who still looked passive. The shoggoth pulled themselves across the little plain on pseudopods, dragging and sliding closer and closer.

"Whisky's gone," Melissa said, but it wasn't, and then Melissa took up the bottle and turned it up into her mouth, puffing up her cheeks. She stood up and took the kerosene lantern and turned the little dial to bring down the wick, leaving only a sliver of orange to glow.

Stephan could hear his heart beating. He could hear Melissa's heart beating too, he thought, even over the wet-shoe squelching noises of the shoggoths. He could hear the human noises he sat there making, not moving at all, as the cave went dark. The shoggoths stretched over the entrance. Then a ball of fire from Melissa's mouth as she spit the Teacher's out and across the burning wick of the lamp. A shoggoth burned and shriveled in retreat, but then a few more came.

NICK MAMATAS is the author of the Lovecraftian Beat road novel *Move Under Ground* and the novel of neighborhood nuclear supremacy *Under My Roof.* His short fiction has been collected in the book *You Might Sleep . . .* and he is co-editor of the anthology *Haunted Legends.* A native New Yorker, Nick now lives in California.

MAMATAS SAYS: *I suppose that in some ways writing Lovecraftian fiction is mercenary—there's an audience eager for it and a market waiting for it. Of course, the Lovecraftian market proper wants little to do with my stuff, since what I like most about Lovecraft is that his themes are ripe for nucleic exchange. Strip away the monsters, or hell, leave 'em in, and you are left with that feeling of being all alone in the universe, which we all are. It's one of the great themes of literature that just happened to be delivered via pulp-paper and tentacle fetishism by Lovecraft. So why not rehab him a bit, by introducing some Lovecraftian elements into a Beat novel or a dirty realist short story or experimental fiction? Keeps me in expired canned goods and a room set to fifty degrees, just as it did ol' Howie, anyway.*

ELLEN DATLOW has been editing science fiction, fantasy, and horror short fiction for over twenty-five years. She was fiction editor of *Omni* magazine and *Sci Fiction* and has edited more than fifty anthologies, including the horror half of the long-running *The Year's Best Fantasy and Horror*, the current *Best Horror of the Year*, *Little Deaths*, *Twists of the Tale*, *Inferno*, *The Del Rey Book of Science Fiction and Fantasy*, *Poe: 19 New Tales Inspired by Edgar Allan Poe*, *Troll's-Eye View: A Book of Villainous Tales*, and *Salon Fantastique* (the last two with Terri Windling). Forthcoming are *Naked City: New Tales of Urban Fantasy*, *Darkness: Two Decades of Modern Horror*, and *The Beastly Bride and Other Tales of the Animal People* (the latter with Windling). She has won multiple Locus Awards, Hugo Awards, Stoker Awards, International Horror Guild Awards, the Shirley Jackson Award, and the World Fantasy Award for her editing. She was named recipient of the 2007 Karl Edward Wagner Award, given at the British Fantasy Convention for "outstanding contribution to the genre."

She lives in New York. More information can be found at www.datlow.com or at her blog, http://ellen-datlow.livejournal.com/.

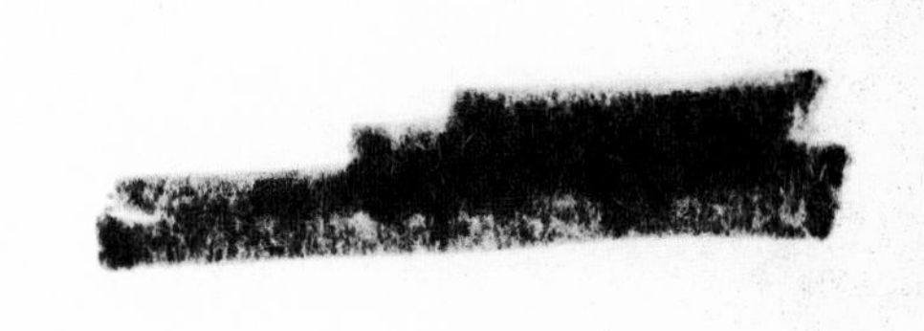